COUNTERPLAY

ROBERT K. TANENBAUM

COUNTERPLAY

ATRIA BOOKS

New York   London   Toronto   Sydney

ATRIA BOOKS
1230 Avenue of the Americas
New York, NY 10020

Library of Congress Cataloging-in-Publication Data
Tanenbaum, Robert.
Counterplay / Robert K. Tanenbaum.—1st Atria Books hardcover ed.
p. cm.
ISBN-13: 978-0-7432-7113-4
ISBN-10:   0-7432-7113-0
I. Title.

PS3570.A52C68 2006
813'.54—dc22   2006042621

First Atria Books hardcover edition August 2006

10 9 8 7 6 5 4 3 2 1

ATRIA BOOKS is a trademark of Simon & Schuster, Inc.

Manufactured in the United States of America

For information regarding special discounts for bulk purchases,
please contact Simon & Schuster Special Sales at 1-800-456-6798
or business@simonandschuster.com.

To those most special,
Patti, Rachael, Roger, and Billy,
and to the memories of my legendary mentors,
District Attorney Frank S. Hogan and Henry Robbins

ACKNOWLEDGMENTS

Wendy Walker and Espey Jackson deserve special recognition for their invaluable assistance. The superior quality of the manuscripts in the trilogy comprised of *Hoax, Fury,* and *Counterplay* is directly attributable to their devoted and brilliant contributions. Also, I must note the sage advice and counsel of my inimitable chief assistant, Georgia di Donato.

COUNTERPLAY

Prologue

CLAY FULTON GRIPPED THE ARMREST OF THE BIG ARMORED Lincoln like he used to cling to the safety bar on the Cyclone roller coaster at Coney Island when he was a kid. At six foot three and two hundred and fifty pounds, plus thirty-odd years on the New York Police Department, there wasn't a whole lot that frightened him. But zipping along a snow-patched country highway in upstate New York at sixty-five miles an hour made him nervous as a cat at the Westminster Dog Show.

You're just out of your element, he told himself. But something more than the drive had put him on edge. In fact, he hadn't felt quite right since waking up that morning.

What's the matter, Clay? his wife, Helen, had asked as he dressed for the day, sensing his disquiet.

Nothing, he'd lied. *Just don't want to mess this up . . . got to make sure my t's are crossed and i's dotted.*

Helen smiled and stretched languorously, making no move to prevent a breast from slipping out of the ancient nightshirt she wore. *Come back to bed,* she said, her voice suddenly husky—with sex or tears he couldn't tell. *Don't go today. Let one of your young guys and the feds handle it. I got a bad feeling, baby.*

Fulton felt a chill run down his spine at his wife's words. He wasn't particularly superstitious, but he was also careful not to tempt fate by ignoring gut feelings and a woman's intuition. Still, there was nothing he could do about it except keep his eyes open. *I've got to go, baby,* he'd argued. *You know I won't ask one of my guys to do something I wouldn't. Besides, I promised Butch I'd ride shotgun.*

Oh to heck with Butch, she'd pouted. *And to heck with your machismo. If you'd rather play cops and robbers than stir it up with your wife, then to heck with you, too.*

Helen had, of course, popped out of bed before he left to make sure he knew she didn't mean any of it. But her unease combined with his own had filled him with a sense of foreboding that he still had not shaken eight hours and more than four hundred miles later.

The road wasn't even that bad. The fields and wooded areas on either side were snow covered, but the potentially slick spots on the asphalt were few and apparently of no concern to his driver—a young, moonfaced FBI agent, who whistled tunelessly and looked back and forth at the countryside like a tourist on holiday.

Fulton wanted to ask the agent . . . his name is Haggerty . . . to slow down a bit, but he didn't want to come off as chickenshit. So he kept his eyes on the unmarked New York State Highway Patrol car on the road ahead of them and maintained a bored expression on his face.

Only normal to feel apprehensive, he thought. After all, a very dangerous individual was sitting in the backseat next to Special-Agent-in-Charge Michael Grover. If not the most dangerous man in America, the prisoner, Andrew Kane, certainly ranked right up there. He was the most cold-blooded criminal Fulton had ever met over a long and "I've seen everything" career, and rich too, which made him even more dangerous.

Fulton glanced up at the mirror in the visor. Kane, the glib, handsome, and fabulously wealthy head of a Fifth Avenue law firm, stared out the side window, his hands cuffed together and locked to a chain-link bellyband. Six months earlier, he'd appeared to be headed for a landslide victory to become the next mayor of New York City. But that was before he'd been exposed by Fulton's boss, New York District Attorney Roger "Butch" Karp, as a homicidal megalomaniac whose tentacles went deep into the NYPD, the city government, and even the Catholic Archdiocese of New York.

Although technically a detective with the NYPD, Fulton worked as the head of the squad of detectives assigned to the NYDAO. He'd taken the job at Karp's request. The two of them had known each other for most of their respective careers, meeting when Fulton was a rookie cop and Karp a still wet-behind-the-ears prosecutor working for legendary DA Frank Garrahy.

Fulton and Karp had not always worked together. Karp had even gone into private practice for a short stretch before returning to the DAO where he'd been working as the chief of the vaunted homicide bureau when the governor appointed him to fulfill the remaining two years on the term of then–district attorney Jack Keegan, who'd been appointed to the federal bench.

The term was nearly up and now Karp was running for the office in November's elections. It was a thought that made Fulton chuckle. His old friend took to politicking about as well as a cat to water; he hated it and few things put him in a sour mood as did the necessity of what he labeled *kissing up to people you wouldn't spend two minutes with otherwise.*

"Are we there yet?" The mocking voice interrupted Fulton's recollections and brought him back to the moment. He glanced up at the mirror and into the smirking eyes of Andrew Kane.

Looking at Kane, it was hard to imagine him as a monster. Despite being approximately the same age as Karp and Fulton, the blue-eyed, blond-haired, and boyish Andrew Kane looked more like a well-preserved former fraternity president than a vicious crime boss charged with capital murder and a host of other major felonies. Nevertheless, they were on their way to a private psychiatric hospital in upstate New York to have Kane evaluated by doctors selected by his defense team, who hoped to have him declared insane and therefore not responsible for the crimes he'd been accused of.

The state's psychiatrists had already examined Kane and declared him fit to stand trial. Fulton had read their reports. Kane, they said, had an antisocial and schizophrenic personality disorder with strong narcissistic tendencies. In other words, he didn't give a shit about anybody else but himself.

Still, the important thing from the legal vantage of the prosecution was that he "knew and appreciated the nature, quality, and consequences" of his acts and that those acts were wrong. If the prosecution could prove that Kane possessed such a state of mind, he would be held accountable for his crimes, and any attempt at an insanity defense would be defeated.

Naturally, however, Kane's dream team of lawyers—the very best that money could buy—insisted that he be tested by their own doctors. The state's psychiatrists were obviously prejudiced, they argued, and the judge in the case, Paul Hans Lussman III, had allowed it. Like most judges, he was inclined to bend over backward on defense motions in a death penalty case so as to give the defendant every benefit of the doubt. Besides, no jurist likes to be reversed, especially on capital cases, which have a way of making it to the U.S. Supreme Court for the entire world to watch.

So now Fulton was riding shotgun on the transport security team. The New York City Department of Corrections was nominally in charge of getting Kane to and from the hospital for his evaluation. But Karp had asked him to oversee the security measures, which to Fulton meant he had to be there every step of the way.

"We'll get there when we get there," Fulton replied to Kane.

"If we get there, Mr. Fulton . . . if we get there," Kane laughed.

Fulton glanced at Haggerty, the driver, who smiled and rolled his eyes upward. They both knew that every precaution had been taken.

In fact, Fulton had taken a page from the past by re-creating a security detail he'd been on back in the late sixties.

Essentially, he was creating a diversion. To transport Andrew Kane, a five-car motorcade had wheeled up the driveway from the city jail known as the Tombs, and proceeded to the Willis Avenue Bridge. Crossing the East River, the motorcade converged with the Major Deegan Expressway, heading north toward Albany.

Meanwhile, an hour after the motorcade left, a hooded Andrew Kane was rushed out of the DA's elevator and into the armored Lincoln with Fulton and the two federal agents. A single unmarked NYPD sedan had escorted them up the West Side Highway and over the George Washington Bridge, where the New York cops were relieved at the sight of two state patrol cars with four armed officers inside each, with one taking the lead while the other brought up the rear.

Not even Kane's defense lawyers had been told what day Kane was to be transported, nor was anyone informed that they would be avoiding the interstates and traveling north on small country highways and back roads. The biggest irritation for Fulton had been having to pass his plan through Special-Agent-in-Charge Grover, now blank-faced as he sat in the back next to Kane. The feds had insisted on participating—Kane had broken several federal, as well as local, laws, and the word was that after "the locals" were through with him, they wanted to talk to Kane about some of his international dealings with suspected terrorist organizations. Thus, the presence of Agent Haggerty and Grover, who'd essentially rubber-stamped Fulton's plan.

"Yeah, well, if something goes wrong, it'll give me a chance to shoot your ass and save the taxpayers a lot of money," Fulton said and looked again in the mirror. The humor was gone from Kane's face, replaced by a mask of such malevolence that the detective was suddenly reminded of one of his mother's old sayings about letting sleeping dogs lie.

"I'll remember that, Mr. Fulton," Kane said, and turned his head to stare out the side window again as he clenched and unclenched his jaw.

Fifteen minutes later, Fulton was grabbing the "oh shit" handle above the door as Haggerty jumped on the brakes to avoid colliding with the car ahead of them. They'd come around a corner and found that the vehicle in front had suddenly slowed to five miles an hour as they approached some obstruction on the road ahead.

Fulton grabbed the radio microphone. "What's the problem, Alpha?" he asked, calling ahead to the lead car.

"Mr. Fulton, there's been an accident," was the reply. "Damn, looks like a school bus turned over on its side. There's an ambulance on scene. Should we lend a hand?"

Fulton opened the window and stuck his head out. He could see the yellow bus and the ambulance; a paramedic seemed to be administering to several children standing near the bus, while a second paramedic trotted toward the lead car waving his arms.

Furrowing his brow, Fulton asked aloud, "How come we didn't hear about this on the scanner?" Each of the cars was equipped with a standard police scanner that should have at least picked up the call for help and the response from the ambulance crew.

Pulling his head back in, he yelled into the microphone and grabbed his gun out of his shoulder holster. "It's a setup! Back up! Back up!"

As Haggerty and the drivers in the other cars began to comply, Fulton looked in the rearview mirror just as a figure clad in black stepped from a wooded area behind and to the side of the rear car. He recognized the grenade launcher on the man's shoulder a moment before the rear state patrol car was struck and exploded in a ball of fire that lifted the vehicle off the ground and flipped it over onto its top.

"Get us the hell out of here!" Fulton shouted at Agent Haggerty, who sat with his mouth open looking in the rearview mirror at the burning vehicle behind them.

Up ahead, Fulton saw a paramedic dive in through the window that the driver of the lead car had rolled down. There was a blinding flash and then a full-throated roar as the man detonated a bomb attached to his chest. The suicidal act was so unexpected that Fulton was as stunned as Agent Haggerty, who looked like a man desperately trying to wake up from a nightmare.

Fulton quickly recovered and reached over to turn the steering wheel violently to the left. He jammed his leg across to hit the gas pedal, and the big sedan lurched off the road, striking another black-clad figure who was pointing an automatic rifle at them but did not fire.

"Drive!" Fulton yelled at Haggerty, who started to respond, but just then his head exploded from the impact of a bullet. A red mist filled the air as the agent slumped forward, his lifeless hands dropping to his sides.

The car continued for perhaps twenty-five more yards with Fulton trying to drive despite the obstacle of the dead man, but finally mired itself in the mud. It's over, he thought. Shoot Kane before they get to you.

Fulton started to turn but saw, in his peripheral vision, that Kane's hand was already moving toward him. He noticed that there was something in Kane's hand, but there wasn't enough time for him to wonder why his prisoner was no longer restrained. He felt a jolt on his neck from the stun gun and then everything went black.

When the lights came back on, Fulton was lying in the snow outside the car. He heard a man's angry voice . . . Kane's.

"You fucking moron!" Kane was shouting. "You could have killed me!"

"They were trying to escape." Fulton recognized this voice after a moment as Special Agent Grover's. "I had to shoot him. I knew the car would slow down in the field."

"Knew?" Kane hissed. "You knew the car wouldn't roll? You knew we wouldn't plunge into one of these frickin' ponds these hicks have out here? What do you mean, you knew?"

Fulton raised himself on his elbows, conscious that two armed, hooded men stood behind him with their guns trained on his back. They did not try to stop him from watching Kane berating the quaking Grover.

"You're an idiot, and I can't abide idiots," Kane said. He reached up with the stun gun and zapped the federal agent in the face, knocking him to the ground. He then bent over and picked up the shaken man's gun.

"No, don't!" Grover pleaded weakly as he struggled to recover from the shock.

"You're too stupid to live, Grover," Kane replied and shot him in the face, blood and brains splattering the snow.

Kane nodded in satisfaction as the body twitched once then stopped. He walked over until he stood directly in front of Fulton. "You owe me one," he said. "Saved you having to shoot him yourself, but I guess you won't be shooting me today."

"Fuck you," Fulton replied. He figured that there wasn't much of a reason for Kane to let him live, so he might as well go out cursing his executioner. Good-bye, Helen. Good-bye, kids. I love you.

Kane laughed and pointed the gun, but turned hearing a shout from down the road.

Fulton looked that way as well. The hooded man up near the first burning police car yelled again. Fulton thought the words sounded Russian.

The smaller of the two guards behind him spoke—surprising Fulton because the voice was that of a woman—in yet another language . . . Arabic, maybe . . . to the guard next to her. This guard also proved to be a woman and replied to her comrade in Arabic, obviously translating what the man on the road was saying.

"He wants to know what to do with the prisoner," the first woman said to Kane in accented English.

Fulton looked at Kane and back to the scene on the highway. He could see one of the state police officers sitting on the ground, apparently wounded.

"Kill him, of course," Kane said.

The first woman shouted a command in Arabic, which the second woman translated to German or Russian, Fulton wasn't sure which, directing the translation back to the hooded man. She drew her hand across her throat for emphasis. The men on the road immediately shot the prisoner.

"Who's injured?" Kane asked the first woman, nodding toward the man who'd been run over when Fulton steered the car off the road. The man lay on the ground, propped up on an elbow and talking to one of his accomplices, who knelt to give him a cigarette.

"Akhmed Kadyrov," she said. "A Chechen."

"Hmmm . . . gives me an idea," Kane said. "Finish him and leave the body. We'll call our friends later and suggest that this presents an opportunity."

"And the infidel children?"

Kane scowled as though annoyed by one too many questions. "Must I tell you everything?"

"God, no!" Fulton shouted looking at the school bus where the children he'd seen earlier were now sitting, obviously crying.

The first woman shouted something else toward the men standing with the children. Apparently, one of the men there understood her and didn't need a translator. Immediately, there were several bursts of automatic rifle fire, which echoed across the fields. An eerie silence followed, which was broken by the cawing of crows and, after a moment, a bellow of rage from Fulton.

"God damn you, you murdering son of a bitch," he yelled. He tried to rise to his feet to go after Kane but was clubbed back to the ground by the two guards. Dazed, he rolled over onto his back. "Better finish it," he swore at Kane. "Or someday I'm going to kill you, you insane piece of crap."

Kane put a finger to his lips. "Oooooh. Down 'Shaft.' Always playing the hero, but it didn't do those children who were kind enough to participate in my little ruse any good, now did it? Or save any of these fine police officers and marshals? Guess being a hero didn't mean shit today."

Waving Agent Grover's gun at the detective, Kane said, "You know, I really should shoot you now. Isn't it always the way in movies: the bad guy doesn't kill the good guy when he has the chance and lives only long enough to regret it?"

Without warning, Kane rushed at Fulton and kicked him hard in the ribs, knocking the wind out of the detective. He kicked him again and again like he was punting a football. "You going to kill me, Detective?" he raged. "You think a piece of shit nigger is going to kill Andrew Kane?" He rained more blows.

Finally, Kane tired and stopped. Panting from his exertions, he said, "However, no, Detective Fulton. As much as I would like to stomp you to death like a cockroach, I'm not going to kill you. Not yet. I want you to have to live with this fine job you did weighing on your conscience for a while, maybe you'll decide to suck on the end of your gun and blow your ugly head off because all those kids were counting on you to deliver crazy Mr. Kane to the hospital safe and sound. But first, I need you to take a message back to our mutual friend Mr. Karp."

"Fuck you," Fulton croaked, spitting blood out on the snow. "I ain't your messenger boy."

"Oh, I think you'll do as told," Kane said, kicking Fulton again. "After all, ol' Butchie is going to want to know everything that happened here today. So tell him I said, 'The game is on.' And that I hope he's up to the challenge. I don't want this to be too easy when I kill every thing he loves—his bitch, his idiot kids, his imbecile friends, and even his fucking dog—before I come for him."

A black helicopter appeared from over the top of the trees and landed on the highway behind the last burning car. "Ah, my ride awaits," Kane said. "Samira, my love, would you do the honors."

Fulton looked back and saw that the first woman had a handgun pointed at his leg. She pulled the trigger and the bullet tore into his knee. He screamed in rage and pain, and then screamed louder as a second bullet blew his other knee apart.

"Just a little something to remember me by," Kane said. "I think your chasing days are done, don't you?" He giggled and took off at a trot for the helicopter with Samira and the other female terrorist on his heels.

As the helicopter took off, Fulton lay in the snow wishing that Kane had killed him. Then he thought of Helen and his children and slowly, painfully, began dragging himself through the snow toward the overturned school bus.

1

March

THE GNOME-LIKE ITALIAN GRANDMOTHER DROPPED HER OVER-
sized purse in the crosswalk as she tried to jostle her way through
the crowd at the corner of Canal and Centre streets in Lower Manhattan. A short, bandy-legged fellow with big ears stooped to pick it
up but was nearly knocked over when she pushed him away and
ripped the bag out of his grasp.

"Watch it, *minchione*," the old crone hissed.

Having essentially just been labeled a "fucking idiot," Ray Guma
backed off as his octogenarian assailant fixed him with what he assumed to be her version of *malocchio,* the "evil eye," while she
scuttled back to the curb.

"I'll call the cops," she shouted at him and gave him *il ditto
medio.*

You got to love us Eye-ties, Guma thought, we're such an ex-
pressive people. He hurried across the street and reached the curb
where he turned right and headed south toward his destination,
the Criminal Courts building at 100 Centre Street.

A storm had blown in Friday, dumping two feet of snow on the city, which by Monday morning was melting slush piles along the curbs and inescapable puddles on the sidewalks. Although the temperature had risen to fifty degrees, the skies were overcast with the weatherman hedging his bets—"a fifty percent chance"—on whether more snow was on the way. But even wets socks and irascible old women couldn't dampen Guma's mood as he approached the courthouse.

From a distance the building, with its four front towers and the jail behind it, looked massive, reminding him of an enormous gray toad towering seventeen stories above the streets and gobbling up the insect-sized humans who passed between the stone pillars at its mouth. The limestone and granite exterior was not welcoming to most, and many of those who went inside had reason to fear they would not be coming out—at least not for a while. But Assistant District Attorney Ray Guma never failed to appreciate the building as the scene of some of his greatest triumphs in life, or to reflect on the irony of the location, a trait that might have surprised those of his colleagues who thought he was not the contemplative sort.

The site on which it stood had once been known as Collect Pond, a large lake at the southern end of Manhattan that had teemed with fish and wildlife, first a favorite of the Indians, and then of picnickers and fishermen. But eventually the tanneries, slaughterhouses, and breweries moved in and polluted the water until it was little more than a cesspool and a breeding ground for mosquitoes and disease.

In 1802, the city had drained the lake and surrounding swamp to make room for houses, and for a brief few years, the area enjoyed a reputation as a respectable, if modest, neighborhood called Five Points for the convergence of streets that met there. But the homes had fallen into disrepair, and the upwardly mobile members of the neighborhood left for greener pasture uptown.

Through most of the nineteenth century, Five Points was a notorious hellhole of rotting tenement houses—occupied by the latest wave of impoverished immigrants and "free Negroes," as well as brothels and saloons. There, the law-abiding residents had been extorted, shanghaied, murdered, and terrorized by gangs and corrupt politicians until the victims, too, could flee or turn from prey to predator.

"This is the place; these narrow ways diverging to the right and left, and reeking everywhere with dirt and filth. Such lives as are led here bear the same fruit here as elsewhere," Guma recited quietly as he wove through the crowd toward the building with his eyes on the deliciously round ass of the woman walking in front of him—a favorite pastime.

The quote was from a passage that Charles Dickens had written about Five Points in *American Notes* after visiting the area escorted by two police officers. Guma's fifth-grade teacher had insisted that her class of Italian, Irish, German, African, Puerto Rican, and other children of immigrants memorize parts of it as being integral to their personal histories. He was surprised that more than four decades later he could remember even that much of it.

"Where dogs would howl to lie, men and women and boys slink off to sleep," said a voice at his side, "forcing the dislodged rats to move away in quest of better lodgings."

Guma stopped and looked over at a dirt-encrusted, bug-eyed bald man who also stopped and stood grinning at him—whether from mirth or insanity, Guma could not tell. With a gaping hole where his teeth had once been and the disintegrating potpourri of indistinct clothing he wore, the man looked like he also could very well have been the moronic great-grandchild of some unfortunate genetic mix from the old Five Points denizens. "All that is loathsome, drooping, and decayed is here," the stranger said and giggled.

Normally, Guma would have merely smiled and nodded to a man who'd done him no more harm than help recall an old passage from a story. You could not live most of your life around the streets of New York, especially working for the DAO, without developing a certain tolerance, even fondness, for the diversity of its huddled masses. But the man's protruding yellow-green eyes and the idiot grin made Guma uncomfortable. "You know your Dickens," Guma said, intending to pass by.

The man jumped back. Giving Guma a wide berth—to the point of rudely pushing other pedestrians out of his way—the madman circled around until he was safely behind, then ran off down the sidewalk, shouting as if he were being chased. "He knows Dickens! He knows Dickens! Beware! Beware!"

Guma shook his head as he watched the man disappear in the bobbing mass of heads. Then he noticed the suspicious glances from fellow New Yorkers and cautious stares of visitors, all trying to assess if he was part of the insanity. He supposed that dressed in comfortable but old sweat clothes and ratty Nikes—part of his on-again, off-again regime to "get back in shape"—and sporting a two-day growth of beard—part of his plan to shave as little as possible—he might have missed the "maturing but still virile" look he'd aimed for and achieved "eccentric old bum" instead. He decided to ignore the looks and hurry on.

Approaching the stairs leading to the building's maw, Guma looked up and paused appreciatively. It was almost the twentieth century before the city fathers got up the nerve to raze the squalor that was Five Points and, in a sort of civic slap to the face of the evil done there in the past, built a courthouse across Franklin Street from the old Tombs prison. The Tombs got its name because the locals thought it looked like an Egyptian mausoleum; it was considered one of the worst prisons in the country for most of the century. Small wonder that the catwalk connecting the courthouse and prison over which prisoners passed was called the Bridge of Sighs.

Guma knew the history by heart and took pride in being able to recall its details. The city jail had been rebuilt several times and was now officially the Manhattan Detention Center, though it had retained its nickname through each of its incarnations. And it was still connected to the Criminal Courts building by an underground tunnel through which thousands of prisoners still sighed on their way to see the judge or return to their cells.

In 1941, the old criminal courts building also had been replaced with the current one. It housed the city's Criminal and Supreme courts, Legal Aid, offices for the NYPD, the Department of Correction, the Department of Probation, and, on the eighth floor the Office of the District Attorney of New York County.

Climbing the stairs to the entrance, Guma began to labor. Once upon a time, before the cancer, he'd entered the building like he owned the place—a young, macho assistant district attorney with the New York DAO. Back then he'd been known as "the Italian Stallion" . . . feared by bad men, revered by women both good and bad. . . . At least that was his story and he'd stuck to it for the better part of thirty or so years.

"More like the 'Sicilian Shetland Pony' these days," he grumbled as he arrived at the top of the stairs winded from the minor exertion. *Maybe it's metastasized to your lungs.* He quickly shook off the dark thought. That's thinking like a loser. You a loser, Guma?

The cancer had started as a constant ache in his gut; then there was blood in his urine, and finally a sharper pain that wouldn't subside no matter how much whiskey he drank or pain pills he swallowed. He'd overcome a standing distaste for doctors, which returned when one told him that he had cancer. A very bad, aggressive cancer that would kill him soon if he didn't take drastic measures, the man said. Those measures had included removing a few yards of his guts, followed by miserable bouts of chemotherapy that made him wish he were dead.

However, he'd survived what might have killed a less strong-willed individual, but it had also made an old man out of him. Sometimes the change was only outward. His once wavy black hair had turned white almost overnight, and the thickly muscled baseball player's body had wasted into sagging skin and aching bones. On cool, wet days like this one, he could feel where he'd been laid open, his diseased parts removed, and then sewn back together.

Most of the time, he still thought like the Ray Guma of old—cocky, headstrong, and convinced that he was God's gift to women. His mind was still as agile as ever, the biting wit razor sharp, even if he didn't have as much energy for lengthy debate or even screwing as he had back in the day.

Yet, some days he had a hard time shaking the feeling that he was just biding his time until "the really bad news." In fact, sometimes he felt like he was walking around inside the outer shell of a man he might have once been, but that man had taken a horrible beating and been left a frightened victim of a crime he couldn't prevent. It surprised him. He'd always thought he would be the sort to scoff in the face of death, but it wasn't the case. There were days when he was sure the pain in his abdomen was more than scar tissue tearing, or the shortness of breath a warning that the cancer had moved north.

Then at night, he'd lie alone in his bed, trying to tune in to what his body was telling him. But all he could hear would be his heart beating through the mattress: *Doom-doom. Doom-doom. Doom-doom.* On nights like that, he'd get up, dress, and go try to walk off the anxiety attacks that threatened to overwhelm him when surrounded by four walls.

The feeling never lasted, usually not even on those nights. The morning light would find him calm and contemplative, sitting on some park bench with the sun on his smiling face like some Italian Buddha, happily listening to the city launch into day mode. Then the pugnacious, womanizing street kid would reemerge ready to fight or make love, whichever came first . . . bad guys and good women beware.

Guma entered the Criminal Courts building and looked up at the big clock that hung down from the exact center of the two-story lobby. It was another impact of the disease that he rarely wore a watch anymore; he didn't need anything telling him how much time was left in the day.

On time, he thought as he headed to the elevator to take him up to the eighth floor. He was thankful to have work. The cancer treatments had forced him to take a leave of absence, and he still didn't have the energy for a full-time caseload. But Karp let him do what he could.

Of late, a period covering the past several months, he'd taken an interest in so-called cold cases—homicides that had gone unsolved and been shelved to await further development. The files—literally thousands of them—were kept in a corner of the basement. With the help of one of the old, retired NYPD detectives hired by Karp to work on special investigations, a tough old-school cop named Clarke Fairbrother, he'd started looking through the files for one that might have some hope of resolution.

It wasn't a case of chasing ghosts. With improvements in forensic investigation tools, like national databases for DNA and finger-prints, cases formerly thought to be unsolvable were being brought to justice more and more frequently. And some just needed a fresh set of eyes.

He'd found several cases that held promise. But the excitement he was feeling at the moment had been initiated not by his investigations, but a telephone call. As he stepped off the elevator, his mind flashed to the photograph of the victim, Teresa Stavros, a beautiful woman when she'd disappeared some fifteen years earlier and whose face had worked its way into his dreams.

Entering the outer office, he was met immediately with the disapproving glance of his boss's receptionist. "Hello, Mrs. Milk-Toast," he said cheerily.

Mrs. Milquetost glared at him. They'd been having this battle over the pronunciation of her name ever since she started working several months earlier.

"There are three syllables in my name, Mr. Guma—Mil-Kay-Tossed . . . it's French, Mr. Guma . . . Mrs. Mil-Kay-Tossed," she lectured. "And I'd appreciate it if you'd be so kind as to remember that in the future."

Guma smiled and said, "Sorry, I was just yanking your chain, Darla. I promise to do better in the future. Is the boss in?"

Just then Butch Karp opened the door and stuck his head out. "Mr. Guma, if you'd be so kind as to join me in my office," he said.

2

"**WOULD YOU MIND NOT ANTAGONIZING MY RECEPTIONIST,**" Karp said after he shut the door. "Mrs. Milquetost may be a bit eccentric, but she is efficient, minds her own business, and, unlike my last receptionist, doesn't seem to be spying on me for Andrew Kane."

"Sorry. Can't help it," Guma laughed. "She reminds me of my fifth-grade teacher, Sue Queen. A real tyrant. But I'll try."

"I'd appreciate it," Karp replied. Then his eyebrow arched, he grinned wickedly, and added, "There isn't something going on between you and Mrs. M, is there?"

Guma looked horrified. "What in the hell do you mean by that?" he demanded.

"Oh, I don't know. You say she reminds you of your fifth-grade teacher, but this reminds me more of a twelve-year-old boy yanking on the ponytail of a girl he likes—"

"Christ on a crutch, give me a break. Are ya blind?" Guma exclaimed. "She must be a hundred years old—"

"I looked at her résumé, she's two years younger than you. A widow, too."

"There's chronological age and there's psychological age," Guma sniffed. "I date women who look closer to my psychological age."

"Yeah, but teenagers under the age of sixteen are off limits in the state of New York," Karp said, circling around to his seat on which he plopped down with a self-satisfied smirk. "Nevertheless, I'll thank you kindly if you'd avoid boinking Mrs. Milquetost should you ever find her drunk at an office party and in a compromised position. Office romances are such a pain in the ass."

"Screw you, Karp," Guma said, smiling as he sat in the leather chair by the bookcase, across the room from his boss's desk. He'd never been one who liked sitting in a chair across a desk from someone else; it made him feel subservient. He glanced at the small stand with a green-shaded reading lamp next to the chair and reached for a small black object. "Black bishop," he said. "Yours?"

Karp shook his head. "Nah, you know I'm too impatient for chess. I saw it earlier on the floor and figured it was yours or V.T.'s, so I put it there."

Guma and V. T. Newbury were two of Karp's oldest friends. They'd all graduated law school and hooked up with the New York DAO within a few years of each other. In contrast to Guma, or Karp, Newbury possessed a dry wit and cool exterior, and had been a handsomely aristocratic Yale Law boy and the scion of a senior partner in one of the city's most prestigious white-shoe law firms; but he'd turned his back on civil litigation and wealth for the low-pay but high-reward task of prosecuting criminals. Guma was the hot-blooded son of Italian immigrants. When just starting out at the DAO, he'd carried quite a chip on his broad, neckless shoulders, especially around better-heeled colleagues, but it had been offset by his sense of humor, abilities in the courtroom, and general joie de vivre.

Both Guma and Newbury possessed rapier-sharp legal minds. But Newbury preferred the complex, thinking-man's cases, which was why Karp had him heading up the White Collar Fraud and Rackets Bureau. The bureau primarily focused on business fraud, organized crime, and public corruption. He and his team, known around the office as "the Newbury Gang," had aggressively and successfully prosecuted high-level politicians, government officials, and other white-collar felons in and out of the justice system.

Meanwhile, Guma liked his cases down and dirty, the messier the better. He hated to plea bargain and was happiest in the courtroom in front of jurors—preferably women jurors—watching him dismantle the bad guy's defense and send him off to prison.

One thing they did have in common was the game of chess. They'd been going at it ever since Karp had known them, both playing in styles that matched their personalities. Newbury preferred the classical attacks and defenses; he could name them and recall the point at which they'd been used in world tournaments. Guma had learned his game at the knee of old Italian men sitting in parks on sunny days. He simply attacked, making up for his lack of finesse with an innate sense for an opponent's weaknesses. *Defense* was a foreign word to Guma, except when applied to the other attorney, at which point it became a curse word.

"Not mine," Guma said of the chess piece, which he put back on the table. "Maybe V.T.'s. It's certainly his taste—expensive—but I've never seen that particular bishop. Check out the detail in the carving. It looks like a little statue."

"I'll check it out later," Karp said, yawning. "Excuse me, guess I'm a little bushed. So what's this case you're all pumped up about? And don't you want to bring it up at the regular meeting?"

Every Monday morning, Karp met with his bureau chiefs and a few other select assistant district attorneys to review cases, which meant grilling each other to ensure that the convicting evidence was trustworthy and looking to shore up weaknesses. The practice had started with the Old Man, Frank Garrahy, who believed that cases were won or lost in the preparation stages, long before they went to trial.

"I will next week," Guma said, reaching into his coat pocket for a cigar, which he stuck in his mouth without lighting. "But I wanted to run it by you first, and for you to meet someone, before I take it to the rest of the law-school underachievers you employ."

"Meet?" Karp said, looking at his watch. "When?"

"In about three minutes, if this kid is punctual, and I suspect he will be," Guma said. "But there's another reason why I wanted to talk about this before the meeting; you know how some people like talking to the media more than they should."

Karp had a standing rule that no one in his office was supposed to discuss anything with the press without prior approval—especially to comment on ongoing cases. But it was only natural for young assistant district attorneys, some of whom got invited to the meeting to discuss big cases, to want to highlight their exalted position as "someone in the know" by leaking juicy tidbits to the media. Karp was also getting uneasy with the way Guma was obviously trying to break bad news to him "gently."

"Spill it, Guma," he growled. "You're getting entirely too much pleasure out of watching me squirm."

"Payback for the Milquetost innuendos." Guma smiled at his friend over the tip of the cigar as he slouched further into the chair. "The 'other reason' is there may be political implications with pursuing this case at this time."

"Great."

"Let me give you a little background," Guma said, taking his cigar out of his mouth and sitting forward. "As you know, I've been spending a lot of time going through old files in that cold, tiny cubicle you so graciously arranged for me in the basement—"

"You asked to be down there."

"Yeah, but you might have installed some carpeting and a light or two more than the single bulb dangling from a wire in the ceiling—"

"Objection: exaggeration. Get on with it, Goom."

"Sure, sure. Anyway, I'm shivering in the near-dark at my minuscule desk when I get a telephone call from some guy who says some other guy saw his dad choke his mother. The guy on the phone says they think the dad killed her because she disappeared suddenly without a word."

"Seems pretty straightforward," Karp said. "Why aren't they going to the cops?"

"Because it's a cold case. The cops aren't interested."

"You believe it?"

"Maybe," Guma said. "I went and talked to the son who supposedly witnessed the murder. At first, he was surprised I knew about it, but then he loosened up and told me the story. Pretty believable as witnesses go, but there are a couple of reasons I wanted to get a second opinion from you before I go forward with this. For one thing, the woman disappeared fourteen years ago."

Karp whistled. A lot of police departments across the country were creating "cold case" squads to revive old homicide cases. There was no statute of limitations on murder and forensic sciences had been making enormous strides in recent years. But not many DAOs that he knew of were conducting their own investigations.

Then again, Guma wasn't on the regular payroll. If he and his former detective pal, Clarke Fairbrother, wanted to knock the dust off some old files and see if they could bring some killer to justice, more power to them. But fourteen years was a long time—witnesses die or disappear or "forget"; evidence gets lost . . . and what about this "political ramification," he thought. That didn't sound good. "You want to drop the other shoe now, please."

Guma sucked on the cigar and looked down at it lovingly before turning his gaze back to Karp. "This kid's father is Emil Stavros."

Karp let out an involuntary groan. Emil Stavros. Wealthy banker, moved in the best social circles, and, of greater concern, a major mover and shaker in the opposition party. The party that had at one time backed Andrew Kane as the next mayor of the Big Apple. The thought of Kane . . . the dead children . . . Fulton crippled . . . he had to focus to hear Guma.

"Hey, I know," Guma said, holding up a hand. "Bad timing with the election seven months away. We can always wait and go after this in December . . . if you win. If you don't, well, I expect we'll all be fired and that will be the last we hear of it."

Karp caught the challenge in Guma's comment. His old friend didn't give a rat's ass about politics, nor did he have much respect for those who let it influence their decisions. "Let's presume for a moment that I win the election, what are the other hazards of waiting so that this doesn't come off as dirty politics?"

Guma shrugged. "Well, I suppose something bad could happen to this kid."

"Kid?"

"Zachary Stavros . . . kid as in almost twenty years old. He and his old man are estranged."

"And you're saying Daddy might have his baby boy whacked?"

Guma studied his cigar. "Who knows?" he said. "A kid who hates your guts is going to end your happy millionaire life and get you sent off to the can? People get killed for a lot less. But I don't think the old man knows what Zachary is saying, so he's probably safe until after the election."

Karp pondered the possibilities. "You know who the caller was? Maybe he has something more."

"No. He didn't give a name. No Caller ID and it wasn't traceable. I had a hunch it might have been Zachary's psychologist, who is supposedly the only other person who knows about this. But I talked to the doc, with Zachary's permission. He, of course, denied revealing 'confidential information,' and, well, the voice wasn't the same."

"Psychologist?" Karp asked as the red flags went up in his head. Great, I can hear the "dirty politics" accusations now, all based on testimony from a nutcase.

Guma looked up at the ceiling as if he'd suddenly discovered something unusual there. "Uh, yeah . . . forgot to tell you, but this is a 'repressed memory' thing."

Karp groaned again. Repressed memory was where someone buried—or repressed—the memory of traumatic events, only to "recover," or recall, them later, usually with the help of a psychologist using hypnosis. It had become popular in the eighties, and he knew of cases in which defendants had been convicted on nothing more than the recovered memory of the accuser. However, it was notoriously unreliable. Instances had been found in which the accuser—usually someone with serious psychological problems that led to the psychologist's couch in the first place—"recovered" memories of events that they had actually read about in newspapers or heard in long-ago conversations. There had even been cases in which the hypnotist, intentionally or unintentionally, had "planted" in the patient false memories, that upon waking, were remembered as real.

From wide acceptance—by both prosecutors and defense lawyers, depending on which side the repressed memories helped—the science had since fallen into a gray area of the law. Anyway, it was a huge battle to get such testimony into evidence and usually only when backed up by corroborating evidence.

For Karp, if the corroborating evidence wasn't sufficiently compelling and independently establishing the defendant's guilt, he wouldn't consider offering the so-called repressed memory at trial. "I remember the Stavros case, somewhat," he said, not wanting to rain on Guma's parade, yet.

"You should," Guma replied. "It was page-one headline material for weeks. 'Wealthy socialite disappears.' 'Banker husband investigated by police.' 'Police clear banker husband when socialite sighted in Buenos Aires.' On and on and on."

"They ever find a body?" Karp asked hopefully. Without a body, the repressed memory hurdle became a wall topped with razor wire.

Guma shook his head. "No. But I might know where to look."

Before Karp had a chance to ask where that might be, Mrs. Milquetost buzzed in on the intercom. "There's a young man here to see you. Says he has an appointment, though I don't see it anywhere on my—"

"That's okay," Karp said. "This was spur of the moment, send him in."

A moment later, a tall young man in a black T-shirt and jeans—stunningly handsome despite the too-pale complexion, dark eye makeup, and a "sleeve" of tattoos that covered his entire right arm down to the wrist—walked in. His nearly coal black hair was short and formed into neat ringlets, and he had the sad, deep-set brown eyes of a poet.

Even the air about him was melancholy, until he smiled, at which point the sun seemed to come in the office windows just a tad brighter. He stepped forward to shake Karp's hand and then turned to Guma. "Hi, Mr. Guma," he said. "I take it I'm in the right place."

Guma got up and shook the young man's hand warmly, then led him over to a couch near Karp's desk on which they both sat. "I know you're nervous, but you can trust Mr. Karp. Despite being the district attorney, he's an all-right guy. I just wanted him to hear your story from your mouth. As I told you, pursuing this would be very difficult."

"I'm sure," Zachary said, the smile disappearing as he looked back at Karp. "My father's a powerful man."

"Well, that may be true, but that's not the issue right now," Guma said. "Whoever sits in that chair over there is pretty powerful, too. There are certainly more important considerations, not the least of which is you would be testifying against your father. He's your only family, right?"

Zachary nodded. "Yeah, my mom was an only child and her parents died a long time ago . . . not long after she disappeared," he said. "My dad's a second-generation Greek immigrant. His family never wanted anything to do with me. In other words, there's not much family to this family. Never was. . . . Now, where should I start?"

3

ROGER "BUTCH" KARP HEARD FULTON GROUSING THE MINUTE
he got off the elevator on the fourth floor at Beth Israel Hospital
and was glad it gave him something to smile about. Butch hated
visiting hospitals, even a nice, modern facility like BI. Above all, he
hated the smell of hospitals—the cleaning fluids that couldn't disguise the stench of urine and blood and the cloying presence of
death and disease.

Ever since high school, he'd associated these smells with the
pain his mother had been put through as she battled cancer. It
didn't matter that she'd died at home, there'd been too many trips
to the hospital for tests and surgeries, too much watching her suffer as the doctors poked, prodded, and shook their heads with long
mournful faces. *Nothing can be done. . . . We'll try to make her as
comfortable as possible. Sorry, son.*

Nor did it matter that atop the list of Karp's happiest moments
had been his presence at the births of his three children: Lucy,
the eldest, and the twins, Isaac and Giancarlo. He still hated hospitals.

Yet he had to laugh as he drew closer to Fulton's room from

which there came the sound of objects crashing to the floor and the detective bellowing at the top of his lungs. "I don't need nobody's help to take a piss, young lady. Now, if you'll just stand aside and hand me the walker, I'll manage to drain the tank just fine on my own."

A young female voice argued back. "Now, Mr. Fulton, you aren't supposed to get out of bed without two nurses here to assist you," she said. "I'm not big enough to support you by myself if you fell. But if you'll just wait a moment, I'll call for another nurse. Or you can use the bottle we've provided next to your bed."

"Ah, for Christ's sake, I just want to take a whiz in a toilet without a couple of women watching . . ."

Karp entered the room and saw Fulton perched on the edge of the hospital bed, waving his outstretched arms at a pretty little blond nurse who stood between him and an aluminum walker. Fulton looked up at the intruder with a scowl, but his expression changed when he saw it was Karp.

"Butch! Just the man I wanted to see," Fulton said. "Now, nurse, my friend Butch here will do just fine with piss duty. As you can see, he's a big strapping fellow; he'll save me if I fall in and begin to drown. Now, hand me the walker."

The nurse—Nancy Hull, if her name tag was accurate—looked at Karp dubiously. But she had to admit that the visitor was a big man—six foot five or so, she guessed—and looked like he worked out. She liked the way he was smiling at her with his curiously almond-shaped eyes which, she noted, were gray and flecked with gold. Nurse Nancy turned and handed the walker to Fulton, who practically jumped out of bed.

Karp quickly realized that the nurse's concerns were not without merit. His friend nearly toppled over to the side and would have fallen except that Karp reached out to steady him.

"Thanks," Fulton said, grimacing in pain from having tweaked a knee catching himself. "I've got it from here, if you'd kindly get the bathroom door."

Karp reached for the handle and held the door open. Fulton half walked and half dragged himself into the bathroom with Nurse

Nancy positioned on the other side, looking as if she was prepared to dive under the big man to break his fall if necessary.

"Out," Fulton demanded as he reached the toilet.

"But—" Nurse Nancy began to complain.

"Out. Nonnegotiable. Vamoose! Butch can stay if it makes you feel any better, but you have to scram. . . . Please."

The nurse stood back with a sniff and shut the door. Satisfied that his privacy was not going to be invaded, Fulton positioned the walker so that he could relieve himself. "They're saying I can go home in the next day or two," he grumbled back at Karp. "But I have to stay off my legs for a few weeks, then gradually rehab back into shape. I can't wait. The worst thing about this place is all these people treating me like a child. A big, helpless child. I just want to get back to work and hopefully someday run into the mo'fo who did this."

Karp listened patiently to the rant, which he'd heard since shortly after that terrible day. A farmer in upstate New York, out trying to discover what all the black smoke over by the highway was about, discovered the massacre. Fulton had been found lying with his head on the body of a murdered child, passed out due to loss of blood and shock. His survival had been touch and go for a bit, and there'd been concern about brain damage from the blood loss. But he'd pulled through with his wife, Helen, at his side, and there appeared to be nothing physically wrong with him other than the damage done to his knees.

The surgeons had been able to repair one knee with the expectation that it would fully recover with physical therapy. *You were lucky,* the surgeon told him. *The bullet damaged a ligament and nicked a pretty major blood vessel, but it didn't hit the bone.* However, the joint in the second knee had been destroyed, requiring a total knee replacement and the honest assessment, *You may never walk quite normally again. There was damage to the perineal nerve that affects how you raise and lower your foot—a condition known as "drop foot" may result, as well as a general loss of strength.*

"I was going to have to have my knees done someday anyway because of football," Fulton said as he finished his business and washed his hands. "This was just a little earlier than I'd hoped." He paused and looked down at the floor. "It's probably going to get me on the department's physically-unable-to-perform list . . . mandatory retirement."

Fulton's voice had gone froggy at the statement, and Karp pretended not to notice him swiping at the tears on his face. He assured Fulton that if the police department forced him to retire, he'd still have the job as head of the DAO's investigations unit. "That won't change," Karp said reassuringly.

"Thanks, I appreciate it . . . but it's not the same," Fulton replied. "I've been part of the NYPD for most of my life. That's who I am . . . a cop with the finest police department in the world. . . . I wouldn't be part of the thin blue line anymore." Fulton seemed to realize the effect he was having on his friend and quickly added, "But that's okay. You and I can still put the bad guys in the can. I'll just do it as a civilian with the DAO, right?"

"Yeah, right, Clay," Karp agreed. He hesitated. "I'm sorry. Sorry I asked you to oversee this one. We should have had the feds handle the whole thing."

Fulton scowled. "To hell with that," he said yanking paper towels from the dispenser. "We've been over this before. The traitor was a fed, Michael Grover. That's how we got ambushed."

Karp nodded. "Yes, I know, I just—"

Before he could finish the thought, Fulton had dismissed it. "I'm the only one who'll have to answer for this fuckup. I knew something wasn't right . . . I could *feel* it. . . . I should have just stuck with my own guys like I wanted; guys I've known practically their whole adult lives. But I didn't follow my instincts and now all those kids and those men are dead."

The last sentence came out as a sob. Fulton's massive shoulders shook as he cried. Not knowing what else to do, Karp put a hand on his back. "We'll get them all, Clay," he gently enunciated, feeling less than adequate at coming up with the right words. "We'll get the bastards who did it."

Fulton nodded and straightened up. He pulled another paper

towel from the rack, wet it, and wiped his face. Karp noted the dark circles under his friend's eyes.

In all, six children, ages seven to twelve, had been on the rural school bus commandeered by the terrorists. Six dead children, one dead bus driver, plus nine dead police officers and federal agents. Ten if Grover was counted, but no one was shedding any tears for him.

"So anything new on Kane?" Fulton asked to break the ice as Karp opened the bathroom door.

The public had not been told much about Kane's escape except that apparent Islamic terrorists had murdered children and law enforcement officers and that authorities believed these terrorists had freed Kane, who was now referred to in the press as "the criminal mastermind Andrew Kane" because of his suspected ties to arms dealers. One of the terrorists had died, and one New York police detective had been wounded and survived, but no identities were being released "at this time."

In the meantime, the nation had been put on Red Alert as the largest manhunt in U.S. history was launched. But Kane and his accomplices had disappeared.

Meanwhile, the press was going bonkers, clamoring for more, filing Freedom of Information Act demands for whatever public records might exist, but none did—or they were deemed part of the "ongoing investigation" and therefore exempt. The media camped out on the lawns of the families grieving for their children and spoke in stage whispers for the cameras at the funerals of the murdered officers. It was a bonanza for retired generals and terrorism experts, who were trotted out by the television networks as being the final authorities on the latest casualties in the War on Terrorism.

"Maybe, I can help answer that."

Karp and Fulton looked over at the doorway as S. P. Jaxon, the FBI's man in charge of the New York office and an old friend of Karp's, walked into the room followed by another man. It was the second man who'd spoken.

"Roger Karp, Clay Fulton, I'd like you to meet Jon Ellis, the assistant director of special operations with the U.S. Department of Homeland Security," Jaxon said. "Jon, this is Mr. Roger Karp, Butch to his friends, the district attorney of New York County. And you know all about Mr. Fulton, one of New York's finest."

Ellis stepped forward and shook hands with Karp and Fulton. "Of course, no introductions needed," he said. "I'm a big fan, Mr. Karp—Butch, if I may—and Mr. Fulton's reputation with the NYPD is legendary."

"Hi, Espey," Karp said, shaking the FBI agent's hand before turning to shake Ellis's. "Special ops?" The man smiled, but Karp noticed that his eyes did not crease with any humor. Botox or that's just the way he is, a cold fish? he wondered.

"Nothing like military special ops, Butch," Ellis replied. "More of a catchall for all the shit—pardon my French, sir—but the shit nobody else knows what to do with. Mostly odds and ends."

Yeah, like I believe that, Karp thought. Something tells me this guy is no odds-and-ends man.

Jon Ellis wasn't particularly large; in fact, he was a shade under five foot ten, but from the way he moved, Karp knew there was a trained, muscular body beneath his conservative Brooks Brothers suit. Ellis's face was tanned and his eyes gray as rain clouds; Karp knew they were assessing him and filing the information into some internal computer.

"Jon will be handling the Kane case, at least the federal side of it," Jaxon said. "The FBI will mostly be assisting. I've been temporarily appointed to be the agency's liaison with Homeland Security."

Karp noticed the tightness in Jaxon's voice and attributed it to the interagency power struggles the feds were known for. Silver haired, lean, and lithe as a cat, Jaxon, known to his friends simply as Espey, was no slouch himself but exuded none of the other man's cockiness.

"We'll do our best to cooperate," Karp said. "Now, you were going to answer Mr. Fulton's question about the latest on Kane?"

Ellis went over to the doorway and looked up and down the hallway before closing the door. He then picked up the television remote control from the bed stand and turned up the volume.

A bit melodramatic, Karp thought. But maybe that goes with the spook business.

"This goes no further," Ellis warned. "I shouldn't really be telling you, but Mr. Jaxon assures me you can be trusted absolutely and need to be in the loop. As to your question, we don't know where Kane is at the moment, although we have reason to believe that he remains in the United States." Ellis looked at Fulton. "However, you were right about the terrorists speaking Russian. We've identified the dead guy as Akhmed Kadyrov, a Chechen terrorist with ties to al Qaeda."

"Chechen?" Fulton asked.

"Yeah, from Chechnya or, as they call it, Ichkeria, in southern Russia. He was one of these so-called Chechen nationalists who want to establish an independent state . . . full of patriotic anti-Russian rhetoric, but really just a collection of thugs, gangsters, and Islamic extremists. The Russians think he was behind several bombings last year in Moscow that killed a lot of civilians. He may also have been involved in the Nord-Ost musical theater takeover in Moscow, 129 people killed, as well as the school massacre in Beslan last September. They killed 341 people in that one, 172 of them children. Obviously, the world's a better place without him. The Russian ambassador will be appearing at the White House tomorrow with the president to use this attack to blast Chechen terrorists as a worldwide threat and renew his country's commitment to the 'War on Terrorism,' whatever that means."

"What have these guys got to do with Kane?" Karp asked.

"Good question. But as you know," Ellis pointed out, "we suspect that one of Kane's 'extracurricular' businesses, while maintaining the public persona, was arms dealing—much of it supplying terrorist organizations and various insurgencies with everything from rifles to shoulder-fired anti-aircraft missiles. Your guy, Newbury . . . who, by the way, is very, very good, we'd like to steal him away—"

"He's spoken for," Karp said with an equally false smile while thinking, This guy certainly likes to work the crowd.

"Ah, the jealous boyfriend." Ellis laughed. "But I'll leave it for the moment. Anyway, your guy Newbury has also uncovered some paper trails indicating Kane was sort of a one-stop supermarket for terrorists . . . weapons, maybe even working on acquiring WMD . . . and banking. He apparently had connections and accounts at a number of U.S. and offshore banks and was transferring, laundering, and funneling large amounts of cash from a variety of sources including, get this, the Little Sisters of Islam Home for War Orphans. . . . Hey, who says these guys have no sense of humor?"

"With Newbury's help, we've frozen a lot of Kane's assets," Jaxon added. "I doubt we have them all, but it had to hurt."

"There are other arms dealers and crooked bankers," Karp said. "Why go through all the trouble—including murdering kids, which they knew was going to bring the heat in spades—for this one guy?"

Ellis shrugged. "What can I say? He's got something they want. We do know that they sent one of their top field operatives to get him."

"Don't tell me," Fulton said. "The girl."

Ellis snorted in disgust. "Some girl. She goes by Samira Azzam, though we don't think that's her real name. More of a political statement—the 'real' Samira Azzam was a Palestinian poet who was vehemently anti-Israeli way back when it all started in the forties."

"What happened to her?" Fulton asked.

"She died of a heart attack during the 1967 Arab-Israeli War when she heard that the Jews had captured Jerusalem. The current Samira Azzam is made of sterner stuff. . . . She does appear to be Palestinian, although there are no known photographs of her. She first surfaced as a militant with Hamas, but switched allegiances to al Qaeda in the late nineties. She's a born killer, ruthless, pitiless . . . as you saw with the children. In fact, while we suspect Kadyrov of being involved with the Beslan school massacre, we *know* Azzam was from reports by survivors and the one terrorist who was captured alive. She apparently supervised the setting of explosives in the gymnasium where most of the victims died, as well as the execution of twenty teachers early on in the siege to let the Russians know she was serious. How she got out of there when everyone else died is the million-dollar question."

"But she's Palestinian," Fulton noted. "These Chechens are Russian, right?"

It was Karp who shook his head and answered. "Ethnically different from Russians. More Asian than Slav, and mostly Muslim. They also speak their own language but will use Russian as a common language." When the others looked at him with raised eyebrows, he added, "My people are from the Galicia area of Poland. I know a little about the region that's down south in the Caucasus Mountains."

"Exactly," Ellis said. "But the question's still valid. What's a Palestinian terrorist, an Arab, doing mounting attacks in Russia, working with Chechen nationalists and local Islamic hard-liners? The unfortunate answer is that these groups are networking far more than ever before, merging into one big happy homicidal family. The bigger question is, what is Samira Azzam doing in the United States helping Kane escape?"

"So do you know the answer?" Karp asked when the agent hesitated.

Ellis looked at him as if trying to decide whether he could be trusted. Karp got the feeling that Ellis was putting on an act, attempting to indicate that they were "in this together." Karp had used this same technique plenty of times himself to lull recalcitrant witnesses and defendants into admitting more than they wanted.

Ellis looked at Jaxon, who nodded. "We're not sure, but we do know that the Chechen nationalists feel that the United States has joined the Russian government in siding against them. They're also Muslim, an alliance with al Qaeda seems likely. So our best bet is something that will strike a blow at both countries . . . or maybe cause a rift between them."

"Any idea what that might be?"

"Nothing for sure, yet."

"What about the Pope's visit?" Fulton asked. It had just been announced that the pontiff would be coming to Manhattan in September for the installment of the new archbishop of New York.

"We've considered it," Jaxon said, "but there are a couple of problems with the theory. One is that security around the Pope is almost heavier than the president of the United States. He's surrounded by his own security people, and the church keeps everything very close to the vest. The ceremony's going to be at St. Patrick's, invitation only inside, and the crowds will be searched and scanned and, along with unauthorized vehicles, be kept at a safe distance. It'd be a tough nut for anyone to crack."

"The bigger problem with the theory," Ellis interrupted, "is that Kane escaped before the Vatican announced the visit. Since the escape was obviously planned for months, and these things take time and money to implement, it's pretty obvious that Kane and the terrorists have something else in mind. We're getting a lot of conflicting information and rumors, but with Kane, the problem is knowing who to trust, even the cops."

Fulton stiffened at the implied criticism, which Jaxon noted. "Sorry, Clay," the FBI agent said, taking over for Ellis. "We all know that ninety-eight percent of the department is clean. But between Newbury's Gang and what help we've been able to lend, we've uncovered a pretty extensive network of cops with ties to Kane. As you know, the DAO has been bringing charges against those we can prove committed crimes. But it would be a mistake to believe that we've found them all . . . any more than we should assume that there are no more traitors within my agency."

Karp silently congratulated Jaxon for taking some of the sting out of Ellis's comment by accepting that they all had better look within before blaming other agencies. He knew that Jaxon had taken the defection of Agent Grover personally. They'd gone through the academy at Quantico together, Class of '76, and he'd considered him as trustworthy as they came, which was how Grover got the nod when he volunteered to be part of the escort detail.

Jaxon had told Karp about the conversation when Grover asked for the job. *Maybe I can get him to chat a bit. He'd probably prefer to spend his time in a federal pen than Attica. So there's a chance he'll want to make a deal.*

Ellis walked over to the window and looked out, peering both ways as if on the lookout for suspicious cars on the streets outside. "We do have a couple of assets going in," he said. "The first is that we have a man on the inside. He's the one who identified Azzam. He's still trying to work out an introduction to Kane."

"Sounds dangerous," Karp said.

Ellis smiled. "It is. But this guy's good. The . . . um, people, he worked for before signing on with Homeland Security planted him with an antigovernment white supremacist group years ago, mostly to feed us information on their plans. We kept him there but were careful not to overuse him or act on everything he told us. We occasionally even took a pretty good hit in order not to blow his cover. Then just before this little debacle with Kane, he learned that Azzam was in the country looking to buy plastic explosives and automatic weapons."

"From white supremacists?" Fulton asked, his forehead furrowed like a freshly plowed field. "Now I'm really getting confused."

"Lots of people are," Ellis said. "But there's an old Arab proverb, 'The enemy of my enemy is my friend.' These Islamic terrorists have one thing in common with our homegrown antigovernment types, like the late Mr. Timothy McVeigh. They all hate the United States enough to put aside their differences long enough to bring us down, then they'll squabble like vultures over the pieces. . . . In this case, 'strange bedfellows' works well for us; we've managed to get our guy set up with plastic explosives and some pretty sophisticated ordnance that Azzam was looking for . . ."

Fulton looked like he was going to jump off the bed and strangle Ellis. "You fucking telling me that the ordnance used on those kids and officers was supplied by a U.S. agent—"

Ellis held up his hand and shook his head. "No. Sorry should have explained that up front," he said. "Nothing's exchanged hands between our guy and the terrorists. That's a deal he's *trying* to set up. Azzam got the grenade launchers and automatic rifles from someone else . . . maybe Kane's connections."

"Why not get the plastic explosives and other stuff from Kane, too?" Karp asked.

"Don't know," Ellis replied. "Maybe he couldn't get it on time, or they wanted to shop around so as not to raise red flags with someone who might get curious about all that sudden influx of money for guns and explosives. The important thing here is that if our guy can get close, we may be able to catch Kane and nip this plan in the bud.

"However," Ellis continued, "we don't want our guy pressing too hard so that they get nervous. If they get wind that we're on to them, they'll just move on to some other target. If you want to trap tigers like Kane and Azzam, you have to stake a live goat to the ground and let them come to you."

"What goat?" Fulton asked.

"Me," Karp said. "I'm their other 'asset.' Me and my family and friends, we're your goats."

Ellis nodded. "As you know, Kane seems to have an ulterior motive besides whatever the terrorists are up to and that's to kill Butch and his family. That's the bad news. The good news is it means he's letting emotions—hate and vengeance—cloud his thinking, and it could be what trips him up. This is personal to him, and our shrinks believe that may be what draws him out of hiding first."

Jaxon pointed out, "There's also the possibility that all of this is about you and has nothing to do with the Chechen issue. You and your gang managed to mess up their plans to blow up Times Square on New Year's. In fact, you've been a thorn in their sides for a while now. They might have wanted Kane freed for other purposes, but Azzam may also be targeting the district attorney of New York before he screws it up for her side again."

"Which is why," Ellis added, "with your permission—and no disrespect to you, Mr. Fulton, I know your guys are providing security for the Karp family—but I'd like to have some of my guys watching, too. As good as I'm sure Clay's guys are, my teams are trained to spot these people and their techniques before they can succeed."

Seeing the look on Fulton's face, Karp started to say that he felt safe with the NYPD providing security—not to mention his wife's former life as a security expert—but Fulton spoke first. "I agree. These assholes already caught me with my pants down once. It can't hurt to have extra eyes and extra firepower around."

Karp closed his eyes and a malapropism of one of his favorite Yankees ever, Yogi Berra, popped into his head. "It's like déjà vu all over again."

4

AFTER THE TWO FEDS LEFT, KARP STAYED TO TALK AWHILE
longer, knowing that the long hours Fulton had with nothing to do
at the hospital weighed him down with thoughts of the future.

In many respects, they couldn't have been more different. Karp
was a Jew, born and raised in Brooklyn, the son of a moderately
successful businessman and a schoolteacher mother.

Fulton had been raised in Harlem, the son of a single mom
who'd worked three jobs rather than have her boys learn to rely on
government handouts. He was the youngest of three brothers. The
eldest, Percy, had been shot and killed by a robber while working
as an assistant manager in a liquor store. The perp had never been
caught, and the injustice of that had been one of the primary reasons that Clay had become a cop. His other brother, Donald, had
been drafted and sent to Vietnam in 1968 just in time for the Tet
Offensive. He'd not returned and been listed as missing in action.

The common denominator between Karp and Fulton was their
shared sense of right and wrong as actually being separate and distinct from one another—no gray areas for them. Fulton had never
accepted so much as a dime or a cup of coffee walking the streets

as a young cop or as a middle-aged detective. Nor did he break the rules to catch bad guys. And Fulton knew that Karp would have quit the work he loved rather than accept a bribe, or give in to a threat, or "do whatever it takes" to win a conviction, unless he could do "it" the right way. His nearly perfect conviction rate on homicide cases was due to intense preparation, a brilliant legal mind, and—as Fulton had seen time and time again in court—a sense of integrity that jurors connected with.

They were an odd pair of brothers, but brothers they were in the truest sense. Fulton lay back on the bed, let out a sigh, and strapped his right leg into a continuous-motion machine that flexed and unflexed the knee joint to keep it from stiffening, and to increase its range of motion. "This thing will drive you nuts," he grumbled as the machine began whirring away. "Every four hours the dungeon masters they call nurses come in and move it to the other leg—hurts like a bitch when the knee is stiff. A man can't get any sleep."

Karp made a motion as if playing the world's smallest violin. "Feeling sorry for yourself, again, Detective Fulton?" he said. "Whatever happened to Freight-train Fulton, the human wrecking machine fullback out of Syracuse who gave out as much punishment as he took?"

"Nobody around here to punish, 'cept Nurse Nancy," Freight-train sulked. "And if I give her too much lip, she threatens to give me an enema when I'm sleeping. She would, too. . . . But on to more important matters; what'd you think of that guy?"

"By 'that guy,'" Karp replied, "I take you to mean Ellis, not Jaxon, who I regard as a friend and the second most honest cop I know. He gives you his word on something, you could bank it. A rare trait these days. But as for Ellis, 'spooks' have always made me nervous, especially if they're ex-military."

"You picked up on the military vibes, too?" the detective asked.

"Yeah, but not a foot soldier; more the born-to-command type. I don't know what it is about these guys . . . they're always just so *sure* that they've got it all figured out, and they're condescending—the rest of us don't know what in the hell is going on, so we shouldn't even try to understand. They're the ones with the data, let them make the decisions, and they don't take it kindly if you question those decisions or their motives. After all, they're out to save Mom, apple pie, and the American Way. . . . Then again, maybe we need people like that these days to deal with the terrorists."

"Why, Butch, are you suggesting that circumstances can sometimes require measures that might be a little bit outside of the letter of the law?" Fulton asked with a lifted eyebrow. "Do I see that stiff neck bending?"

Karp knew his friend was only giving him grief, but scowled at him anyway for effect. "No, of course not," he answered. "While I'm sure it's going on, and maybe is even in our best interests, anybody—*anybody*—breaks the law in New York County, even in the name of national security, and they will answer to the NYPD and the DAO."

"Just asking," Fulton replied with a grin. "Wanted to make sure the rules of the game weren't changing around here."

Mention of the word *game* brought on an awkward silence, broken first by Fulton. "You know, they're right about Kane coming after you and the family. He may be the world's biggest liar, but he was telling the truth when he said the game was on between you and him. The worst thing about it is, I'm not in any position to protect you and it's eating me up."

Karp patted him on the shoulder. "Well, if it makes you feel any better, your guys are mother-henning me worse than Nurse Nancy does you. I can't sneeze in my bedroom without someone stepping out of the closet to hand me a tissue and say 'Bless you.'"

Fulton laughed. "They're good men, but this Kane, he's something else, and that Samira Azzam. . . . They killed those kids without blinking an eye, and I don't expect they'll blink when it comes to the twins, or Lucy, or Marlene, though I expect that wife of yours can take care of herself. . . . How's she doing, by the way?"

Karp hesitated—not because he wanted to keep anything from Fulton, who was as trusted as a brother, but because sometimes it was just plain hard to tell how Marlene was doing. They'd been together for almost thirty years—about as long as he'd known Fulton—having met when they were both young assistant district attorneys. But he never quite knew what was going on in that head of hers.

Marlene Ciampi was a violence magnet. She'd quit the district attorney's office after a letter bomb meant for Karp caused her to lose an eye, and started a firm that provided security to high-profile and wealthy clients. One of her "hobbies" had also been protecting women from abusive, often dangerous men.

Now, she was trying to deal with the recent death of her mother. Karp sensed that she was troubled about something regarding the death but wasn't ready to talk to him about it.

"She's still trying to adjust to her mother being gone and deciding what to do about her dad. He's reaching that point where he can't really live alone," Karp said. "But he doesn't want to leave the family home. . . . And she's still going through the ups and downs of trying to stay out of trouble, and the trouble on New Year's Eve didn't help much."

Both men were quiet for a moment, reflecting on what might have been. An Iraqi terrorist had nearly pulled off blowing up Times Square on New Year's Eve by planting explosives in an abandoned subway tunnel beneath the area. Tens of thousands would have died except for the actions of Marlene, a spiritual Indian police chief from the Taos Pueblo in New Mexico named John Jojola, as well as an old Vietnamese gangster, Tran Do Vinh, a cowboy, Ned Blanchet, and a millennialist vigilante, David Grale.

As strange a team of superheroes as ever walked out of a comic book, Karp thought. "It's tough to play by the rules when the other guys don't have to," he said.

"Yeah, the question is how do we win this game with Kane under those circumstances?" Fulton mused.

"Last man standing, I expect," Karp replied before his eyes glanced at the braces and he immediately regretted the comment. "Clay, I didn't mean—"

Fulton held up a hand. "No offense taken. I understood where you were coming from. But you're right; it's going to be him or you.

Just stay on your toes, Butch. Whenever you think you've got him figured out, try to look at it from another angle. We can win this one, too. This is a game to him, he's going to make a mistake, and we have to be ready."

When Karp was at last ready to leave, he stood and put on his coat. He felt something in the pocket and reached inside, pulling out one of Guma's Cuban cigars, which he tossed to Fulton. "It's from Ray. Don't tell Nurse Nancy where you got that," he said.

"I won't, and tell Goom thanks," Fulton said, giving the cigar a lingering sniff. "Hey, Butch?"

"Yeah, Clay?"

"When we're ready to catch this guy, if there's any way possible, I'd like to be in on it."

Karp smiled grimly and nodded. "Sure . . . as long as you promise me that he won't have any 'accidents' before we haul his ass into court."

"Of course," Fulton replied with a chuckle. "But if I'm lucky, he'll try to escape again."

As Karp left the hospital, he pulled the peacoat around him to ward off the chill. Officially, it was spring, the last snow had melted, and there had certainly been those days he loved best when, washed clean by winter's snows and rains, the city gleamed and trees began to put forth tender green leaves, as the grass in the parks woke from hibernation. But tonight Old Man Winter was reminding the citizens of Gotham that he might have one last punch to throw before he was counted out.

Walking out of the entrance, Karp was quickly flanked by two brawny plainclothes cops, each of them with a neck bigger than his thigh. The cheap suits did little to disguise their occupations; they even walked like guys who were carrying guns and hoping for a chance to use them. Criminy, has it come to this? he thought. An armed escort.

Karp would have settled for the driver of his official city car, an armored Lincoln. But Fulton wouldn't hear of it.

In fact, when Karp complained about his new shadows, Fulton had fixed him with his "don't fuck with me" glare and spat, "I already screwed up once this year and got people killed, and the year's just started. Now, I know I can't guarantee I'll do any better this time, but let me try to do my job."

The look in Fulton's eyes had told Karp it was pointless to argue.

Karp's two escorts drove him back to the family loft on the corner of Crosby and Grand and parked in front of the building. They were still there when he brought out the trash two hours later. They started to get out of the car, but he motioned for them to remain where they were. It was getting colder, and he was only going to toss the garbage in a Dumpster in the alley.

Karp closed the lid on the Dumpster and was about to turn to leave when a shadow emerged from the deeper dark of the alley. He chided himself for letting the security detail remain in the car and prepared to fight. Go down swinging, you big dummy, he thought.

"Good evening, Mr. Karp," said a soft, raspy voice.

Before he could say anything else, the speaker was racked by a fit of coughing that sounded deeper and wetter than was healthy. But Karp had recognized the voice and relaxed. "David Grale," he said. "I guess the question is, what brings you out on a night like this?"

The last he'd seen Grale, the former Catholic social worker–turned–homicidal maniac, was on New Year's Eve when Grale had been pivotal in helping thwart the terrorist attack on Times Square. Since then, he'd disappeared back into the labyrinth of man-made and natural tunnels that honeycombed subterranean Manhattan Island with his army of Mole People, homeless wretches who lived beneath the city, venturing out only to find, beg, or steal the basic necessities of life.

Some years earlier, Grale had started to take it upon himself to hunt down and kill men who at that time had been preying on the homeless of New York City. He believed that his victims were men but possessed by demons. At least that was the story according to Karp's daughter, Lucy, who'd first met Grale when he was serving soup to the poor by day and killing by night in a perceived battle between good and evil.

Now Grale, according to Lucy, was some sort of spiritual leader and avenging angel for the Mole People. They'd rallied behind his cause, and quite a number had given their lives to stop the bombing plot.

Karp wasn't sure how to feel about Grale. The man was by his own admission a serial killer—even if his targets were themselves discovered to be murderers and rapists, and wanted by the police. "The others," as Grale referred to them, also lived below the city streets or in dark places where regular citizens did not go if they knew what was good for them. No one would mourn their loss, but the law did not hold a special place for vigilante killing.

Then again, that was also a line Marlene had tiptoed around on behalf of defenseless women. It all added up to a conundrum for Karp.

Whatever else Karp thought of the man, Grale seemed to have some inexplicable tie to his family that wove his mad purposes into the fabric of their lives. He was dangerous, probably insane, and yet he kept showing up in the proverbial nick of time to save them from, for lack of a better word, "evil" men. Karp couldn't quite bring himself to condemn Grale's actions when there'd been times these actions were all that saved his family from tragedy.

Even in the dim light that filtered into the alley, Karp could see that Grale's lifestyle was taking its toll. Always tall and thin, his face now appeared drawn and haggard, almost skeletal. Lank dirty hair hung raggedly around his pale face, a thin beard filling in the hollows. He shivered beneath the hooded Xavier College sweatshirt as he tried to wrap his arms around his thin chest for warmth.

"Yes, what would bring me out on a night like this," Grale responded, "away from the warmth of my underground kingdom. . . . I'm afraid that I have been waiting for the opportunity to warn you."

"Warn me?" Karp asked.

"Yes," Grale said. "Warn you that Kane is coming. His vengeance will begin soon."

"You know where he is or what he plans to do?"

Grale shook his head, which seemed to set his whole body trembling, and he was racked again by the damp cough. "No. Nothing concrete or I would be there, not here. But haven't you noticed the sudden jump in your crime statistics, especially those for violent crimes like murder, rape, and assaults?"

As a matter of fact, Karp had been apprised of the numbers just that morning. His aide-de-camp, Gilbert Murrow, had come into the office, worried about how a spike in the stats would be portrayed in the media. Karp had assured Murrow that a fluctuation seven months before the election wasn't going to turn the population against him. He wondered how Grale knew. . . . Or was it just a lucky guess?

"What does that have to do with Kane?" he asked Grale.

"Evil men are getting bolder and their numbers are growing," Grale said. "They're drawn to the city like rats to cheese. Those of *the others* we've managed to catch jabber on and on about 'something big' brewing."

Karp was not a big believer in Grale's theories about the gathering forces of darkness and an upcoming Armageddon-like battle with New York City at its center. His daughter gave them credence, but Lucy was something of a spiritual eccentric herself. It all sounded like something either out of the Bible or a comic book, whereas professionally he preferred to rely on the State of New York Revised Criminal Statutes such as they applied to crimes committed in the County of New York.

"I can't do much with that, David," Karp said. "I need to be able to charge people with crimes so that, if convicted, they can be put behind walls and razor wire."

Grale looked at him, his dark eyes burned with either madness or fever. Karp couldn't tell which, but they also seemed to be judging him. Grale appeared to be about ready to say something else but was interrupted by a coughing fit. When it stopped, he wiped at his mouth with his hand, and glanced at the dark stain on the sleeve of his sweatshirt.

Karp saw it, too. "You want to come in and warm up?" he said, looking up at the light shining out of the windows of the fifth-floor loft where his wife and twin boys waited. Faint laughter and happy shouts could be heard through the century-old brick walls.

Grale gazed up at the windows with obvious longing. He'd been in the loft before, back when he was still just a handsome young social worker dedicated to helping the poor and the object of Lucy's schoolgirl crush. He smiled, perhaps at the memory, or perhaps the gesture, but then shook his head. "No . . . but thank you for the kindness of the offer," he said. "I think that may cross the line of this 'professional' relationship between the two of us, Mr. Karp, and we will both need all the friends we can get in the coming months. Anyway, I need to be returning to my flock."

Grale suddenly stepped back into a doorway where Karp could not see him though he was only a few feet away. A spotlight stabbed into the alley, catching Karp in its beam.

"You okay, Mr. Karp?" the voice of one of his police bodyguards called from the Lincoln, which had silently rolled to a stop in front of the alley.

"Yeah, sure," he answered. "I was just looking at the stars for a moment."

"No problem," the voice said. The car pulled a U-turn to take up a position across the street.

Karp glanced back over his shoulder. "David?" He peered into the darkness, but there was no answer, just the whispering of shadows.

5

ON HIS WAY UP TO THE MONDAY MORNING MEETING, GUMA decided to stop at the small cafe inside the Criminal Courts building to grab a cup of coffee. He wanted to be bright and alert when he presented the Stavros case to the other assistant district attorneys. Not that he wasn't ready—on the contrary, he felt in fighting trim, having done his roadwork and gone numerous rounds with his sparring partner, Karp.

Feeling saucy, he gave the young Hispanic woman behind the counter an extra dollar on top of his usual tip and got what he was sure was a "come back and see me when I get off" smile. But as he turned, he nearly had the coffee knocked from his hand by a young pasty-looking man with long, stringy brown hair and the straggly beginnings of a beard. The man appeared to be trying to escape from a very angry, very thin middle-aged woman who wore her Clairol blond hair tightly piled on top of her head, which accentuated a thin, elegant neck that led his gaze to a black dress cut to reveal the wonders of modern plastic surgery and a string of white pearls that accented her cleavage. She looked like she was dressed for dinner at the Waldorf rather than the courtroom . . . unless the purpose is to soften up the judge, Guma thought.

"Albert, you come back here this minute," the woman hissed, trying not to be gauche and yell. "Albert, you're not going to fail to appear again, or your stepfather will not bail you out again."

Albert stopped and turned so that Guma was pretty much in between the two. "Which one?" Albert asked with a sneer. "Stepfather Three or Stepfather Four?"

"Albert! That was unkind," the woman said with prep school enunciation.

"It's Rasheed, Mom," the young man complained. "My name is Rasheed, not Albert."

"Oh nonsense," the woman replied, waving the name change away with a perfectly manicured hand. "You're not even black."

"What's that got to do with it? I'm Muslim. I don't recognize the authority of secular governments; I answer only to the imam and Allah."

"Pshaw, once a Lutheran always a Lutheran," the woman said. "And you answer to me. Now, you get your little fanny back in that courtroom or no more money for rent. You'll just have to move back home."

Having fixated on the woman's breasts, which looked even larger on her emaciated frame than they probably were, Guma decided to attempt the gallant tact, just in case Stepfather Four wasn't performing up to standards. "Excuse me, I'm Assistant District Attorney Ray Guma, may I be of some help?" he offered her with a slight tilt of his head and his sexiest half smile.

"You can mind your own business, grandpa," the woman replied, giving him a look he figured she probably used on the maids when they spoke without being spoken to first.

"Yeah, mind your own business, grandpa," the youth echoed.

Normally, such an affront would have called for a witty comeback. *I wasn't so picky, why are you?* But "grandpa" had thrown him for a loop. Guma sipped his coffee and slunk off for the elevator.

A few minutes later, he sat in the reception area waiting for Karp to arrive. He'd tried to walk right into the inner office, but Mrs. Milquetost had primly informed him that the office was locked until its owner arrived. He was still too crushed by the incident with the blonde and her son to battle with the receptionist, so he decided he'd spend the time reviewing his case while sitting on the couch.

After Zachary Stavros left Karp's office the week before, Guma had asked, *So what do you think?*

Karp sat back in his chair and looked up at the ceiling, deep in thought. *I don't mean to throw water on this, Goom,* he said. *But without a body, you're going to have a tough time getting a conviction based on Zachary's memory . . . if you can get it into evidence in the first place. Any defense lawyer worth his salt is going to fight it tooth and nail. And if it gets in, he'll go after the kid without mercy.*

I know, Guma said. *I'd sure like to get a backhoe and dig up Emil's yard.*

You'll never get a search warrant, Karp said, *without something the judge can hang his hat on. Without a body, you're not only going to have to prove that Emil Stavros killed his wife, you're going to have to prove beyond a reasonable doubt that she's even dead. That's twice the normal burden for any prosecutor, even you. What else you got?*

Guma gave him a rundown of what the early police investigation and a subsequent investigation a few years after Teresa's disappearance had turned up. *Unfortunately, the investigation seemed to have ended rather abruptly. I'm still trying to locate the detective who worked on the case.*

You suspect Emil Stavros might have pulled a few strings?

Who knows? Guma replied. *But I'd sure like to find out.*

As he waited now for Karp, his balloon deflated by the bitchy blonde, Guma wondered if he was just spinning his wheels. It just galled him that a wealthy man could get away with murder and go on with his life . . . his mistress, his parties, and fast cars and expensive vacations . . . while his wife laid buried in some unmarked grave. But then, he'd gotten into the prosecution business to stick up for people who had no voice of their own.

A baseball player in college, good enough for a shot at the pros even if it didn't turn out, Guma had a competitive nature that made him a tough, even ferocious, prosecutor whether he was going after some crack addict who blasted a clerk in a liquor store robbery or a mob enforcer who slipped up and got caught. Occasionally, those who slipped up were members or associates of his own extended family, some of whom were "mobbed up." But there was understanding in the "connected" members of the family that if they got caught in Manhattan, they were fair game for Ray Guma and it wasn't unusual to get a letter from Rikers Island or Attica letting him know that there were no hard feelings.

Karp entered the reception area. "What's up, Goom? Or as my kids say, 'Sup, Goom?"

"Huh? Oh, sorry. I'm just a little preoccupied with the Stavros case."

Karp nodded and led Guma into his office. The case seemed to have affected his old friend and colleague more than most. A few days earlier, he'd visited Guma in his basement office and noticed an eight-by-ten photograph of Teresa Stavros tacked to the wall. She was a beautiful woman, indeed, but he was only teasing when he said, *You should get it framed.*

Guma had shrugged the comment off. *It's just a reminder when I get here in the morning and when I leave at night that someone is still waiting for the wheels of justice to turn for her,* he said. *Anything wrong with that?*

No, nothing at all, Karp had replied. *Just a bad joke.*

Now, Guma was fretting like any rookie ADA. "You've done a thousand of these at least," Karp said. "Relax."

Guma nodded. "Thanks, but this one is pretty complicated, and I'm a little rusty since the . . . since my illness. I realize there's no body, but I worry that if I let this go now, I won't get back to it and neither will anyone else. Those wheels of justice will have ground to a halt for Teresa."

Karp noted the reference to the victim by her first name. He knew that Guma had a heart of gold, but when it came to trials, Ray had always approached them more as a competition than something he took personally. He was tough, tenacious, and in court could be quite impassioned when addressing the jury. But he'd never seemed particularly sentimental about the victims he was championing.

Now Karp wondered if Guma was getting too close, but he wasn't going to say it. He extended a hand to his friend. "Come on, you wuss. The worst that can happen is they'll tear you to pieces and leave you a quivering blob of Italian gelato."

"That all?" Guma replied, but at least he was smiling again.

When everyone was assembled at the conference table inside the office, Karp nodded to Murrow, his administrative maven, campaign manager, and numbers cruncher for the DAO, who smiled broadly and said, "Everybody, I'd like to formally introduce Susan Halama as the new chief of the sex crimes unit. Of course, most of you know she's been the interim chief, but this makes it official."

The room full of lawyers erupted in applause and cheers for the pretty brunette at the end of the table, who blushed and shoved the files in front of her around with a finger. Karp smiled and clapped along with the rest. He couldn't help but think that the former head of the unit, Rachel Rachman, would have never received that sort of approval from her colleagues. Soft-spoken and hardworking, Halama was not the sort to put herself forward or treat the law like some sort of personal crusade. Yet she was every bit the prosecutor Rachman had been—he couldn't remember her losing a felony case.

The meeting progressed with reports from the various chiefs about the major cases they or their assistants were trying or preparing for trial. Then Kipman, the appeals bureau chief, reviewed the various stages of appeals before the meeting turned to dissecting each other's cases.

The practice of presenting cases so that colleagues could rip them apart had been a staple of the Garrahy years. Old Man Garrahy, the legendary district attorney and Karp's mentor, believed that cases were won or lost long before they got to the jury. *You win by being the best prepared lawyer in the courtroom, not the flashiest,* he'd once told a young Karp, who'd taken it to heart.

Each attorney with a major case would be called on to present the evidence, and then it was open season for the others to ask probing questions and pick apart weaknesses. Many an assistant district attorney had crumbled under the onslaught, some so badly that they'd disappeared into misdemeanor court oblivion, rarely to be heard from again. Or worse, they became defense attorneys.

Although some of his predecessors had let the practice slip, Karp had revived it. Now, he looked forward to Guma's presentation of the Stavros case.

Guma had asked to go last. *I may have to run to the crapper to throw up and wouldn't want to interrupt the flow of the meeting,* he'd joked when he made the request. But Karp sensed that there was a grain of truth to it and now, as he watched Guma wince as he stood, he wondered if there was more than a grain.

Guma began by giving the basics of the case. Teresa Aiello Stavros, the child of a wealthy Italian jeweler, had married Emil Stavros twenty-five years earlier. She'd borne a son who by all accounts she'd doted on, even as her marriage fell apart, mostly due to a philandering husband.

"One night fourteen years ago, she suddenly disappeared," he said. "One theory is she grew tired of her husband and, I guess, her five-year-old son, Zachary, and ran off to start a new life. The other theory is that she was murdered that night by her husband. . . . And I have one witness who is prepared to testify that he saw Emil strangle Teresa. The witness is Zachary, who has recently, through hypnosis, recalled a memory he has repressed all these years."

Guma ignored the eye-rolling and shaking heads of some of the older ADAs and moved on to other aspects of his case. The original police investigation had turned up very little to suggest foul play before it was shelved. "A little abruptly, though, as we haven't located the detective assigned to the case to ask why," Guma noted. "He retired five years ago, and we understand moved up to Bar Harbor, Maine—so that remains on the list of things to do.

"However, according to police investigation reports, someone had continued to use Teresa's credit cards after her disappearance and withdrew cash from her private accounts," Guma said, looking at his notes, "for a period of about five years, according to bank records we've obtained, until the money was gone.

"A story about 'missing persons' that had appeared in the *New York Times* several years later touched on the Stavros case. Apparently, Emil hired a private investigator who turned up 'evidence' that Teresa was living abroad, leaving tracks in the form of hotel registrations and shopping sprees from Madrid to Buenos Aires. However, somehow the PI just never quite caught up to her, though he supposedly snapped this photograph"—Guma held up a fuzzy black-and-white photograph from the newspaper—"of a woman in a hat and dark glasses getting into a taxi in Paris, who he claims was Mrs. Stavros."

When he finished, Guma sat down—a bit wearily, Karp thought. But when he picked his head up, it was again with the look of a prize-fighter eyeing his opponent at the weigh-in. "Come on, guys, take your best shot," he challenged.

"So what do we know about the husband's whereabouts when Mrs. Stavros disappeared?" Kipman asked.

"Emil Stavros was questioned a number of times, but he stuck with his alibi—that he'd attended a very public fund-raiser that night, apparently not concerned how the press would react to being accompanied by his mistress, a former Radio City Music Hall Rockette by the name of Amarie Bliss," Guma replied.

"I take it they were seen by others then?" Susan Halama tossed out.

"Lots of people saw him at the fund-raiser. He and the little gold digger even got on the *Times* society page," Guma said.

"So maybe he whacked her after the party," Murrow suggested.

"Well, he spent the night in bliss with Ms. Bliss at her apartment. A doorman at her building saw them going in about 1 A.M. and Emil leaving about eight the next morning. Told the cops that he was on duty all night and would have noticed if Emil left."

"Before the party, then?"

"Not according to a report from the chauffeur, a Mr. Dante Coletta, who said he saw Teresa when he returned from dropping

Emil and Amarie off. She was apparently upset and talking to someone on the telephone."

"Have you talked to the chauffeur?" Kipman asked.

Guma shook his head. "Not yet. That's from an old police report. Clarke Fairbrother is looking for him, as well as the detective originally assigned to the case."

"Anybody else recall hearing any arguments that night or other sounds that might have seemed out of place, like gunshots?" Karp asked.

Guma shook his head. "No. The neighbors reported that Emil and Teresa argued frequently and sometimes publicly. But no one heard anything unusual that night . . . then again—it was the middle of August. Most people, especially in that neighborhood, would have the windows closed and the air conditioners cranked. Even if they'd had a window open, traffic noise and city sounds would have muted even a gunshot, especially if the gun had a silencer."

"Maybe she moved on," one of the young assistant district attorneys chimed in, trying to look serious and thoughtful.

"Maybe," Guma conceded. "According to Zachary all this activity—the credit card use, bank withdrawals, plus a few typed Christmas cards and birthday wishes sent to her son—all stopped about the same time, about five years after she disappeared."

"Well, that makes sense," the ADA persisted. "She blew through her money or transferred it to other accounts so that Emil couldn't get at it and then got rid of the personal baggage."

"Which included a son she was very devoted to," Guma replied. "She was also a good daughter to her mother, but all contact with her family ceased. She didn't even attend her mother's funeral."

"So she's good at disappearing and made a complete break," Murrow said. "Maybe she wasn't as close to her family as the reports indicate. Or maybe she had some sort of mental breakdown."

"Or maybe she died," Kipman noted. "But not here. Maybe she's been dead for all these years and buried in some other country. Like you said, the husband has an alibi—"

"Wouldn't be the first time a mistress lied for her sugar daddy," Guma retorted, his face flushing. "Maybe. Maybe. Maybe. I thought we dealt in common sense. A devoted mother and daughter disappears suddenly; writes to her son until the money runs out and then nothing; plus misses her mother's funeral."

"Doesn't prove Emil Stavros killed her or that she's even dead," Karp said. "We're short on the thing we call hard evidence around here."

Guma shrugged. "You could be right. But here's the kicker . . . at least it was for me. Emil Stavros didn't file for divorce and remarry for five years . . . not until her bank accounts were emptied."

"So?" Murrow asked.

Guma shot Karp a look that Karp had seen plenty of times before in the courtroom when his friend had led a witness into painting himself into a corner. "Teresa was the much wealthier of the two, worth millions from her parents' trust. Emil made good money as a banker, but rumor had it that around the time of Teresa's disappearance he'd made some poor financial decisions . . . and a lot of it involved other people's money. Other people who don't bother going to courts to recover their money."

"Anybody you're related to?" Newbury asked to general laughter.

Guma laughed with the others, and then did his best imitation of Marlon Brando playing Don Corleone, "If I told you, I'd have to have you whacked." Then he reverted to his normal voice. "Let's just say I have a little insider information about Emil's financial straits. Funny, but after his wife died, he was able to make good on his debts."

"So maybe he was waiting for his wife to return?" Murrow said.

"First of all, they'd signed a prenup," Guma said. "He had full access to her accounts so long as they were married. However, if they divorced, he got nothing that wasn't his from before the wedding or earned in his current employment. Second, her will stated that if she died, all of her money would go immediately into a trust to be held for her son, Zachary, until his twenty-first birthday. Dad would get nothing."

"So he doesn't move to have her declared dead, otherwise the kid gets the entire bankroll," Kipman summed it up.

"And he doesn't divorce her until the money's all gone," New-bury added. "Got to admit, it's pretty good stuff."

"I still think it's weak," Murrow shot back. "You can't prove a negative—just because there's no evidence that she's alive, doesn't mean she's dead. . . . Without a body you're toast."

"There have been successful prosecutions of so-called body-less homicides," Guma said.

"But they're rare," Kipman noted.

"I'm aware of that," Guma said, "but I'd rather try and fail for the right reasons than regret doing nothing at all." He looked at Karp, who nodded. "I've done something a little different this morning. I knew many of you, rightly so, would have some concerns about my witness's 'recovered' memory. So I've invited Zachary Stavros here; you can judge for yourself how you think he'll do on the witness stand."

Guma got up and opened the door. "Come on in, Zachary," he said.

Zachary looked nervous as he entered the room, clutching an old cigar box in front of him as though to ward off an attack. "Don't let this pack of jackals bother you," Karp added, "most of them bark but don't bite."

Zachary was seated with his box on the table in front of him. Guma stood beside him and said, "Why don't you tell us a little about yourself. What you do. That sort of thing."

Zachary smiled. "I'm an Unemployed Vampire," he said.

"An unemployed vampire?" Guma replied. "You come out at night and suck people's blood, but you're out of a job?"

Zachary laughed. "No, sorry," he said. "It's an old childish habit, but I like to see people's reactions when I say that. . . . I really am an Unemployed Vampire, but that's the name of my band. We play the club scene, mostly in SoHo and sometimes over in Brooklyn or Jersey. Head-banging, three-chord shit, played real loud. . . . You ought to come see us sometime."

"I'm more the blues sort of guy," Guma said, "but maybe I will. Where do you live?"

"Well, that's sort of funny," Zachary replied. "Spanish Harlem.

Personally, I dig Latin music. In my secret life, I like to dance salsa. Just don't tell my fans."

There was a minute of silence while Guma poured himself a glass of water. Quiet before the storm, Karp thought.

"Okay, well, why don't you tell us your story?" Guma suggested.

"My story," Zachary repeated, looking down at the box, his face suddenly haunted. "Yes, I have to admit that it seems more like a story than reality." He cleared his throat. "My mom's name was Teresa Aiello Stavros. I don't really remember much about her, because I was five years old when she . . . disappeared. I know what she looked like because of photographs and sort of dreamy memories of her face smiling at me. But one thing I do remember distinctly was this blue dress she used to wear—it might have been sort of a housedress or nightgown because she wore it a lot. It was probably satin or silk because I remember how cool it felt against my face when she held me."

Stopping for a moment to gather himself, Zachary tried to clear his throat again as tears welled in his eyes. He wiped at the tears, which left a streak of makeup on the side of his face. "Sorry I'm being such a baby," he said. "Anyway, I was about to say, one thing I am sure I remember is that she loved me. I felt it whenever she was near me and knew it was missing when she was gone. That's why I know she didn't walk out on me . . . us, if you include my old man, but that's what he says. She walked out and abandoned us, like he cared."

Zachary opened the cigar box he clutched in his hands. "This is the only supposed contact I had with her after she disappeared," he said, removing a small bundle. "A few Christmas and birthday cards. They never said much, all of them typed, just saying some shit like 'someday you'll understand. Love, Mom.' Don't even know why I kept them, except I guess I hoped that someday I'd see her again and I could show her these and ask her to explain. But they stopped coming after I was about ten or so—Emil said it was because she wanted to forget about me entirely. But now I think it's because she was already dead. . . . I think these, these are fake."

Placing the bundle back inside the box, which he handed to

Guma, Zachary continued. His father had waited for about five years and then married his mistress, the former Rockette dancer named Amarie Bliss. That was about the time the cards and letters stopped, as well as his introduction to boarding schools throughout the Northeast.

"I've been kicked out by all the best," Zachary said. "Fighting, drugs, suicide attempts. They say I'm quite the poster child for manic depression."

Zachary took another drink. "I hope I'm not boring you," he said looking at Karp, who shook his head but didn't say anything.

"You're very kind," the young man said. "I think I'd be bored to tears by now. Anyway, about the third time I cut myself—here you can still see where I messed up my body art . . ." Zachary rolled his tattooed arm over to show where ugly pink scars ran through a blue, black, and white wave that formed a ying-yang symbol. He snorted derisively as he added, "The psychologists say that 'cutting' comes from anger and a lack of self-esteem. . . . My dad paid thousands of dollars for someone to tell him that."

Zachary turned his arm back over and sighed. "But then some friend of my dad's suggested I go see this psychologist, Dr. Donald Craig. And for once, my dad did something that actually helped me. The short version is that Dr. Craig hypnotized me and when I came to, all these memories were swimming around in my head like fish in an aquarium. It took some time to sort them out—the stuff that was obviously imaginary from those that Dr. Craig said were 'repressed memories,' shit I'd submerged into my subconscious when I was a kid because I didn't want to deal with it."

The young man bowed his head. "You okay to go on?" Guma asked. Zachary nodded.

"Yes, I want to finish, then you guys can decide what to do about it," he said. "If it's nothing, fine, I understand and I'll forget about it. Going up against my dad will be tough, even for the district attorney; he's got a lot of powerful friends. And even if that doesn't bother you, what have you got here: Emil Stavros, self-made millionaire immigrant, philanthropist, and political heavy-hitter versus his whacked-out, suicidal kid who suddenly remembered his mom's murder after fourteen years. Believe me, I still have my own doubts."

"Why don't you let us be the judge of that," Guma, said. "Just tell us your story like you told it to me."

Zachary looked at Guma, then Karp and nodded. "Okay, I've come this far. . . . Here's the deal: one of those repressed memories is the crystal-clear image of watching my dad with his hands around my mother's neck. He's screaming in her face as she tries to tear his hands off her throat. But he chokes her until she falls to the ground and didn't move. I remember this was at night. They were on the back patio, and I was watching from inside the house—probably supposed to be in bed, but I got up for some reason. I remember seeing my dad stoop over her. I remember her lying there in that blue dress."

Zachary stopped and looked at Guma as though waiting to be challenged. Carefully selecting his words, Guma said, "First, I'm not saying I don't believe you. No one in this room is; however, there are some big obstacles to pursuing this case, the biggest is that we're going to have to prove it with evidence that we can get in front of a jury. For instance, we know for a fact that your mother disappeared fourteen years ago under what were at first considered suspicious circumstances. A concern right now in this room, however, is with the so-called science of forensic hypnotism. If we were to go forward with this case with the idea of pursuing a murder charge, there would be a significant legal hurdle just to get you on the witness stand."

Zachary took a drink of his water and nodded. "Yes, implanted memories," he acknowledged. "To be honest, after I was hypnotized the first time, I had a hard time dealing with the whole idea. I mean, I want nothing to do with Emil, but he is my father and the idea that he killed my mom then pretended she'd left me was not something I really wanted to believe. So I looked for all sorts of reasons why this was a bunch of crap. At first I wrote it off as fortune-teller nonsense. But I also read a lot of the literature on repressed memory that's out there, including some of the case law that's available on the internet. I know it's not always accurate and has been rejected by some courts, sometimes with good reason."

The agitated young man got up and walked over to the window and looked down on the street. "You know what I'd give to be any one of those people out there? Maybe I'd be more miserable. But I'd take a chance that maybe I'd be one of those with a happy life," he said. "You know, my dad used to tell me that the reason my mother left was that she was selfish and had never really loved either of us. I was just a burden to her, so she ran off so that she could enjoy her life."

Zachary stopped speaking, his entire body slumping. "When Dr. Craig told me about these repressed memories, I wondered if I wanted them to be true so that I could stop dealing with the idea that she left me. She hadn't left me at all, she'd been murdered. Maybe, I thought, I wanted it so bad, my subconscious had made it all up. Maybe the doctor accidentally implanted this memory by something he said. But all I can say is, to me, they're real."

The young man seemed to have finished, but the attorneys in the room remained quiet to let him compose himself. At last Guma spoke. "If you can, tell us the rest, Zachary."

Slowly, Zachary turned to look at the ADAs sitting around the table, his pale cheeks wet with tears. "Yes . . . there are a couple of other things I remember distinctly from that night. The first is that when I was back in my bedroom, too scared to sleep, I heard two 'pops.'"

"Pops?" Guma asked.

"Yeah, I'd say like gunshots, I guess, 'pow, pow,' except muffled—one right after the other. And I think . . . this isn't quite as clear and who knows, maybe this is my subconscious mind working, but I can't get it out of my head—"

"What's that?" Karp asked when the young man hesitated.

"Well, my bedroom was right above the backyard where we used to have these beautiful rose gardens. What I can't get out of my head, is the sound that night of someone digging."

❋   ❋   ❋

Five minutes later, Zachary was gone from the room, but the ADAs were still quiet, lost in thought. "Well, what do you think?" Guma said. "I could wait and keep trying to find a way to search Stavros's backyard. But that might not happen, and even if he killed her, she might not be buried there. Or I can try to get an indictment, throw the dice, see if I crap out."

No one else spoke. Then Kipman cleared his throat. Of all the ADAs there, chief of the appeals bureau "Hotspur"—so named because of a surprisingly quick temper—Kipman knew best the hurdles the case would have to overcome. "Even a conviction won't end this, Ray," he said. "But I say you roll the dice. If we can get him on the stand, that kid might just do it for you."

All the ADAs agreed. Several stopped to pat Guma on the back and wish him luck on their way out. Then only Guma, Murrow, and Karp were in the room.

"If we go after Emil Stavros, you know all hell is going to break loose on the political front," Murrow said miserably. He was running Karp's campaign for district attorney and looked like someone had just told him that they'd booked the victory party on the *Titanic.*

Karp understood where he was coming from. Part of him wanted to put off the move for an indictment until after the election. What are another few months after fourteen years? said the little voice in his head. But another side of him was recalling the image of a young man still grieving for a lost mother. "I know," he said.

"Want to put it on a back burner until after the election?" Guma asked.

Murrow didn't bother to look up from where he was doodling the word *Doomed* on his yellow legal pad. He knew his boss and knew what the answer would be.

"Nah, if what Zachary says is true, Teresa Aiello Stavros has already waited fourteen years too long for justice," Karp said. "Let's take it to the grand jury and see what they have to say."

Guma grinned like a wolf contemplating which little pig to eat first. "That's my guy," he said. "Damn the torpedoes, full steam ahead."

"Yeah, well, I hope we don't get blown out of the water on this one," Murrow said.

To which Karp added, "Let's figure out a way to find her body, Ray. Also, check with forensics and see if they can make a match with her signature or any other handwriting we have that she allegedly signed off on during that period after she disappeared. Let's hope it works, because right now this case is as thin as it gets."

6

April

SAMIRA AZZAM'S HEART WAS LIGHT AS SHE WALKED DOWN
the breezeway connecting the mansion in Aspen, Colorado, to the
"guest cottage" where *he* waited. It was a good day . . . the plan was
in motion, martyrdom assured.

She was sneeringly aware that the two bodyguards poised at the
door ahead couldn't take their eyes off her bouncing breasts and
the promising swing of her hips wrapped as they were in tight blue
jeans. She knew that fundamentalist Islamic men like the two at
the door viewed women dressed like she was as whores—to be
used, perhaps, but not respected. But these two also knew to keep
their mouths shut as she drew close; Samira Azzam was a dangerous woman to insult.

As a modern Palestinian woman, she believed that the traditional roles between Muslim men and women were outdated and
would have to change someday. But not until the Zionists and their
puppets, the Americans, had been cast out of Palestine, and one Islamic State, a caliphate, established to rule the world. *In sha' Allah,*

she murmured to herself . . . *God willing.* Not that she planned to be around for either the cultural revolution in the Muslim world or the final defeat of the enemy. She sought *istish-haad,* heroic martyrdom, and she'd been promised that the moment was near at hand.

She was well aware of her effect on men and used it to full advantage as an al Qaeda field leader and assassin. Personally, she preferred women in bed—they were so much more civilized in their sexual desires than the gruntings and groanings of men. She especially despised it when men made their infantile inquiries as to whether they had "pleased" her. Depending on her mission, she might coo, "Oh yes, like no other," and ply them for information. Or, her preference, she'd snarl "no" and kill them. Her current love, Ajmaani, a Chechen, was a strong woman like herself; tall, beautiful, and blond, the result of some holdover DNA from ancient Thracian incursions into the area. She'd also proven to be invaluable as a strategist, a Russian translator, and a guide who had led Azzam into and out of the sieges of the theater and the school. They'd sworn their eternal love for one another and promised to die in martyrdom by each other's side so that they could enter paradise together. Their sexual appetite for each other had made them stronger, more impassioned for their work.

Sex, however, weakened the men she dealt with. They were all molding clay in her hands, even those of her masters who had used her for their own pleasure without realizing that she was using them as well. She could manipulate any man, except for *him,* the man in the room beyond the guarded door. He never asked whether he had pleased her, he knew he had not, nor did he care. Sex was a brutal, savage way to please himself, anyone else be damned.

Still, Azzam pretended to enjoy his attentions. His narcissism demanded it, and her al Qaeda masters seemed to consider him an important asset in the struggle and, therefore, she had been ordered to do whatever he wanted.

Of course, he'd been more beneficial before being exposed by the Jew Karp and his rabble of family and friends . . . *the targets.*

That al Qaeda's ally Kane might otherwise have become the next mayor of New York had been so very Arabic in its irony. It was disappointing that it had not come to pass, but the man was still valuable. He had a network of arms dealers and banking institutions that had survived his fall. And, more importantly, he'd conceived the plan that would at once satisfy his requirements, as well as strike a blow that would make the infidels tremble.

It had been up to her and Ajmaani to plan and carry out the operation to free Andrew Kane. Since then, she hadn't given the murdered children or other victims a second thought, any more than she had the schoolchildren at Beslan. If ever she had been troubled by such embers of a dying conscience, it was long before and short-lived, giving way to the mantra, There are casualties in every war.

The subterfuge with her "lover" Kane was not difficult. Even her name, Samira Azzam, was not her own. She had been born Nathalie Habibi, the child of Palestinians living on the West Bank. Her father had driven a taxi—an ancient, dilapidated Volkswagen van he kept running with scavenged parts, curses, and constant prayers to Allah—while her mother crossed to the Israeli side every day to work in a factory that made parts for irrigation machines. They didn't own much, just their simple cinderblock home, a few changes of clothing, and family heirlooms, like the old and somewhat tattered Quran that had been handed down for generations. But there'd been food on the table, as well as love and laughter, especially if the laughter came at the expense of the "damned Israelis" as the butt of some joke.

However, her eldest brother, Jamal, had joined the Palestinian Liberation Organization, promising his worried parents that he was working for a "political solution" to create a Palestinian state and wouldn't get involved in the violence. Ten years older, strong and handsome, he'd been his little sister's hero, carrying her around on his shoulders whenever he came home, saying it was practice for the celebration on the day of liberation. But then there'd been the terrible night when a man from Arafat's office arrived to tell the family that Jamal had been killed by Israeli soldiers near the border with Syria.

The Israelis claimed that Jamal had been part of a team that had tried to ambush one of their patrols and had been killed in the firefight. The family was sure the Zionists were lying; Jamal had promised them that he was working for a peaceful resolution. Nevertheless, the next day the tanks with the blue Star of David on their turrets had roared into the Palestinian enclave accompanying a bulldozer. The family was allowed only ten minutes to pack up their meager belongings before their home was razed as punishment for Jamal.

Suddenly, the family found themselves out on the streets—sometimes living in the van, other times with friends for a day or two. The situation grew worse when Nathalie's mother was fired from her job by her Israeli employer because of her dead son's activities. Humiliated that without his wife's income, he was unable to support his family, her father loaded them into the van one night and left for a refugee camp just inside the Jordanian border. He was sure that the taxi business would be better and they would not have to live humiliated among their former neighbors.

Nathalie was twelve years old when Jamal died and she went with her family—her father, mother, and younger brother, Ishmael—to live in the rat's maze of the refugee camp. They were fortunate to get an apartment in one of the insect-and-rat infested cinder-block government housing projects—the four of them crowded into a single room with blankets strung up for privacy. But they were lucky; many others lived under whatever roof of wood or tin they could scrounge up.

The taxi business wasn't much better, but somehow they managed to survive for the next six years. Yet, fate was not through kicking the Habibi family. On a visit back to the West Bank to visit friends and relatives, Ishmael was arrested when an inspection at the border of the VW van—which had been loaned for the trip—uncovered a box of detonators packed inside a crate of oranges.

Though Ishmael denied knowing the detonators were in the

crate, he was taken to an Israeli prison to await trial. But he'd died before he ever saw a judge. *A virulent strain of pneumonia,* the Israelis said. Another lie, thought the distraught family. Adding insult to injury, the Israelis had confiscated the van. The taxi business was no more.

It had been too much for her mother, who could not get over the deaths of her sons and the loss of her home. She lay down to sleep one night complaining of a headache and didn't wake up the next morning. *A stroke,* said the doctor. But her family knew that her death was due to a broken heart.

Upon the death of his wife, Nathalie's father had essentially given up as well. He spent his days begging for money to buy hashish to deaden his pain and railing against the "Zionist pigs." He paid little attention to the comings and goings of his remaining child, until one evening, while crossing the street in a daze, he was struck by, ironically, a speeding taxi and killed.

Just nineteen years old, Nathalie burned with a desire for vengeance against the Israelis. As she got older, she became enamored with the poetry and writings of Samira Azzam that exposed the "liar claims" of the Jews to Palestine. She swore that she would carry on her hero's struggle, but with guns and bombs, not words. Soon after her father's death, when a recruiter from Hamas came to the camp looking for young people willing to kill and die for Allah, she'd eagerly signed up.

Nathalie, who took the name Samira Azzam when she swore to give her life to *jihad,* grew into a beautiful woman on the outside. Only a large mole on her right cheek marred her perfection, but even that seemed only to make her other attributes—the green eyes, olive skin, thick dark hair, and perfect body—stand out all the more. But inside there was little room for anything but hatred. Early on, she hoped to be granted the honor of blowing herself up in the middle of a crowd of Jews. However, a Hamas leader had taken a fancy to her and, under the guise of "training" for important missions, also took her virginity. He smiled whenever she begged *istish-haad* and promised that her time would come, but for now she should accept whatever role she was given.

She was, after all, a woman and therefore subject to the commands of men.

This went on for a year before Nathalie/Samira found a way to pursue her dream. The man's wife received an anonymous letter telling her of the affair. He suspected that his young lover had sent the letter herself, but regardless he had no choice but to send Azzam away. He arranged for her passage to an al Qaeda training camp in Afghanistan, allowing himself a certain satisfaction in knowing that his betrayer would probably not be long for the world. Too bad, he thought. A wonderful body, but there will be other young desert flowers to nurture.

Azzam turned her hatred into her motivating force to learn martial arts, especially the killing techniques, as well as weapons training. She'd excelled and soon returned to Jordan. There she led sorties into Israel and detonated roadside bombs to kill passing Israeli army patrols. She also ambushed a school bus full of Israeli children.

The first time she'd seen a dead child as a result of her work, Azzam experienced a curious regret. The lifeless eyes of the child, the strangely pale skin, and blue lips had haunted her sleep. Once, the face had been that of her brother, Ishmael, and for the first and last time she'd questioned the morality of her actions. But then she'd remembered that Ishmael had died at the hands of the Israelis, and she'd quickly suppressed any more feelings of remorse. After all, she reasoned, her own childhood had been destroyed by the Israelis, why shouldn't their children suffer, too. There are casualties in every war, she told herself and thought no more of it.

The only downfall to her new path was that she was still alive. Several times, she'd accompanied some young man to the entrance of a disco or shopping mall, and then waited at a safe distance, listening with envy for the sound of the explosion, the screams, and the wailing of the ambulances.

After a time, Azzam learned that she was to be arrested by authorities in Jordan who were under pressure from the United States and Israel to crack down on militants coming over the border. She'd fled only minutes before the Jordanian secret police kicked down the door of her apartment. Watching the agents rush her building, she'd listened for the *"CRUMP"* of the booby-trapped land mine she'd set and then left the country.

She'd arrived back at the training camp in Afghanistan, where she'd been noticed by a high-ranking lieutenant in the al Qaeda organization who took her under his wing and into his bed. *Hamas has grown soft,* he said. *Now they talk about negotiating with the enemy. All they care about is a Palestinian state. Their leaders fail to understand the big picture of Islamic* jihad *and the drastic measures and sacrifices it will take to achieve a world-encompassing Islamic state. Join us, Samira, and you will find the martyrdom you seek.*

Tired of being put off from her destiny by the leadership of Hamas, disgusted by the "peace talks," and flattered by the offer, Azzam switched her allegiance. She liked how her new masters thought in terms of big blows against the infidels, right where they lived—not these insignificant attacks on the Israelis, who merely picked up the pieces, retaliated against some Palestinian neighborhood, and then moved on. She hoped someday she would be allowed to lead such a mission, so she remained with her current mentor/lover.

After he'd hammered away at her body and finally spent himself, he liked to pontificate on subjects he'd learned from the great man himself, Osama bin Laden. Driving the United States out of the Middle East so that Israel could be destroyed was only the beginning of the *jihad,* he said—the beginning of the end of Western culture, and the reign of the one true faith.

After the Jews had been driven into the sea, the apostate regimes of Egypt, Turkey, and the most corrupt of them all, Saudi Arabia, would be toppled by revolution with the assistance of *mujahideen* from other countries. Then the entire Middle East would be melded into a single fundamentalist Islamic state governed by one man, the Caliph, who as the successor of the Prophet, would be the final word in all things spiritual, temporal, and military.

Once in control of the world's most important oil supply and with nuclear capabilities already nearing completion in Iran, the Caliph would unleash the worldwide *jihad* in which all Muslims would be obligated to rise up and destroy the infidels wherever they lived. All those who survived but would not then bend to the teachings of the Prophet would be put to the sword. *In sha' Allah . . . God willing.*

Although she'd hardly opened the family Quran growing up, Azzam now studied the book until she was *hafiz*—someone who knew the book by heart. She considered herself fortunate that whenever she ran into some troubling contradiction between the Quran and what she was being told by the leaders of al Qaeda, her mentor was there to explain. For instance, she'd noted that according to the book, *jihad* prohibited the harming of women and children, yet bombs detonated in civilian populations didn't discriminate between gender and age.

"While the Quran does prohibit the killing of women and children in principle," her mentor said, "it is also written that if their deaths are in retaliation for the killing of Muslim women and children, or to prevent such killing, then it is allowed. The Crusaders and Zionists have been murdering our women and children for hundreds of years; this is merely payback and to stop them."

So she had accepted the deaths of noncombatants, combined with her more immediate goal of self-destruction. She begged for a suicide mission but kept getting told, "You are more valuable to us alive now. There will be plenty of time to die later."

In the meantime, he said, the leaders of al Qaeda had a special mission for her. They were sending her to Chechnya in southern Russia. There she would meet Muslims yearning to break free from the yoke of their Russian oppressors. The Muslim population in Chechnya, he said, had a story similar to that of Palestinians. They, too, had their lands stolen and were victims of wars of aggression, first by tsars, then the Soviets, and now the army and secret police of the Russian Republic.

However, she was cautioned, the Russians were not the only enemy. Worse in some ways were Chechen nationalists who wanted to form an independent republic. These nationalists were

Muslim in name only and intent on forming a democracy in which Islam would be the state religion but have little power.

Not only were these nationalists a disgrace to Islam, her mentor explained, but they represented a danger to the ultimate goal of a united Islamic state. Muslims who were lured into the evils of Western-style democracy—whether in Iraq or Chechnya—might be loath to give up their elected governments and submit to Islamic law. Therefore, any such attempts to install a democracy in the Middle East had to be stamped out.

Chechnya had been in a state of war off and on since the early 1990s. However, the secular nationalists were trying to negotiate a peace settlement with the Russians and establish their republic. It was therefore imperative that the Russians be forced to continue to fight Chechen independence. To accomplish this, the al Qaeda movement in Chechnya was planning a series of bombings and other violent acts in Russia to keep the Russian population angry and unwilling to deal with the nationalists.

However, al Qaeda had to be somewhat circumspect. It had to appear that al Qaeda was aligned with the nationalist movement; it was important that the Russians, and the Western governments, associate the independence movement with Islamic terrorism.

"Let the nationalists complain all they want to the Western press that they are being blamed for acts they do not condone," her mentor said. "We will make sure to give them credit, along with ourselves, for every death. It is the way of these Crusader nations to lump all Muslims into the same pot anyway; they see no difference between any of us and will eventually drive even the moderate nationalists into our camp."

So Azzam had been sent to Chechnya to work with local Islamic hard-liners to implement the strategy. She understood the importance of the assignment, but she couldn't help but feel she'd been sent to a backwater in the struggle. However, it was also how she met Ajmaani, who claimed to be an orphan with no last name and was to serve as her liaison with the Chechens, so she thanked Allah for that small favor. It was difficult to say when professional respect had turned to lust and even, though Azzam had thought herself incapable, to love. Somewhere in the adrenaline rush of placing their lives on the line and the periods of inaction—a congratulatory touch had turned to a kiss that had turned to the wild, sometimes violent, meshing of their bodies. And then it had been easy to return to the cause, satiated for the moment, willing to die while still high on the scent of her lover.

Azzam had been nearly beside herself with both pride and envy when her brothers in al Qaeda flew the planes into the World Trade Center. More than twenty-seven hundred dead! *Alhamdulillah . . . praise to God,* she'd shouted with the others when word reached their camp in the Chechen mountains, and then more softly later in the arms of Ajmaani. She wished that she had been there, listening to the screaming of the jet engines and the passengers just before they struck the building. To be in the cockpit, shouting *Allah akbar! . . . God is great!*" and see the frightened faces of the people in the offices and on the planes when they realized they were about to die.

Shortly after the glorious event, she'd returned for a visit to Afghanistan. She allowed her mentor to have his way with her body so that she could learn more about future plans and beg to be allowed to take on a mission of similar importance. She had actually wept—one of the few times since childhood—with frustration that others were getting the glory that should have been hers. But he'd only told her to be patient and that her time would come.

Azzam left Afghanistan before the Americans attacked in retaliation for the World Trade Center. She was disappointed that the *mujahideen* and the Taliban had hardly put up a fight. But she had not wept when she learned that her mentor had been vaporized by a cruise missile that had zeroed in on his cave in Tora Bora and caught him standing at the mouth enjoying the fresh air. *There are casualties in every war.* She shrugged and went back to planning attacks against the Russians with Ajmaani.

They had begun with bombings at Russian bus stations and marketplaces. The Russians, as they had for years only now more viciously, retaliated with their own brutality against the Chechen population, leveling whole towns, raping women, and murdering the men. When the Chechen nationalist complained to the Western press that the acts had been committed by Islamic hard-liners and outsiders, the Russians pointed out that they, too, were fighting the War on Terrorism against Islamic extremists, and the West turned their backs on the abuses.

Azzam was overjoyed when Ajmaani suggested they ramp up the violence by seizing the Nord-Ost musical theater in Moscow. She'd hoped to die with the others, but had been ordered to escape before the Russian troops stormed the building. It was Ajmaani who led her to a tunnel, once used to carry coal beneath the streets to the furnaces that heated the buildings, and out behind the surrounding Russian forces.

As successful as it was, the attack on the theater had paled in comparison to their greatest achievement, the seizing of the school in Beslan, Russia, on September 1, 2004. The attacking force was comprised of the more radical element of the secular nationalist movement—those for whom negotiation was too slow, or driven to more extreme tactics by Russian brutality—as well as Islamic hard-liners and Arabs intent on the establishment of an Islamic state. More than three hundred Russians had died in the school—two-thirds of them children—and she would have gladly died with them. But once again, her lover Ajmaani was there to lead her to safety during the confusion when the building was stormed. Once outside, they'd blended into the crowd of Russian parents who waited word of their loved ones.

The attack had been a public relations success for al Qaeda. The Western press, which had begun to turn a sympathetic ear to the nationalists and even reported on Russian atrocities, swung 180 degrees. In their eyes, Muslim nationalists were no different from Islamic extremists—murderers all.

With the climate too hot in Chechnya—the nationalists and the Russians were hunting for her—Azzam and Ajmaani had fled to the wild country on the border between Pakistan and Afghanistan where al Qaeda and the remnants of the Taliban were regrouping. There Azzam fretted as al Qaeda grew bolder in Europe, and still she wasn't called upon to give her life. She grew more outspoken and critical of the planning. The attacks on the Madrid rail system had been too little, she said. *The work of amateurs.*

Then she heard about the plan to blow up Times Square on New Year's Eve, a blow that would have been even more glorious than that which had destroyed the World Trade Center. But the mission had been placed in the hands of *that idiot, al-Sistani, who somehow managed to botch a perfect plan.*

Tired of listening to a woman criticize their plans, she had at last been given a mission that would get her out of their hair. She didn't care about their reasons; all she knew was that this attack would make all the others, even the World Trade Center, pale by comparison.

Odd, she thought as she entered the room of the house in Aspen, considering how much I hate him. But she owed her good mood to the plan of the man sitting at a table near a window with his back to her. He was looking out of a large window across the valley at the ski slope on the other side. Aroused at her approach, he reached out toward her. "Ah, the lovely Samira Azzam." He gestured at the seat across from him. "Please, sit down and let us resume our game."

Games, she thought scornfully. He plays too many games and allows himself to be distracted by revenge. I use vengeance to help me focus on the task I am assigned. He uses his for petty personal vendettas.

Andrew Kane turned his gaze from the window and the tiny figures sliding down the slope and faced her. "Silly sport, skiing," he said, his voice partially muffled by the wrappings of gauze that covered his face. "It's cold and you could fall and break something. And for what?"

Azzam smiled and looked into Kane's newly designed brownish appearing eyes peering at her from under the bandages. "It does seem to be a waste of time."

She did wonder about these Americans. She'd expected them to panic and collapse after the destruction of the World Trade Center and the attack on the Pentagon. When they didn't, and instead seemed to find some inner reservoir of strength, she'd felt trepidation, a moment's wavering in her resolve. Perhaps, they can't be brought to their knees, as her al Qaeda masters preached. But the anger had returned and she'd determined that it would simply take more and better blows.

They are a stupid people. Surely they knew there were killers in their midst, plotting against their cities, hoping to take down their economy. Yet, here in Aspen, they wandered around in their fur coats, lived in mansions that would have housed a dozen Palestinian families from her old neighborhood, and acted as if the struggles going on in other parts of the world were annoying inconveniences, not matters of life and death. Aspen was the epitome of everything she hated about the United States—superior, wealthy, comfortable, and safe. *At least for the moment,* she thought with satisfaction.

The owner of the home where Kane was staying was one of the myriad members of the Saudi royal family, a distant cousin of the king, living off the oil proceeds that belonged by rights to the Saudi people. He was a flabby, lazy man who secretly supported al Qaeda with cash donations and by playing host to the occasional operative who needed a safe place to stay. She supposed he was hedging his bets for the day when the royal family was brought down and Saudi Arabia turned into a theocracy, like Iran.

Azzam snorted. Fools like her host and his piggish little wife and their fat, Westernized daughters and corpulent sons would be purged from the Islamic state. In the meantime, they served a purpose greater than themselves.

"I believe it is your move," Kane said.

Azzam studied the board. She hated games, but he'd insisted that she learn to play chess. He said it sharpened the mind and was "good training for staying a step ahead of your opponent" and had started a daily "tournament." So far she had yet to win a game and was growing tired of the loser's penalty.

She studied the board carefully. To open, Kane had moved his king's pawn ahead two spaces. It seemed harmless enough, so she mirrored his move by jumping her king's pawn two spaces forward, too.

"Has it begun?" Kane asked casually, moving his king's side bishop diagonally through the space opened by his pawn until stopping in front of his other bishop's pawn.

This move required more study. Moving the bishop seemed to presage an attack from that side. She moved a pawn forward one space toward his bishop. The move freed her queen to sally forth and meet the danger on that side.

"In sha' Allah," she said.

"Yes, God willing," Kane said dryly, "though I don't suppose He will have much to do with this. Just remember, don't rush. These first moves are not the ultimate targets. They are insignificant pieces on the board, not the king." He studied the board as if surprised by her move. His hand went to his bishop but then retreated. Instead, he moved his queen diagonally to the right, into the space in front of his bishop's pawn, facing her bishop's pawn across the board.

Azzam's eyes narrowed as she glanced at his queen. He was up to something but seemed to be building toward one of his precious "classical attacks" that he used over and over to break down her defenses. She thought she might gain the upper hand by attacking before he was prepared. She moved her knight's pawn ahead two spaces, placing his bishop in danger. He would either have to move the bishop, allowing her to bring out her queen on the next move to go on the attack, or lose it.

"I want them all guessing when it will be their turn . . . Karp, most of all," Kane said. "I want him to suffer. . . . I know you think that my plan has too many . . . um . . . shall we say, 'nuances.' But I want them distracted, looking the wrong way when we make our move. . . . You see, my dear Samira, there is much to be gained when things aren't as they seem." He moved his queen across the board and took her bishop's pawn, exposing her king. "Checkmate."

Azzam sat looking at the board, stunned. He'd defeated her in four moves. Backtracking, she saw that his intent had been clear the moment he moved his queen. Yet she'd been preoccupied with his bishop because it was closer to her side and had seemed the greater danger.

"Disappointing, Samira," he said shaking his head. "You are still too easily distracted, too committed to your little wars of attrition . . . you take my bishop, I take your pawn, you take my knight, I kill your queen. That's not chess . . . nor is it the way to win in the real world."

Azzam sighed and rose from the table. "I'll go see if there is a message yet from California?"

"Ah ah aah," Kane chided as he turned back to the window. "Not so fast. You forget, there is always a price to pay for losing."

She heard the sound of his zipper, and her shoulders sagged as she walked around the table and knelt in front of him. Sometimes it seemed the glorious day of her death would never arrive.

"Come on, come on," Kane urged impatiently. "What's taking so fucking long? I haven't got all night."

7

As AZZAM SANK TO HER KNEES, AN OLD MAN WALKED INSIDE a barn on a prison work farm outside of San Diego and carefully placed the rake he'd been using against one of the dairy cow stalls. He lingered momentarily in the shadows, inhaling deeply the fragrance of bovine excrement, fresh hay, and mechanic's oil. Good, honest smells.

For just a moment, he allowed himself to fantasize that he was just a simple farmer, finishing up after a hard day's work; dinner would be on the table soon, a wife removing a pie from the oven as children gathered noisily. But he didn't allow himself to dwell there long. He felt it was a sin to try to escape the reality of the greater sins he'd committed, so he rarely let himself indulge in such simple pleasures.

The other inmates, and even most of the guards and administrators at the prison farm, knew him as Richard Ely, supposedly an old bank robber serving out a life sentence. He kept to himself. When he wasn't in the garden tending to the rows of vegetables, he remained as much as he could in his cell, reading his Bible and praying for forgiveness, coming out only to eat, shower, and attend mass.

Even his cell was bare of anything that might be considered comforting, except perhaps the crucifix on the wall. There were no photographs of family and friends; no pictures of nude women or men (as preferred by some of his fellow inmates). When he did speak to the other inmates, he had a habit of calling them "my son," but otherwise he was just a tired old man who apparently had no one else in the world and was just biding his time until he checked into the big house in the sky . . . or the hot one down below.

And yet, he was no bank robber, nor was his name Richard Ely. His true identity was much more shameful. He was Timothy Fey, the former archbishop of New York, who dreamed of the day he would die . . . hoped that it would be in his beloved garden, his head lying on the warm, good earth, his eyes turned to heaven and the promise of salvation. He wanted nothing except to meet God, whom he thought he had served all his life only to fail so miserably, and ask for forgiveness.

In moments of contemplation, lying at night on the cold cement floor of his cell, Fey sometimes still wondered how he'd ended up as he had. He'd not sought to commit any crime or hurt another human being. He had not plotted to steal, or rape, or murder. Yet he had been partly responsible for all those things.

As a onetime parish priest in Ireland, he'd sought all of his life to care for the sick, nurture the poor, and spread the word of eternal salvation . . . free for the asking. His rise to power had been in large part due to his reputation for honesty, piety, and dedication to God. His greatest sin, he had thought, was the sin of pride. He'd wanted to build a new cathedral—grander and more magnificent than even St. Patrick's—to be located next to Ground Zero where the World Trade Center had stood. He wanted that to be his legacy to his flock and, he now admitted, to his own name. So he had not seen—or more honestly, had turned a blind eye—to other sins, bigger more horrible sins, being done in the name of the church through evil men at the bidding of the most evil of them all, Andrew Kane.

He'd trusted Kane, as both a friend and the church's attorney—

listened to the whispered lies. He convinced himself that what was being done was for the greater good of the church and its believers, and that he needn't trouble himself with the uncomfortable details.

After Kane was caught, and the truth thrown in Fey's face, he'd wanted only to live long enough to testify against his Judas. He wanted to do whatever he could to make sure the man was sent where he could do no more harm. But now Kane had escaped, and Fey only went through his days because to take his own life would simply compound his sins.

Fey turned at the sound of the barn door opening behind him. He squinted against the bright afternoon sun that flooded in. The dark silhouette of a man passed across the blinding light. It was difficult to make out his features, other than he was a big man. Then Fey saw the white collar.

"Ah, Father," Fey said as the man stepped into the barn. "I did not recognize you." He squinted more as the man moved just out of the light. He could see that the man had wavy dark hair and a pale complexion but little else to distinguish him. "Do I know you?"

"I am new," the other man said. "They told me I could find you here, Your Excellency."

Fey was startled at the reference to his old life. "You know who I am?" he asked.

"Yes," the man said circling around until he was nearly behind Fey. "I was sent to . . . find you."

So this is how it ends, Fey thought, feeling both fear and relief. "Tell me this, at least," he said. "Are you an ordained priest?"

The man stopped. "I am," he said. "In fact, I was ordained by you, Your Excellency. . . . But that was a long time ago, in another life."

"Yes. I seem to recognize the voice. Would you do me the favor of hearing my final confession and then, when you are finished with what you need to do, perform the rites."

"Even from a hollow priest? One who no longer believes in God?"

"If that is all I have—better a man who once knew Him than never."

The man sighed. "Then sit, Your Excellency, and I will do as you ask, although I do not know what good I will be as an emissary between your soul and your god."

"Our god," Fey said gently. "And He will understand and forgive me, as He will understand and forgive you someday."

Fey sat on a milking stool, facing the open door through which the light had softened and was turning to gold as the sun dipped toward the ocean. As he had since he'd been a boy on the violent, troubled streets of Belfast, he asked forgiveness of a priest "for I have sinned."

When Fey was finished, he paused. "Are there no acts of contrition?"

The man behind was silent for a moment then said, "An Our Father and one Hail Mary. Is there anything else?"

"Only that I forgive you. . . . Our Father . . ."

"Thank you, Your Excellency," the man said softly. So softly that Fey wondered if his executioner was crying when the garrote dropped over his head and tightened about his throat.

The man was strong, but it wouldn't have mattered if he'd been a weakling. Fey made no attempt to struggle or escape. Dying, he thought, isn't as painful as I imagined it might be. His lungs cried out for air and his head throbbed for want of blood to his brain, but they were overwhelmed by the feeling of release. He let himself slip away, overjoyed to discover it wasn't into darkness but toward the light beyond the barn door.

When Fey's killer was sure the old man was dead, he relaxed his grip and wiped at the tears that rolled down his cheeks. He'd murdered many times now, but none had been so hard as this man who had reminded him of the soul he'd lost. He cursed the devil for the weakness of his flesh and Andrew Kane for exploiting it, turning him into the monster he'd become.

The priest glanced one last time at Fey, whose face was bathed in the last beams of light from the nearly defeated sun. The old man seemed to be smiling ever so slightly. "I hope you find peace," said the priest. Turning to leave, he left the garrote around Fey's neck as he'd been instructed. The murder weapon was comprised of a set of rosary beads strung onto thin, tough wire from which dangled a gold medallion on which was embossed the image of St. Patrick's Cathedral in New York City.

Closing the door behind him, he walked rapidly toward his car, got in, and drove to the main gate.

"Take care of all the sinners, Padre?" the guard asked with a smile as he waved him through.

"Just one, my son," he replied, rolling up the window. "Just one."

8

AT THE SOUND OF LOUD VOICES IN HIS OUTER OFFICE, KARP
glanced up from the political finance reports he had to sign off on
and tapped his pen on the desk. He knew he should be irritated at
the inevitable interruption. While the normal workday was just
about over, he had hours' more campaign work to do, which he did
on his own time. Karp didn't feel right soliciting votes on the taxpayers' dollar. However, anything was better than dealing with
minutiae of his campaign, so he got up from the big mahogany
desk to see what was causing the ruckus.

Opening his door, he was confronted by the sight and smell of a
filthy and wide-eyed individual in a stained and deteriorating tie-
dyed T-shirt on which were stenciled the words Jerry Garcia Lives!
With his wild mane of wiry gray hair and unkempt salt-and-pepper
beard, the man reminded Karp of what Moses might have looked
like coming down from the mountain after a particularly grueling
session with God. . . . That is, if Moses had lived in Haight-Ashbury
during the late 1960s. The man certainly sounded like a prophet,
even if he smelled like bad wine, sweat, and cheap marijuana.

"JEHOVAH KNOWS HOW TO DELIVER PEOPLE OF

GODLY DEVOTION OUT OF TRIAL," the man thundered, "BUT TO RESERVE UNRIGHTEOUS PEOPLE TO BE CUT OFF ON THE DAY OF JUDGMENT! . . . SECOND PETER TWO!"

The preacher was not alone, however. Indeed, he was performing a spoken-word duet of sorts with Mrs. Milquetost, who was darting around to face the man no matter which way he turned, demanding that he leave the premises "or face the consequences." Every time he shouted some new Biblical passage, she shouted back. But he ignored her until she finally gave up and hurried to her desk where she began to dial for security.

Karp reached out and gently took the receiver from her and hung it up. "That's okay, Mrs. Milquetost," he said, careful to pronounce her name as she insisted. "I know this man and will deal with this." He turned to the intruder and said, "Good afternoon, Mr. Treacher. To what do we owe the pleasure of your visit?"

"ON THAT DAY A GREAT PANIC FROM THE LORD SHALL FALL ON THEM, SO THAT EACH WILL LAY HOLD ON THE HAND OF HIS FELLOW, AND THE HAND OF THE ONE WILL BE RAISED AGAINST THE OTHER! ZACHARIAH FOURTEEN, TWELVE!" The man's voice boomed as if speaking to a multitude in an auditorium, not two people in a small room, but then he seemed to notice Karp for the first time. His jaundiced and red-rimmed eyes focused and he smiled. "Why, good afternoon, Mr. Karp, hail fellow and well met," he said pleasantly and at a normal volume.

"Is there any particular reason for these rather forbidding quotations, Mr. Treacher?" Karp asked. "You're frightening my receptionist."

"I'm not afraid of him," Mrs. Milquetost hissed. "I just want him out. This is a place of business . . . not some street church."

Edward Treacher bowed gallantly to the red-faced receptionist, who couldn't seem to decide whether she resented the intruder more or Karp for stopping her from calling security. "I shall leave promptly, dear lady," he said, "after I have delivered a very important message to your employer."

"And what is that?" Karp asked. Treacher had once been a philosophy professor of some note at New York University during the Flower Power years. Legend had it that he'd taken too much LSD during one rock festival and had never quite returned to planet Earth. He'd certainly never returned to teaching or any other fulltime employment, preferring to live homeless on the streets. He was full of doomsday quotations and had a habit of turning up at the most unusual times and places—in fact, he was a material witness in the murder of rap star ML Rex by a cop working for Andrew Kane. But otherwise he was harmless.

Leaning toward Karp conspiratorially so that Mrs. Milquetost, who strained to hear, was thwarted in the endeavor behind her desk, Treacher whispered as he winked, "Oh, just the usual end-of-the-world stuff, Mr. Karp. You know, if I keep it up long enough, I'm bound to be right; the world has got to end—sooner than later at our current pace. . . . However, I have been sent here on a more immediate mission and that is to warn you, and I quote, 'Take care, Mr. Karp, the forces of evil are gathering and the pale rider is returning to Sodom' . . . otherwise known as our beloved Big Apple. 'A harbinger of bad tidings will soon arrive from California as proof that what I say is true.'"

Treacher glanced suspiciously at Mrs. Milquetost, who narrowed her eyes and looked like she'd wanted to gouge his out. "On a personal note, I myself only just escaped an evisceration by one of their number before dawn this morning and was narrowly saved by our mutual friend Mr. Grale," he said. "Apparently, Mr. Kane does not take kindly to those who interfered with his plans to take over the city. But I'm just a small fish in this pond, the attempt was unprofessional and halfhearted, and the would-be assassins are now rat meat beneath the city. Oh, and it was our Mr. Grale who asked me to deliver the warning."

Karp grimaced inwardly at the thought of Grale dispatching yet more "demons," though it sounded like it had been in defense of another. "All right, Mr. Treacher, I'll certainly take it under advisement," he replied.

In all honesty, he was growing tired of all the "forces of evil gathering" stuff. There are good people and bad people, he thought, not angels and demons. But Grale and his Mole People, of whom he figured Treacher was one, certainly had their ears to the ground when it came to word from the streets, and it paid to listen to what was being said beneath the mumbo jumbo.

Treacher reached out and clapped Karp on the shoulder. "Good . . . well, that's about it, unless you have something to eat," he said hopefully. His hopes were dashed by the stern countenance of Mrs. Milquetost. "I see you do not, so if you'll excuse me, I have the Lord's work to do; places to go, folks to warn about the end of the world. . . . Sort of like a spiritual Paul Revere, don't you think? One if by land, two if by sea."

"Wait," Karp said. "If you're in danger, maybe we can find a safe place for you to stay for a while? After all, I've got to keep my witnesses alive."

Treacher chuckled. "Safe? For how long would you keep me a pampered prisoner? There won't be a trial; the defendant has escaped and even now plots against you and others. No, I am as safe as you can be in New York City, and there are bigger fish in the pond that Mr. Kane is trying to land than me. Have a care, Mr. Karp." With that he turned on his heel and strode purposefully from the office.

"Shall I call security to escort him from the building?" Mrs. Milquetost inquired, starting to reach for the telephone again.

Karp shook his head. "No," he said. "I don't think that will be necessary. He really doesn't like to stay indoors any longer than he has to."

Mrs. Milquetost was still muttering about "lax security" when Gilbert Murrow walked in a minute later and wrinkled his nose. "What is that smell?" he asked. "The garbage union on strike again?"

"One of Mr. Karp's friends came calling unannounced," Mrs. Milquetost complained. The stench of Edward Treacher had a staying power that overwhelmed air fresheners and defied open windows.

Karp returned to his office and walked back to his desk, followed by Murrow. He looked down at the campaign finance papers and slumped into the seat, feeling the first storm clouds of a headache approaching. "Do I really need to know all this?" he complained. "Isn't this why I pay you?"

"Yes and no," Murrow replied, sitting down in the chair across from him and whipping out a PalmPilot day planner with the flourish of a matador drawing his sword from its scabbard. He began reading off the various upcoming speaking engagements, ribbon cuttings, fund-raising events, and black-tie parties Karp was expected to attend.

The reluctant candidate put his hands to his head, groaned, and said something disparaging about Murrow's immediate ancestry. Sometimes Karp wondered if the brain damage of running for political office was worth getting elected. In fact, he often wondered why he wanted to be the district attorney of New York.

Fighting crime on the island of Manhattan was like building sand castles against an incoming tide, what with some 600 murders, 1,700 rapes, 27,000 robberies, and 34,000 aggravated assaults, plus a deluge of other felonies in any one year. But that wasn't the bad part; he enjoyed putting criminals away and standing up for the victims.

No, the onerous part of being the district attorney was putting up with an exploitative and sensationalizing media and dealing with a myriad of special-interest groups, all of whom thought they were being ignored, or discriminated against, or deserved more, and all of whom *knew* that they could do his job better than he could. He was also tired of watching incompetent judges and ethically challenged lawyers make a mockery of the system.

More than any of that, though, he worried about the impact on his family. He'd made plenty of enemies over the years, some of whom had tried to get back at him by going after his wife and the kids. Not that Marlene hadn't brought some of the violence on herself or them, but as long as he remained The Man, they would always be a potential target.

Maybe it's time to let someone else carry the ball, he thought, leave the city and find some small town and practice law. Maybe

Marlene would consider practicing again. Karp and Ciampi, LLC, has a nice ring to it.

Yeah, right, said the little voice that seemed to have camped out in his cerebellum of late. Butch Karp, the lion of New York County's DAO, going to hang his shingle in some little place in the sticks and take on divorce and shoplifting cases. Your ego couldn't handle it.

That's not fair, he responded. This has nothing to do with my ego. I'm doing this to return the office to the integrity and respect it had under the Old Man. Somebody has to keep building sand castles or the tide will have nothing to slow it down.

Liar, said the voice. That may be part of it, but face it, you're as competitive as ever. You want to WIN this election. You just don't like the grunt work.

"I want to *win* this election because it's important for the public," Karp said before realizing he was now speaking aloud.

"I know, I know," Murrow said, putting up his hands in mock surrender, like he did every time the boss started grousing. "The polls are looking good, too, but we've got to continue to counter Rachman's ad campaign with personal appearances. That's where you shine."

Murrow furrowed his brow, a very studied move that he'd practiced thousands of times in front of a mirror back in law school. "I wonder where she's getting all that money?" he mused. "Her own party seems barely lukewarm to her candidacy."

Karp cringed at the mention of the former head of his sexual assault unit. "She should be in prison, not running for political office," he growled. "But there's plenty of people out there who would prefer her to me, and some of them have pretty deep pockets."

"Yeah, criminals," Murrow said. "I still can't believe the AG's decision."

Rachel Rachman, who years earlier had taken Marlene's place as the head of the sexual assault unit, had gone off the deep end in January and been caught trying to withhold exculpatory evidence from the defense in two rape cases, as well as preparing to put a witness on the stand who she knew had lied to the police. She'd always been something of a crusader—a virulently effective trial lawyer when it came to prosecuting rapists. But somewhere along the line, she'd decided that all men were rapists and all female complainants honest . . . justice and the rules be damned.

He'd had to recuse his office from prosecuting her but had turned over the evidence to the New York Attorney General and asked him to seek an indictment for obstruction of justice, false imprisonment, and withholding evidence in a criminal case. He'd been both surprised and disgusted when the AG declined to prosecute, saying that Rachman's action could have been interpreted as carrying out the job she'd been hired to do, albeit unethically, but it didn't rise to the level of criminal intent. The AG suggested that it was a matter for the state bar association, not the courts.

Seething, Karp had then tried to have Rachman disbarred. But again, he'd been stymied unexpectedly when the bar association would go no further than send his former employee a letter of reprimand. He sensed a rat.

The whole thing had been kept hush-hush from the public. Because the AG declined to file criminal charges, and the bar association letter was considered confidential, Karp's office—in the form of Murrow, who would have loved to expound on Rachman's shortcomings—was not free to comment on the reasons for her leaving the DAO.

Murrow's girlfriend, the ubiquitous journalist, Ariadne Stupenagel, had done her best to get to the bottom of the scandal in the DA's office. Even to the extent of promising Murrow sexual experiences almost unheard of, and possibly illegal, in the civilized world. But he'd refused to crack, and she'd otherwise run into a stone wall as far as official comment.

However, she had written a story noting that Rachman had been dismissed shortly after two of her sexual assault cases had fallen apart for unknown reasons. One of the complainants in the case, a young woman named Sarah Ryder, who'd accused her professor of Russian literature at NYU of drugging and raping her, turned out to be a real nutcase. In fact, she'd stabbed Karp's appellate chief, Harry Kipman, in the shoulder with a pair of scissors.

In both sexual assault cases that Rachman mishandled, the accused had been set free, the charges dismissed by Karp. And now corporation counsel, the city's attorney, was holding his breath, waiting for the expected lawsuits.

However, Rachman had countered by taking advantage of Karp's refusal to get into a war of words in the press. She'd announced her candidacy for the district attorney's seat and then gone on the attack. Her dismissal, she told her friends in the press, was due to "dirty politics." She claimed that she'd informed Karp that she intended to run for the office and her termination had been an act of revenge because her boss felt "betrayed."

When questioned about the cases noted in Stupenagel's story, Rachman angrily denied that there was anything materially wrong with them. She said she would have preferred "going forward and letting the juries decide on guilt or innocence. Not some arbitrary decision made by a male district attorney who can't seem to understand the trauma that women go through in a sexual assault that might leave them psychologically precarious."

Karp had ignored the attacks and insisted that Murrow and the others working on his campaign do the same. He believed that the public was bright enough to understand that Rachman was blowing smoke.

Still, he had to admit that her campaign was gaining ground. She had a long ways to go to challenge his position in the polls, but she was outspending him four-to-one with television, radio, and print ads. She'd even assembled a small group of former rape victims whose attackers she had put behind bars to give testimonials to the press that she was their "champion" while Karp was nothing more than a figurehead.

Murrow had complained bitterly that he was hobbled by Karp's refusal to get into negative politics. "I don't like dirty politics, either," he griped. "But it's the way things are done these days. If someone hits you, people want to see you hit back. Otherwise, you're a big wuss."

"A wuss?" Karp said. "Well, I guess I've been called worse."

"And still are," Murrow said. "We're taking more 'KKKarp' hits for the Coney Island Four case." He handed Karp a copy of the *New York Post* that had a huge headline over a photograph of flamboyant, race-baiting black attorney Hugh Louis that read: New York DA a Racist?

Karp barely glanced at the paper before tossing it into his wastepaper basket. The so-called Coney Island Four was a gang of young black men who'd brutally raped and almost killed a young woman who'd been jogging along Coney Island's Brighton Beach one morning more than a decade earlier. They'd been serving time when a vile sex offender named Enrique Villalobos came forward to claim that he'd been the only one to assault the woman. Their attorney, Louis, had immediately demanded that they be exonerated and released from prison, and the King's County DA had immediately capitulated. Louis had then sued the city of New York and NYPD for what he called a "racially motivated railroading" of his clients by overzealous prosecutors.

Although it wasn't part of his job description, Karp had taken on the case at the request of the city's new mayor, Michael Denton, who didn't trust the corporation counsel, the city's attorney at the time. At trial, Karp had proved that the original prosecution had been a good one and that, in fact, Villalobos had been forced by the gang of rapists into testifying otherwise.

Karp considered the trial a win, although justice had been meted out in an unusually lethal manner. In garish courtroom cross-examination, Karp forced Villalobos to recant his "confession." The leader of the gang, Jayshon Sykes, had than seized a court officer's gun and killed Villalobos. The uncommon fireworks ended when the rape victim shot and killed Sykes.

Hugh Louis was arrested for his part in the planning of the schemes and charged with capital murder among other major felonies. He would be going to trial later that fall, and was now claiming again that Karp's defense of the city had been racially motivated.

It is immaterial that my client, who is no longer here to defend himself, may or may not have committed a crime, the former dapper Hugh Louis, now dressed in his jailhouse jumpsuit, ranted to the press from the Tombs dayroom. *The big picture here—are you with me—is that the city called in its "top gun," a man who has been accused before of racist acts, because my clients were African-American, and is now after me because—although I was duped by my clients—I am African-American. It is another example of The Man sending a message to people of color, "Do not attempt to seek justice or we will silence you one way or the other." Well, no one silences Hugh Louis.*

When an incensed Murrow read the quote to Karp from the *Times* and demanded that they issue a press release to counter it, Karp told him to drop it. *I think the public sees through this crap. I'm not going to dignify it by responding every time Louis, or Rachman, or anybody else wants to play the race or gender or religion or politics card.*

Murrow winced at the mention of Rachman. As he'd predicted, when Guma had convinced Karp that he had enough to reopen the Stavros case, a decision that was vindicated when the grand jury indicted Emil, she'd howled with outrage. She'd blasted Karp, saying he was *showing his true colors* by resorting to *Tammany Hall politics* to stay in power.

Stavros's attorney had, of course, joined the chorus. The attorney, Bryce Anderson, a glib, frequent commentator on legal issues for CNN, was beside himself with indignation at a hastily called press conference on the steps of the Criminal Courts building.

This is an absolute outrage, he huffed. *It's obviously a shameless attempt by the district attorney to pull out old rumors to embarrass and damage a man who opposes him politically. It's vengeance, pure and simple, for all the funds that are pouring into his opponent's war chest, and he's starting to feel the pinch in the polls. Mrs. Stavros abandoned her family fourteen years ago, at which time Mr. Stavros was completely exonerated of any wrongdoing. Should this farce be allowed to continue, we will fight these charges with every ounce of our energy, and when we are victorious, we will work to make sure that this new "Boss Tweed" is chased from office by the good people of New York City.*

Murrow had wanted to go on the attack then, just as he did now. But Karp wouldn't let him answer Rachman or Anderson, other than a brief comment: *A duly formed grand jury heard the evidence and determined that probable cause existed to warrant the charges against Mr. Stavros. We will reserve further comment for the courtroom.* Nor would he let Murrow go off now. "If I can't run on my record and what I have to say, then I don't want to win anyway."

"Well, then, that means you agree to all these appearances," Murrow said.

It was Karp's turn to hold up his hands. "You win, Gilbert," he said. "As long as it doesn't interfere with doing the job or cut into all of my family time."

"That doesn't leave much," Murrow groused. "I think you're getting stretched pretty thin."

Karp downplayed the comment but thought: He's right. I am feeling a little stretched. It wasn't just the day-to-day stuff of running the District Attorney's Office, either. The hunt for Andrew Kane and his accomplices was running into dead ends, according to the almost daily reports he got from Jaxon. Nor was there much to indicate what Kane was up to beyond revenge. *Apparently, there's been an increase in internet chatter that seems to indicate that something's up,* Jaxon said. *And the NSA's "man on the inside" is still trying to get close. In the meantime, Ellis said to tell you he's "got your back."*

Karp had rolled his eyes at that one. It was almost a game now trying to figure out who among the hundreds of people walking the sidewalks around Crosby and Grand every hour were really federal agents assigned to protect him and his family. Was it the street workers who'd showed up one morning but didn't seem to do much except pop in and out of a manhole down the block? Or was it the old couple he'd never seen before walking their miniature poodle? *You don't like this guy Ellis much, do you?* Karp said to Jaxon the last time they talked.

The telephone was silent for a moment before Jaxon spoke again. *It's not that I like or don't like him. I mean, the guy's obviously a pro. He's just not much of a team player, if you know what I mean, or maybe he doesn't see me as being on his team. But I might just be grousing about playing second fiddle in my own neck of the woods.*

Karp tried not to dwell on Andrew Kane and what he might be up to, especially as it affected his family. But it was pretty hard to entirely ignore a homicidal maniac who has promised to wipe your DNA from the planet.

So he'd tried to turn the negative into a positive by focusing on spending quality time with his family, in particular Marlene. Their marriage had survived a few recent rocky patches, but was still challenged by recent events. If it wasn't Kane, then she was dwelling on the January death of her mother and the increasing mental deterioration of her father. So he'd taken to sending the kids out to a movie or some other activity—with a police escort— so that he and Marlene could spend more time together just necking on the couch or discussing the issues of the day. They'd even managed a couple of dinners out, which she seemed to appreciate, especially when she'd spent the day dealing with her father.

Meanwhile, Lucy was living in New Mexico, but there was nothing much he could do about that. He liked her boyfriend, the cowboy Ned Blanchet, who'd proved himself more than competent in tight situations, and John Jojola, the Indian police chief of the Taos Pueblo, was also out there keeping an eye on them.

Somehow, he'd even found more time to spend with the twins. Zak and Giancarlo were studying for their bar mitzvah, which unfortunately had just been scheduled for late October, right before the election. Karp was still teaching classes at the behest of the young rabbi at their synagogue for those taking their bar mitzvah (and even a few girls studying for their bat mitzvah). That ate up another night of the week.

With all that attention to the family and the job, he knew he wasn't being fair to Murrow, who'd been working his butt off on the campaign. "I'll try to pass off some of this office stuff so that I can attend as much as I can," Karp told his assistant.

Karp saw that the next item on Murrow's yellow pad was "Television Ads" for which he had a particular aversion, but was saved by the buzzing of the intercom. He reached forward and punched the answer button. "Yes, Mrs. Milquetost."

"There's a Mr. Espey Jaxon on the line for you," she said. "He says he's calling from California and that it's urgent."

Karp felt his stomach muscles tighten. *I believe a harbinger of bad tidings will soon arrive from California . . .* "Put him through, please," he said, hitting another button to engage the speakerphone.

"Hello, Espey, you taking up surfing?" he asked, leaning back in his chair and wishing the conversation would remain as light.

"I wish," Jaxon replied. "Can I talk freely?"

Karp glanced at Murrow who asked with sign language if he should leave. But Karp shook his head. "Gilbert Murrow is here, if that's okay," he said. "I'd trust him with my life." He winked at his aide who blushed and smiled.

"Yeah, sure, I know Mr. Murrow . . . hi, Gilbert. . . . Anyway, I'm afraid I have some bad news. Fey's been murdered."

Karp knew his jaw was hanging open, hopefully not as far as Murrow's, but he couldn't help it. He felt suddenly prescient in that he knew the information was only going to get worse. "When?" he asked, not sure why that was important at this point.

"Apparently, last night," Jaxon said. "But nobody counted him missing until this morning. They found him out in the barn. . . . I have no idea why it took so long to discover he was missing and get word to me, but I flew out as soon as I heard."

Karp heard the disgust, and the suspicion, in the agent's voice. "How'd it happen?"

There was a pause on the other end of the line. "I'd rather talk about some of this in person, tomorrow morning when I get back," he said. "But he was strangled . . . with a set of rosary beads."

There it is, Karp thought, the other shoe . . . or maybe better, the ax, has fallen. "Kane," he said.

"Looks like it," Jaxon replied. "I'll see you tomorrow."

He'd hardly hung up when the intercom on his desk buzzed again. "Your wife is here to see you, Mr. Karp?"

Karp slapped a hand to his head. "Shit. I forgot," he said to Murrow, who got up and started to leave. "I'm having dinner with Marlene and . . . some old friends." He was about to tell Mrs. Milquetost to send Marlene in when there was a squawk—some sort of strangled cry really—from the intercom and Karp's office door flew open, nearly knocking Murrow off his feet.

"Well hello, Gilbert," Marlene Ciampi said, her eyes narrowing. "Are you the reason my husband is having the gendarme stop me from entering?"

"Don't hurt me," Murrow squeaked, only half in jest, and scooted past her.

Marlene slammed the door on the still protesting Mrs. Milquetost. "The next time that woman tries to stop me, I'm going to scratch her eyes out."

9

TEN MINUTES EARLIER, THE SECURITY GUARDS AT THE JUS-
tice Center tensed as the attractive woman with the dark hair
and Mediterranean features nonchalantly pulled the Glock 9 mm
from her purse. She'd already shown them her license to carry a
concealed weapon and told them about the contents of the
purse. But it wasn't until she expertly slid the magazine from the
handle, pulled back the slide to demonstrate there was no bullet
in the chamber, and handed it to them that they were able to
relax.

"Hold on, boys, there's more," she said, her hand moving slowly
to the small of her back and lifting her shirt above the top of her
blue jeans to expose the smaller Colt .380 tucked into a belt holster. She removed the gun, went through the same motions as with
the first weapon, and handed it with a smile to the slack-jawed
guards.

"Oh, and you'll find a knife and a can of pepper spray in here,"
she said, shoving her handbag toward one of them.

"Expecting a war today, Marlene?" asked Harry Kipman, the
brilliant chief of the DAO's appellate division. His security pass had

allowed him to waltz in the building ahead of her though they'd arrived at 100 Centre Street at the same time.

"I'm expecting a war every day," Marlene Ciampi replied.

"I thought your hubby told me you'd given up gunslinging," said Ray Guma, who'd seen them enter the building and had waited beyond the security desk.

"Times change," Marlene said.

"Criminal masterminds escape," Guma added.

"It's just plain frickin' dangerous out here," noted Kipman, who absently patted his other arm, which was being supported by a sling. He was still recovering from being stabbed in the shoulder by Sarah Ryder and subsequent surgeries to repair nerve damage.

"I know, poor Harry," Marlene said, passing through the metal detector and walking up to kiss him on the cheek. "Threw himself in front of me just like Superman and took the bullet."

"Scissors."

"Bullet . . . scissors sounds like you got in a fight with Hillary Clinton and she won."

"Okay, bullet," Kipman agreed.

"Machine-gun bullet, fifty cal," Guma laughed.

"'Twas only a flesh wound," Kipman replied with what he thought of as his "stiff upper lip" English accent as they walked to the elevator.

Even though it was almost closing time, they had to navigate through the human flotsam and jetsam that floated about the lobby. They skirted a mother who slapped her son, a hulking three-hundred-pounder, and scolded him for "hanging around that bad element." The young man hung his head and took his medicine, though he looked like he would have preferred hearing it from a judge. "Yes, Momma. Sorry, Momma."

A little further toward the elevators, a frightened young woman huddled against her husband and told an earnest assistant district attorney that she just didn't think she could face the man who raped her. "I can't handle having his eyes looking at me again. I'd rather drop the charges."

Over near the water fountain, a wild-looking vagabond in a tie-dyed shirt shouted that the end was near. A cop moved to silence him.

A bleary-eyed drunk sailed out of the crowd to offer Marlene a business card proclaiming Jimmy Jones Bail Bonds to be the best. "Come on, lady, the faster I give these out," he complained to Marlene who'd declined, "the sooner I get a drink and can stop this shakin'."

Every step of the way toward the elevator there seemed to be someone crying, or a lawyer chasing a frightened or sullen client insisting that he "accept the deal or I am out of here," or bewildered citizens running around with official-looking documents in their hands and lost looks on their faces. "God, sometimes I forget how depressing this place can be," Marlene said as they stepped on the elevator and hit the button for the eighth floor and the offices of the New York District Attorney.

"You certainly see an interesting slice of the human pie down here," Kipman remarked somewhat awkwardly, his face turning red. He hadn't been kissed *anywhere* by *anyone* in quite some time, not since before his wife had died, and he was intoxicatedly aware of the lingering presence of Marlene's perfume.

Marlene smiled up at Kipman, her one good eye sparkling with a bravado she wasn't really feeling. She'd lost the other eye more than two decades earlier when as an ADA she'd opened a letter bomb intended for Karp, whom she was dating. The injury marked the beginning of what had surprisingly veered from the normal life track of a Catholic schoolgirl raised in Queens, educated at Sacred Heart High School, then college at Smith and finally Yale Law School. Right after law school, she'd entered the DAO, eventually heading the sex crimes unit. Frustrated with the system's inability to not only mete out true justice, but also its pathetic ineptness at protecting the innocent, her path had deviated away from the practice of law and entered the realm of dispensing street justice.

Whether as the head of a firm providing security for high-profile VIPs or volunteering to take on men who were terrorizing women and ignoring court-issued restraining orders to leave them alone, Marlene had discovered a latent talent for violence. Even the dogs she raised on a farm in Long Island weren't the usual fare for a Manhattan housewife. No poodles or schnauzers for Marlene, no it was Presa Canarios, massive, potentially ferocious guard dogs that could be trained for bomb, drug, or simply protection duties.

At some point, the lines between protecting the weak and vigilantism had grown increasingly blurred; her response to confrontation more violent. In a sort of last-ditch effort to pull out of the dive into moral oblivion, she'd gone with her daughter, Lucy, to a retreat in Taos, New Mexico, for women suffering from post-traumatic stress syndrome. The retreat had steadied her nerves and left her psyche open to possibility. A possibility realized when she met John Jojola, the police chief of the Taos Pueblo who was investigating the murders of young Indian boys.

She'd liked Jojola right away—from his self-deprecating humor to his air of a man who was comfortable in his own skin. But it had taken some time to realize the depth of him. Jojola wasn't allowed to talk to her about the details of his people's beliefs. *We are an ancient people—one of the few American Indian tribes still living in the lands of their ancestors,* he explained. *There are secrets we don't share with anyone, friend or foe. Just like we don't teach people our language, Tewa, though Lucy has assimilated enough to almost carry on a conversation. Sorry, it's not meant to be rude, just sacred.*

It was the beginning of Marlene's return to the world, but not an easy road to travel with her family's propensity to attract trouble. She'd been forced to call on her violent tendencies again on New Year's Eve to save her son Zak and help stop terrorists from blowing up Times Square. But she had done it with a clear conscience, quite sure that killing terrorists fell under the heading of protecting the community.

After that, she'd hoped for a respite from danger. But then

Fulton had been shot and Kane escaped. She hadn't needed to hear Fulton's message from Kane; she knew that the game was on and had been back to packing heat ever since.

And yet, her concerns recently had more to do with her father than Kane's escape or her husband's election campaign.

At noon she'd gone to take her father to lunch with the purpose of trying to talk him into moving out of the family home in Queens and into a nice assisted-living community.

He'd been living alone ever since her mother had died earlier that year, and she worried that he wasn't coming out of his funk. The last years of her mother's life had been rough. Concetta Ciampi had developed Alzheimer's and had become increasingly difficult to deal with. Half the time she couldn't remember Marlene's name and had taken to walking out of the house and wandering the neighborhood, lost.

Mariano Ciampi had grown increasingly frustrated and frightened by the whole process. The woman he'd been married to for more than sixty years no longer knew who he was most of the time or thought he'd replaced the "real" Mariano. And he no longer recognized her as the woman he loved since meeting her on the boat on the way to the United States from Italy. His frustrations had made him angry, and Marlene had worried that he might physically harm his wife in a fit.

Then came the morning when he called. Her mother, he said, wasn't breathing. He was afraid that she was dead. She'd arrived to find her father grieving downstairs and her mother lying on her back upstairs, her sightless eyes fixed on the crucifix above her bed. She'd bent over to close her mother's eyes and noticed the tiny spots that indicated hemorrhaging in the eyes, sometimes an indication of strangulation or smothering.

She'd gone back downstairs and gently questioned her father. He said they'd gone to bed early, like normal, and when he woke up that morning, her body was cold and she wouldn't respond when he called her name and touched her.

The medical examiner, who knew Marlene and didn't want to extend the formalities any longer than necessary, did a cursory examination and pronounced the verdict "natural causes." There'd been a quick burial, a service attended by dozens of people Marlene didn't know as well as family, then a period of grieving in which she had not allowed herself to entertain the thought that her father might have killed her mother. Gradually the immediate sadness passed, but the question continued to trouble her sleep. Many nights she got up and made her way across Crosby to the loft building on the other side and up to the little art studio Butch had created for her. There she'd paint away into the morning, imagining how to ask her father if he'd murdered the woman he loved.

Using the excuse that she was working on a case, Marlene had questioned another medical examiner to see if there were other explanations for the hemorrhage spots besides murder.

Oh sure, he said. *She might have had a stroke or even choked on something . . . although an autopsy should have revealed it if that was the case.*

Marlene had decided then that her mother's death had been through natural causes. She was wrong to think otherwise of her father, a good and gentle man all of his life, dedicated to his family, and absolutely and madly in love with his wife. But that didn't answer the problem of what to do with him.

He wasn't as bad off as her mother had been, but he wasn't all there anymore, either. He often forgot things—whether it was a doctor's appointment, or something as simple as his key and locking himself out of his house. A couple of times he'd called her, his voice weepy and on the edge of panic, to say he had driven somewhere but couldn't quite figure out how to get back. He was lost but too afraid of strangers to ask for directions, so Marlene would have to go retrieve him, or call the neighbor she'd left a spare house key with to let him in.

Ever since the death of her mother, he'd grown more frail. She was worried that he wasn't eating or sleeping well. She had plenty of money from the sale of her security company—more than she or

Butch or their children would be able to use in their lifetimes—and wanted to use it to make his life, and hers, easier. She'd found a fabulous assisted-care facility, "more like a permanent vacation in a five-star hotel," she told him. But he refused to go.

"I will not go into a nursing home," he'd shouted.

"Take it easy, Pops," she replied in as calm a voice as she could muster. "It's not a nursing home. I would never do that to you. It's a community for senior citizens. You'd have your own apartment, a social center, including a pool and a billiards and card room. There's someone around 24/7 if you need help, and all your meals and laundry and stuff is taken care of. . . . It's like Club Med."

"Call it whatever you want, but it's where you send people to die who are no longer useful," her father shouted again and retreated up to his bedroom.

"I plan to die in the same house I lived in with your mother for more than fifty years!" he yelled through the door when she asked him to open it. "This is the house where you and your sisters and brothers were brought the day you was born. You were all raised here . . . this is where we were a family, goddammit!"

Marlene used a bobby pin from her hair and unlocked the door. He didn't seem to notice but looked around behind her as if he expected to see someone spying. "You know I've seen her," he whispered.

"Who, Pops?"

"Your mother. She sometimes shows up in the doorway at night when I'm in bed. If I get up and try to find her, she disappears. But I can hear her moving around out there. . . . I think she's waiting for me. But if I go to this living facility, she won't know where to find me so that we can go to heaven together."

The old man had sat down on the bed and started weeping. "I miss her so much," he said. "I'd even take the crazy version back."

Marlene had laid down on the bed next to him and pulled him close. In some ways, it was romantic, the way her old man looked forward to spending eternity with his sweetheart. But his visions of an unsettled ghost made her wonder if the manner of her mother's death was weighing on her father's conscience. But she couldn't ask him. She just couldn't, and instead she said, "It's your imagination, Pops. Mom's in heaven with Jesus waiting for you there."

She repeated an offer for him to come live with her, Butch, and the boys, but not even the promise of daily contact with his beloved grandsons could get him to budge. "We'd get on each other's nerves," he said, "and then I'd have no place to go that was my own. I want my house, where I can do what I want, when I want. Besides, the guys at the VFW would miss me."

So she'd left the debate for another day. Marlene had arrived at 100 Centre Street a bit unsettled, but she brightened when she saw Harry Kipman walking up to the entrance. She adored Harry. He liked to play the irascible intellectual, but she knew he was not just bright, but kind and warm. She hadn't minded the teasing about her weaponry, but it did remind her that she was falling back into old patterns.

Doesn't matter, she thought, I'm defending my family, and I'm not about to leave their security up to someone else.

As soon as he could start barking orders, Fulton had immediately beefed up the police presence around her husband until wherever Butch went, he looked like a presidential candidate surrounded by Secret Service agents. She accepted the extra police patrols around the loft and even the presence of escorts when the boys went out. But she'd declined her own bodyguard.

You lose your edge when you depend on someone else, she'd told Fulton. And he'd known her better than to argue.

She'd fought it again when Butch came home and announced that the Department of Homeland Security was beefing up the detail. However, Jaxon, another longtime friend of the family, had persuaded her that the new teams were professionals who knew how to stay out of the way but would be ready just in case.

Marlene wasn't the only one who wasn't thrilled with being shadowed by federal agents. Even more adamantly against the whole idea was Lucy. She was back in Taos, New Mexico, with

Ned, and didn't want anybody spying on her. *I've got Ned,* she pointed out before she left. *He's the only secret agent man I need.*

No one's doubting Ned's abilities, Marlene had said as the subject of the conversation stood bashfully to the side with his head down and Stetson in his hand while mother and daughter argued in the loft before they left that past January to return to Taos.

Like her husband, Marlene liked the young man and acknowledged that his hobby as a quick-draw gunslinger at Western competitions had come in handy when Lucy's life had been threatened several times over the past year. But again, that had all been about reactions; he wasn't trained to be proactive when dealing with a security threat. *He's only one man, and he may be a target himself. Kane, or whomever he sends, is not going to step out onto the street and ask for a fair fight. You won't even know the feds are there.*

Yes, I will, Lucy said, placing her hands on her hips with her feet apart, an obstinate stance she'd inherited from her mother. *And I'm not going to give up my privacy for the latest madman du jour who has it in for this family.*

Looking at her defiant daughter, Marlene was struck again by the changes in the thin, pale, and frightened young woman who'd gone to Taos, New Mexico, almost a year earlier to help at a Catholic mission for Taos Indian kids. Bookish and wrapped up in Catholic mysticism, she'd done little up to that point to make herself attractive to members of the opposite sex. A savant at picking up languages—having mastered nearly sixty already—she'd accompanied her mother to Taos, hoping to learn Tewa, one of the oldest and most individualistic languages left in the world from the Pueblo Indians there. Whether it was the outdoor life or her love for her young cowboy, Lucy had blossomed into a tanned, muscular but well-filled-out young woman, who if not pretty in the classical sense of a rose was certainly beautiful in the sense of a desert flower.

Marlene then turned to John Jojola to persuade Lucy, but he'd been no help. *These federal agents might be okay in the city,* he said. *But every time some guy from the FBI shows up in town, it's all over the reservation faster than you can pick up the telephone.*

And the people in town can smell the difference between the tourists and out-of-town cops. One spends money on doodads, the other doesn't. I'm worried that if the bad guys show up in town, we won't know which is which, and they might spot the feds first, which would make them more cautious. I'd rather they were over-confident. He'd put his arm around Marlene's shoulders. *Come on, I'll keep an eye on the young lovebirds. Us cowboys and Indians blend in better in our West. If Ned doesn't see them first, me and my guys will.*

Marlene chatted briefly with Kipman and Guma after they arrived on the eighth floor. The men then preceded down the hallway toward the appeals bureau, while Marlene walked into the reception room outside of Butch's office and found Mrs. Milquetost blocking the way.

"I'm here to see my husband."

"Is he expecting you?"

Marlene stared at the woman dumbfounded. "Well, yes, now may I go in?"

"Let me see if he's available," Mrs. Milquetost said, giving her a look that said "stay where you are" while she walked around her desk and pressed the intercom button.

"Yes, Mrs. Mil-kay-tossed?"

"Your wife is here to see you, Mr. Karp?"

That was too much for Marlene, who threw her legs into gear and breezed past the the receptionist, who responded by grabbing for her, too late, and an angrily squawking, "You can't—"

Marlene burst through the door nearly knocking Gilbert Murrow off his feet. "Well hello, Gilbert," she said. "Are you the reason my husband has the gendarme—"

"Don't hurt me," Murrow squeaked, only half in jest, and scooted past her.

Marlene slammed the door on the still protesting Mrs. Milquetost. "The next time that woman tries to stop me, I'm going to scratch her eyes out," she told her husband.

"What if I was having sex with my mistress and you burst in like that?" Karp teased as she reached up to place her arms around his neck.

"I'd have to kill you to avenge my Italian honor."

"But you wouldn't know if you didn't barge past Mrs. Milquetost and had waited in the reception area like a good wife until my mistress had enough time to get her clothes back on. Ow!"

Karp rubbed at his lip where she'd bitten him hard enough to draw blood. "Oh, I'd know, buster," she hissed and kissed him again, gently on the wound. "The woman always knows . . . even if she doesn't want to admit it to herself. Now, are you ready to go to dinner? Oh, by the way, it's the street workers."

"What street workers?" Karp replied.

"The spooks," Marlene said rolling her eyes. "The guys watching the loft."

"What made you change your mind?" Just the night before she'd guessed the poodle people as they lay in bed playing Guess the Spooks. *They aren't really old and that's probably a bomb-sniffing poodle . . . yaps and pees all over itself when it finds one,* she'd said. *Isn't that right, Gilgamesh?*

The huge Presa Canario who camped at the foot of the bed responded with a mumbled "woof" and shifted his enormous head from one paw to the next, hoping that would be the end of it. The couple in the bed had been keeping him awake with their sexual antics, and he was tired. It took a lot of energy to haul his 150-pound frame around all day. He, too, was trained to sniff for bombs, as well as dismember human threats upon the appropriate command. But mostly he just wanted to go for walks, eat, and nap.

"What makes you so sure it's the street workers?" Karp asked.

"Well, when I came out of the building tonight to walk over here," she said, "I went right by those guys—both of them clean-cut Ivy League sorts and neither one of them whistled, or yelled, 'Hey baby, hubba hubba,' or asked me for a date. And I'm wearing my tightest jeans. You tell me how many street workers in New York would ignore this cute little tush? It's just not normal."

"You have a point," Karp said. She did look hot in the tight jeans that molded to her still perky rear end. The compliment got him another kiss and he was feeling a bit distracted by the feeling of her body pressing up against his. "Can't we just go home?"

Marlene kissed him again but broke the embrace and fended off his attempts to reengage. "No," she said. "Now, calm down, tiger. The boys will be home anyway, so it's hours before you would be able to act on that notion anyway. And Uncle Vladimir said it's important."

10

"So now he's 'Uncle Vladimir'?" Karp inquired as their cabdriver wove his way down Centre and turned onto the Brooklyn Bridge for the ride over to Brighton Beach.

Karp wasn't sure how he felt about her adopting his "other" family. "Uncle Vladimir" was actually his great-uncle Vladimir Karchovski, his paternal grandfather's brother and, of greater concern, a power in the Russian mob over in Brighton Beach.

He did not know the man well. He'd always been a distant relative, seen rarely on childhood visits to his grandfather's house. Back then he'd just been a nice old man who liked to lift him up to eye level, ask if he'd been a good boy, and when he responded in the affirmative, gave him pieces of licorice candy he kept individually wrapped in his coat pockets.

Only when Karp had grown older, probably about the time he entered law school, did his father spill the beans and tell him the truth about his uncle "the gangster." The announcement had stunned him. His dream was to become a prosecutor with the New York District Attorney's Office and somehow "gangster" and "prosecutor" didn't seem to mix well. But his father had assured him that "that" side of the family had always kept their affairs to themselves, and after Karp got on with the DAO, it had been understood that so long as no laws were broken in the County of New York, there would be no cause for family strife.

Other than the rare birthday card, a present of Russian crystal wine goblets for his and Marlene's wedding, and gifts of Russian nesting dolls when the children were born, there'd been very little contact between Karp and the Brooklyn Karchovskis. That was until that past fall when Vladimir Karchovski asked his son, Yvgeny, heir to his father's criminal empire, to arrange a meeting with Karp and Marlene on Ellis Island to pass on information that had helped Karp unravel the Coney Island Four case.

A short time later, the Karchovski family crossed paths again with the family Karp. Yvgeny Karchovski's half brother, Alexis Michalik, an NYU professor, was accused of raping student Sarah Ryder. Ryder had been the one to stick Harry "Hotspur" Kipman with the scissors when Marlene had proved she was a liar out to get Michalik.

The case had gone a long way in getting Yvgeny, a former colonel in the Soviet Red Army who'd illegally immigrated to the United States to join his father, to acknowledge that the legal system in America could and did work. But after that, Karp and his Brooklyn relations had gone back to their respective turfs.

That distance, however, had not included all the members of Karp's immediate family. Marlene, who'd met the older man and been charmed by his Old World manner and kindness, surprised her husband one evening by announcing that she'd been painting over on the boardwalk at Brighton Beach and decided to stop by that afternoon to see Vladimir at his St. Petersburg Tea Room restaurant. She'd been greeted by both the old man and his son like a long-lost daughter and sister, respectively. Her money had been no good as they dined on honey cakes, cabbage pies, and pickled tomatoes, washed down with lemon *kvas* and green tea, while they talked about their lives and families.

Vladimir would like to see the twins again, Marlene had said that night.

Now, we're arranging family visits? Karp had sighed in response.

To be sure, he was curious about his family's history. They'd all belonged to a Jewish community in the Galicia region of Poland. But Cossacks had burned the village, murdering Jews of all ages and genders. His father's side of the family had immigrated to the United States; the other side had escaped into Russia where they'd eventually joined the Bolshevik Revolution and became heroes of the Red Army. He knew that Yvgeny had served in Afghanistan until his tank had been struck by a rocket, leaving a portion of his face and upper body scarred.

There were questions Karp would have liked to ask his cousin, and to be honest, in the brief instances they'd been together, he'd found that he liked his Brooklyn relatives. Yet, at the heart of it all, he was ill at ease with the whole criminal enterprise business. The relationship, which both sides understood, would always remain at arm's length.

Moreover, ofttimes, he wondered how many people they might have killed. Probably no more than Marlene, he mused, which caused him to wince. His wife's propensity for acting the part of the avenging angel made it difficult to point the finger at others sometimes.

Marlene had taken the boys to see their great-great-uncle and cousin by herself. She'd started to explain to Vladimir that Butch would have come except he had to work, but the old man put a finger to his lips. *We are family, and I understand why these meetings are . . . difficult for him. When you see him, give him my love . . . an old man's affection for his brother's grandson. And thank him for loaning his beautiful wife and darling boys for a few hours to brighten an old man's afternoon.*

From his large but not ostentatious home in the middle of the Russian community, they'd walked past the knish shops and furriers to the boardwalk along the beach. Marlene had done her best to ignore the dark sedans that slowly preceded and followed them, as well as the two burly Slavic types who walked behind them at a discreet distance as if out for a mob-guy stroll.

Vladimir wore a light-colored linen suit with a black beret, which she discovered was his favored mode of dress when out for his daily walk along the boardwalk. While the twins ran off to play along the breakers on the beach, the old man and Marlene got a chance to talk about his role in the community. She noticed how ordinary people greeted Vladimir warmly and treated him with extreme deference, but it didn't seem borne of fear so much as genuine affection for a benefactor.

Yes, they don't see me as a . . . a gangster, he said. *I dislike that term myself. It is for people who seek a life of crime because that is what they want—it is the way they are made. I suppose it can be argued that I didn't have to lead this life either. For instance, my brother, your husband's grandfather, he was a success as an honest businessman. But I came later, with no money and up against a lot of . . . of discrimination because I was "stupid" immigrant, a Russian Jew, maybe a Bolshevik. . . . I did not feel I had the choice if I wanted to support my family and myself, and to protect them from bad men with evil intent who would have preyed upon us. It has been this way for many people when they come here—the Irish, the Italians.*

Vladimir had walked a little farther, pointing and laughing at where the boys chased through a crowd of protesting seagulls. He stopped and looked out to sea, as if to imagine those ships full of immigrants. *We had to organize ourselves, the strong leading the weak, when the larger society wouldn't help. I made my living by sneaking people into this country, yes, for profit, but I also feel good about that. And I make money off such things as gambling and some of man's other vices—but those are his choices, I am merely a provider of goods and service. Never drugs, and I would not demean women by making them prostitutes. And if I have . . . at times . . . resorted to violence, it has only been in defense of me, my family, or my people. As such, I offer no apologies and any sins I have committed will be judged by God.*

Marlene had been over to visit the old man several times since, occasionally running into Yvgeny, who had always treated her warmly. Then one day, while drinking tea with Vladimir at his restaurant, he'd suddenly asked if she and Butch would consider coming to dinner at his house.

I wouldn't ask . . . or risk my nephew's reputation if I did not think it important to discuss something directly with him. It is the sort of thing best discussed in person and not over the telephone lines.

Marlene had accepted. Later, when she told Butch, he'd agreed with an uncharacteristic solemn nod.

As the cab rolled over the Brooklyn Bridge, the couple grew silent, each lost in their own thoughts. Then Butch said quietly so that only his wife could hear. "Fey was murdered last night."

Marlene blinked hard once. "How?"

"I don't know much," he said. "Jaxon called just a few minutes before you arrived and didn't want to talk until we're face-to-face tomorrow. But apparently, Fey was strangled . . . with rosary beads."

"Kane," she said, echoing his response a half hour earlier.

"Yeah, looks like it," he answered. "I'd like to know how Kane found him. The feds had him buried pretty deep."

Marlene wasn't so surprised. "The feds had a traitor who got a bunch of kids murdered and Fulton shot to help Kane escape."

"Yeah, but Michael Grover's dead, and supposedly he didn't know Fey's whereabouts. Anyway, I'll know more tomorrow."

Marlene stared out her window. She clutched her handbag to her lap, glad of the heavy presence of the Glock inside but upset that her family was in danger again. "It's getting dark outside," she said wiping at the tears that had formed in her eyes.

When they arrived in the Karchovskis' neighborhood, the streets were oddly empty of cars and pedestrians. As they pulled up to the house, a large man whose head seemed to almost disappear into his massive shoulders waddled out from the gated courtyard to pay the cabbie and escort them into the living room of the house. He then waddled back the way they had come without saying a word the entire time.

They didn't wait long. Vladimir Karchovski soon appeared, leaning on the arm of his son, Yvgeny. He immediately disengaged himself and came forward to hug Marlene and kiss her on each cheek. He then greeted Butch in the same way. "Welcome, welcome to my home," he said and led them to the sitting area.

Marlene took a seat on the couch next to the old man. Butch and Yvgeny remained standing, which gave her a chance to compare the two. They were nearly identical in height, weight, and age. Anyone who did not know them might have guessed that they were brothers, maybe twins. They both had high, wide cheekbones and would have had the same eyes, gray flecked with gold and curiously slanted, except that Yvgeny had lost one of his during a battle in Afghanistan and now wore a black patch. They were both handsome men in a rugged way, and even the scars from the burns on his face did not subtract from the overall attractiveness of Yvgeny. Careful, old girl, Marlene cautioned herself, keep thinking this way and you'll be fantasizing about a Marlene sandwich.

"Penny for your thoughts," Vladimir said.

"Uh, they aren't worth that much," she replied, wondering if the old man's sly smile meant he'd read her mind.

A chessboard was set up on the coffee table in front of the couch. When Yvgeny noticed Karp's attention drawn to it, he asked, "Do you play?"

Karp shook his head. "Not really. Or perhaps I should say 'horribly,' a real amateur . . . a sort of 'last man standing' strategy that would get me whipped by either one of my sons."

"Ah, but so very American," Yvgeny said, picking up a silver cigar box and opening it to offer one to Karp, who declined, and to Marlene, who accepted. "The subtleties don't interest you, you'd rather . . . how do you say it . . . 'slug it out.' Always rushing in where the proverbial angels fear to tread."

"Are you saying Americans are fools?" Karp asked with a smile. He knew his cousin was trying to bait him and he was willing to rise to it for the time being.

"Perhaps," Yvgeny said. "Or maybe just naïve, a sort of innocent belief in yourselves. But there must be something to it that allowed the United States to become the most powerful nation ever on the planet, more powerful than even the old Soviet Union. Maybe it is your bigger-than-life mythology . . . good guys in white hats always beating the bad guys in black hats . . . you don't believe you can lose, and so you don't lose. You are always so reluctant to start a fight—or, more importantly in today's world, to strike first—even though you know you are being threatened. It is almost as though you cannot fight back until pushed nearly to the brink of not being able to fight at all."

"How do you mean?"

"Your history is replete with examples of what I am talking about. The easiest is, of course, American reluctance to enter World War Two. If the Japanese had not been so stupid as to attack and waken the sleeping giant, you would have probably not started fighting until it was too late . . . your allies already gone down in flames, and you would have been standing alone against the darkness. It is the same now with this so-called War on Terrorism. You have been attacked—repeatedly—and yet you treat each incident as if it were some sort of separate crime, instead of an act of war. You worry about such things as 'profiling' young Muslim men because of your sense of fair play and not wanting to discriminate, yet it is young male Muslim extremists who are intent on murdering all of us. You have the power to obliterate entire regions where you know your enemy is hiding, yet you send in your troops to do the slow, dirty work—and to die—because you don't want to risk harming 'innocent' civilians."

"Is that so bad?" Karp asked.

"Only if you want to survive," Yvgeny countered. "For one thing, those citizens are probably not so innocent if they are lending support, recruits, and a base of operations to your enemies. You cannot fight this war the way you are going about it, not if you want to win it. You are simply not killing them fast enough, or enough of them, to discourage the rest, even in Iraq. But you are reluctant to bring the full force of your military power down on their heads because it would look like you are the bully, and Americans hate bullies."

Yvgeny shook his head. "Once again, you will wait until you are pushed to the brink, before you will act as you did against the Japanese and Germans in World War Two, brutally, ruthlessly, and accepting nothing except unconditional surrender or death. The problem is that when you wait too long, you start at a disadvantage, which will cost more lives than it otherwise might have—innocent lives as the terrorists kill until finally you say 'enough' and do what it takes to put a stop to it. But this time, if you wait too long, you might not win at all, your culture—all Western culture—could be wiped out except what is allowed according to the whims of a despotic religious leader, a Caliph. Even now it will be difficult to turn the tide. I know these people; I fought them in Chechnya and Afghanistan. It is nothing for them to lose their lives."

Karp's eyes had widened at the mention of the Caliph and again at Chechnya. He would have liked his cousin's take on the issue, but Yvgeny reached out and clapped him on the shoulder.

"Come, let us go eat," Yvgeny said. "This is not the time for political discussions. I am sorry to have climbed up onto my soap stand."

"Box . . . soapbox," Karp said. "It's an expression."

"Yes, soapbox—an interesting concept; you'll have to tell me the derivation of it sometime," Yvgeny said. "But I shouldn't have given such a speech. Besides, what effect can an American district attorney and a Russian . . . ah . . . businessman have on such enormous affairs of state?"

"You never know," Karp said. "It's why we have a First Amendment protecting free speech and a free press. Without discussion and debate—whether between two people or among two million—we will indeed be lost."

"Well said, cousin," Yvgeny laughed. "Spoken like a true American."

Dinner was soon served in the formal dining room, a collection of dark teak, leather, brass, and crystal that could have been brought piecemeal out of Tsarist Russia with its portraits of ancient nobility, tapestries, and Greek Orthodox icons of varying sizes on the walls. Even the meal was Russian—several courses consisting mainly of *pelmeni,* which were small balls of minced meat covered with pastry, *shashlik,* a seasoned and broiled lamb dish, potato *vareniki* and mushrooms in sour cream sauce, all of it accompanied by a powerful red *rkatsiteli* wine from Anapa. "That's a famous wine-producing resort area on the Black Sea," said Vladimir, who had enjoyed pointing out where each dish and wine had come from in Russia, as well as giving a bit of the history of either the course or the region. His tales were accented by a young man playing the balalaika in the background.

The wine kept flowing and none of them were feeling any pain by the time they rose from the dinner table and retired to the library. The room was another tribute to Russian dramatics with its enormous fireplace in which a roaring blaze had been laid, and row upon row of books from floor to ceiling, some of which could be reached only by rolling ladders. Again Marlene sat down on a couch next to Vladimir, while Karp sank into an overstuffed leather chair next to her.

Yvgeny poured a round of cognac for each and then passed his cigar box. Karp was going to turn him down again, but saw that Marlene had already cut the tip off of another and was happily puffing away with Vladimir, so he decided what the hell and followed suit.

"Thank you for your wonderful company this evening," Vladimir said, toasting the others. "Still, I realize that it comes at some danger for your political aspirations. I apologize for asking you to come here, but I cannot travel to Manhattan to see you— there are too many people watching you and your family, not all of them well intentioned, but I'm sure you know that. We made sure that you were not followed here; my men were waiting when you came over the bridge and would have intercepted any intruders. The cab driver was also one of my people, and he will take you home."

Karp, who was feeling a little light-headed after just two puffs and a sip of cognac, waved off the apology. "We should have done this sooner, Uncle Vladimir," he said. "Marlene's right: families need to touch base."

The old man smiled. "Yes, Karchovski or Karp, we are the same blood. Which is why I felt the need to talk to you tonight, but mostly have you listen to my son, Yvgeny. It involves Andrew Kane, which is why I thought it important enough to discuss it face-to-face and away from prying eyes and ears. . . . Anyway, the first part of this, I can fill you in on. Quite simply, you have probably noticed a large influx of money into your opponent's campaign coffers. This *sooka*—pardon my Russian, Marlene—this Rachman has . . . what is the expression? . . . hitched her wagon to a dark star. The money behind her campaign is coming from people and businesses with ties to Mr. Kane."

"Are you sure about that?" Karp asked, sitting up and trying to clear his head.

"Yes," the old man replied. "I confess to have taken some amateurish interest in your campaign—not to interfere, mind you—and was perusing the campaign contribution public records on the computer and noticed first the influx of money, and then a trend of who it was coming from. Some of it is from members of the social elite, as well as law firms and businesses who had ties to Kane's former election campaign; some is being generated among a more secretive group of people whose names you might not recognize unless you travel in certain 'less desirable' circles more attuned to Mr. Kane's illegal activities."

Vladimir leaned forward and pushed a sheaf of papers that had been lying on the coffee table toward Marlene, who picked them up and began looking through them. "I've highlighted some of the more interesting contributors," he said.

Marlene whistled. "There are some heavy hitters on this list. Millionaires, lawyers, doctors, politicians . . . and a few who, if I'm not mistaken, are in prison. It would appear that Mr. Kane's influence is still being felt in Gotham's public and private sectors."

As his wife ticked off some of the names, Karp's mind was whirling from the cognac, cigar smoke, and possibility that his campaign opponent was being subsidized through the efforts of a man sworn to kill him and his family. He searched for another explanation. "They may just be people upset that we spoiled his bid for mayor," he pointed out. "It could be that they'd support anybody, so long as it wasn't me."

Vladimir shrugged. "Maybe so, but I doubt it. This money poured in almost overnight; there was a sudden push that had to come from somewhere. Rachman had nothing—not so much as a tissue to wipe her . . . well, I won't say with a woman present—but now she has what the newspapers are calling 'one of the best-financed campaigns for district attorney since Garrahy' . . . I am thinking that if this information got out to the press, it would pretty much sink her airplane."

"Boat," Karp corrected. "Sink her boat. But I'd prefer to keep this quiet, at least for now. I don't want to run a campaign based on innuendo against my opponent. It would be hard to prove that Kane is behind this influx of cash and might even come off looking like I was getting desperate and afraid to run on my record. I've got enough accusations of playing 'dirty politics' because of the Stavros case. Besides, I'd like to figure out what Kane is up to with this. Why should he care whether I win or lose the election if his aim is to kill me? It doesn't make sense to call in all those 'favors,' if that's what he's done, unless he has something to gain by supporting Rachman."

"It is a good question," Vladimir agreed. "I will give it some thought as well. And the information stays here for now. . . . So let us move on to Yvgeny."

All eyes turned to Vladimir's son, who was standing in front of the fire, holding his snifter of cognac, watching the flames. Without turning, Yvgeny said, "Forgive me if this is all rather melodramatic. Blame the cognac, good food, good company, and the fact that Russians must turn even the smallest gathering into an occasion to tell a story full of dark moods, tragedy, and impending doom."

Yvgeny walked over to one of the bookcases and, reaching up, pulled down a map of the world. He pointed to a spot in southern Russia and looked back at his guests. "Chechnya," he said. "Russia's pathway to the Caspian Sea, as well as vital oil lines. It is part of a region that has known little peace throughout its history and a succession of invaders from Mongols to Cossacks to Bolsheviks to Soviets to Russians."

He turned away from the map and faced his audience. "In the late forties, Stalin ordered the Chechen people—mostly Muslim, as well as native Muslim peoples in the neighboring regions—to be 'relocated' to camps in Kazakhstan and Siberia. A quarter to perhaps half of these populations—hundreds of thousands of people— died under the brutal conditions of the deportation and the camps. The reason they were removed was twofold. One was to replace them with Russians. The other was Stalin did not want any Muslims, who might have had questionable allegiances, living in the contemplated invasion routes to Turkey, which he coveted for its oil and warm water ports.

"In the fifties, the 'reeducated' Chechen—which is a Russian word, they call themselves *Nokhchi*—were allowed to return to their homelands, only to find that they had been given to Russians and others. They had to buy back their homes and fields, if they could afford it, and many could not. They were second-class citizens in their own lands.

"In 1991, Chechen nationalists declared independence rather than join the new Russian federation. They even held an election and voted for a president. But it was a government plagued by corruption and men looking out for themselves rather than their new country. However, I have come to believe that some of the failings of this government were actually a planned sabotage by the Russians, who used the instability to send in troops and establish their own puppet government. It was the start of a long and bloody civil war with the illegitimate puppet government—a collection of criminals and gangsters, some of them actually released from prison by their masters—and Russians on one side, Chechen nationalists on the other. I personally have seen the results as an officer with the Russian army—before I was sent to fight Muslims in Afghanistan, I was fighting them in Chechnya."

Yvgeny walked over to the desk and poured himself another cognac and then offered it to his father, Karp, and Marlene, all of whom held up their glasses. "Am I boring you yet? No? Good," he said. "I promise the point of all this will become clear in a moment. Continuing . . . this puppet government, which in truth is controlled by gangsters in Moscow, is allowed to prey upon its own people so long as payments are made to their masters and the oil flows into Russia undisturbed. In the meantime, the Russians get to keep their troops in this vital region, supposedly by 'invitation' of this illegitimate government, although a lot of what has occurred since 1991 falls more under the description of 'ethnic cleansing' than warfare.

"Fortunately, most of the worst atrocities committed by Russians are done by the 'special purpose detachments' of the Ministry of the Interior and the Federal Security Service, OSNAZ, which used to be the KGB. These are paramilitary units created to deal with internal conflicts and terrorism, although they are certainly quite capable of terrorism themselves. They call it *bespredel,* which translates literally to 'no limits.' It means acting outside the rules, violently and with impunity. Women and children are raped, tortured, and killed. Prisoners are maimed and executed. The barbarity of this war—out of sight of most of the Western media—is unimaginable.

"Meanwhile, Chechnya has become a quagmire for the Russian army, which is taking significant losses—sort of like your Vietnam and Iraq, and our Afghanistan. Meanwhile, young, half-trained Russian soldiers are being sent to fight and die there, but for what? There has been no effort to bring peace to the region, either by winning this war or by negotiated settlement with the nationalists. It is more like the Russian government would rather keep the region inflamed so as to explain the presence of their troops and legitimize the present government to the outside world. Russian officers who question these things and try to rein in the excesses of the troops are sent home or on dangerous assignments from which they often do not return. Some of my friends and former fellow officers have been among these."

Yvgeny paused long enough to throw back his cognac and pour another. "One of the effects of this civil war, especially in the past five years or so, has been to attract other groups to the fighting. The worst of these are the Muslim extremists, many of them influenced and supported by al Qaeda and other groups from the Middle East. Their purported goals are the same as the nationalists: to kick the Russians out of Chechnya. However, they do not want to see the formation of a secular democratic republic, but rather an Islamic theocracy that would eventually be melded into a single Islamic state, the caliphate I mentioned earlier that would stretch from North Africa to the Far East. Imagine such resources all brought under the control of a single religious fanatic whose rule would be based upon a hatred for Western culture. Such a man might be impossible for even the great United States to stop."

Yvgeny let the image sink in for a moment. "The Muslim extremists brought a new form of fighting to the battle. While the Chechen nationalists are fierce fighters and would slit the throat of any Russian soldier for fun, their targets have always been primarily military. But these new Islamic hard-liners favored the terrorist acts aimed at the civilian population of Russia—"

"The nationalists don't commit acts of terror?" Karp asked, thinking of Ellis's description of the nationalists as murderers and thugs.

Yvgeny pursed his lips and nodded. "Sure, there are some in the nationalist movement who, either through frustration or because it fits their personality, welcomed the new tactics. But they are not the mainstream of the secular independence movement, which has been trying to negotiate a peace settlement so long as it includes an independent state of Ichkeria. The moderates in the nationalist movement struggle to disavow the acts of terror against civilians and being aligned with Islamic extremism. But there is an interesting marriage occurring: the Islamic extremists and certain powerful people within the Russian government seem determined to link the nationalists to the more fanatical groups, especially al Qaeda, which almost guarantees that whatever the Russians do to suppress the nationalists will be accepted here."

Karp put his cigar down, it was making him queasy. "You fought these Chechen nationalists, but now you sound more like you're on their side. Why is that?"

"Why?" Yvgeny repeated, looking over at his father who had seemed to be nodding off but suddenly perked up. "Because I am a Russian patriot. I do not like what has been done and what is being done in the name of the Russian republic to a people who want only independence. What's more, I am a former Russian officer who led good, young men into battle and watched them get killed. But it is one thing to die for your country, and another to die for a lie. Myself and some like-minded others think that the Russian government is actually in . . . how is the expression? In cahoots? . . . with the Islamic extremists to prevent the Chechen nationalists from forming a legitimately elected democratic republic. They want chaos and instability, even if it costs Russian lives."

"But why?" Marlene asked.

"From the Russian government's point of view, it's easy," Yvgeny replied. "If there was a stable, independent Chechnya, they would no longer have an excuse to station troops there to ensure that the oil pipelines kept delivering. Access to the warm water ports is also important. And, not unimportantly, if the corrupt government in Chechnya was replaced, the graft and bribes, as well as the proceeds from criminal enterprises, would stop coming to Moscow to line the pockets of government officials and gangsters."

"But why would Islamic extremists cooperate with the Russian government?" Karp asked, feeling a bit slow. "Don't they want the Russians out of Chechnya, too, so that they can establish their caliphate?"

"Yes and no," Yvgeny replied. "Eventually, they want the Russians to leave. However, there are several reasons they are willing to delay that fight. One, every time they strike a blow at infidels, in this case Russian civilians and soldiers, it is a wonderful recruiting and money-raising event. Without Russians to attack in Chechnya, they'd be left to fight other Muslims, the Chechen nationalists, which wouldn't go over as well in other parts of the Muslim world, which is part of why the hard-liners publicly are careful to align themselves with their 'Muslim brothers' within the nationalist movement.

"Another reason is that a foreign infidel government is not nearly the threat to the Islamic caliphate as a single Islamic democracy. Once even Muslims taste freedom and get used to the concept of self-determination, they are not going to want to turn everything over to a single man to make decisions for all the rest. And if there is one such democracy, there will be more—the concept of a caliphate would be shattered by the formation of separate states based on national and even ethnic, but not religious, identities. Why else do you think they are fighting so desperately in Iraq and Afghanistan, killing Muslims by the thousands in direct violation of the Quran, to prevent the establishment of stable democracies? It is the democracies, not you Americans, which are the real threat to their plans. So in Chechnya, they are willing to work in an unholy alliance with their enemies the Russians to first defeat the nationalists."

Karp cleared his throat, privately swearing off cigars and booze. "I don't mean to be dense," he said, "but what has this got to do with Kane? If it still does."

Yvgeny looked at Karp quizzically, as if to tell him that he was on to him. "I am taking it that by now you have heard that a woman called Samira Azzam was instrumental in Kane's escape and that she is a member of al Qaeda," he said. When Karp didn't answer, he nodded and said, "I understand you have probably been sworn to secrecy, so let me tell you what you already know and, perhaps, add a little to it."

The tall Russian picked up a sheet of paper from the desk and handed it to Karp, who gave it to Marlene. It was a fuzzy photograph of a young, dark-haired woman walking down a sidewalk, looking back over her shoulder. Marlene noted the large mole on her cheek.

"That is the only known photograph of Azzam, whose real name is Nathalie Habibi. It was taken accidentally in 1999 by a tourist as Azzam walked away from an Israeli shopping mall. Moments later, a suicide bomber blew himself up inside the mall, killing thirteen people, including a new mother with an infant. As you may already know, she was also behind the seizing of hostages at a musical theater in Moscow that ended with more than one hundred deaths, as well as the slaughter of more than three hundred innocent people, mostly children, at a school in Beslan. In both instances, the theater and the school, nearly all the terrorists were killed along with their victims, but Azzam always walked away unscathed and undetected by authorities even though the scenes were cordoned off."

Marlene frowned. "You're saying the Russian government allowed her to escape to fight again another day. And that means they're allowing terrorists to murder their own people."

"Exactly," Yvgeny said, "though it should come as no surprise. We Russians have always been good at killing our own people. Stalin killed millions more than Hitler ever dreamed of."

"But all those children," Marlene said.

Yvgeny nodded sadly. "Yes, I know. It is a cold thing to contemplate. But you also have to understand that after all this time, Western journalists were beginning to actually look into complaints by the main nationalist party about Russian atrocities, including the bombardment of noncombatant towns and cities, and examples of ethnic cleansing—sometimes the population of entire villages wiped out—by the OSNAZ. The press was beginning to lend a sympathetic ear to the cries for independence and human rights abuses. A few brave journalists were even writing stories about the corruption and organized crime that dominates the Chechen puppet government. But then Beslan happened and good-bye sympathetic press. Despite denials by the main body of Chechen nationalists that they were involved at all, the Russian government went to great lengths to link Chechen nationalism to Islamic extremism for the massacre; for all intents and purposes, they were one and the same. Of course, any mention of a connection to Islamic terrorists to the Western press sets off their alarm bells. The Chechen nationalists went from being called freedom fighters to Islamic terrorists, thugs, and murderers."

"Which brings us to why Azzam is in the United States helping Kane," Karp said.

"Yes, my impatient cousin, forgive the lengthy discourse," Yvgeny said. "As effective as Beslan was at discrediting the nationalist movement, it wasn't enough. It was too far away and would be soon forgotten in the United States. They needed something here, something so horrific and international that any sympathy for an independent Chechnya would evaporate forever."

"So what do you think they are going to do?" Karp asked.

Yvgeny paused and looked at the fire. "We are concerned that it has something to do with the Russian president's speech to the United Nations in September. He is supposed to talk about the situation in Chechnya and the continued Russian presence there."

"But I thought you said the Russian government was in on this," Marlene said. "Are they willing to assassinate Putin, not to mention blowing up the United Nations?"

Yvgeny shrugged. "In some ways it does not make sense. You'll remember that Putin is an ex-colonel in the KGB, the secret police that is now the Federal Security Service, which runs OSNAZ. It was our feeling at first glance that this conspiracy against the Chechen nationalists might go to the very top of Russian government and that he might be involved. After all, a leopard does not change its spots and this leopard was under pressure to withdraw from Chechnya both at home and abroad.

"It is no secret that the Russian people's support for the war in Chechnya was waning; mothers were tired of their sons coming home in body bags. After Beslan public opinion in support of the war soared, as did Putin's approval rating for his promises to root out terrorism, which by the way was met with great enthusiasm at the White House and Ten Downing Street. There has been a lot of discussion on the internet as to whether the terror bombings in Moscow and the massacre at Beslan were actually tailor-made for our president and his government."

"So we're barking up the wrong tree on that one?" Karp asked.

"Barking up trees?"

"An expression meaning 'concentrating on the wrong possibility,'" Marlene said. "In other words, Putin wouldn't be a target."

"Ah, thank you for the explanation, but no, not necessarily,"

Yvgeny said. "Assassination is a time-honored tradition in Russia, especially among its secret police agencies going back to the tsars. There are plenty of powerful people in Russia who would not shed any tears over the death of Vladimir Putin—some find him too weak, some find him too strong . . . sort of like your fairy tale of Goldie and the Three Bears. It would certainly mean all-out war in Chechnya, perhaps the use of nuclear weapons, to destroy the nationalist movement and complete the permanent absorption of Chechnya into the Russian federation. There would be no one left who opposed it. His death would serve that purpose."

"But if Azzam and al Qaeda have this working agreement with the Russian government," Marlene said, "that means the Russians were involved with the escape plot too . . . and the murder of those children and police officers."

Yvgeny hung his head. "I am ashamed to say it, but yes, I think it is possible."

"I still don't understand what this has to do with Kane," said Karp, who was wishing he had not had the last cognac. "Maybe it's the liquor, but I seem to be the only one who doesn't get where he comes in."

Yvgeny smiled. "No, cousin, the liquor I'm sure has us all well grease—"

"Lubricated—" Karp said.

"Well lubricated, then. But we are all in the dark on that question. It may be that Azzam and al Qaeda need his connections with the New York Police Department, which provides security for big events at the UN. He also had a lot of nefarious dealings with some of these rogue governments, so who knows which ones might be willing to listen to him and his schemes. But it could be as simple as his banking connections, too. Something big like this will cost a lot of money, preferably untraceable cash, and it's a lot harder to move cash around without getting noticed than it was before 9/11." He laughed. "I can tell you that from personal experience. . . . We have little to go on at this moment . . . just rumors being passed to us by associates in Moscow and in Chechnya . . . but an attack on Putin, real or not, makes sense. Azzam was sent to Chechnya to help destroy the nationalist movement—our spies know that much—and this would be the coup de grâce for that mission."

"So what does that leave us with?" Marlene asked.

No one answered right away. Instead, everyone was tuned in to their thoughts and the crackling of the burning logs.

Inside one of the logs, boiling sap built up pressure until the wood exploded with a shower of sparks and a sound like a gunshot. The hosts and their visitors all jumped, then laughed in embarrassment at their discomfiture.

"What does that leave us with, my dear Marlene?" Vladimir Karchovski chuckled. "Why, the most Russian of all stories . . . a dark mystery full of intrigue and danger. I bet if you look outside that window, the snow will be falling in the moonlight and somewhere in the distance wolves will be howling."

Marlene shivered at the thought. "Can I have another cognac, please?"

11

May

SOMEBODY WAS TALKING ABOUT THE WAR IN IRAQ. WHETHER establishing a democracy was worth the deaths of two thousand American soldiers.

"Terrorists need sympathetic governments . . . they need access to banks, a place where they can recruit, train and operate freely . . ."

"There's no proof Saddam had any connection to terrorists, any more than he had WMD . . ."

"He allowed al-Zarqawi, who had an international warrant out for his arrest in connection with 9/11, to be treated in a hospital in Baghdad after he was wounded in Afghanistan, and then continue to operate in Iraq. He should have been turned over to the World Court for trial . . ."

"So all these deaths because one terrorist wasn't apprehended?"

"How about over twenty-seven hundred deaths in the World Trade Center . . . and how many the next time? We had to fight these guys somewhere, might as well be Iraq . . ."

Karp hardly followed the conversation; his mind was elsewhere. It was seven o'clock, Monday morning. One hour before his weekly meeting, but first he'd wanted to meet with his "inner council," those he trusted most in his office, to update them on Fey's murder and what little there was on efforts to recapture Kane. The group—consisting of Murrow, Newbury, Kipman, Guma, and his wife, Marlene—were still getting settled, getting their coffees, and debating Iraq.

Karp's eyes strayed to the plastic bag on his desk. On the outside of the otherwise plain container was an FBI evidence label marked Timothy Fey, 04/26/05, Encinitas, CA and some other coded case number. Inside was what appeared to be an ordinary set of dark amber-colored rosary beads, though he knew that they'd been re-strung on high-tensile wire strong enough to cut off a man's air supply. The gold pendant depicting St. Patrick's Cathedral glinted in the early morning sun that peered over his shoulder.

He'd seen similar rosaries—even had two locked away in the evidence vault. They'd been labeled in a similar fashion, just the New York DAO's version with the victims' names, that of two young boys, and the date they'd been found. Only the location was different; the other rosaries had come from Central Park graves.

The two rosaries in the DAO vault had been the calling card of the child killer priest Hans Lichner, who'd tossed them in the shallow graves of his victims. It was how they'd eventually tied to-gether the apparently unrelated rape and murder of Indian boys in Taos, New Mexico, to Andrew Kane and his schemes in New York City.

Karp smiled grimly recalling an argument he'd had with his daughter, Lucy, over Lichner's intent. He'd called Lucy after Fey's murder to warn her that the stakes had gone up and to ask her to reconsider having federal agents with the U.S. Department of Homeland Security watching out for her.

Lucy's reply had been half-angry and half-frightened. *Oh puleeze, like you didn't know there's been a couple of square-jawed fed types hanging around here for a week, trying to play*

*tourist—very stiff tourists—who just happen to turn up wherever
I go with Ned. One even showed up at the cabin where Ned stays
in on the ranch, pretending to be lost when it was obvious he just
wanted to get a look around. Some others have been following
John Jojola around, too, but he's been making a game out of ditch-
ing them.*

Still, Lucy hesitated. *But I guess if they can stay at a distance,
I'll have to accept it. I'd hate to have something happen to Ned because Kane was after me.*

It's just until we catch him, Karp had replied. It had been some
time since they'd had a good father-daughter conversation, so he'd
happily stayed on the telephone when the conversation turned to
philosophy as it applied to Hans Lichner and the rosary beads. His
daughter, who liked to believe that within every human being there
was some goodness, *some spark of the divine that binds us all to a
loving and forgiving God,* argued that it was that spark that caused
Lichner to expose himself. *Maybe, he wanted to get caught. Maybe
that spark worked subconsciously to try to stop the demon in him
from hurting any more children; maybe, it even acted in Lichner to
lead you to uncover the real Andrew Kane.*

Why in such an oblique way? Karp had replied leaning back in
his chair and putting his size fourteens up on the desk. *Why not
just write it out? Why take a chance that your dim old dad
wouldn't be able to decipher the message?* He enjoyed verbally
sparring with his insightful daughter; she could hold her own in any
debate, even if he found her reliance on the existence of angels and
demons to explain human behavior long on emotion but short on
facts.

Maybe the demon wouldn't let him, she'd replied slowly. *Maybe
he had to sort of "sneak" it out.*

Secrets from the devil? I didn't think that was possible, Karp had
teased and been rewarded with a Bronx cheer over the phone.
Um . . . I don't think your rebuttal would hold up in court.

*Well, you can just keep those blinders on, buddy, and refuse to
see that there's more to the rather unusual series of events that have
followed this family like a plague of locusts than mere chance,* Lucy

scolded. *Hell, call us the Koincidence— spelled with a K—Karps. Or accept that we've been selected to play a large, uncomfortable, and maybe even fatal role in a bigger plan that is unfolding all around us.*

I see, "All the world's a stage . . . And all the men and women merely players," Karp said.

Yes, that's sort of it. "They have their exits and their entrances; And one man in his time plays many parts," Lucy said, shooting the Shakespeare right back at him.

Perhaps, Karp laughed. *But I believe that for the most part— with some weight given to behavior caused by nature or nurture— a man chooses the parts he plays. It's the basis of the legal system's insanity rulings. People choose to do good things, and other people, at least those who are not legally insane, CHOOSE to do bad things. I don't discount at all the existence of God, some sort of creative, even moral force in the universe. Nor do I discount the truth that "Bad things happen to good people" for no explicable reason, and we can call that evil, if you like—the sort of evil that tortured and killed my mother with cancer. But I think the vast majority of evil in this world is committed by people who think it's okay to hurt other people. The worst of them we call sociopaths, men like Andrew Kane, who certainly recognize that there is a difference between right and wrong; they just choose to ignore it for their own gratification, whether it's rape, murder, or all of the above. Kane chose the role he is playing, which makes him guilty, not insane.*

In a limited sense, yes, Lucy replied, determined to match him monologue for monologue. *But just because people choose a role for whatever reason—money, power, whatever else turns Mr. Kane on—it doesn't necessarily mean they understand how their part will play out in the end. Judas chose to betray Jesus, but did he know that by doing so he caused the most far-reaching social and spiritual revolution ever? But let's say you're right . . . maybe there's no demon that possessed Hans Lichner and there never was that spark inside of him. That it's all bullshit. Maybe he chose to play the part of a monster who did that to little boys . . . but when he threw the rosaries into the grave, was he choosing to be the instrument for justice that brought down his master, Andrew Kane? Because that's what happened. Or maybe there was something left of the divine in him that made him do it in order to alter the role his conscious mind, or the demon, chose?*

Or maybe it was just a part of his personality disorder, Karp countered. *Maybe it just fed his ego to say, "I did what I wanted, and I want you to know it was me and not some other brute. And I'm leaving this clue because you're too stupid and weak to catch me anyway." . . . And by the way, you just contradicted yourself.*

How's that? Lucy replied, a little testily he noticed.

You said that this "spark of the divine" in him CHOSE to assume a different role for good, Karp said. *But earlier, you were arguing that it's all some sort of enormous play that's already been written, that we've already been cast, and we're just playing out our parts . . . no choice in the matter.*

No contradiction. You're just not giving God enough credit to anticipate where free will would take us, Lucy said smugly. *He works in mysterious ways, you know.*

Lucy had ended the debate with a parting shot at his "advanced age" from the *As You Like It* soliloquy they'd been tossing back and forth. *I guess Old Bill knew what he was saying when he wrote, the "Last scene of all, That ends this strange eventful history, Is second childishness and mere oblivion. Sans teeth, sans eyes, sans taste, sans everything." Sound familiar, old man? Oops, Ned's here, gotta go, love you, Daddy.*

Karp picked up the evidence bag containing the rosary beads. He'd handled a lot of murder weapons in his career—axes, guns, daggers, golf clubs, an oil-soaked rag that had been stuffed down a bookie's throat suffocating him and then lit on fire . . . you name it, it had been used to commit homicide. But there was something about the rosary beads, perhaps the horrible irony that caused the skin on his hand to crawl as he put the bag back down.

Jaxon had been livid when he returned from California. *Only a few people were supposed to know Fey was there,* he sputtered in

Karp's office. *Even the warden only knew that the old man was under the Witness Protection Program. Other than that, a couple of people in my agency knew—but not Grover, who would have been the logical choice for traitor. So that leaves me with another mole and very few people I can trust.*

What about the Homeland Security guys? Karp asked. *Did any of them know?*

Jaxon looked like he was going to say something and then thought better of it. *I don't really know what they know,* he said. *They're worse than the CIA with the "need-to-know" stuff. I don't even know what kind of access they have to FBI files—some of this stuff is being handled at the very top, director to director, and us low-level flunkies are not privy to those conversations. . . . But I'd say no simply because they didn't get into this until after Kane's escape and the connection to Samira Azzam was made. . . . And considering Grover was one of mine, it would be pretty ballsy of me to point the finger at some other agency.*

Hoping it would lift Jaxon's spirits, Karp presented him with a copy of the photograph of Samira Azzam given to him the night before by his uncle. *Apparently, the Israelis can vouch for its authenticity,* he said.

This could be invaluable, Jaxon said. *Where did you get it?*

I'm not at liberty to say at the moment, Karp replied. He didn't feel like explaining his relationship with a Brooklyn crime family to an FBI agent, even one with whom he'd been friends for years. *But this same person has a theory that Kane and Azzam might be after the Russian president, Vladimir Putin.*

Jaxon had stared at Karp like he'd just told him the name of the man on the grassy knoll in Dallas. *I'm really not supposed to say anything about this, but between you and me that scenario has emerged as the number-one theory. Apparently, the terrorist who was killed when Kane escaped, Akhmed Kadyrov, had a telephone number in his pocket—no name or anything else with it, but it rings into the office of the Iranian ambassador to the United Nations. Maybe that means something, maybe not. But there's also been some chatter on internet websites we monitor that al Qaeda has something big planned in the United States for September, which is when Putin is scheduled to speak.*

What's Kane get out of this? Karp had asked. *He's not the "political causes" type.*

I don't know . . . money. Jaxon shrugged. *Al Qaeda has almost limitless funds, which Americans contribute to every time they fill up their cars with gas—either directly, or to governments that support these hyenas. So Kane arranges whatever they need and gets a flat fee and maybe asylum, some sweet penthouse overlooking downtown Tehran. Or maybe there's more to it than that. The important thing will be to learn as much as we can about their plans, and then try to lure them into a trap. This photo will help us spot Azzam.* His brows knit. *If the Israelis have this, I wonder why we didn't?*

Someone spoke to him. Karp looked up from the rosary beads.

"So the killer was a fake priest?" Murrow asked again.

"Uh, sorry, Gilbert, I was somewhere else," Karp apologized.

"I was just saying that Fey's killer was a fake priest," Murrow repeated.

"Well, if he was a fake, he was a good one," Karp replied. "According to Jaxon, he even delivered mass in Latin for the Hispanic population and took confession from at least two staff members who said he knew all the rites."

"So maybe a former priest who found a new line of work," Newbury said. "He was obviously sent by Kane, so maybe he'll turn up in the 'No Prosecution' cases. Espey Jaxon can send one of his feds over, and we'll take a look at the possibilities. Maybe somebody at the prison farm will recognize this guy from a booking photograph, if there is one."

Newbury was referring to hundreds of criminal complaints against cops, and, in a separate section, Catholic priests accused of sexual assault and other crimes. The city and archdiocese—trying to avoid lawsuits and the media—had hired Kane's law firm to settle the cases quietly, as well as vet them to determine if they should also be turned over to the DAO for prosecution. Some, chiefly those Kane had no use for, or he disliked for some reason, had been sent to the DAO with the recommendation that criminal charges be filed. But many others had been stamped "No Prosecution" and forwarded on to Karp's predecessors, who had filed them away in a secret cabinet.

Kane had used the cases to manipulate "dirty cops" into working for him as his own private army of enforcers, up to and including murder. He also had protected sexual offenders within the ranks of the priesthood in part to gain control of the archdiocese but with the ultimate goal of eventually having the accusations "discovered" by the press, thereby destroying the church through scandal and debasement. It was through his counsel that then–Archbishop Fey chose to remain ignorant of what was going on; believing, as Kane whispered in his ear, that he was protecting the church for the greater good.

However, while working on a cleanup crew at the Criminal Courts building, an emerging rap singer named Alejandro Garcia had discovered the "No Prosecution" files, recognized what they contained, and turned them over to his mentor and friend, Father Michael Dugan, a confidant of Marlene. The priest had then arranged to get the files into Karp's hands.

After Kane's arrest, Karp had turned V. T. Newbury loose on the "No Prosecution" inquiry, telling him to bring charges where warranted. V.T. and "Newbury's Gang" of retired NYPD detectives and eager young assistant district attorneys had already charged a dozen police officers and priests with a variety of crimes from malfeasance to assault. One of the main NYPD henchmen on Kane's payroll, Detective Michael Flanagan, had pleaded guilty to murder and was at Rikers Island. He'd been willing to testify against Kane, but now that was moot.

"Jaxon was hoping you might be able to help," Karp replied to Newbury. "But he'll be visiting you himself; once burnt, twice remembered, he's playing things a little close to the vest right now."

"What I don't get is why go through all that effort to find and kill Fey?" Murrow said. "I mean, I could understand if Kane was still in jail, awaiting trial, and was trying to knock off the witnesses. But it's not like he's helping his case now. Even if we had to drop the charges in Manhattan because of a witness's death—and that's not the case, we've got plenty to hang him without Fey—the feds certainly have enough from his escape to earn him a lethal dose in the execution chamber at the federal pen in Indiana."

"This wasn't about taking out a witness," Karp replied. "This is about vengeance. That's why the killer made sure he left the rosary. This is Kane playing his little game."

"But what's this game all about?" Murrow asked. "He's working with some terrorist, but he also wants to kill our DA and everybody he knows."

"What's to understand?" Marlene said. "He's a vicious, cruel animal and he wants to frighten and torment anybody who gets in his way, or he thinks betrayed him. The terrorists have a score or two to settle with Butch and the rest of us, too. What better bedfellows?"

"I can think of two," Karp teased.

"Oh brother, big talker," Marlene laughed, which helped break the tension.

"I just want you all to be careful," Karp said as he passed out copies of the photograph of Azzam. "NYPD now has these, so do the feds. This, we think, is Samira Azzam. She's the one who sprang Kane, and we assume she's still working with him."

"Who's 'we,' *we'd* like to know," Murrow asked.

"I could tell you but—" Karp smiled.

"Yeah, I know, you'd have to kill us."

"You."

"Me."

"Anyway, Fey's killer is described as tall, dark-haired with severe acne scars, a big guy. I'm not trying to alarm anybody, but Kane has made good on one of his threats, so it pays to be careful. There'll be a few more cop drive-bys around your homes than you're used to, and you might occasionally notice the presence of federal agents—probably disguised as homeless derelicts so give 'em a buck when you walk by." Karp's announcement was met with groans but, he noted, no one demanded that they be excluded from the added police surveillance.

When the meeting was over, Marlene jumped up to give him a kiss. "I'm off to see Daddy, and maybe Uncle Vlad," she said with a mischievous grin.

"Uncle Vlad?" asked Guma, who remained seated, as did Murrow.

"An Old World family she's become attached to," Karp said.

Karp was relieved when Newbury interrupted the line of questioning by whistling over near the bookshelf. "Hey, where'd you get the Carlos Torres chess pieces?" he asked. He held up the black bishop that had been sitting on the reading table, but then held up a black knight as well.

"Carlos who?" Karp asked.

"Torres. He's the artist who carves these, though they always come as a set, no two sets alike," Newbury said.

"Never heard of him," Guma said.

"Of course you wouldn't have, you Neanderthal," Newbury said. "But anybody who actually enjoys the more refined aspects of chess knows a Carlos Torres piece. The guy's an artist and expensive. Depending on the material he uses—which could be anything from petrified ivory to sperm whales' teeth, and gemstones he inlays—they can cost a hundred grand easy."

"I thought the first one might be yours, and I guess the second, too, though this is the first I've seen it," Karp said.

"I wish," Newbury said. "But no, I haven't succumbed to that sort of ostentatiousness, for God's sake. I have a beautifully carved oak set by Hannah Aowyn, but they only run about twenty K."

"Only," Guma said.

Karp laughed. "It's all relative, Goom. Anyway, I'll have to ask Mrs. Milquetost if she knows anything about it."

Newbury set the pieces down and left the room. But Guma and Murrow remained seated, obviously waiting for this moment alone. Karp raised his eyebrows and asked, "Yes?"

Guma cleared his throat. "I want you to do the Stavros trial with me."

Karp looked from Guma to Murrow, from whom he expected an instant complaint. When one wasn't forthcoming, Karp looked back at Guma and shook his head. "I don't think that would be a good idea. We're already taking a lot of flak and I don't want to turn this into more of a circus than it already is."

He suggested Murray Osborn, an aggressive young ADA who was starting to make a name for himself in the homicide bureau. "He's a lot like you and me, back in the day."

"He's good and will get better," Guma conceded. "But I'm asking you."

Before Karp could say anything, Guma got a surprising vote from Murrow. "It's a great idea," Murrow said, getting up to pace the room with his thumbs hooked into his omnipresent vest. "We cast this as: 'District Attorney leads by example, helps prosecute rich white guy for a murder committed fourteen years ago.' I can see the billboard now. 'Nowhere to go. No place to hide. Sooner or later, if you do the crime, you're going to do the time with Roger "Butch" Karp.'" He sighed happily.

"What about all the political fallout you were worried about before?" Karp asked.

"We'll take some hits," Murrow conceded. "But we already have, and I don't see how Rachman can make it any worse. Plus, I think we'll make inroads with that part of the voting public that thinks rich white guys always get away with murder. *And* . . . this will also show the press that you're not afraid to pursue a case—no matter who it is, or what the circumstances are—even though it will be obvious to them that you're leaving yourself open to more attacks from Rachman and the loyal opposition. Best of all, despite Kane's threats, the public will see that you're not off hiding in some hole; you're out there convicting murderers. This trial will mean daily exposure on the newscasts. The television stations won't even have to give Rachman equal time because it will be in the normal course of your duties. This is just *soooo* sweet."

"There's a reason right there to stay out of this trial," Karp said.

"I wouldn't want you turning this into a sideshow in the election campaign. Not to mention this is Guma's case."

"Sure, sure," Murrow agreed. "I think that's good. Guma does all the speaking to the press and you're just helping out. It looks even better if you're 'just there to lend a hand to a colleague' and avoiding grandstanding. Then the more Rachman criticizes your involvement, the more it will look like she's blowing smoke and protecting a killer because of who he is in her party."

"Look," Karp shot back, "you wanting me to get involved in the risky biz of trying a high-profile case where the defendant could walk is totally counterintuitive coming from one bow-tied Gilbert Murrow. Moreover, we don't try cases around here because it's politically cool."

Guma turned to Murrow and held up a hand. "Gilbert, would you mind if I talked to Mr. Clean here alone for a moment?"

Murrow clearly didn't like it, but he left, closing the door behind him. They soon heard Mrs. Milquetost, who for some reason had adopted him as sort of a long lost son, cooing over him. She'd been known to bring him cookies she'd baked at home and had even brought one of her former husband's bow ties as a gift when she noticed he favored them as a fashion statement.

"Why's she so nice to Murrow?" Guma asked. "He boinkin' little old ladies with Ariadne out of the country?"

"Maybe it's because he comes off so well compared to you," Karp suggested. "Cuddly, harmless gentleman as opposed to hairy, high-octane bull in the pasture. I've never understood why some little alarm bell doesn't go off in the minds of women whenever they see you coming."

"The only bells going off are the bells of ecstasy after a little time with Ray the Impaler," Guma laughed. But the smile disappeared off his face as he sat forward and looked Karp in the eyes.

"I've been having a few minor glitches with my health lately," he said. "Nothing major, but some days are better than others. I would hate to get into this trial with an inexperienced ADA and then have a couple of off days and have to leave it on his shoulders. Even if I was medically unable to go forward, and we could get the judge to declare a mistrial, we would be kissing Emil Stavros good-bye. The judge would simply continue his bond, and he'd skip the country even though we already froze his assets pending the trial. I got that court order based upon the submission that the dough was legitimately Zachary's and looted from Teresa's accounts. But he's probably got plenty stashed somewhere, and I'll bet it's somewhere that we don't have an extradition treaty with."

"Then we'll get one of the senior ADAs, or even a deputy chief, to be your co-counsel," Karp said.

"You're not getting it," Guma said. "Look, it's been a long time since you and I did one of these together . . . more than a decade . . . and, well, there won't be many more chances."

Karp scowled. "What kind of talk is that? Is there something you're not telling me?"

Guma shook his head. "No. Like I said, someone cuts a few yards of your guts out of your body, it's pretty hard to feel 'normal.' There's a new normal. But as of my last checkup, I was still clean. But with the election coming up and another four years of getting the DAO back on track, you won't have much time for trying cases with your old pal Goom. And I'm not sure how much longer I'll keep practicing. Occasionally I get this instinctual Guinea urge to move to warmer climes, and I think about flying south to Miami to hang with the cousins, buy some big gold chains to hang around my neck, shave my back, get a tan, find some divorcée with . . . big assets . . . and settle down."

"Doesn't sound too bad," Karp said.

"No, it doesn't," Guma agreed. "In fact, I swear sometimes when I fall asleep at night, I can hear waves and smell suntan lotion warming up on a pair of thirty-six double-Ds. So let's do this trial together, for old times' sake. Come on, it will be fun."

Karp sat still for a moment, staring at his old friend, lost in thought. *Did I fall asleep and wake up twenty years later? It all does pass in a blink of the eye. So this is it, the swan song trial.* He shook his head and said, "Wow. Okay, okay. It will be fun to be ringside with the Italian Stallion back in the ring for another title bout. I'll be proud to be in your corner, kiddo."

When they invited Murrow back in and told him, he'd practically skipped around the office. "This is great. *Cold Case Detectives* is the hottest show on television," he chortled. "And people just eat this forensic files stuff up. What can I tell the press?"

The look from Karp sent him scurrying out of the office.

12

KANE STABBED FOR SAMIRA AZZAM'S CHEST. BUT SHE PAR-
ried the blow with her *Bantay-Kamay,* or guardian hand, and then
countered with a slicing backhand that narrowly missed his eyes.

"Careful, Samira, my love," he hissed. "Wouldn't want to ruin
this fine work by Dr. Buchwald, now would we?" He dropped to a
knee and slashed at her thigh, but she'd anticipated the move and
spun backward, delivering a kick to the side of his head.

The blow was glancing but still enough to daze him for a moment, so his mind didn't quite follow the classic *Lipat-Palit* technique of an unexpected flip of her knife from right hand to left. It
left him open for the fatal blow, the point of her knife pressed
against the carotid artery in his neck. She wanted to plunge the
knife in and feel his hot red blood gush over her hand. But now is
not the time, she reminded herself, and probably never would be
unless the al Qaeda leaders tired of the insane infidel and allowed
her to go forward with "the plan" without him.

Samira felt something tickle her and looked down. Kane's knife
was poised with its tip ready to plunge into her crotch. "Hardly a
lethal blow, as mine would have been." She smiled sweetly.

"Ah, but nevertheless, you would have been worthless as a whore." He was smiling, too, but the look in his eyes was cold, sneering. He withdrew his knife and backed away from her blade. "Of course, you know that if you had used yours, your next order would have been to blow yourself up in some meaningless little attack on a kibbutz that wouldn't rate three inches in the newspapers."

Samira kept the smile on her face though she seethed at the insulting insinuation that she was nothing but a whore to be used by al Qaeda. "I look forward to dying for Allah and Palestine in any way I am called upon," she said. "Perhaps, you will martyr yourself with me . . . my love."

Kane laughed. "I love it that you hate me so much, my dangerous little bitch," he said. "It makes fucking you that much more pleasurable for me."

Indeed, Samira wanted to kill him so much at that moment that tears came to her eyes and spilled down her cheeks. But she still kept up the pretense and pouted, "You say such cruel things."

Again, Kane mocked her. "Ah, such a perfect assassin, but a lousy actress. You're here doing whatever I say because your masters want to keep me happy and for some perverse reason, I'm sure, using you like a piece of meat gives me great pleasure and relieves the stresses of such a . . . pressure-filled life. It is so much fun watching you choke on the words you'd like to say."

Samira studied his face, wishing she could carve it with her knife. He didn't look like the Andrew Kane she'd first met, not anymore. Even she had to admit that the work of Dr. Buchwald, a plastic surgeon, was amazing. Gone was the formerly, rather effete-looking blond with the pale blue eyes. He'd been replaced by a more rugged-looking man with a cleft in his rounder chin, wider cheeks and fuller lips, as well as larger, crooked nose—presumably from some old injury. The hair was now chestnut; the eyes no longer blue but brown, thanks to contact lens. He even had a thin white scar beneath his right eye, evidence of a traffic accident that never happened . . . at least not to Andrew Kane.

Still, she knew that the real Andrew Kane had never been what she'd seen on the outside. In her mind, the real Kane merely wore the physical characteristics of a man as a disguise or cloak. He reminded her of childhood stories her parents had told her from Arabian folklore and the Quran regarding the *jinn.*

Allah created man from sounding clay like the clay of pottery, her father would begin, gathering his children around on cold winter nights in Palestine. *And the* jinn *He created from a smokeless flame of fire.*

The *jinn* were spirits—sometimes formless, sometimes inhabiting the bodies of men and animals—and there were different sorts. Some were essentially harmless, even helpful. But others were evil and dedicated to tormenting humans—deceiving and guiding them away from the true path.

The worst are called shayateen, her father had whispered, looking around and over his shoulder as though leery of eavesdroppers in the shadows. His children followed his gaze, half-expecting to see some furtive movement in the dark corners or a shadow pass across a doorway. *They serve Iblis, the Evil One, and the strongest among them are called* afreet.

Of course back then, in better times, such bedtime tales would end with her father jumping up with a shout to startle his boys and girl, who would shriek, then laugh and never seemed to grow tired of the game. The memory stirred a rare longing in Azzam, who blinked back the tears. She wondered if her father knew that the *jinn* were real and inhabited men like Andrew Kane. *"Audhu billah,"* she muttered.

"What was that, my darling?" Kane asked. "Did you say 'I seek refuge in Allah'? Isn't that something you superstitious desert folk say to ward off evil?"

"It is just a saying," Azzam replied. "Like 'bless you' when someone sneezes."

"Hmmm . . . could have sworn it was a little stronger than that," Kane said, and then chuckled. "But I am doing rather well with my language lessons, don't you think? Good thing, as it looks like I may have to spend some time in your part of the world after we've accomplished our task in New York."

"Yes, you are learning quickly," Azzam replied. And yes, she thought, it will be difficult for anyone to recognize this Andrew Kane. The scars from the surgery were mostly healed and one had to look close to see them. Even his body had changed. Although reasonably fit in the manner of a wealthy New York lawyer who visited the gym a few days a week to work out and talk business when she first met him, ever since his escape, he'd trained religiously until there was tight definition to his muscles and more speed and coordination in his movement.

The training included working out almost daily in martial arts with Samira, who was teaching him the Filipino knife-fighting techniques of *Kali.* Kane had proved an apt student there, too. The cold and efficient nature of using a knife as a weapon suited his personality. He was now sparring with her nearly at full speed. She always won the encounters easily if she concentrated and went all out, but he was progressing rapidly and was growing more difficult to beat if she wasn't on her game.

The practice session ended when several large Arab men entered the room, half-dragging, half-pushing a blindfolded prisoner. Behind them, smiling uneasily, walked Dr. Buchwald and Bandar Al-Aziz bin Saud, the minor Saudi prince whose home they were using as a base of operations while Kane healed from his surgeries and set his plan in motion.

"Ah, Agent Vic Hodges of the U.S. Department of Homeland Security," Kane said to the blindfolded man.

"What the hell is going on here?" Hodges replied angrily. "And what do you mean 'Agent.' I ain't no goddamn federal agent. I'm just a redneck nigger hater trying to make a buck and screw the U.S. government at the same time. Now, are we going to talk guns and money or play this little game?"

"'I'm just a redneck nigger hater,'" Kane mimicked, doing a passable imitation of his prisoner's Deep South accent. "No, Agent Hodges, we will not be doing any business, except the business that I'm about to propose. So let's drop the bullshit, which by the way, you are neck deep in right now."

Kane nodded to one of the guards. "Remove the blindfold so Agent Hodges can see who he's talking to."

When the blindfold was pulled off, Hodges stood blinking in the sunny room as his eyes adjusted and his mind raced to find a way out of the fix he was in. His cover was that of an Aryan Nations gun dealer—that's how he'd been introduced to Azzam, who'd been looking for a half dozen Colt M4 assault rifles and enough C4 plastic explosives to bring down a good-sized building. He didn't like the idea of selling terrorists such a lethal arsenal, but his superior, Assistant Director Jon Ellis, had assured him that they were tracking Azzam's every move and would know where the weapons were at all times. When they had a positive idea of what the target was going to be, they'd swoop in and catch the terrorists red-handed.

It was risky business, but then that was the nature of war. And make no mistake, there was a war going on beneath the American public's radar that guys like him—a former agent with the U.S. Department of Alcohol, Tobacco and Firearms who'd volunteered for reassignment with Homeland Security after 9/11—had better win or Americans were going to have to get used to praying on their knees while facing east.

Besides, the arms deal had been the only way to get to the big prize—Andrew Kane, who was planning some major event with Islamic terrorists. The idea was for him to meet and win Kane's trust, then, like a worm in an apple, destroy the plot from the inside out.

The meeting with Kane had finally been arranged. He'd been taken to a private airfield in Dade County, Florida, where he'd boarded a Learjet. But that's when his predicament began. After he was seated next to Azzam, he'd suddenly been grabbed from behind, his arms pinned back, and she'd produced a hypodermic needle that she stuck in his thigh.

The next thing he knew, he was waking up with an intense headache, blindfolded with his wrists and ankles tied together, in what was a small dark room or closet. There he'd been kept for what he estimated to be several days—his only company, rough guards who entered on occasion to give him a drink of water and stuff a few handfuls of tasteless rice in his mouth.

Finally, he'd been dragged from the room, after which his soiled clothes had been cut from him, as had his bonds—though he was warned not to remove the blindfold—and allowed to shower and dress in sweat clothes. His guards had refused to answer any of his questions or talk at all except to give him curt orders in broken English.

Now, as his eyes got used to the first light since his abduction, he tried to focus on the features of the man in front of him. A confused look crossed his face. He closed his eyes and shook his head. The knockout drug must be causing hallucinations, he told himself. But when he looked again, he realized that what he had seen was real.

"What the hell," he said as boldly as he could muster, knowing that for all intents and purposes, his life was over. "You look like me."

"Very observant, Agent Hodges," Kane replied. "Yes, thanks to Dr. Buchwald, the little gnomish man standing behind you, I am nearly the spitting image of you. I do have to compliment the good doctor . . ." he said, turning to the doctor, ". . . for working from nothing but photographs, you did an incredible job."

"Thank you," the doctor said nearly bowing in delight at the rare compliment. "I am rather—"

"Shut the fuck up, Buchwald," Kane said mildly. "Nobody cares what you think."

The doctor stopped and shut his mouth while trying to manage a smile to let everyone know that he understood that everybody was just a little tense. Hodges, however, still wanted answers. "What's this all about?"

"Tut, tut, Vic . . . may I call you Vic?" Kane said as he circled around his prisoner, noting the cleft in the chin, the broken nose, the thin, white scar below the brown eye. "That's need-to-know information, and you don't need to know. However, I *do* need to know some things from you—such as everything about you and your job. Your code words, how the Homeland Security operates, your contacts with the agency. That sort of thing."

Hodges knew he was doomed, but tried to talk his way out of it anyway. "I don't know what your bullshit is about, punk," he bluffed. "But if you don't let me go, my boys back in Mississippi will kick your ass."

Kane laughed and slapped Hodges in the back of his head. "When I told the boys in Mississippi that you were a federal agent and had been spying on them for years, they begged me to ship you back to them so that they could . . . let's see how'd that moron who leads the group put it . . . 'skin that asshole alive and then use an acetylene torch on him.' Sounded absolutely painful, so I'm sure you'll be willing to help me in exchange for keeping you right here. So what about it, Agent Hodges? You going to tell me what I need to know?"

The agent hung his head. "Go fuck yourself, Kane."

Sighing, Kane walked over to the desk and picked up a remote control for the big-screen television in the bookcase. He turned the television on and then pressed a button on the desk intercom and said, "Barak, would you please get me the satellite feed now?" He turned to Hodges and said, "I'm really sorry that it's come to this, but since you insist on being difficult, you leave me no choice."

The picture on the television screen was fuzzy at first, but then it cleared. Someone was videotaping a woman and a little girl walking some distance in front of the photographer at a shopping mall. Hodges gasped audibly.

"So you recognize your wife and darling daughter?" Kane giggled. The agent gave no reply so his tormentor went on. "Looks like they're out spending some of that meager civil service pay, Agent Hodges. Girls can be such drains on the old bank account. Isn't that right, Samira?"

Hodges glanced over at the young woman. She stared back with a look in her eyes that told him there would be no mercy shown here.

"Anyway, Vic, see that man walking about ten feet behind your lovely family? Oops, now that was poor directing, he looked right back at our cameraman," Kane said. "I'm afraid he's not a very nice man, and certainly not one you'd want following your wife and daughter. His name is Liam, and he used to be a Catholic priest until some spoilsport teenager reported him for raping her at a church camp. Turned out, he'd raped quite a few women and little girls, the younger the better, in the neighborhood around his parish, so I had to help him out of the mess he'd made. Now he works for me—putting his, how shall we say it, 'passions,' to use when I need to persuade someone like you. Oh, and I regret to inform you that he's been getting more brutal . . . his last young victim didn't survive his attentions."

"Bastard," said Hodges, as his mind screamed, How? How did Kane find them? Even the Aryans, who'd checked out his undercover identity, had not.

"I've been called worse," Kane laughed. "But there's no reason for this to go any further. You cooperate and that bad man doesn't rape your daughter in front of your wife. Oh, and I'm sure we can provide a videotape of his antics for your viewing pleasure."

Defeated, Hodges asked, "What do you want?"

"Like I said, I need to know everything you do," Kane said. "Believe it or not, but I want to be just like Mike. And we don't have much time so we better get busy."

Hodges lunged for Kane but was slammed to the floor by his guards. At Kane's command the guards picked the agent up.

Kane leaned forward until his lips were just inches from Hodges's ear. "You are a dead man," he said. "Your mind knows it. Accept it. However, make this easy and your ugly little wife can look forward to whatever miserly survivor's pension your grateful but cheap government provides her and your brat. Make it tough, and you'll still die, but not before you watch your family go through hell. So what's it going to be?"

Hodges knew that he should refuse—that many people, not just himself and his family might die if he cooperated—but he didn't know or love those people. "I'll do what you ask," he said.

"That's wonderful." Kane beamed. Another weakling, he thought. No wonder the West will lose this War on Terrorism. They don't have the stomach for what it's going to take to defeat religious fanatics like Samira, who will stop at nothing and aren't afraid to die.

Things were going so well. In the months he spent in jail since his arrest the previous August and his escape in February, Kane had hatched a plan that was part revenge and part the beginning of his "new career," as he'd taken to thinking about it.

The plan was brilliant and efficient because it fit both his own purposes and those of al Qaeda. Through his lawyers, he'd managed to convey the general outline of the plan to the group; Kane's requirement was that they first had to help him escape and then allow him to accomplish his personal goals regarding Karp et al.

The risky escape while en route to the psychiatric hospital had become necessary when his original idea to have himself declared legally insane had been thwarted by the state's psychiatrists. Their examination had been a loathsome experience, but he'd put up with it for his greater good.

Without admitting anything regarding the charges against him, he'd answered most of their other questions quite truthfully, including that his father had screwed his daughter, which is how baby Andrew had been conceived. His sister/mother had been sent away to give birth; after which, his father/grandfather, through bribes and "donations," had arranged with the adoption agency run by the Archdiocese of New York to "adopt" the bastard child. Kane had learned the truth as a teenager from his sister/mother shortly before she killed herself.

A rather disconcerting event at a vulnerable age, Kane told the psychiatrists. By that he meant the circumstances of his birth; however, they thought he was talking about his mother's suicide, until he corrected them. *That didn't really bother me all that much,* he said. *She was a slut. I caught her screwing the old man one day when I came home from school early, you know.*

Kane left out the part about blackmailing "the old man" into blowing his brains out in the family library. Otherwise, his purpose in being honest with the state's psychiatrists was to engender their sympathy, after which they would, of course, declare him legally insane. That would have meant a short stint at a nice psychiatric hospital where, at worst, he'd sit around with a bunch of wackos talking about their dysfunctional childhoods, playing the game, and arrange a relatively easy escape. Ship off to a country with no extradition treaty and resume his master plan.

Only it didn't go the way he wanted. The bastards had issued their report: while he suffered from several personality disorders as defined by the *Diagnostic and Statistical Manual of Mental Disorders,* the shrinks' bible on such things, he was legally sane. More specifically, he knew right from wrong at the time of the crimes— as demonstrated by his elaborate schemes to cover up his actions. He knew the nature of the charges against him and was capable of assisting in his defense. He was therefore deemed both legally responsible and competent to stand trial.

Someday Kane planned to have the state shrinks brutally dismembered, but for the time being they were quite a ways down on his list of people targeted for vengeance. First, Karp and his bunch.

Plan B had required that his lawyer win the motion to have him tested by a private psychiatrist at a hospital in upstate New York. Kane's firm had once defended the doctor from a malpractice suit in which he'd been accused of sexually molesting several of his patients. They'd won mostly by painting the women as nutcases suffering from mass delusions. The man could be counted on to say Kane was nuts. The private psychiatrist was just a last resort if something went wrong with the escape plan he worked out with Azzam.

He'd first met Azzam when she accompanied his lawyer to the Tombs, posing as a legal assistant. During subsequent visits he'd discussed the master plan—making sure she understood that it could not be done without his help—including his escape. *I want what happens to the guards and any "spectators" to be as brutal as possible,* he whispered to her out of the hearing of even his lawyer. *I want them insane with anger—with their minds set on recapturing me and bringing us all to "justice," they won't be anticipating us to strike such a blow that they'll wish they'd never heard of Andrew Kane.*

Or al Qaeda, she'd reminded him.

Yes, yes, al Qaeda. He'd smiled.

Kane had been attracted to the young Palestinian woman's cold-blooded nature. Her arrogance and disdain for him made him want to subjugate her to his sexual whims. Again through his attorney, he'd conveyed his wishes to her handlers, who'd responded by ordering her to make herself available to him when he was free. He was aware how much she despised him the first time he took her, and it had just excited him more. He also knew about her lesbian lover, Ajmaani, and had gone out of his way to demean Azzam in front of her. He'd hoped to evoke some hint of jealousy but was disappointed when the woman didn't react.

After escaping, Kane had been quickly and quietly transported to Aspen and the home on Red Mountain of the Saudi prince, Bandar. The facial reconstruction surgery by Dr. Buchwald had been performed in the house. Meanwhile, Bandar's family was told that the visitor was a distant relative who had a fatal, and contagious, disease and wasn't to be disturbed or talked about with their friends in town. Bandar's self-involved wife and children had shrugged at the information and paid little attention to the comings and goings at the guesthouse.

As Kane healed, he dreamed of taking revenge against those who'd ruined not only his bid to become the mayor of New York City but also, given his malevolent grandiosity, taking up residence in the White House. Then he would have been among the wealthiest men in the world and the most powerful man in the world.

There was no telling what he might accomplish as president. He could use his influence with al Qaeda to terrorize the American public into being willing to accept the "temporary" relaxing of certain parts of the Constitution, including the number of terms a president could serve. Hell, when they see you tame the terrorists, who will have been bought off in exchange for his cooperation with establishing the caliphate in the Middle East, he thought, and bring Pax Americanus to the Western world . . . my world . . . they'll make me president for life . . . emperor.

Along the way, he would destroy the Catholic Church in the United States. He blamed the church for having gone along with his father/grandfather to keep the shameful secret of his conception. They'd all let him think that he was the bastard son of some trashy whore who'd given him up for adoption like one might throw out spoiled milk. Every day of his young life, he'd had to live with being told how lucky he was that his adoptive "father" had "rescued" him from a life of waste and drudgery.

Of course, all the blue-blood sons at the boarding schools he'd been packed off to had laughed at him both behind his back and to his face. They'd called him "the bastard" and spread rumors, such as his mother had been a prostitute. It got worse after his sister/mother swallowed a medicine cabinet full of pills and then slit her wrists in the bathtub while he was home on vacation. Then the rumor became that he'd been "porkin'" her and that was the reason she killed herself.

He'd hated them. But the talk in front of his face had largely disappeared when he castrated the bully who'd been raping him in the dormitory. It had been a good lesson in how to deal with difficult people. Cut their balls off, figuratively or literally, whichever did the job.

And until Karp stuck his Jew nose where it didn't belong, he had been setting up the Archdiocese of New York. He had just been biding his time before leaking to certain friends in the media that the archbishop and other church officials had been protecting rapists, child molesters, and even murderers. It would make the sex scandals that had rocked the Boston archdiocese pale in comparison.

Then Karp had fucked it up—him and that bitch wife, Marlene Ciampi, and their disgusting mongrel horde of family and friends. Should have killed Ciampi when I had her last fall, he thought. She's the hardest to predict. Then he smiled, remembering what he'd told Detective Fulton before Samira shot him in the knees. There's that stupid movie thing again. Kill them quickly when you can, or it will just come back to bite you in the butt.

The thought crossed his mind that he should now kill Karp and the others as soon as possible. But what fun would that be? No, he wanted to make them suffer and to be afraid . . . *very afraid* . . . before he finished them. And so he'd plotted out the moves of his "game" with Karp and the others, as part of the larger plan with al Qaeda.

He had to admit that the plot was a bit complex, like a chess game, and, as in chess, there were many plays and counterplays. The plan had taken more than just al Qaeda's eager acceptance; it had required certain other parties in the United States and Russia to cooperate, each according to their own schemes.

Then when he was ready, he'd made his first move. The Escape. The authorities had reacted as he expected and launched a massive manhunt. Shooting Fulton had ensured that Karp would take it all personally. The next move had been to have Fey located and strangled. The man was a weak-spined traitor. Also, Kane wanted to keep Karp's attention and build toward the feeling that his own doom was approaching.

Each step took him closer to his goal. The plastic surgery. The capture. And now reduction of Agent Hodges.

"Take him away," Kane said to the guards. "But I want him watched 24/7. He better not escape or manage to kill himself. And Agent Hodges, just so you know, if you choose either route, I will make sure your wife and child pay for it."

When the guards and their prisoner left the room, Kane turned to Dr. Buchwald. "Have you ever practiced martial arts, Dr. B?"

The man smiled nervously, wondering where this bit of insanity was going. "Uh, no, no, never had the time or inclination," he said and laughed as heartily as he could under the circumstances. "Medical school and all that—there's not much time for anything else."

"Too bad," Kane said. "I could have used the practice against someone with some skill. But you'll have to do. Samira, would you loan your knife to the good doctor, please."

"What do you mean?" the doctor cried, his voice cracking into a squeak like a nail being pulled from a board. "I'd rather not." He attempted to wave off Samira who offered her blade. "Uh, no thanks . . . sit this one out."

"I'm afraid you have no choice," Kane said. "I can't let you live; you might have a couple of belts down at the Hotel Jerome and start blabbing. Next thing you know, the FBI's all over the place. Loose lips, sink ships, you know."

"I wouldn't, no, doctor-client privilege," Buchwald cried. "I can keep secrets."

"Take the knife, Doctor," Kane urged. "I've never killed anyone with a knife so this is as good a time as any. Besides, you might get lucky and stick me a good one. If that happens, Samira, let the good doctor go free, would you?"

"Whatever you say," she replied in a manner that told Buchwald he was never leaving the house alive. Still, he had no choice but to take the knife and thought, Maybe I can fight my way out of here.

"Good, good," Kane said assuming the on-guard thrust position unique to *Kali*. "Now, do your best for as long as you can."

The two men circled each other, the doctor holding his knife out in front of him while he blubbered and wiped at his nose with the sleeve of his other arm. Prince Bandar started to protest. "Gentlemen, there is no need for this," he said in a calm and reasonable voice. "I'm sure Dr. Buchwald can be trusted to keep a secret."

"Shut up, Bandar, or take Dr. B's place," Kane said.

Bandar ceased his complaints immediately. He sank with a sigh into one of the overstuffed chairs to watch the duel.

As he circled, Kane lectured the doctor on the art of *Kali*. "Note the smoothness of *Saksak-Hatak,* the classic thrust and cut," he said, executing the move, which resulted in a small slice on the doctor's arm. The man began crying as Kane continued his lesson.

"By constantly keeping the blade and point toward the opponent, the strategic positioning of the knife's edge is never lost even when"—he sliced the doctor again, this time above his right eyebrow—"reversing from a backward to forward cut."

Blood flowed into Buchwald's eye. He wiped at it with his free hand, then made a desperate lunge at what had appeared to be Kane's exposed chest. But his opponent dodged sideways and parried the thrust with his own knife.

Kane slashed down, opening a deep cut on the doctor's wrist. The blow caused Buchwald to drop his knife and cry out in terror and pain. "Pick it up," Kane insisted.

"No, no, no . . . please, stop this. Don't kill me," the doctor begged. "I'll do anything."

"Pick it up or I'm going to let one of the guards gut you like a pig and then let the dog pull your intestines out while you watch," Kane snarled.

Buchwald had seen the dog Kane spoke of—a snarling, piebald pit bull that he was quite sure would be happy to eat him alive. Hardly able to see through the blood and tears, the doctor leaned over and picked up the knife. He felt light-headed and nearly passed out.

"It might interest you to know that what I'm doing here is known as the *Palis-Tusok*," Kane said, "which essentially means making a lot of small cuts to bleed you. Gradually, you'll weaken until you will be unable to defend yourself."

Buchwald swung his knife wildly at his tormentor's face. But Kane dropped to a knee beneath the blow, the same move he'd tried on Samira, and slashed open the muscle of the doctor's thigh. The man howled in pain.

As he staggered around to continue facing Kane, Buchwald recognized the proximity of death. But as men and beasts will sometimes do when cornered, he found a small reservoir of courage. He stopped crying and his face grew grim. He gripped the bloody handle of the knife and charged, stabbing for Kane's chest.

This time Kane stepped to the side and parried the knife. But instead of slashing down at the exposed arm again, his blade continued its circular path until Buchwald's neck was open to his thrust. The blade sunk into the man's throat and continued up, piercing the skull and into the brain.

Kane gave the knife a violent twist and then withdrew the blade, stepping back from the falling body. The air was filled with the sweet coppery smell of blood.

Bandar moaned from his chair. "My rug, my beautiful rug," he complained and pointed at the growing pool of blood beneath the twitching body of Dr. Buchwald. "That is a five-hundred-year-old Persian original. Now it's ruined."

Kane looked at the prince and shrugged. "I guess you shouldn't have had it on the floor if you didn't want people to walk or bleed on it." He started laughing at his joke, and then laughed louder when the prince got up and rushed from the room in a huff.

Kane turned to look at Samira, who was standing over by the chessboard. "So how'd I do?" he asked.

"You talk too much and take stupid chances," she said. "If you're going to kill a man, kill him . . . don't give him the motivation or time to kill you first. That's why I don't like this game you want to play. It is not a necessary part of the plan."

Kane formed his face into a pout. "Darn, I'd hoped I'd made you proud," he said. "But it is important to me, and that means, it's important to you . . . or your chance at martyrdom won't be granted, at least not in the grand way you anticipate. . . . And by the way, have we made another move?"

"Bishop to black knight?" she said.

"Perfect," Kane said, clapping with delight.

Fifteen hundred miles away in a segregation cell at the Rikers Island prison, former NYPD detective Michael Flanagan looked up from his steel-framed bed when the guard opened the door to take him to the chapel to receive Holy Communion. He closed the Bible he read constantly and got up with a sigh.

Prison had aged him. Raised a good Catholic who'd followed in the footsteps of several generations of Flanagans and joined the New York Police Department, he'd considered himself a good cop, even when he started going after scumbags and sinners the regular application of the law seemed to overlook. He saw it as just helping an overcrowded justice system. When he first started taking orders from Kane, he thought they actually came down from the Archbishop of New York. After all, the world was a better place for Christian men and women when sinners were sent to the fiery pit . . . albeit a bit earlier than planned.

It had been devastating to realize that the only master he was serving was the evil one, Andrew Kane. Like Fey, he wanted to live only to testify against Kane, and then if some inmate wanted to shank him in the prison yard, he was ready. He'd been doing his best to prepare to meet his Maker and ask for forgiveness by reading his Bible and attending mass and confessing as frequently as the guards would let him. When Kane escaped, he felt as though he'd been robbed of a chance at partial redemption.

As he made his way down to the chapel, he felt tired, and his legs heavy; he attributed it to having fasted since midnight in preparation for receiving the Blessed Eucharist.

Because of his "status" as a segregated prisoner, kept away from the general population who might just want to kill an ex-cop for the fun of it, he was alone when he entered the chapel. He walked to the railing at the front where he dropped to his knees to accept communion.

After a few minutes, he was aware of the rustle of robes. He looked up at the scarred face of the priest, a big man with sad eyes. Must be new . . . wonder where Father Woodard is today? he thought as the priest began the rite of communion.

When Flanagan accepted the wafer representing the body of Christ into his mouth, he noticed an unpleasant metallic taste. It was there even stronger after he drank the wine representing Christ's blood.

The poison in the wafer was powerful but slow acting. Slow enough to allow the priest who fed it to Flanagan to check out of the prison for his drive back to Manhattan where he was the caretaker of St. Patrick's Cathedral.

The priest did not enjoy killing. He hated Andrew Kane for sending him on these missions and hated himself for creating the circumstances that had doomed his immortal soul. Even if those circumstances had evolved from love.

All of his young life since entering puberty, he'd been taunted for the acne that had ravaged his face. No girls would have anything to do with him, even when he starred on the football field. A freak, they called him, Freddy Krueger. Even his own family seemed repulsed; his parents had urged him to go into the priesthood "since no decent woman will marry you."

So he'd committed himself to God, a young priest known for his compassion and love of children, which is what had drawn her to him. She was not what others would have called pretty, either, though as he got to know her, he thought she was the most beautiful of all women. The mutual attraction had led to love, which had led to sex—not only forbidden by his vows, but illegal in the eyes of the law because she was only seventeen. She'd become pregnant and given birth to their child, and suddenly he had two people who loved him unconditionally.

However, when the girl's parents, who had never cared much about her before, discovered who the father of the child was, they threatened to sue the church and go to the law. But Andrew Kane had settled with the parents and recommended against prosecution to the DAO. Then he called the young priest into his office.

So you love this woman and child? Kane had asked.

Yes, he'd said enthusiastically, hoping this attorney would understand that such was his motivation. *I am prepared to leave the priesthood to be with them.*

Oh no, you misunderstand, Kane said. *I don't want you to leave the priesthood. In fact, I am going to get you a special appointment to serve the Archbishop of New York, but really you'll be working for me.*

I don't understand, the priest said.

Kane grinned—a wolfish look, the priest would later recall, his blue eyes predatory and mean. *I've had your little whore and brat "relocated,"* Kane said. *But don't worry; they're safe as long as you do what I ask.*

And what if I don't? he asked.

I'll send them back to you in pieces, Kane replied and grinned again.

The priest had never seen the young woman or his child in person since. Every once in a while, Kane gave him a photograph of a small blond girl who looked like a cross between the priest and her mother as she grew older. And so he had been corrupted, turned into a spy, a heretic, and eventually a killer. He lost his faith in a God who would allow such a thing—not for himself, he accepted that he had sinned with the young woman, but for her sake and the child's. Whether they knew it or not, they lived at the whim of a madman. The archbishop had been just one of many victims, and now the police detective.

An hour after returning Michael Flanagan to his cell, a guard walked past on a routine welfare check and noticed the former police detective was lying on the floor curled into the fetal position. When the prisoner did not respond to verbal commands to get up, the guard entered the cell and rolled Flanagan over onto his back.

"Jesus Christ!" the guard exclaimed and threw up.

Flanagan's face was difficult to look at; his eyes were bugging out of his head, the whites turned bright red from burst blood vessels. White foam was caked around his mouth, and his swollen tongue protruded from between purple lips. His face was stretched into a mask of intense pain.

"Holy shit!" the guard later told his colleagues during a coffee break. "Whatever fragged that asshole must have hurt like hell!"

13

THE TWENTY-SOMETHING ARAB-AMERICAN BICYCLE MESSENGER
rode briskly down Crosby, hopped the curb up onto the sidewalk,
and came to a stop at the old brick building on the corner with
Grand. He dismounted, leaned his bicycle against a railing, and
walked up the small flight of stairs to the security door where he
pressed the buzzer and waited.

A young boy's voice answered over the intercom. "Yes?"

"I have a package for Roger Karp," the messenger said. *Oh no, a
kid. They can take forever, and there ain't going to be no tip.* He
had plans to go out dancing that night with some of his fellow NYU
students and was already running behind on his deliveries. He
leaned toward the intercom. "Uh, kid, you don't have to sign for it.
I can leave it right here, and you can get it when you want."

"Sure," the boy said. "I'll be down in a couple minutes."

The messenger put the box down on the doorstep and turned to
leave. He didn't get far as he was surrounded by three men—one
in jeans and a hooded sweatshirt, another in a business suit straight
off the rack, and the third in dreadlocks, and all of them pointing
guns at him.

"Police! Get your frickin' hands in the air," the one in jeans and a pullover sweatshirt yelled. He waved something that looked like a badge. "Step away from the door and walk slowly toward me. . . . Don't drop your hands or I'm going to put a hot one in your frickin' head."

"Don't shoot!" the terrified young man shouted. "I'm just a bike guy!" He hurried to the bottom of the stairs, where he was instructed to lie on the ground with his arms extended above his head. The cop in the cheap business suit stepped forward and frisked him from head to toe, then ordered him to roll over— "keeping your fuggin' hands where we can see them if you don't want to get shot"—and frisked him again.

"He's clean," the frisker yelled and stepped back with his gun still trained on the young man. "Okay, get up."

The young man did as told and was escorted by the arm across the street from the entrance to the Karp family's loft. "Of course, I'm clean," the messenger complained as they walked, regaining some of his courage now that he realized that his assailants really were cops and he probably wasn't going to get shot. "What's the matter, you see an Arab guy these days, you take him down?"

The cop ignored him. "What's in the package?"

"How the hell should I know? I'm just a delivery guy for Manhattan Bicycle Services," he replied. "They give me shit. I take it where I'm supposed to. If they don't need a signature and the person isn't there or tells me I can go, I just leave it."

As he was talking, two more men came running up. They were wearing New York City Public Works Department jumpsuits, but they looked more like businessmen dressing up for Halloween than men who made a living with their hands. For one thing, their fingernails were clean and there wasn't a spot on the twin aviator sunglasses they wore.

"Nice of you guys to show up," the cop in the sweatshirt said.

"We figured you NYPD guys might be able to handle one kid," one of the federal agents from Homeland Security shot back. "We were watching the street to make sure nothing else was on the way while you three were distracted. So what's this guy's story?"

"Bicycle messenger dropping off a package," the third cop, a black man with the dreadlocks and a Bob Marley Lives T-shirt, said.

"If you're going to jump on every bicycle messenger in town who comes by, you might want to call in more help," the agent said with a smirk.

"Maybe we should, if it's going to take you two such a long time to put down your Starbucks coffees and get your fat asses back out on the streets," sweatshirt cop replied. "We were told all packages, whether they're from the post office or FedEx, whatever, were being held for inspection before delivery by one of our guys. So this guy comes wheeling up at a hundred miles an hour and drops off a package without giving it to nobody, you bet we're going to err on the side of caution."

Business suit cop, who had been speaking into his radio, turned to the others and said, "The guy checks out. He's been working for the messenger service for two years."

"They were profiling, is what they were doing. Violating my constitutional rights," the bicycle messenger said to the federal agents, having decided that the guys with the public works department were on his side. "See an Arab and down comes the law, right?"

Sweatshirt cop, whose face looked like he might have once fought for a living, glared at the messenger. "Don't you have someplace you need to be?"

The messenger got the hint and went back across the street and retrieved his bicycle. As he pedaled off, he raised his right hand and extended the middle-fingered salute. "Fuckin' racists!" he yelled over his shoulder.

Sweatshirt cop was about to yell something back when the door across the way opened and two boys appeared, saw the box, and were about to pick it up. "DON'T TOUCH THE FRICKIN' PACKAGE!" the cops all shouted at once.

The boys stopped in their tracks, looked at each other and then, skirting around the package, jumped down the stairs, and bounded across the street to the cops. "Is it a bomb? Is it a bomb?" the Karp twins, Giancarlo and Zak, shouted with excitement.

"Mom and I told you the public works department guys were the feds," Giancarlo yelled in triumph at his brother.

"Doesn't mean the guys selling the purses on the sidewalk aren't feds," Zak replied hotly. "They've been watching us every day, too."

"Maybe they're the terrorists," Giancarlo suggested.

"One of 'em's got blue eyes," Zak pointed out.

"Lots of Muslims have blue eyes, especially if they're from Persia. There's a lot of Slav and Thracian—you know, Thracian like Alexander the Great—influences in the population. But they're Muslim now."

The cops listened as the boys debated whether they had terrorists eyeing their apartment like they were debating the Yankees' chances of winning the World Series. "Is it a bomb?" the twins repeated. "And did you catch the guy who left it?"

"We don't know what it is, so we want to play it safe for the moment," sweatshirt cop said. "The guy who brought it was just a bicycle messenger. He doesn't know what's in the box."

"That's what he says," said Zak, who had always been more given to intrigue and danger than his brother. "Maybe you should have tortured him a bit and squeezed the truth out of him."

"Would you suggest I rip out his fingernails or break every bone in his body?" sweatshirt cop asked, smiling.

"Both," Zak replied but further comment was stifled by the deep-throated bark of a large dog. They all turned to see Marlene Ciampi exiting the building behind them where, the cops knew, she had an art studio on the top floor. She was accompanied by the biggest dog any of them had ever seen.

As she approached, Marlene noticed the men, especially the presumed federal agents who'd had no contact yet with Gilgamesh, glancing nervously at the dog. "It's okay," she said, "he's friendly, unless I tell him not to be." As if to prove her right, the animal licked enthusiastically at their outstretched hands and rubbed up against their legs to beg for scratches and pats. "You want to tell me what's going on?"

"Oh, uh, sure, Mrs. Ciampi," sweatshirt cop said. "We just saw a guy dropping off an unscheduled package across the street and we were checking him out."

Marlene turned and started walking across the street toward the package, but the officer asked her to stop. "Sorry," he said. "I know it's probably okay, but I'd like to call in the bomb squad just in case."

Marlene looked back over her shoulder at him. "That's okay, officer, Gilgamesh, my dog, is certified in bomb detection. I'll have him take a whiff and save your guys the trouble." She continued across the street.

Gilgamesh gave the box a cursory sniff, turned a bored expression to Marlene, then walked back to the curb where he barked at the twins who were still standing across the street. He was ready for a romp and wanted to know what they were waiting for.

"Nothing to worry about," Marlene shouted as a dark Lincoln pulled up. Her husband and Special-Agent-in-Charge Espey Jaxon got out.

After she explained what had occurred, Jaxon knelt down by the box. "There's no return address," he said. "The shipping label isn't complete either; there's nothing under sender."

Business suit cop walked over and said, "The messenger company says it received the package from Denver, Colorado—no return address and the bill was paid in cash."

Jaxon took a pen from his coat pocket and inserted it into a flap to pick up the box. "We'll send this back to the folks at Quantico," he said, referring to the FBI's crime lab in Virginia. "But let's see if we can get a peek first at what's inside."

Karp, Marlene, Espey, the two twelve-year-old boys, and one disappointed dog entered the building and crowded onto the elevator that took them up to the landing outside the door of the loft. Inside, Jaxon placed the box on the dining room table as they all gathered around to watch.

Using a borrowed pair of tweezers and his pocket knife, the agent carefully opened the package without touching it to avoid messing up any fingerprints, even though it had already been handled by who knew how many people in transit. Once he had the box unsealed, he began removing the contents. First, he took out the packing material—handfuls of newspaper shredded into spaghetti-thin strips—which he placed in a plastic zip-lock bag Marlene got from the kitchen.

A folded notecard emerged with the second handful of shreds. Using the tweezers, Jaxon opened the card, which he read aloud. "It says, 'I hope you didn't shoot the messenger. Your move.'"

"This is soooo cool. Secret messages," Zak said as his parents rolled their eyes at their adrenaline junkie son.

Jaxon peered inside the box and then tipped it on end so that a small white object tumbled out.

"A bishop," Karp noted of the chess piece that lay on its side on the table. He didn't need V.T. to tell him that it was a Carlos Torres; the detail was exquisite and the inset jewels had to be worth his annual salary.

"Awesome," Giancarlo, the chess player in the bunch, said and reached for the piece only to have his mother, who'd anticipated his avarice, smack his hand.

"Don't touch, buster," she growled looking at Giancarlo but also turning her glare on Zak, who had a tendency to believe that warnings given to others didn't necessarily include himself.

Jaxon took out a handkerchief and touching as little of the chess piece as possible, dropped it into another zip-lock baggie. "Looks expensive. Neither of you ordered it, right?"

Marlene shook her head. But Karp said, "It's carved by a guy named Torres. Apparently, it is very, very expensive and each piece is hand carved." He explained how he had come by his sudden knowledge. He bit his lip before adding, "I think we're being told that Kane has selected another target."

"You think Kane sent this to you?" Jaxon asked.

Karp nodded. "Yeah, it's looking that way." He told them about the two black chess pieces that had been found in his office. "First, I thought it might be a couple of my guys misplaced them. Then I asked my receptionist about it. She said they'd appeared on her desk on two different mornings and, thinking the same thing I did, put them in my office so they could be given back to their rightful owner."

"She working for Kane, too, maybe?" Jaxon said.

"Nah, if she's anything more than she appears to be—an uptight, efficient, widowed receptionist—then I'm Winston Churchill," Karp said. "She's going to check with the janitorial company that cleans the office. No, I think this is part of Kane's little game—first the black bishop and Fey is killed; then week before last, the black knight, and the target is Flanagan, the dirty cop. I should say that Lucy thinks it's not Kane sending us these pieces, but someone close enough to him to know his plans and is sending these as some sort of coded message. But I think Kane's telling us he's about to make his move and is challenging us to counter him."

"So who's the white bishop?" Marlene asked.

"Good question," Karp replied. "If the type of piece has something to do with occupation and which side of the fence you sit—bishops for church people, knights for cops, white for good, black for bad—then one of the 'good guys' with the church."

"What about Father Dugan?" Marlene said. "He and Alejandro were the ones who uncovered the 'No Prosecution' files and gave them to you."

"That's a possibility," Karp said. "I'll call Bill Denton and ask him to assign some guys to Dugan. Where is he now?"

"St. Malachy's Church on West Forty-ninth," Marlene said. "The Actors' Chapel."

Karp picked up the telephone and placed a call to his friend Denton, the brother of the current mayor of New York and recently appointed chief of police for the NYPD. When Denton answered, Karp quickly explained what had happened and asked for the extra set of eyes on the priest. "Thanks, Bill," he said. "Let's talk over lunch one of these days soon." He hung up the telephone and turned back to Jaxon. "You want to send somebody by to pick up the other pieces. Unfortunately, I didn't understand their significance and they've been handled, but maybe your people can still find something of value."

Jaxon nodded. "We might even be able to piece the newspaper Kane used to pack the box and find out where it's from. But what if this chess piece doesn't represent Dugan? What if it's just white for good and black for bad, in which case, the white bishop could be someone else?"

"You know, I may have seen someone suspicious watching the loft the past couple of days," Marlene said. "I just happened to be looking down across Grand and noticed a couple of guys, looked Mediterranean or Middle Eastern. I hate to stereotype, but they were paying a lot of attention to what's going on here."

"The guys selling the purses!" Zak crowed and punched his brother on the arm. "I told you."

"You thought they were federal agents," Giancarlo replied, punching back.

"I never said that," Zak contended. "I said they're watching the loft. I didn't say if they were feds or terrorists."

"So you saw them, too," their mother interjected. "They were certainly more interested in watching the loft than selling purses, especially after the boys got home from school. I was about to go visit them when that poor bicycle guy delivered the package and got jumped."

"Well, if you see them again, sic the cops on them," Jaxon said.

"Oh, I'll sic more than that." Marlene smiled and scratched Gilgamesh behind his ears.

14

THE NEXT AFTERNOON KARP WAS STILL MULLING OVER THE chess pieces—the two from his office had been picked up at eight sharp—when Mrs. Milquetost buzzed him. "Mr. Karp, Mr. Guma is here with another . . . gentleman. Shall I tell them you're too busy to see them now?" she asked hopefully.

"That's okay, Mrs. Milquetost, he'll probably just outwait me; he doesn't have much else to do," he replied. "Send him in."

A moment later, Ray Guma walked in the door. "Hey, thanks for all the support with Eva Braun out there."

"You deserve it," Karp said, then spotted the man behind Guma and grinned as he stood up. "Well, hello, Jack. I heard Ray had been talking to your group but didn't know you were in town."

"Top secret . . . worried about the paparazzi, you know," Jack Swanburg replied with a chuckle. "A handsome face like this drives the girls wild, and if they knew I was here, I'd never get any work done."

Karp laughed. While Swanburg was one of the preeminent forensic pathologists in the country, he was no Tom Cruise in the looks department. In fact, he looked a lot more like Santa Claus on

holiday with his white beard, twinkling blue eyes, and a pronounced round belly that—Karp suspected—probably shook like
the proverbial bowl full of jelly. The gut was covered with a bright
yellow aloha shirt and red suspenders holding up a pair of baggy
cargo shorts that exposed hairy white legs that obviously rarely saw
the sun. The pipe that hung perpetually from his mouth, even
when he wasn't smoking, completed the jolly old elf picture, and
Karp half expected him to break out in a "ho ho ho."

Swanburg had appeared as an expert witness more than a thousand times to testify about the cause of death in homicide cases. It
should have been enough morbidity for any one man. However, he
also had what he called a "hobby" as the president of 221B Baker
Street, Inc., a loose affiliation of scientists who volunteered to help
police solve difficult homicide cases by combining their expertise
into what their literature described as a "many-headed Sherlock
Holmes."

In fact, the name of the group—221B Baker Street—was a reference to their fictional hero, the master of deduction and the her-
ald of the real-life collaboration of science and police work.
Holmes was said to live at 221B Baker Street in London. Many of
the group's members were forensic scientists, whose work—such as
forensic anthropology or blood-splatter analysis—was regularly
used by police agencies. But most of the others made a living in
other scientific endeavors, such as geology and entomology, not
normally associated with crimes but applicable in the right situations.

Karp had first heard of the group from Marlene, who'd met one
of the members, Charlotte Gates, a forensic anthropologist from
the University of New Mexico in Albuquerque. Gates had been
called in to exhume the clandestine graves of Indian boys murdered by the demonic priest Hans Lichner; she'd been the first to
discover the rosary beads.

Karp had met Swanburg when he needed a forensics expert to
testify in the Coney Island Four case. The old man had essentially
dismantled the rapists' version of events.

When Guma presented the Stavros case to the bureau chiefs

and questions were raised about the need to find the victim's body, Karp recalled that 221B Baker Street's specialty was locating hidden graves of murder victims. When the meeting was over, he'd suggested that Guma give them a call.

Like most law professionals, Guma was leery of amateur sleuths who wanted to play detective. *They'll give you the shirts off their backs,* he'd explained his hesitation. *But they'll tear them to pieces in the process.* It was clear he was putting the 221B group in the same category as psychics and tarot card readers who regularly call the police to help "solve" crimes. But with nothing left to lose and a major obstacle to overcome to win at trial, Guma called Swanburg. He'd been impressed by the man's questions and was soon thereafter on his way to Colorado, the group's home base.

There, the tables were turned. He was asked to present his evidence, as well as his theory on where the body might be located. This time, he was the one peppered with questions by the two dozen 221B members in the auditorium at a local sheriff's office.

I'll be honest, Guma told Karp when he returned, *I wasn't expecting that much . . . but they really put me through the wringer. If nothing else, I learned that I wasn't half as prepared in this case as I thought I was.*

They'd asked him if the moon was absent or full on the night Teresa Stavros disappeared. It might indicate, they said, how much light the killer would have had to work with in the backyard if he hadn't wanted to turn on the lights. They asked if he knew the composition of the soil, which could affect how deep the killer might have been able to dig. Could Stavros have moved the body from the premises without being seen?

"I basically had to say, 'I don't know,' to a lot of the questions," Guma said now recalling the inquisition for Karp.

"But he also said, 'I'll find out,' " Swanburg added, "which is what we wanted to hear. We don't take all the cases presented to us. We simply can't with our limited resources and time. So if the cops or, in this case, the DAO, aren't willing to do their homework, we shake their hands, wish them well, and politely decline."

Swanburg walked over to Karp's desk and opened a large manila envelope he was carrying and withdrew two large black-and-white photographs, which he placed on the desk. "One of the questions we asked Ray was the availability of aerial photographs of the Stavros home from before the 'disappearance' and after," he explained. "These photographs are more available than people think—if you know where to look. Places like surveyors' offices, zoning commissions, the United States Geological Survey, even declassified military photographs—which have the highest resolution, those guys can read a license plate from a satellite. Take a moment and look at the photographs I handed you and tell me what you see. The former Stavros house and yard is the one surrounded by the circle I've drawn to make it easy."

Karp stood up and, resting his knuckles on the desk, leaned over to get a bird's-eye view of the side-by-side photographs. He felt like a kid being put on the spot in a geography bee. However, when he compared the circled areas on the photographs, he quickly noticed a difference between the two. "The backyard . . . the one photograph there seems to have more bushes and less of this white space; the other, there's more white space, with something on it, and fewer bushes."

"Very good!" Swanburg exclaimed like a proud parent overseeing a homework assignment. "Photograph number one, as you correctly noted, has more vegetation, and was taken by a photographer in a Piper Cub in 1989, two years before Mrs. Stavros disappeared. The photographer was creating a coffee-table book called *A Bird's-Eye View of Manhattan Neighborhoods.* Photograph number two, which was taken in conjunction with the experimental mapping of Manhattan with a new satellite, was taken in 1991, three months after she disappeared. By the way, the white space is a patio, probably cement, and that's a hot tub on it."

"That's pretty cool, but what's it prove?" asked Karp. "Emil got tired of the garden and wanted a hot tub for his mistress . . . or was she a wife by then?"

"Still a girlfriend," Guma said. "There was still money in the account, so he hadn't divorced Teresa yet." He used the eraser end of a pencil to point to a corner of the house above the former rose-garden-turned-patio. "Zachary said that he remembered the sound of digging that night. And his bedroom was here, above the former rose garden."

Karp looked at his friend. The old Guma energy was radiating from him, he was gearing up for the fight with relish. Karp looked down at the photograph again. "I'd say if your instincts tell you a judge will grant a search warrant based on this photograph, then go for it."

"I've already got an appointment with Judge Paul Lussman in a half hour," Guma answered, grinning. "Want to come watch?"

Two hours later, Guma looked up at the opulent brownstone on Manhattan's Upper West Side as his car pulled up behind a marked police cruiser with a flashing light. A second unmarked car was behind them, followed by another cruiser with its light flashing. He might never get to bring Emil Stavros to justice, but Guma wanted to remind the neighbors that Emil Stavros had killed his wife.

Teresa Stavros had been on his mind a lot lately; in fact, her face as it appeared in the photograph on his wall at work stayed with him long after he left each evening. He'd always made it a point when prosecuting a homicide trial to get to know the victim as well as he could. It was important to make the victim real to the jury, not some character out of a story who had never been flesh and blood.

So he'd talked to anyone he could find who'd known Teresa. There wasn't much in the way of family outside of Zachary, who could only recollect bits and pieces. But she'd had quite a few friends, especially before she'd married, and some of them dating back to when she was a student at Marymount School of New York. They'd painted quite a picture of a wealthy Italian Catholic girl who was a little bit angel and a little bit devil. She'd been known to leave white mice in the desk drawer of the mean sister and skipped school to try parachuting. She loved the author Tom Robbins, and had once been expelled for bringing his sexy, funny novel *Even Cowgirls Get the Blues* to school to share with her classmates.

In her college days at Columbia, she would have been the first to strip naked for midnight swims in the Atlantic. A strong swimmer, on a dare she'd even tried crossing the East River where it met the Hudson on the north end of Manhattan at a particularly treacherous spot known as Spuyten Duyvil. Many a strong male swimmer had drowned in its strong currents and undertows, and she had nearly succumbed as well, but crawled out on the Washington Heights side and collected on the bet.

Most of her friends spoke of Emil Stavros with disgust. They'd tried to talk her out of getting serious about him. He was a big talker and had all sorts of grandiose plans—they always thought he was more interested in her trust fund than her love. But it seemed the more they tried to break them up, the harder Teresa fought to stay with him. Then she got pregnant and agreed to marry Emil, determined that her son—she was sure from day one it was a son—wasn't going to be born a bastard.

She was the best mother any child ever had, one of her college roommates said. *She adored that baby from the moment she knew she was pregnant. Then when Zachary was born, she fell in love. He made living with Emil almost bearable.*

That guy Emil is a piece of work, said another old friend. *The guy cheated on her all the time, and we suspected he was slapping her around. He wouldn't let her see us much, but when she did, we noticed a lot of bruises on her face and arms—a lot more often than could be explained by clumsiness. But she was a devoted, old-fashioned Catholic. She refused to have an abortion when she got pregnant with Zachary. And she wouldn't divorce Emil. So she just devoted herself to her son.*

She was a wonderful friend, said yet another. *It didn't matter if her own life was a mess, she would drop everything for any one of us in a heartbeat. She was an unusual woman in that as beautiful as she was, other women weren't threatened by her—everyone wanted to be her friend. And I don't have to tell you that men fell in love the moment they met her.*

The fourth woman Guma interviewed laughed at some recollection, then added, *I'll tell you what . . . she would have melted your heart, Mr. Guma, like butter in the sun.*

Ray Guma didn't tell the woman that Teresa Aiello Stavros already had. It had come as quite a shock that he'd fallen in love with a dead woman. He'd always adored women in just about all their myriad shapes and sizes, and he'd made it a mission to bed as many of them, in as many ways and as many places as possible.

Yet, in spite of the playboy image he'd carefully cultivated, he'd always believed that someday he'd meet the woman who would make all the others superfluous. Then he'd settle down and have the sort of marriage his parents had enjoyed for nearly seventy years. There'd be a handful or two of kids—who'd have been out of college by now if you'd met her twenty-five or so years ago, he thought as he looked out the window of the car at Teresa's former home. And later, he and the ball-and-chain would retire and spend half the year in Miami and half the year in Manhattan, right up until the Yankees won the World Series every October.

There'd been a dozen "future Mrs. Ray Guma's" he'd joked as he introduced each to friends or family over the years, but there'd never been a present Mrs. Ray Guma. Part of the problem—he was willing to admit after years of therapy, which he'd kept secret from even his best friend Karp—was that he'd never been good at keeping his zipper up. He looked at sex as fun and games; none of it meant anything. Unfortunately, the women who had meant something more to him than a passing lay never seemed to see it the same way.

When he was being less than honest with himself, Guma would contend that he'd messed around on the others because none of them were "the one." He wondered now if Teresa had lived, and they'd met, would he have known she was the one.

Face it, a voice in his head said, you're just all sentimental right now because you're worried your guts are rotting again and you'll be alone in your apartment to face it. And she's dead, so she's no threat to your "independence." You can cheat on a dead woman, so you're free to screw around.

"That's not fair," Guma said aloud to his conscience.

"It never is—bad things happen to good people," Swanburg said. The old man cocked his head to one side and gave him an appraising look. "Talking to the dead, Ray? Don't worry, it's okay. I do it all the time. It helps me remember why I'm in this business."

Guma patted Swanburg on the shoulder. "Thanks, Jack," he said and pulled the handle to open the door.

As they stood on the sidewalk waiting for the others to unload their equipment and gather, Swanburg looked up at the brownstone. "Whoo-whee," he said and whistled. "Nice digs . . . more impressive from eye level than the aerials. What's a place like this cost? A million?"

Guma snorted. "Yeah . . . for the fence around it. Land is at a premium in Manhattan and single-family residences a rare breed. This probably runs more like five or six million."

Swanburg whistled again, then chuckled. "All the more fun digging it up. Isn't that right, Mr. Clarkson?" he said to a tall, lanky man who walked up carrying what looked like the handles to a large lawnmower. Behind him two cops struggled with a large case. "Damn straight, Jack," Dave Clarkson said. "So enough flapping our gums, let's get to it."

Guma asked Detective Clarke Fairbrother to do the honors of leading the charge. The old gumshoe, hobbled a bit by arthritis in his hips, knocked on the door as the rest of the team gathered behind him. They included several police officers to secure the scene, plus Guma, Swanburg, and Clarkson.

The door opened and a butler appeared, the look on his face as if he'd just got a whiff of a bad odor.

"Afternoon," Guma said stepping up next to Clarkson. "Ray Guma, New York District Attorney's Office. Is Mr. Stavros in?"

The butler couldn't have looked more uninterested if Guma had just announced himself as a Fuller Brush salesman. "I'm afraid Mr. Stavros is . . . indisposed at the moment," he said and began to shut the door.

With a dexterity born of practice, Fairbrother blocked the door with his big foot.

"I'd suggest that your boss might want to be disposed," Guma said, "or maybe I get my friend Detective Fairbrother here to arrest you for obstruction. Then you'd get to experience a night in the Tombs, see if the rumors about what happens there in the dark are true."

The butler blanched, then nodded. "I'll inform him you're here, Mr. Guma."

"Thank you," Guma called after the man and led his party into the foyer. The butler walked up a flight of stairs and disappeared down a hallway. There were shouts from wherever he disappeared and then the butler reemerged. "He'll be here in a moment," he sniffed and left the room.

A minute later, Emil Stavros appeared at the top of the stairs in a jogging outfit and looked over the railing. "What do you want?" he demanded. "I just got home after a long day and was going out for a run."

Guma noted again that the once movie-star handsome face with its strong Mediterranean features had grown jowly and the features more pronounced until he was almost a caricature of his former self. But otherwise he looked to be in reasonable shape; his hair, though a pewter gray, was still full, and the tan looked real.

Reflecting how his former ballplayer's body had shriveled, Guma felt a twinge of envy. This asshole was her lover, he thought, and he's still in better shape than me. He shook off the feeling and shrugged apologetically, "I'm real sorry about that . . . right now, I'm asking your permission for me and my colleagues to nose about the premises a little, if you don't mind."

"But I do mind. As I said, I'm about to go out, and then I have a dinner engagement. . . . Perhaps, if you call my secretary at the bank tomorrow, you can make an appointment, and we can discuss why you think you get to look around my house. Even then, I'm sure my lawyer will insist on a search warrant."

"Afraid it can't wait," Guma replied. "Tomorrow's too late . . . you see, this search warrant I have in my hand is specific for today . . . right now, as a matter of fact. I was asking more as a courtesy." A courtesy you don't deserve, you scumbag, he thought.

"Now, you can watch, go for a run, call your lawyer, whatever it is you want to do, but we'll be going about our business. Come on, guys."

With that Guma led the troop farther into the house toward the back. Stavros followed, protesting "this outrageous invasion. I am calling my lawyer. This is all obviously the Tammany Hall tactics of your boss."

Guma ignored him and wasted no time getting to the backyard where the team reassembled on the cement patio. The butler was sitting on one of the lawn chairs, smoking a cigarette. "What *are* you doing?" he asked.

"Looking for Jimmy Hoffa," Clarkson answered, then noticed the strange, pained look on Guma's face. "Sorry, Ray, bad joke."

"Fuhgitabowdit," Guma said, waving him off with a lightness he did not feel. He'd met Clarkson on his trip back to Colorado and after the meeting, they'd gone to have a few beers at El Rancho Historic Inn off Interstate 70 near the little mountain town of Evergreen.

The topic of conversation had turned to the dark sense of humor most of the members of the 221B Baker Street Irregulars, as they sometimes called themselves, revealed when working on cases. *Most of us are "civies." When we got into this, I don't think we knew the emotional impact working with families of murder victims, as well as the cops and prosecutors who get so involved. I think it's either we laugh at tragedy or we'd start crying.*

Clarkson now leaned over the large aluminum case the two police officers had carried for him like Moses approaching the Ark of the Covenant. He flipped the latches and gently lifted the lid. Reaching in with both hands, he lifted a large red but otherwise almost featureless rectangle on wheels. He placed it on the ground and attached the handles, then plugged a cable into the top of the box. It kind of resembled an electric lawnmower.

"Gentlemen," Clarkson said as he plugged the other end of the cable into a computer he set on the patio table, "meet ground-penetrating radar, the closest thing there is to Superman's X-ray vision."

Guma smiled at the reference. When they went before Judge Lussman for the warrant bearing the photographs and a summary of the case, the jurist had scratched his head and then started asking questions. A Fordham law graduate and former Navy pilot who despite the gray in his crew-cut hair looked like he could probably still fly, the judge was probably the most liberal judge on the bench. But he also ran a tight, no-nonsense courtroom.

Lussman taught law at NYU at night and expected both his students and the lawyers who came before him to be prepared and to avoid wasting his time. That or risk a glare from his cobalt blue eyes that many a young law student or careless attorney had sworn could see through every excuse and attempt at subterfuge.

There were a lot of legitimate reasons why a homeowner might get rid of rosebushes and replace them with a patio and hot tub, Lussman had said after Guma explained his reasoning for the search warrant. But at last he'd conceded that combined with the other evidence there was probable cause to issue a search warrant; however, he was going to make it conditional.

You can go look around, but unless you come up with something stronger than this, I'm not going to let you tear up the man's house or backyard, Lussman said. *Mr. Stavros is a well-known and respected member of the community. He's still presumed to be innocent and owed the benefit of the doubt in this one.*

Guma had started to protest. How were they going to find "something stronger" if they couldn't dig? But Swanburg, who'd been allowed to attend the meeting to explain how the photographs were taken, leaned over to Guma and whispered.

As he listened, Guma's frown changed to concentration. Then he'd nodded to the judge and said, *No problem, Your Honor, but if I find something stronger, I might be back tonight for permission to dig.*

Lussman raised an eyebrow. *Well, you know where to find me, Mr. Guma. And ask my secretary to give you my cell phone number in case I'm gone for the day before you find what you're looking for.*

When they left the courthouse, Guma asked Swanburg to explain in more detail what he'd meant by Superman's X-ray vision.

It's called ground-penetrating radar, or GPR. It works by shooting an ultrahigh-frequency radio wave into the ground through a transducer or antenna. Part of that signal from buried objects or differences between, say, compact soil and loose soil reflects back up to the antenna, which stores them in a digital control unit.

Huh? It was getting complicated for Guma.

Uh . . . think of it sort of like taking an X-ray of what's underground, Swanburg had said. *When you take an X-ray of your arm, the picture you get back shows the bone as a denser white, while things like ligaments are more a shade of gray.*

So we'll be able to see Teresa's body? Guma asked.

Well, yes and no, Swanburg explained. *GPR produces a cross-sectional profile of what's under it—a record of subsurface features. It isn't as exact as that X-ray at your doctor's office. It could indicate when it's reflecting off something hard, like bone, but it's more for finding "anomalies" in the soil—like a pocket of natural gas or looser area soil of a size and shape to indicate a grave.*

Seems like a lot of trouble, Guma said. *Why not just go in there with a backhoe?*

Well, a couple of reasons, Swanburg said. *As you just heard, the judge isn't going to let you go on a fishing expedition and dig up holes all over this guy's yard without narrowing the search. Another reason is, unless you know exactly where to dig, you could miss a grave by a few inches and never know you were that close— unless you're intending on bulldozing the entire backyard.*

I might, Guma said.

Well, that would be a mistake, Swanburg said. *When we excavate bodies, we do so very carefully with small hand trowels and whisk brooms. We try not to miss a single shred of evidence, like bullet casings or pieces of clothing, that could be overlooked from a bulldozer. Also, any human remains might be disturbed, likely damaged, by machinery—sometimes even the position of the bones in a grave can tell us a lot. GPR, while not perfect, can give us a good idea of where to dig.*

Swanburg had referred any other questions to Clarkson, who was a geologist working for an oil company "in my real life." GPR,

Clarkson said, was used by geologists to evaluate the location and depth of buried objects—from buried cables to mineral deposits. It was capable of penetrating to one hundred feet in loose soils, like sand, but was more limited in denser soils, *such as only a few feet in clay, which is why we asked if you knew the soil composition.*

"The question is," Clarkson said now as he ran the GPR antenna—the red box—over a test area on the patio, "where exactly beneath the cement we should dig?"

"What if it's under the hot tub?" Guma said.

"Then we're screwed," Clarkson replied. "GPR sends its signal straight down, not sideways."

Swanburg saw Guma look over at the hot tub with concern. "Funny thing, Ray," he noted. "We've done a couple of these—and so have other groups like ours—and for some reason, killers who hide their victims on the property, don't like to put things like hot tubs or even new rooms or outdoor furniture directly over the graves. Maybe it's superstitious or disconcerting for their consciences, but they avoid it."

Over the next two hours, Clark slowly pulled the GPR device over the patio area, which had been divided by Swanburg into grids, as the digital recorder made a printout. Guma looked at the printouts but couldn't make heads or tails of them—they just looked like a bunch of different-colored bands and squiggly lines.

After they were finished, and the scene secured with a sign NYPD, the ensemble went back to the hotel where Clarkson and Swanburg were staying. Ordering a half dozen beers and ice up to the room, they pored over the printouts.

Clarkson showed Guma what the bands and lines meant. "Here's one that clearly indicates the electrical line just under the concrete, which is about six inches thick, that goes to the hot tub."

But it was the printout taken in the corner of the yard closest to the house that caused the two scientists to get excited. "Here you can see that this light area is looser soil and begins a foot beneath the concerete and goes about three feet below the surface, approximately six feet long and thirty-one inches wide," Clarkson said. "If I were looking for a grave, that's exactly where I'd dig."

"It's also right below Zachary's bedroom window," Guma said. "So what's our next step?"

Swanburg answered first. "Me? I'm going to get on the phone and call Char Gates, the leader of our forensic anthropology team. We'll need her for the excavation and, if we're right, the exhumation of the remains. . . . You, call the judge and ask what's the earliest we can see him with our 'something stronger.' We can assure him that we only need to dig one hole."

"What about the concrete pad?" Guma asked.

Clarkson cracked another beer and grinned as he took a sip. "Know any guys with the public works department who might have a jackhammer at their disposal?"

15

EVEN AS GUMA AND THE 221B BAKER STREET IRREGULARS CELE-brated with another round of beer, the two plainclothes police officers parked outside of St. Malachy's Church were trying to stay awake. "Hey, Dan, check out the legs on this hooker," Jose Villa said, nudging his partner and nodding toward the rearview mirror.

Dan Solomon turned his beefy body so that he could see the woman walking down the sidewalk toward them from Broadway. The ass-high short skirt, acres of visible cleavage, as well as the knee-high boots and the bad platinum blond wig identified her as one of the streetwalkers who hoped to make a buck from horny tourists in Times Square.

They had been told that terrorists wanted to assassinate the pastor of St. Malachy's and to keep their eyes peeled. But they'd had the evening shift duty for three days and "nothin' doin'." Tonight, their backups, a couple of federal agents, who'd been staking the place in a hotel linen supply van hadn't even bothered to show up. Chatting it up with a prostitute was better than listening to each other talk about the same shit they had the night before—and who knew what favors she might offer for free.

"Hey, sweetheart," Solomon called from the passenger window when the woman was nearly even with the car. He flashed his badge. "You wouldn't be doing nothin' illegal that maybe I should run you in?"

The hooker smiled and sauntered over. "Hi, boys, thinking about going to church?" she said. "Maybe you want to do something worth confessing first?" She leaned down to look in through the passenger window, giving Solomon a clear view of her ample free-swinging breasts.

"Hey, where you from?" Villa said leaning over from the driver's side to get a better view of her tits. "India? You have a nice accent . . . and your tan ain't half bad either."

"Actually, Palestine," Samira Azzam purred, "which is unfortunate for you."

The first bullet tore a hole in her purse, where she'd kept the gun to muffle the sound, on its way to Solomon's brain before exiting and lodging in the roof of the sedan. She then turned the gun on Villa whose smile was just beginning to fade as his mind comprehended what had just happened. The bullet caught him in the throat. He raised a hand and tried to ask her to spare him as she pointed the gun again, but all he could do was gurgle until the second bullet shut off the lights.

Azzam stood and tossed the gun in the car. It had been reported stolen from a home in Martha's Vineyard two years earlier. No sense getting caught with it later, and she wasn't going to need it for what she planned to do next. Looking up and down the mostly empty street to make sure no one was paying attention to a whore stopping to talk to a couple of possible customers, she quickly ascended the steps to the church and pushed the door open.

Inside, Father Michael Dugan finished his evening prayers at St. Malachy's and prepared to lock up for the night. He was in a hurry as an old friend . . . a young, old friend, he thought with a smile . . . was in town for a visit and there was a lot to talk about regarding Andrew Kane.

The last of the worshipers had left, and there was no one waiting in the confessional. All that remained was to lock the front door, and then he was done with his duties for the night. He missed the days when churches left their doors open, even at night, as a place where the desperate and cold could get in out of the dark—but to do so anymore would be to turn the church immediately into a homeless shelter. Remember to wave good night to the police officers out front, he thought as he walked toward the front of the church. He wasn't very happy with their presence, but Karp had convinced him that the threat was real.

Dugan winced as he stepped awkwardly on his way up the aisle to the front of the church. His arthritis had been acting up a lot lately; but that was to be expected of a seventy-year-old man who'd once played middle linebacker for the Fighting Irish at Notre Dame. He had the ruddy, rubbery face of the stereotypical Irish peasant, but he was no stereotypical priest. He'd worked in Latin American war zones and inner-city ghettos; he also ran the foundation created by Marlene Ciampi from millions she'd reaped in a stock market deal when she sold her security firm.

Lost in thought, he didn't see the beautiful young woman slip into the church at first. When he did, his initial thought was that she was awfully good-looking for a streetwalker—not just the body, which even the priest in him couldn't ignore—but she looked strong and vital, not the usual spent look of even formerly attractive hookers.

This ought to be quite a confession if that's why she's here, Dugan thought. "Good evening, my child," he said, "I'm afraid we're closing for the night. But if there's something I can help you with quickly—"

The young woman didn't reply except to stoop and quickly withdraw a thin double-edged knife from her boot. Recognizing the danger, Dugan showed some of the old athleticism by turning on a dime and running for the back of the church. But about five steps into his flight, his knee buckled and he stumbled. Immediately after there was a heavy blow and a sharp pain in his shoulder. As he fell forward, he saw a man step out of the shadows with a gun.

Azzam cursed: *"Zasranec,"* a Russian word Ajmaani had taught her that translated roughly to "asshole." She regretted picking up the recent habit of cursing, but Ajmaani's mouth was full of such things and she adored the woman.

Unfortunately, the priest had stumbled at the exact moment she'd thrown the knife, so what should have been a mortal blow stuck into his shoulder blade. She started to spring forward to finish the job when she, too, saw the man at the back of the church step out of the shadows. Then she saw the gun, just in time to throw herself behind a pew as it fired. The bullet, which would have caught her in the chest, tore into a column behind her. The next bullet chewed into the wood of the pew behind her.

"THAT'S RIGHT, BITCH, YOU BETTER RUN, 'BOOM' IS IN THE HOUSE," Alejandro Garcia shouted as he began a game of cat and mouse with the woman. He'd come looking for Father Dugan in time to see his friend turn to run and the woman throw the knife. He'd pulled the gun out from under his sweatshirt and shot.

Marlene Ciampi had been right when she called to tell him Dugan was in danger and she wasn't sure all the police could be trusted. A former gangbanger from Spanish Harlem turned rap musician in Los Angeles, Garcia had sworn off guns and changed his life. Central to that had been the support of Dugan, whom Garcia regarded as both Father figure and father figure. Arriving in New York City that morning, he'd checked in with some of his former running mates back in the 'hood and borrowed his weapon of choice, a Colt .45, whose loud report was the impetus for his nickname Boom.

"Come on out, bitch," he yelled. "You stuck the wrong priest. Now, I'm gonna cap your sorry ass."

Garcia had to make a choice which side of the row of pews he was going to cover best. He'd seen the woman's act with the knife and knew she was no one to take lightly, especially because he didn't know if she had another. He listened for a moment, then chose the side closest to the stone wall.

Four pews away, Azzam cursed herself for getting rid of the gun.

However, her information was that only two police officers would be in front of the building and that the old priest, who would have chased other visitors out by then, would be by himself in the church. Now, the only weapon she had left was a razor-sharp throwing star; she was going to have to make it good as her adversary had another ten rounds at least in his clip. She listened for the stealthy approach of the man's feet and at the moment she expected him to come around the end of the pew she stood, ready to throw.

He wasn't quite where she expected him to be. Cunning, this one, she thought, he came forward and moved back. And he was aiming at her. She threw at the same moment, he fired.

Dodging to the side, Alejandro saw his bullet strike the woman on her upper shoulder, spinning her to the side and down. At the same time, he felt a sting on the side of his neck. Instinctively, he reached up and felt a surprising amount of blood. He jumped up on a pew to try to see her but wasn't prepared when she stood up ten feet farther down the aisle than he'd expected and sprinted for the church door. He felt faint as he aimed and fired, but she was fast and his hand was growing less steady by the moment. She reached the door and was gone into the night, even as he sank to his knees on the pew.

The next moment, he was lying on the floor looking up at Father Dugan, who leaned over him and was pressing something against his neck. "Lie still, 'jandro," he said.

"Am I going to die?" the young man asked.

"You don't hear me giving you last rites, do you?" Dugan said. "No, you got a pretty good cut, but I don't think she got anything major. And help is on the way. Do you feel strong enough to keep this pressed against your neck? I want to check on our police guards."

Alejandro nodded though at that moment he would have preferred that the priest stay with him. Dugan patted him on the shoulder and got up, a groan escaping his lips. Alejandro saw that the knife still protruded from the priest's back. "You okay?"

Dugan glanced over his shoulder at the weapon. "Hurts," he

conceded. "But I've had worse." He hurried to the front of the church, but was back in a minute.

"I'm afraid the police officers are dead. There's no sign of the woman, except a trail of blood. I think you got her pretty good."

"Shoulder," Alejandro said. "She took off running like Reggie Bush on first down. That was some tough, bitch . . . oh, sorry, Father."

"An extra Hail Mary on the way to the hospital," Dugan said and smiled as he sank down onto one of the pews, the sound of sirens drawing nearer. "You saved my life, Alejandro. You are truly a blessed soul."

Alejandro's round face was split by his trademark ear-to-ear grin. "Denada, Padre," he said. "You saved mine a long time ago. Besides, it's not every day a gangster gets to shoot up a church and it's okay."

"Well, let's not make a habit of it."

"Nah, once in a lifetime, Father, once in a lifetime."

16

MARLENE WAS IN BED WITH BUTCH, NEGOTIATING THE TERMS
of a quick romp before sleep when the telephone rang. It was Fulton calling to tell them about the attack on Dugan and Alejandro, as well as the deaths of the two officers.

The detective could scarcely contain his rage when he arrived at the loft with a driver to take them to the hospital. "The two feds who were supposed to be backing them up said they got a call from NYPD that the stakeout had been called off. I'd like to know whose cluster fuck that was, ours or theirs." But he was also angry at the two NYPD officers as well.

"They knew this was a hot assignment and that people had already been killed. But they let themselves be lulled to sleep, and now they're dead."

When Fulton, Marlene, and Karp arrived at the hospital, Dugan was in surgery to repair damage to his shoulder. "Nothing too serious," said the surgeon, when he came out to announce he was finished and the patient would be back in his room soon, "mostly, ligament and bone. But he lost quite a bit of blood, probably more because of the blood thinners he's on for his heart, and at his age everything is more dangerous than it was forty years ago."

The cut on Alejandro's neck had required fifteen stitches, but the doctor had released him. He was sitting in Dugan's room when they got there. The short, barrel-chested young man greeted Marlene warmly, embracing her with his heavily tattooed arms. He was more reserved with Karp, shaking his hand and then stepping back and crossing his arms in the instinctive manner of a gangbanger in the presence of The Man.

They talked to Alejandro about what happened. "Good thing you called," he told Marlene.

"Good thing you came," she replied.

"Nothing else I could do," Alejandro said. "He's the only family I got."

"Feeling's mutual, Alejandro."

The three turned to see that Dugan was looking at them through half-lidded eyes.

"What's the matter with your heart?" Marlene asked him in an accusing tone.

"Nothing," the priest replied.

"Priests shouldn't lie," Marlene scolded. "They know better. The doctor said some of your blood loss was due to blood thinners you're taking for your heart."

"It's nothing. The oil's just a little thick in the engine," he growled in a manner meant to discourage further probing. His eyes flicked to Alejandro, whose smile at seeing the priest awake had been replaced with a look of concern.

Marlene got the idea and changed the subject until Dugan fell asleep again. Then she and Butch left Alejandro, and a pair of police officers sent to guard the room and went home to bed. Neither was in the mood for romping anymore.

Early in the evening two days later, Marlene was back in Dugan's hospital room when the priest received a package from "a well-wisher." The priest was still too weak to open it so he'd asked her to. "At least it's not flowers," he said. His room already looked like a florist shop.

"Or a card, and hopefully not candy." Marlene laughed as she slid the wrapper from the box and opened it. "Two white knights," she said quietly.

"Beautiful," Dugan said when he saw the pieces. A fan of chess himself, he started to reach for one. "They're Torreses, he's a famous sculptor of—"

"—chess pieces. Yeah, I know," Marlene said.

"Exquisite detail, inlaid jewels. Regular works of art," Dugan said. "Which means they're not really for me. What do they mean?"

"The next two intended victims of Andrew Kane. It's a nasty little game he's playing," Marlene replied and gave him the rundown on what was going on.

"Any idea who the white knights represent?"

Marlene pondered the question. "My first thought was the twins," she said. "A mother's conclusion; but much to their dismay, I don't think they quite rate knighthood. If Flanagan was a black knight, I think it's going to be someone at his level—only on the white 'good guys' side."

"Butch?" Dugan said.

"Nah, don't tell him or he'll get a big head, but I think we'll know Kane is after him when we get the white king," Marlene answered. "Besides, I think the whole point of this stupid game is to torment Butch. He'll be last. One could have been Alejandro; it's pretty clear Samira Azzam wasn't expecting him to show up packing heat."

"Who's Samira Azzam?" Dugan asked.

"The black queen, I suspect—a Palestinian terrorist, linked to al Qaeda and now apparently working with Kane."

"Is that all? I thought maybe she was dangerous or something." Dugan chuckled, then sobered at the thought of the dead police officers. "I feel for their families—leave home to go to work, and someone shoots them dead because a terrorist wants to kill some old priest. I'll pay my respects as soon as I get out of here. . . . So maybe the white knights are cops, like Fulton, or one of the attorneys who works for Butch?"

"Maybe," Marlene said. "But he's already had a whack at Fulton and seems to have moved on. However, you could be right, and Guma played a role in Kane's downfall, so did V.T. But somehow I think it's more dramatic than that."

"Who then? Lucy? Tran?"

"Beats me. But Lucy doesn't seem to fit the knight mold, and I don't know that Kane is aware of Tran—he sort of showed up in the proverbial nick of time after Kane nabbed me and then disappeared back into the woodwork. He wasn't mentioned in the newspapers or the police reports. But it does make me think that if I was planning on coming after Butch and me, I'd want to make sure John Jojola and Ned Blanchet were out of the way first. Now, there's a couple of knights, right out of the *Le Morte d'Arthur* or at least Zane Grey's *Riders of the Purple Sage*."

"Maybe you should warn them, then," Dugan said.

"Yeah, in fact, I'm out of here, Father Mike," Marlene said patting him gently on his forehead as she stood to leave. "I don't have Jojola's cell phone number with me, and Lucy refuses to carry one, so I better scoot." She looked at her watch. "Ooh, and I'm running late for picking up the twins. They're taking the subway home and I want to meet them at the station. They've been messing with the bodyguards, playing a game by trying to ditch them. Normally, Butch would be with them, too, but he's helping Guma dig up some body, literally, on the Upper West Side. So I want to make sure they're okay."

Marlene left, pausing at the door to admonish the police officers sitting outside the door to "watch out for the old geezer for me." Dugan had finally forced Alejandro to go back to his apartment at St. Malachy's to sleep, but he had done so complaining that the cops couldn't be trusted to stay alert. However, this pair was on edge and angry after what had happened, and she knew they wouldn't be caught napping.

It was getting dark, and as Marlene got out of the cab at Houston and Crosby she spotted the twins exiting the subway station across the street. She started to call out to them but froze.

The twins had turned for an instant to look back at a tall man wearing a brown hooded sweatshirt who was walking directly behind them. It was hard to see their expressions in the failing light, but he obviously said something to them, and they turned back around and kept walking. She noticed that the man's hands were in the front pocket of the sweatshirt. He's got a gun, she thought and started to run south on Crosby. She wanted to get ahead of them, cross the street, and then meet them coming the other way.

As she ran, Marlene reached inside her purse for her gun. When she was almost to the intersection with Spring Street, she paused and looked back. The situation was worse than she thought. There weren't many pedestrians on the sidewalks, and she immediately spotted the two men she'd seen selling purses on the sidewalk across Grand. They were tagging along behind her sons and their captor, trying not to look obvious. He's got backup, she thought.

Marlene raced ahead and crossed Crosby at Broome Street and headed back toward her boys. She saw the twins again just as they reached the mouth of an alley halfway up the block. The man in the sweatshirt said something and the boys turned and went into the alley as the man followed.

Fearing that her children were about to be slaughtered, Marlene began to sprint, pulling the gun from her purse as surprised pedestrians made small exclamations of fear and surprise as they moved to get out of her way. Although they apparently had not seen her, the two purse sellers also broke into a run, reaching the alley thirty feet ahead of her. They hesitated at the entrance to the alley, then pulling their guns they plunged in.

Marlene arrived and looked into the shadows. She thought that she saw figures moving in the dark and heard sounds of a struggle. She shouted for the twins to lie down and charged in, nearly stumbling over a body lying ten feet into the gloom. She looked down and could just make out the features of one of the purse sellers. His throat appeared to have been slashed, and he lay in a large pool of blood. She nearly jumped out of her skin when a voice spoke from the dark only two feet to her side.

"Good evening, Marlene. . . . Please don't shoot, the twins are safe."

"David? David Grale?" she asked as one shadow separated itself from the darker shades behind it and touched her on the arm.

"Yes, it's me," he said.

She realized that he was the man in the hooded sweatshirt. "Where are the boys?"

"I sent them out the other end of the alley to circle around and wait for you at the Housing Works Bookstore. It's a well-lit wholesome place; they should be safe for the moment."

Marlene looked down at the corpse. "Is the other one in the same condition?"

"No, though perhaps not feeling quite up to snuff," Grale replied. He raised his hand and several more shadows stepped forward and threw the other purse seller to the ground. "I thought you might want to ask him a few questions before I allowed my people to 'escort' him to his new home."

Marlene shuddered. She had been down into the bowels of the city where Grale and the Mole People lived and still had nightmares about being lost in the dark as thin, translucent hands reached out of damp holes for her. "Who sent you?" she asked the man on the ground.

The man spat and looked straight ahead. Grale moved instantly and stomped a heavy-booted foot down on the man's hand. He screamed. "Allah, curse you, *shaytan.*"

"Were you going to kill my sons?" Marlene asked.

The man again refused to answer as he held his crushed hand. Grale moved again, a blade flashed and the man howled with pain as he grabbed his wounded cheek. "I'll carve the flesh right off of you and leave you here for the rats if you don't start talking," he said.

"No, no, they were not targets . . . not tonight," the man cried. "We were just supposed to follow them . . . learn their habits."

"So you could kill them some other day, right?"

The man nodded. *"In sha' Allah."*

"God willing? Murder two little boys? I don't think that has anything to do with God, you cowardly piece of shit," Marlene said in disgust. "But if you weren't supposed to kill them tonight, who are the two white knights?"

The man looked puzzled. "White knights? I know nothing of this." He hazarded a look at Grale and added. "As Allah is my witness."

Marlene looked at Grale. "I don't think this scumbag knows much of anything," she said. "Kane probably hasn't let him in on 'the game.' He's all yours."

Grale nodded. "We'll see how much he knows when we take him to our home sweet home and have the time to whittle it away from him . . . so to speak." He raised his hand again and the shadows stepped forward and became people—emaciated with half-mad, glittering eyes, but people, not monsters. Four picked up the dead body and hauled it off into the dark. Several others grabbed the man on the ground and pulled him roughly to his feet.

"Where are they taking me?" the man cried, recoiling at their appearance and the smell of their unwashed bodies. "Are they turning me over to the police?"

Marlene smiled grimly. "Nah, it would just be a waste of taxpayer dollars. I believe where you're going, even in Islam, you would call it hell."

The man started to cry. "I am *mujahideen,* a holy warrior, I have been promised paradise . . . I have—" His voice was muffled as one of his captors threw a cloth sack over his head. He screamed and was cuffed into silence as they dragged him off.

Marlene turned to Grale. "I better go track down the twins," she said. "Thanks, I owe you."

Grale nodded. "You're welcome. We've been watching these two for a while, hoping they might lead us to Kane. But as you suspect, they are just witless pawns." He stopped and listened. Satisfied or at least not alarmed, he continued. "Get your family out of Manhattan, Marlene, there's death and a gathering of evil. Kane is coming . . . his assassins are already here. I don't know what they're planning yet, but it's big, and I fear you and your family figure prominently in his designs."

"I'll think about it," she replied. "Want to come back to the loft and take a shower, get a hot meal?"

Grale laughed. "Are you trying to tell me I stink? I guess I've gotten used to it. Living in hell, as you put it. Anyway, that's the second time I've received such an invitation, first from your husband and now from you, and it's much appreciated. However, that would not be for the best. Nor, as much as I love your family, should you always trust me to look out for your best interests." He paused. "I am not . . . I serve a higher power whose purpose for me might not be safe for you and yours. And sometimes . . . sometimes I worry that I am in such constant contact with evil, willing my mind to think as they do so that I can anticipate them. It's like standing too close to a plague victim; sooner or later you notice the buboes under your own skin."

Marlene felt a sudden surge of compassion for the young man. Insane or not, Grale believed that he was fighting the good fight against evil, and time and again had saved her family from tragedy. She reached up and touched his face, surprised when tears popped to the surface of his eyes. "I will never be afraid of you, David Grale; you will always be a hero to me."

Grale bowed. "I couldn't ask for a better compliment. But our paths—all of us, for good or evil—are running toward each other and there will soon be a collision. Now, care to tell me the significance of your questions about the white knights?"

For the second time that day, Marlene explained about the chess pieces.

"Perhaps it's not Kane who's sending them," Grale suggested.

"What do you mean? It's part of his 'game's on,' threat," Marlene said.

"Maybe, but what if they were being sent as a warning by someone who knows Kane's plans?" Grale said. "Maybe they can't be any more specific . . . or don't want to make it too easy on you. Maybe they're playing their own game."

"I guess anything's possible. But if it's a warning, it's pretty hard to decipher in time for it to do any good," Marlene said. "I think it's just a sick mind enjoying playing cat to our mouse. Sorry, have to run." She stood on her tiptoes and kissed Grale on the cheek. His skin felt warm and dry.

Grale mimicked looking at a watch, then exclaimed, "Oh dear! Oh dear! I shall be too late . . . time for me to pop down my rabbit hole." He started to turn away, then stopped. "By the way, sorry to hear about your mother, Marlene," he said softly. "She's resting in the arms of the Lord now."

The comment caught Marlene off guard, and the sudden lump in her throat made it hard to catch her breath. But she mustered enough to say, "Thank you, David, I think so, too."

Then he was gone.

Marlene trotted down the street to the bookstore where she found the twins hobnobbing with the owner over iced frappacinos. The Housing Works Bookstore—the proceeds of which were used to provide housing for people infected by HIV and AIDS—was a favorite hangout of the family's. Only a couple of blocks from the loft, it was a great place to sit down peacefully with an old book and a good cup of coffee that didn't come from one of the ubiquitous Starbucks that had sprung up all over the city.

"Come on, you two, that stuff will stunt your growth," she said, escorting each by an arm and calling over her shoulder to the owner. "Good night, Georgio. No caffeine for these two after six or we're all up all night."

"Understood Ms. C," Georgio replied. "But they coerced me by promising to tell me a story about terrorists and Mole Men. I'm a sucker for a good story."

Marlene gave the twins an extra shake when she got them on the sidewalk. "Let's not be spreading rumors, boys," she warned.

"What rumors?" Giancarlo said. "Our lives are like one big Arnold Schwarzenegger action flick. Zak and I are thinking about writing a script."

"We'll insist on starring in it as ourselves," Zak added. "At least at this age—we'll probably have to get some actors to play us when

we were little kids. Like the time Giancarlo got shot by those hill-
billies."

"Or when Zak stuck his switchblade into the leg of that terrorist
who was trying to abduct him."

"Or when that psycho murderer Felix Tighe tied up Lucy and—"

"Enough! Don't remind me," Marlene said putting her hands
over her ears. "Just let me know before the Academy Awards. I'd
like to buy a new dress, something becoming for the mother of the
stars."

"Who said you're invited," the twins laughed.

Marlene made a face. She sent a curse Georgio's way for dosing
the twins with caffeine. They were bounding around her like dogs
invited to go for a walk.

"What happened with David and those guys who were following
us?" Giancarlo asked.

"Bet David sliced them into pieces," Zak said with a sigh for
missing the imagined mayhem.

"He caught up to us when we got off the subway and told us we
were being followed and needed to walk fast until we got to the
alley," Giancarlo explained. "Then he told us to run for the bookstore and not look back."

"I bet they died a horrible death," said Zak.

"You shouldn't be so quick to celebrate violence, Zak. Violence
doesn't solve anything," Marlene scolded, trying to sound like a responsible parent.

"But sometimes violence is the only way to stop the violent," Zak
replied. "I've heard you say that to Dad."

"Don't listen to me," Marlene instructed. "I'm not a good role
model."

"No, you're not," the twins agreed.

"But you're a lot of fun," Zak said merrily to soften the blow.

"Never a dull moment," Giancarlo added somewhat less enthusiastically.

"Gee, thanks, boys."

When they reached the loft, she rushed to her desk to retrieve
telephone numbers for Jojola and the Sagebrush Inn, where her

daughter had taken up semipermanent residence. She tried the inn first, but there was no answer. Nor did Ned have a telephone at the rustic cabin where he stayed on the ranch. She sent an angry mother thought west in the direction of her obstinate daughter.

Next, she tried Jojola's cell phone and was happy to hear his voice. "Hey, Marlene, were your ears burning? I've got Tran here in my truck, and he's been talking trash about you. Ow! That hurt, you old gook."

Marlene heard something shouted about "drunk Indians." "You drinking again?" she asked sternly. When she met him the previous summer he'd been a recovering alcoholic, dry for more than twenty years.

"Nah, we're just giving each other shit," Jojola said. "So what's up?"

Marlene told Jojola the latest news and her fears about the implications of the white knight chess pieces. "I'm worried about Ned being one and you the other," she said.

"Well, I've seen these fed agents around a lot," Jojola said. "They're about as obvious as Custer at the Little Big Horn. But I haven't noticed anybody else who struck me as something other than a local or a tourist. . . . However, you'll be happy to know that we're on our way to see the young lovebirds at Ned's place. Tran just flew in this afternoon, and we're trying to get there before sunset to surprise 'em. But this place is a ways out here, middle of some of the prettiest nowhere you've ever seen."

Jojola was quiet for a moment and she could hear him saying something to Tran. "Hello, Marlene, you still there?" he asked.

"Yeah, what's up? I thought you forgot about me with your drinking buddy there."

"Nah, he's Vietcong, they were into opium," he said. "Anyway, there's a car pulled over on the road up here, we're going to check it out. Looks like the one these feds have been driving around. A dark Ford Taurus four-door in truck country if you can believe that."

Marlene heard Jojola and Tran talking again and the sound of his truck slowing down on gravel. Suddenly, there was an exclamation that sounded like it came from Tran. Then Jojola was back on the telephone.

"Marlene, I need you to call my office. You got the number, right?"

"Yes, what's going on, John?"

"There's a couple of dead agents sitting in a car out here. We're about five miles from Ned's place. I need backup, but there's a big mesa in between here and the res, and I usually can't reach them. Use your land line and tell whoever answers, 'Jojola needs you ASAP at the old . . . cabin . . . and come ready for a war party.' It's going to take them more than an hour as it is."

"What was that?" Marlene asked. "Your phone cut out. What was the cabin?"

"The Josh . . . Steers . . . ," Jojola yelled. "They'll understa—"

Marlene heard Tran shout, "Shots fired." She heard the truck accelerating.

"Make the call, Marlene. Got . . . go."

As soon as Jojola hung up, Marlene hit the speed dial for the Taos Pueblo's police department. A young woman answered and Marlene relayed her message. "I think he said the Josh Steers cabin, but I'm not sure." The other woman didn't waste time with pleasantries and hung up.

Not knowing what else to do, Marlene called her husband. Or, more accurately, she called Murrow because her husband was just as much a Luddite as her damn daughter and wouldn't carry a cell phone.

17

THE UNMISTAKABLE CALL OF THE *WILLIAM TELL OVERTURE* brought the work going on beneath the array of portable floodlights in Emil Stavros's backyard to a momentary halt. Murrow quickly snatched the cell phone from the holder on his belt and flipped it open.

"Hi, Marlene," he said. "You really should stop calling me like this. Your husband is standing right here." His smile disappeared as he listened and then handed the telephone to Karp. "It's your wife. Sounds like trouble . . . again."

"My wife's number is programmed into your cell phone, Gilbert? The Lone Ranger's theme music?" Karp asked with an arched eyebrow. "Is there anything I should know?"

Murrow blushed. "She's always riding to the rescue . . . shooting guns out of the bad guys' hands—"

"—or if she misses, the bad guys themselves," Karp said dryly. He put the phone to his ear. "Hi, babe, what's the trouble?"

Like Murrow, Karp's smile quickly turned into a frown. "The twins are okay?" he asked. "Good. Look, Jojola and Tran are on the way, and Lucy's got Ned with her. That's a pretty tough combination. I'll be right home." He flipped the telephone shut and turned to Guma, who'd walked over from where he was keeping a log-book.

"Sorry, got to go," Karp said. "Looks like you've got this in the bag. You don't need me."

"Trouble at home?"

"Yeah, and maybe in New Mexico. But everybody's all right, you just keep on this and call me when you know something." Karp left with his driver in tow.

Guma watched him go. New Mexico . . . hope everything's okay with Lucy, he thought before turning back to the gaping hole in the ground above which a petite middle-aged woman knelt brushing away at something below his line of sight.

Early that morning, he and the two scientists from 221B Baker Street arrived at 100 Centre Street to meet with Judge Paul Lussman and ask for an expanded search warrant. With Clarkson's expertise on the technical stuff, Guma presented the results of the GPR investigation.

Your Honor will find in the sheaf of papers I handed you a com-pilation of instances in which this supposedly "pseudo-science" has aided law enforcement in locating clandestine graves, Guma said. *While this is a relatively new use for geophysics equipment, the sci-ence and technology have been used for decades. The anecdotal evi-dence I've given you demonstrates that this is more than some carnival act.*

Lussman patiently sat through Geophysics 101 and asked several probing questions of his own that indicated that he understood the basics. When Guma was finished, the judge bowed his head and appeared to be thinking. *Very well,* he said, looking back up at both parties. *I'm going to grant the amplified warrant as the people re-quest, but on the condition that any disturbance of Mr. Stavros's backyard be limited to the excavation of this one "anomaly." Con-sistent with what the scientists have stated. Is that sufficient, Mr. Guma?*

Yes, Your Honor, thank you, Guma had replied with a nod. Then he and the 221B scientists rushed from the courthouse building.

By the time the team could be reassembled again at the Stavros home, it was midafternoon.

It now included a New York City public works department employee, who when introduced to Swanburg, a criminologist, and Clarkson, a geologist, declared himself *a jackhammer-ologist. There ain't a man in this city can handle a 'hammer better than yours truly, Norris A. Marshall the Fourth.*

Norris A. Marshall the Fourth? Guma asked.

Yeah, long line of workingmen, Marshall replied. *Just call me Norris.*

Marshall had done the prerequisite griping about "extra" work. But in reality, he couldn't have been happier to be part of a project right out of a movie instead of sweating over some city sidewalk. He'd arrived dressed for work with a sleeveless, dirty blue T-shirt that didn't quite cover a protruding beer belly of prodigious proportions, counterbalanced by a butt of equal tonnage. But his tan forearms were the size of fence posts, and there didn't appear to be an ounce of fat on them.

Once in the backyard, Clarkson led the way over to the patio table on which he laid out the printout from the GPR, as well as a to-scale map depicting the anomaly from above and its relations to Global Positioning Satellite reference points he'd established the previous evening. He now marked those points with chalk and then drew a rectangle eight feet by four feet on the concrete.

Emil Stavros had watched the proceedings from the doorway. When Clarkson stood up from his chalk work, the banker announced, *I'll be stepping out to run a few errands. Please clean up your mess from this wild goose chase before you leave.*

According to Detective Fairbrother, who'd kept watch from his sedan, Stavros then left the house, walking ahead of Amarie Stavros, who walked after her husband as fast as her high heels would allow shouting, *Where we going, Emil? And what are those men doing? I thought you said they were here to fix the hot tub. Why do they need a police officer to fix the hot tub? Does this have something to do with your trial? I'm confused.*

Just get in the car, Amarie, please, he said walking up to the limousine that had pulled up to the curb.

Fairbrother watched the limousine pull away and, giving it plenty of space, began to follow. As he tailed the limo, he relayed Amarie's complaints to Guma, who laughed, *I guess she's not the brightest bulb in the chandelier.*

Yeah, but what a set of gabonzas, and still looking pretty good for a forty-something Rockette, the detective said. *I'd say he didn't marry her for her ability to balance a checkbook. Let me know when it's time to pounce.*

You're a good man, Clarke, Guma said. *Wish I could be there when you do. Make the cuffs extra tight for me, will ya?*

You got it, Ray, Fairbrother answered and left with one of the younger plainclothes cops from the DAO's investigations unit.

Clarkson then called Marshall over and explained that he had to be careful not to damage any potential evidence beneath the concrete. *We just want to crack the concrete and lift it out piece by piece without disturbing anything underneath. Think you can do it?*

Marshall reacted like an old platoon sergeant who'd been asked by his commanding officer if he was capable of taking a machine-gun emplacement. He walked over to where he'd leaned his jackhammer against the hot tub and shouldered it like a rifle before returning. *I'll go through this slab so gently it wouldn't dent a baby's bottom,* he said.

Right along the chalk lines then, Norris, if you please, Swanburg said.

Marshall stood for a moment surveying the slab. He took a moment to flex the muscles in his arms and chest, then like a surgeon preparing for work, he pulled on his work gloves, taking the time to secure the leather over each finger. Dragging out the moment for as long as possible, aware that he had a rapt audience, he placed the business end of the jackhammer on one of the chalk lines. He glanced at Guma, who gave him a nod, and squeezed the trigger.

Cracking the six-inch thick slab took Norris Marshall the better part of two hours, during which he'd stopped on occasion to help the others lift the pieces out and pile them in a corner of the yard. When he was finished, there was a nearly perfect rectangle cut out of the patio.

Beneath the slab was an oblong depression in the soil. *Common occurrence,* Swanburg explained. *When soil is removed, it never goes back in quite as compact. It's a lot looser with air pockets and such. Over time, gravity and moisture will cause the soil to settle and compact, leaving a depression.*

Nice work, Norris, Clarkson said. *Not a dent in the dirt. You're a true artist.*

Thank you very much, Norris replied. He would have bowed but his belly prevented anything more than a slight inclination of his massive head forward. *We aims ta please. Anything else?*

Nope, Clarkson said. *I think we can take it from here.*

Maybe Jack can, but not you, said a tan, middle-aged woman being escorted through the house by a police officer. *Leave an exhumation to a geologist and next thing you know, they'll be in here with a stick of dynamite and a pickax.*

Nothing wrong with a boy who likes things that go boom. It's only natural. Clarkson pretended to pout, then broke into a smile. *Why, it's the ever-lovely Dr. Charlotte Gates. So glad you could make it, and with your usual impeccable timing.*

Just got into LaGuardia about an hour and a half ago, Gates replied, *and got over here as fast as I could. I kept seeing you trampling all over my "dig" with those gunboat boots of yours.*

Guma stepped forward to shake the hand of the woman he'd heard a lot about but hadn't yet met. Gates worked at the Human Identification Laboratory at the University of New Mexico in Albuquerque and hadn't been at the grilling in Denver. However, he knew that she was one of the top forensic anthropologists in the world.

Gates was a small woman but had an energy about her that made her seem larger. She walked with confidence, like a woman who'd spent twenty-some-odd years trekking about in the deserts of the Southwest, working for law enforcement agencies, as well as her "hobby" of helping Indian tribes locate and preserve ancient sites. She wasn't especially pretty, but the clarity of her opal green eyes against the mahogany of her face was striking.

She'd brought with her a bundle of white plastic pipes about an inch around and in various lengths. She looked at the hole in the cement, grunted *it will do,* and began to fit the pieces of pipe together to form a rectangle the same size as the hole, only broken into a half dozen squares. Each section was labeled and corresponded to similarly marked buckets she set on the patio.

Gates was assisted by Mackenzie Lorien, a young graduate student from the University of New Mexico who was studying forensic anthropology. When ready, the pair laid the pipe grid over the depression and then they got to work.

Working from either end, Gates and Lorien each chose a square and began carefully removing the soil and placing it in the appropriate bucket. As a bucket was filled, it was then carried by Clarkson over to a large, wood-framed screen set up on legs. The geologist would dump the bucket on the screen, then he and Swanburg would sift the contents *looking for anything out of the ordinary—things that don't belong in a bucket of dirt.*

If they found anything of interest, Swanburg noted it in a logbook, including which grid it had come from and at what depth it had been located. In the meantime, whoever filled the last bucket moved to a different square so that gradually the depression became a hole in the ground and then began to look like a grave.

The anthropologists used garden trowels to dig and even then were careful not to just plunge the blade into the soil, but scraped up each layer gently. When the others saw how the process worked, they started helping out by carrying the buckets so that the two men could sift and the women dig. Even Marshall, who had begged to be allowed to stay, made himself useful by hauling away the debris that piled up under the screen.

They'd been digging for two hours when Gates, who was working again near the top of the depression announced, *I just hit something solid. It felt like bone.* Lorien stopped what she was doing and crawled over to help her professor while the others gathered around, careful to stay outside the taped area around the grid so as to not contaminate the site.

Gates put her trowel aside and began digging with a spoon while using a small whisk broom to brush the dirt away. *She doesn't want to take a chance that she might leave a mark that could be open to some false interpretation,* Swanburg announced for the spectators, *such as a nick on the bone that would leave a question of whether it was caused by an anthropologist's trowel or a murder weapon.*

Spoonful by spoonful, brushstroke by brushstroke, Gates worked for another half hour before she stood up to stretch and allow the others to see what she'd been working on. A dome of yellow-white was emerging from the ground that even the laymen among them knew was the top of a skull. *Gentlemen,* she said quietly, *I believe we've found what we came here to find. I'd like to ask for a moment of silence to reflect on the fact that these are not just inanimate objects but the remains of someone who was once just like you and me . . . someone who loved and laughed and didn't deserve to be forgotten in an unmarked grave.*

Gates and Lorien worked steadily as centimeter by centimeter the earth gave up a skeleton, which was lying on its back, the head slightly tilted down with the chin on the chest. At a break in the work, Gates told those who were watching, *This is not absolute, mind you, but judging by what I can see now, these are the remains of a female, probably Caucasian and, looking at the teeth, between the ages of, oh, late twenties and forty.*

You can tell that just by looking at her? Guma asked. *Teresa was thirty-five.*

Gates nodded. *I can be more exact after I've got her back to the lab, but I can make reasonable guesses based on certain visible criteria. For instance, the muscles in the jaw are much larger and stronger on a male and thus cause more scarring on the bone where they attach. The area on the jaw of this person is not very pronounced and thus probably belongs to a female. Although we're not as far down in that area, I can see enough of the hip structure to also identify the remains as female. Later, I'll be able to tell you if she's borne children. The shape of the skull tells me that she was at least part Caucasian. And maybe you've seen a Western TV show where the cowboy looks into the horse's mouth to tell its age; the same thing, basically, can be done with humans.*

Guma looked at the skull and tried to picture the woman in the photograph hanging above his desk. *Teresa,* he said aloud.

Probably, Swanburg agreed but warned him, *Nothing's set in stone yet. This could be someone else . . . we've seen it before . . . or, more importantly, we're going to have to prove it's her to a jury and that isn't always easy.*

Guma nodded, but he also got out his cell phone and punched in a number. *Clarke, you still got an eye on our errand boy?* he asked.

Oh yeah, Detective Fairbrother responded. *Apparently, these errands required heading out of town on Interstate 87—in violation of his bond, I believe—and making good progress for . . . oh, I don't know . . . maybe Canada? Should I take him down now?*

No, not yet . . . not unless you have to in order to prevent him from crossing the border, Guma said. *Canada won't extradite him if he faces the death penalty. And I might just want that to be the case. But I'd also like the judge to see that he is a flight risk, so let him run a little longer.*

Not a problem, Fairbrother said. *We've got a "bird dog" GPS locator planted behind his bumper. We couldn't lose him if we tried, and the state patrol guys are following a few miles back. See you later, alligator.*

See you later, alligator? Aren't we supposed to say ten-four out or something like that? Guma retorted whimsically.

Oh, almost forgot, TV cop shows, and you overdosed on Broderick Crawford. Ten-four. Feel better now, Ray? Fairbrother said.

The team from 221B Baker Street continued to work meticulously and now every bucket seemed to contain items for the logbook. Buttons. Metal pieces from a bra. A spent shell casing from a .22-caliber gun.

It got dark, but the 221B Baker Street team had already prepared for that eventuality and set up the floodlights they'd asked Guma to arrange for, courtesy of NYPD special services. About that time, Karp had showed up with Murrow, who'd been disappointed when his boss told him *absolutely no press.* Then Murrow's cell phone went off, and Karp left in a rush.

A few minutes later, Guma was standing near the grave as Gates whisked away the dirt near the base of the skull. She pulled a flashlight from her pocket and peered closer.

"Whaddya got?" Guma asked.

Gates sat up. "An entry wound," she said. "Looks like she was shot behind her left ear."

"One wound or two?" Guma asked, recalling that Zachary heard two *pops.*

"I can only see one," she replied.

It wasn't entirely what he wanted to hear, but there was no need to wait any longer. Guma called Fairbrother again. "It's me. Collar the bastard."

Well north of Albany and darn close to the Canadian border, Fairbrother hung up the telephone and flipped the car's police radio to the state patrol frequency. "Okay, boys, time to bring this chicken back to the roost," he said.

"All right, finally," his young driver yelled. He pulled the red bubble light off the dash and, reaching out the window, set it on the roof of the car, and stomped on the gas pedal.

The readout on the bird dog locator, which appeared as a map on the laptop sitting between the two cops, let them know how far they were from the target. A mile, then a half mile . . . now they could see the red taillights of the limousine and didn't need the equipment. "There they are," Fairbrother said. He looked in the rearview mirror and saw the flashing red and blue lights of the state patrol cars approaching fast.

When the occupants of the limousine realized that they were being pursued, the car started to speed up. But one of the state patrol cars dashed past Fairbrother's car and jumped in front of the limo while the other state patrol car hemmed it in from the side with Fairbrother's car bringing up the rear. Then in unison, they slowed down, forcing the limousine to pull over to the shoulder of the road.

The state patrol officers and the two NYPD detectives were out
of the car with their guns drawn and spotlights on the limousine.

The chauffeur got out. "What? You guys got nothin' better to do
than harass Mr. Stavros," the chauffeur said.

"Shut your piehole and get your hands up," Fairbrother yelled.
"You thinking about trying to run?"

"No, hell no, you just surprised me. I was just speeding up because I thought you needed me to get out of the way."

"Yeah, sure," Fairbrother said. "And I'm Derek Jeter. Now, tell
your passengers to put their hands out of the car where we can see
them."

The driver leaned back toward the car and said something. He
nodded and stood back up. "Mr. Stavros says he's not getting out of
the car until his lawyer gets here."

The young cop walked up to the limousine and flung open the
door, then stepped back with his gun pointed at the interior. "Get
the hell out of the car, now!"

A woman screamed and a man bellowed with rage. Emil Stavros
climbed out of the limo with his hands up in the air and his face a
textbook example of apoplexy. "This is outrageous," he sputtered.
"I'll see that you never work in law enforcement again."

"On the ground," Fairbrother ordered.

"What? That's preposterous—"

The younger detective walked up to Stavros and still pointing
the gun at him, spun him around and shoved him up against the
car. He patted the man down and then pulled him away from the
car. "On the ground."

Stavros sprawled in the gravel on the shoulder of the road. "I'll
get you for this," he hissed.

"Yeah, yeah, tell it to the judge," Fairbrother said, pulling
Stavros's arms behind and cuffing him. "Now listen close . . . you
have the right to remain silent, anything you say can and will be
used against you in court, and you have the right to have an attorney present during questioning. If you cannot afford an attorney,
one will be provided. Are you with me so far?"

"Yes, yes, you son of a bitch," Stavros whimpered. "These handcuffs are killing me. What's the charge? I'm out on bond."

"You're under arrest for flight to avoid prosecution and for violating the terms of your bond. Now, do you want to stay quiet until we get back to the city and you can lawyer up? Or maybe you have something to say about the body in your backyard and save the taxpayers of New York City a lot of dough."

Stavros didn't answer.

"I'll take that as you wish to remain silent," Fairbrother said.

The woman in the car peeked out. "Officer?" she asked timidly.

Fairbrother turned to see Amarie Stavros. "Yes, ma'am?" he replied.

"Am I under arrest too?"

"No, ma'am. In fact, we can probably let the limo driver take you back to the city or wherever you want to go."

"Good," she said getting out of the car and scurrying toward a clump of bushes. "'Cause I gotta tinkle . . . if you know what I mean. Emil wouldn't let me stop at the rest area, and I'm about to wet my pants."

18

THE FIRST SIGN OF TROUBLE FOR THE YOUNG LOVERS HAD appeared as a growing cloud of dust beyond where the gravel road leading to the cabin disappeared over a hill five miles distant. Ned stood up in his stirrups to gain a few inches, the westering sun casting a bronze glow on his angular face.

He was such a picture of an Old West cowboy that Lucy felt like she should swoon or do something else ladylike. However, what she really wanted to do was to knock him out of his saddle and have at him on the prairie. Her conversion from vestal virgin to wanton woman shortly after meeting Ned, who'd also been a first-timer, had been sudden and complete. That was a year ago, she thought, and we're stronger than ever. I wonder what that means?

"Someone's in an awful big hurry," he said sounding miffed. "They better have a good reason to be haulin' ass like that on a private ranch road, stirring up the dust and risking hitting a steer. Guess we better wait here and see what's up."

Run! Lucy recognized the voice in her head as that of a martyred sixteenth-century saint named Teresa de Alhuma. Ever since childhood, St. Teresa had appeared to her in times of stress and danger with warnings and sage advice. The fact that she now no longer saw the saint but only sometimes heard her in her head, had convinced Lucy what she had suspected all along—and that was that the apparition was a figment of her imagination, a psychological response to traumatic events.

Run! The voice pleaded.

Why? Lucy asked herself. Ned doesn't seem to be alarmed. She'd come to trust the rock steadiness of her lover, who when times got iffy remained as unperturbed as the rugged land he loved.

He doesn't understand the danger, St. Teresa or her mind replied. And he won't until it's too late, unless you RUN!

"Ned," Lucy said aloud, "I'd rather not meet whoever this is."

Ned turned to her with a puzzled look. "Any particular reason, pardner?"

Lucy smiled. She loved it when he called her his pardner. It sounded so . . . together. Still, she didn't want to sound crazy, even though she'd told him about her *imaginary friend I've had since childhood . . . this sort of saint who got shot full of arrows in the fifteenth century.* She'd appreciated that he listened without rolling his eyes or laughing out loud. She realized that tolerance came from living in a land where the native people, like their friend John Jojola, believed that the spirit world was just as real and part of their lives as the rising and setting of the sun. And Ned had been raised on a ranch where his playmates had mostly been Indian children in whose homes he'd spent a great deal of time, learning as much of their culture as the secretive Taos Pueblo Indians would allow.

"Just a feeling." She shrugged.

Ned studied her with his steel-blue eyes. Life with Lucy was like riding a bucking bronc at the rodeo; one moment you're sitting on top of the animal, all nice and peaceful in the chute, then the gate flies open and all hell breaks loose. Ever since he'd asked the stranger visiting from New York City to dance with him at the Sagebrush Inn bar, there'd been one adventure after another. If it wasn't fighting what he thought of as the Morlocks, straight out of H. G.

Wells's *Time Machine,* one of the many books he'd read during the long winters he'd spent alone in the cabin, he was rescuing Lucy and her mother from a corrupt and murderous sheriff, or shooting it out with international terrorists. He'd once heard that love wasn't easy, but this was ridiculous.

Especially after Kane's escape, he took his role as Lucy's protector seriously. He'd regularly carried a Winchester 30/30 rifle for varmints and "shooting stuff" as he rode the range, caring for the cattle. But only since Kane's escape had he regularly carried his grandfather's Colt .45 Peacemaker, the gun he used in his quick-draw contests, either on his hip, under a coat in a shoulder holster, or at the very least in the glove box of his truck.

Ned looked back in the direction of the dust cloud. "They must have stopped," he said. "The dust is settling. Probably just some lost tourists. The Men in Black will get them turned around."

Lucy giggled. Men in Black. Secret Agent Men. Dumb and Dumber. They were all pet names the couple had come up with for the federal agents who had obviously been assigned to watch out for them. Whenever Lucy and Ned were staying at the cabin, the feds had regularly parked on the road about five miles up the road. Or, if the couple was staying in Lucy's room at the Sagebrush, they actually checked in and stayed at the same hotel, lurking around the bar and restaurant. They made no attempt to talk to Lucy or Ned, who returned the favor.

"The Secret Agent Men will get them even more lost," Lucy said. "They'll probably end up here—" Whatever she was going to say was interrupted by the distant crackling of gunfire. The shots were rapid and over quickly, but there was no denying what they were. Then in the distance, two vehicles appeared on the road heading for them at a high rate of speed as the rust-red dust again billowed into the shimmering New Mexican air.

Ned reached into his saddlebag and pulled out a pair of binoculars and trained them on the trucks. "I think we should go to the cabin," he said.

"Why?" Lucy asked, fighting the fear that was rising like bile in her throat.

"Those are pickups with a bunch of guys in the back hanging on for dear life. They're armed and something tells me they ain't out here huntin' coyotes. Now, no more jawin' about it. Ride!" He leaned over and gave her horse a slap on the rear to jump-start her.

One of the benefits of having a ranchhand for a boyfriend was that Lucy had become a passable horsewoman and now leaned forward, her legs back and grabbed as much of the horse's mane with her right hand as she could—a sure way, Ned had once told her, to stay in the saddle of a running horse. She knew Amos, the big bay gelding Ned had given her, would head for the barn behind the cabin, so she didn't worry about trying to guide him.

Behind her, Ned rode in perfect harmony with his horse, turning every once in a while to judge the distance between themselves and the trucks, and themselves and the cabin. It was a half mile to the cabin and the trucks had four to go on a bumpy, rutted road; he figured they'd make it if they hurried. But two hundred yards from the cabin, Lucy's horse planted a leg in a prairie dog hole and tumbled, throwing Lucy, who rolled like a denim-clad ball across the alkali flats.

Ned yanked his horse around to go back for her when the first bullet from the trucks kicked up a geyser of dirt ten yards from Lucy, who was already up and sprinting toward him.

"Keep running," he yelled as he thundered past her heading for the trucks, which were now only a half mile away. His first thought had been to pick Lucy up, but he didn't think there'd be time unless he could slow the pursuit down.

Placing the reins in his teeth, he pulled the Winchester from its scabbard and stood forward in the stirrups, his legs pumping like shock absorbers and his horse responding to the pressure of his knees. His upper body hardly moved as he aimed at the first truck, fired, and missed. The men in the trucks fired back, bullets sending up geysers of dirt all around him but generally inaccurate due to the bouncing of the trucks until something hummed by his head like a giant bee.

They were only separated by a hundred yards. He fired again and saw the windshield of the truck shatter. The truck swerved, then veered off the road until it flipped and rolled, throwing the men in the back. The second truck braked to a stop, the men piling out to run to their fallen comrades, some shooting in his direction but ineffectively.

Ned reined his horse in. The men from the second truck were shouting in a foreign language. Some helped pull the remaining passenger, who appeared shaken but otherwise all right, from the cab but made no attempt to retrieve the driver. Others went to check on the men thrown from the truck. One was standing, though he appeared to be favoring a leg; two others were apparently beyond help as no one stopped long to assist them; the fourth man was alive and trying to crawl. The others held a short conference around him, and then one pointed his rifle and shot the man.

Ned didn't need any more encouragement to spur his horse back to the cabin. He hoped that the attackers would lose heart and leave, but they were well armed and had come to do a job that wasn't finished.

Riding back toward the cabin, Ned came upon Lucy's horse, which he'd picked out especially for her because of its gentle gait and patience with an inexperienced rider. The horse was thrashing about, trying to get up on a broken leg. Cursing the men in the trucks and promising revenge for what he had to do, Ned drew his Colt and put the animal out of its misery.

Reaching the cabin, Ned dismounted and removed the saddle from his mare. He gave her a whack and sent her scampering off, kicking and bucking in delight at what she thought was a day off to spend on the prairie. He took another look at the men with the trucks, who confirmed his fears that they weren't finished as they had jumped into the remaining truck and were approaching the cabin, although at a more circumspect pace.

Ned started to reach for the handle of the cabin door when he was slammed against the wood. Realizing he'd been hit and that other bullets were striking the logs of the cabin near him, he flung himself through the door as Lucy opened it.

Lucy saw the blood on his denim shirt and screamed. "Ned!" she cried. "You've been shot."

Reaching down to feel his side and then looking at the hand now covered with blood, he winced. "I don't think it's bad."

Ned got to his feet and took a quick look out the window. The truck was stopped fifty yards away, partly behind a large cottonwood. The men were standing around talking and gesturing toward the cabin, which lay across a fairly flat expanse of dirt and rock without much cover, except the occasional knee-high bit of sagebrush. He broke out the glass of the window with the barrel of his rifle and fired off a quick shot. It missed but had the effect of sending the attackers scrambling for cover behind the tree and truck.

Ned ducked back as they returned fire with their automatic rifles. Soon the windows were shot out, but the stout ponderosa pine logs absorbed the bullets like rain drops into a sponge.

Lucy crawled over to where he leaned against the cabin wall. She insisted on lifting his shirt—to her relief, the bullet appeared to have struck him in the lower ribs and exited clean out the other side. He wasn't even bleeding as profusely as she would have thought, but she still felt she ought to bind the wound and get pressure on it.

"Hold on a sec," he said. He figured he was up against eight men and wanted to try to even the odds a bit and make them think twice about rushing the cabin.

John Jojola had told him about a trick he'd used when outnumbered in Vietnam. The trick, Jojola had explained, was to *expose yourself while taking a picture in your mind of where your adversary is before you duck back, drawing their fire. When they stop shooting, good chance whoever you picked out will still be standing there looking to see if he hit anything. Just keep that picture in your mind, then stand and shoot without thinking about it.*

Ned stood next to the window then jumped into view before jumping back as the bullets flew. As soon as the others stopped shooting, he turned with the rifle already on his shoulder and eye sighted down the barrel. He pulled the trigger when the scene outside matched the one in his head.

Lucy who'd peeked out of the other front window, yelled, "Got one! And the others are staying low."

Ned hoped he'd live long enough to tell Jojola that the trick worked. He risked a quick glimpse and saw his target trying to crawl back to the truck. There was a shot and the target lay still. "Guess these guys don't think too much of each other," Ned said.

"Or they don't want anybody left behind to answer questions," Lucy replied as she crawled back to where Ned was again resting against the wall. "Pretty soon, they'll figure out that they can surround us." She pulled her shirt off and started ripping it in strips to make a bandage.

"Who cares as long as I can look at those puppies," he said, his eyes on her breasts as they jiggled in her bra, a little red push-up number she'd bought at Victoria's Secret in Santa Fe, hoping to entice him into a little lovemaking under the stars later.

"Get serious, idiot," Lucy said. "I swear, one look at a tit and men lose their minds. You're bleeding and all you can think about is getting your grubby hands on my mammary glands. Now, let me get this wrapped around your ribs . . . and keep your mitts off the merchandise."

"Yes'm," Ned pouted, then his face got serious. "They don't seem to be in a hurry, so maybe they know we don't have a way of calling out. The good news is there's only one way to come at us, through the front door and the front windows; the bad news is that's the only way out of here, too, so they don't have to watch a back door. They might try to burn us out, but that could be tough with the tin roof and these old treated logs. So I 'spect they'll wait until dark before they try to rush us."

An accented voice taunted outside. "Hey, cowboy, why do you hide behind a woman's skirt. Come out and play!"

"Why don't you come in and get us, you son of a bitch!" Lucy yelled. "The cops are on the way."

A chorus of derisive hoots and laughter followed. "The woman speaks for him," the voice shouted. "There are no cops . . . except two dead ones on the road." Someone shouted in Arabic.

"Guess no one told them I speak the lingo," Lucy said.

"What did he say?" Ned asked.

"He was telling the others that I'm not to be harmed, if possible," she said.

"What?"

"Yeah, for some reason they'd prefer not to shoot me," Lucy said. "Probably so they can take me alive and do all sorts of unspeakable things to my body."

"You wish, you strumpet." Ned grinned.

"Watch this," Lucy said, jumping up suddenly and flinging the door open, standing in full view as Ned shouted for her to get down. Lucy stuck her tongue out at the men and calmly shut the door.

"What in the hell did you do that for?" Ned yelled at her.

"Calm down, cowboy," she smiled. "I was just testing my theory. They'd like to shoot you, but they want me alive, warm, and wiggling."

The man outside shouted again, this time in English. "You see, the girl is safe," he said. "We only want you, cowboy. Come out and she lives."

Ned thought for a moment, then got up painfully. He leaned the rifle against the wall and started to reach for the door, but Lucy pushed him back. "What in the hell do you think you're doing?" she yelled.

"Giving myself up," he said. "At least you'll be alive and maybe John or somebody will be able to rescue you. If we wait until dark, they might shoot you whether they mean to or not."

"Like hell you are," she said and burst into tears. "I don't want to live if you're not here with me."

"My choice, Lucy," he said and pushed her to the side. He opened the door and stepped out with his hands up. Two of the attackers stood up when they saw he was unarmed. Grinning, one of the men raised his rifle . . . and was blown two feet backward as the bullet from the 30/30 crashed into his chest.

The others ducked as Lucy fired wildly in their direction, which gave Ned the opportunity to jump back inside the cabin. "What in the hell did you do that for?" he yelled as a fusillade of bullets splintered the door, sending him sprawling to the ground.

"Keeping your ass alive," Lucy said grimly, wiping at the tears on her face. "I mean it, Ned, I'm in love with you, and I don't want to grow up to be an old lady unless you're my old man."

Ned blushed. "I love you, too, Lucy. I've had more happiness in the past year than I expected to have in my entire life."

"Then quit the brave cowboy shit. Besides, what do you think these assholes are keeping me alive for?" she said.

"Carnal desires?" he said, purposefully letting his eyes fall to her breasts again.

"Raise the gaze, buster," Lucy said. "I realize this body is to die for, but that's not why they want me." Her face grew serious. "If they capture me, Ned, it's to take me to Andrew Kane. I'd rather be dead ten times over than be in the clutches of that man."

Suddenly, the cruel, leering face of Felix Tighe, a homicidal wacko who tortured her until she was rescued by David Grale and company, flashed in her mind and she shuddered with fear and revulsion. Kane would be much worse. "I can't go through something like that again, do you understand, Ned?"

Ned Blanchet, high school dropout, steady ranchhand, a cowboy straight out of the pages of American mythology, looked at the woman he loved, realized what she was saying—*what she expects you to do, if it comes to that, pardner*—and nodded. "I understand," he answered.

Lucy smiled. "Oooh, you know when you do that Western man thing it gets me all hot and bothered."

Ned touched his index finger to his straw hat and threw an extra heaping of country on his twang, "Well, ma'am, you're jist gonna haf-ta rein in that lil' mare in heat and pay attention," he drawled. "I've been trying to conjure up a way to save our hides, and I might just have come up with something."

When darkness had fallen, the sliver of the moon still behind the mesa, Ned slipped from the cabin. Squirming forward like a snake, he dragged along a milk gallon jug full of kerosene he'd siphoned from the cabin's lanterns. Every couple of feet, he stopped to listen; he didn't hear anything, which made him think there wasn't much time left.

He doused the hay bales with kerosene and started to turn back for the cabin when he spotted the other man crawling toward the house. Ned had been obscured by the bales or the man might have seen him as he wormed his way past only fifteen feet away.

Drawing his gun, Ned picked up a pebble and tossed it so that it struck the man on his head. "Pssst," he whispered, not wanting to shoot a man in the back. Faster than he'd anticipated, the terrorist tried to turn and bring his rifle to bear. But the heavy slug from Ned's Colt knocked him into the next world.

Ned sprang up and bolted for the cabin. Fortunately for him, the other attackers were surprised by the sudden shooting and didn't know if it was their man or one of the defenders who pulled the trigger. Their aim was off by the time they figured it out and tried to stop Ned from reaching the door.

Ned burst through the door and rolled across the floor as bullets slammed into the wood. Jumping up, he yelled to Lucy, who was standing over by the window directly opposite the hay bales, "Wait until I give the word." He tossed her his Colt, grabbed his old rifle, and moved into position next to the window on the other side of the door. "Okay, now," he said.

Lucy stepped in front of the window and aimed the flare gun he'd given her earlier from his emergency gear at the spot she thought would be right for the hay bales. She pulled the trigger. The flare streaked across the yard and, skipping once off the ground, struck the bales, which went up with a *whoosh.*

The sudden explosion of light caught two of the terrorists halfway across the yard to the cabin. Blinded by the intensity of the fire, which caused their night-vision goggles to overload momentarily, they were sitting ducks for Ned, who shot them both before ducking back.

Ned looked out and saw two more terrorists running from the shadows toward the house, their guns winking red flashes as bullets crashed into the logs on the front of the cabin and came in through the window striking the back wall. Lucy dropped the flare gun and fired the Colt .45 over and over, attempting to hit anyone trying to make his way to the door.

Trying to jack another bullet into the chamber, the old rifle jammed. Ned looked up just as one of the terrorists started to throw something. The man stumbled but still managed to toss whatever he was throwing forward. Ned heard it bounce off the cabin just before it exploded with a deafening clap and a flash of brilliant light, knocking him against the back wall.

Stunned and half-blind from the blast, Ned looked over at Lucy who was frantically trying to reload the revolver, just as the door of the cabin was kicked in. One of the attackers stood there with his rifle aimed at Lucy. He held his fire and instead swung his gun over to Ned.

At the exact moment Ned expected a bullet to end his life, the man lurched forward a step, dropping his rifle. He looked down, as if in amazement, at the razor-tipped arrowhead and six inches of shaft that protruded from his chest. Dropping to his knees, the man murmured, *"Allah akbar. Allah akbar. Allah—"* and collapsed.

Ned and Lucy looked at the dead man, not comprehending. But they were grinning a moment later when they heard a familiar voice from just outside the cabin door. "Ned, Lucy . . . don't shoot. It's John Jojola."

"Yahoo!" Ned shouted. "It's the cavalry!"

"Don't be insulting," Jojola answered stepping into the cabin. "It's the Indians who are saving your pale butt."

"One of them is a Vietcong Indian," Tran added, slipping in behind him.

"Okay, yahoo, it's the Indians and Vietcong," Ned laughed.

"If you guys are finished talking nonsense, I'd like to get out of here," Lucy said. "It's been a really long day."

Jojola turned on his flashlight, the beam of which caught Lucy standing half-naked in her bra.

Ned whistled. "Yeehaw! Now, that's what I call a nice pair of hooters."

"Hooters?" Lucy hissed. "Ned Blanchet, you're a dead man."

The room went dark again as Jojola turned off the flashlight. The door opened and a dark figure ran out of the cabin. "Not if you can't catch me," Ned shouted over his shoulder.

"Here's my jacket," Jojola said, holding it out in the direction he'd last seen Lucy.

Lucy's angry face loomed out of the dark and into the partial light from the moon and stars outside. She glared at Jojola. "Men," she muttered, then left the cabin yelling, "Ned, you cowardly piece of shit, you get your ass back here so I can kick it."

Over by the cottonwood tree a "coyote" yipped with glee. Then laughed. Then Ned howled in pain. "Damn, getting shot hurts."

19

JOHN JOJOLA'S DEAD . . . AND THEY TRIED TO KILL MY KIDS. Karp stood near the witness stand, waiting for the hearing to start, anxious for it to start and take his mind off the news from New Mexico. It was three days later, but the anger still boiled up inside his gut until he had to force himself to look about the courtroom just to keep from hitting something.

Fortunately, everyone else was also occupied. Guma was behind the prosecution table but with his back turned to Karp as he leaned over the bar in earnest conversation with Detective Fairbrother.

Over at the defense table, Emil Stavros sat surrounded by his defense team, trying to look involved though his three main attorneys hardly acknowledged his existence while they conferred behind him. Stavros was wearing a bright orange jail jumpsuit, having been locked up in the Tombs ever since violating the conditions of his bond. The judge had agreed with Guma's argument that the little jaunt to upstate New York proved he was a flight risk. Every once in a while, one attorney or another would lift his head and peer over at Karp or Guma, like a quarterback surveying the opposing defense from the huddle, then go back to talking strategy.

Or lunch plans, Karp thought, surveying the defense lawyers. Someplace they could be seen by the media, like the Tribeca Grill. They'd protest that they weren't supposed to comment, *there's a gag order you know, however, you are aware that . . .*

Three days since the attack in New Mexico and Karp was still fuming. Marlene had gone to Taos to check on her daughter and Ned, and more tragically, to attend the memorial service for John Jojola. According to the *Taos News,* the police chief of the Taos Pueblo had been killed by suspected Islamic terrorists. Although there had been very little official information provided by the U.S. Department of Homeland Security's man on the scene, assistant director Jon Ellis, the aggressive little weekly newspaper speculated that the assassination of Jojola had something to do with his having played a role in stopping a terrorist plot in New York City on New Year's Eve. *"It's possible that this was a revenge thing,"* the newspaper quoted a *source close to the investigation.*

Apparently, Jojola, a decorated Vietnam veteran, put up quite a fight as the entire gang of a dozen terrorists also died in the gun battle that took place at the old Josh Steers homesteader cabin, the newspaper stated.

According to Taos County Sheriff Chris Ferguson, Jojola is credited with saving the lives of Taos residents Ned Blanchet, who he said also fought bravely and was wounded in the fight, and Lucy Karp, a newcomer to Taos from New York City where her father is the district attorney. Jojola was apparently killed by one of the terrorists, who had been wounded in the fight . . .

God, you'd think I would be used to it by now, Karp steamed silently as the judge's clerk entered the courtroom, an indication that the judge was on his way and it was time to amble over to the prosecution table. In fact, you'd think I'd have gotten past telling myself that I should be used to it by now.

He wondered what Marlene was up to and could only hope it didn't involve more guns. She'd called after arriving in New Mexico and told him that Lucy was fine and that Ned, while grazed by a bullet and knocked around a bit, would heal completely, too.

However, she was mourning the loss of Jojola, who apparently died just when it appeared that the fight was over. One of the terrorists who'd survived had apparently hidden a weapon and killed Jojola.

The entire reservation is locked down; no one but tribal members are allowed on the property. However, there's going to be a memorial service tomorrow for everyone else, Marlene had said. *He had a lot of friends in this area and elsewhere, and the tribal council wanted to give them a chance to get back here for the memorial service.*

Marlene's voice caught. Karp thought she might be crying and kicked himself for not going with her. He'd liked Jojola a great deal from the moment they'd met—a man at peace with himself and his view of the world. *I wish I could be there,* Karp said. *But this hearing—*

John would understand, Marlene said. *He'd tell you he's not here anymore anyway, at least not physically. I'm here to pay my respects out of consideration to his people. Maybe if I'm lucky, his spirit will find me.*

Karp hung up the telephone not sure what he thought of Marlene's faith in Jojola's spirit-filled world and Lucy's Catholic mysticism. Then again, *I suppose they're no different than Judaism and the concepts his boys were studying for their bar mitzvah. Spirits. A God risen from the dead. Or a God who parts seas and hands down laws written in stone tablets. It all takes faith,* he thought. *You believe what you believe.*

What he believed right now was that Kane was trying to make good on his threat to kill the people he loved, and it had shook him. Most of Karp's adult life he'd been exposed to the most heinous side of human nature, of which the slaughter of the children and officers during Kane's escape was as bad as it got. But there was still a big difference when the intended victims were your flesh and blood, and if Kane had walked into the courtroom at that moment,

Karp would have gladly wrapped his hands around his neck and squeezed.

Karp was still indulging his homicidal fantasy of watching Kane's face turn blue when the bailiff entered the court, followed by the judge, and cried out the traditional, "Oyez. Oyez. The Honorable Judge Paul Hans Lussman III."

As they waited for the judge to be seated, Karp, who was standing next to Guma at the prosecution table, glanced back to where Jack Swanburg and Charlotte Gates were sitting, waiting to be called to the stand. Gates smiled at him and Swanburg added a nod; they looked relaxed and slightly bored. During witness preparation in Karp's office the night before, Swanburg and Gates had assured him that their scientific expertise was convincingly persuasive.

Between us, we've done a couple thousand of these, Swanburg said when they met in his office before walking to the courtroom. *We've found that keeping an even keel—simply testifying about the science without appearing to favor one side over the other—tends to go over well with juries and jurists.*

After the body was exhumed, Bryce Anderson, Stavros's lead lawyer, had filed a motion to controvert the search warrant and to prevent the prosecution from entering the remains found in the Stavros backyard as evidence. The defense's main contention was not only deficient probable cause to justify the issuance of the warrant, but there was insufficient proof that the body was that of Teresa Stavros. So the judge had granted the defense request for an evidentiary hearing.

"Good morning, Your Honor," Anderson said. "I'll leave alone the question of the district attorney's motives for suddenly pursuing this case just five months before the general election. However, this case is awash in irregularities, including the DAO pursuing an indictment for murder when there was no proof that Mrs. Stavros is even deceased. Then they go all the way to Colorado to 'find' some group that claims to locate bodies with divining rods, or some such thing, and now claim that they 'know' whose bones are buried in the backyard at the Stavros residence. The defense contends that the state should have to at least prove that the remains are truly those of Teresa Aiello Stavros. If they are not prepared to do that, or simply cannot do that, then we are asking the court to suppress the bare bones, pun intended," he said smirking while looking back at the press, "upon which this case rests. And I might add, Your Honor, to order the District Attorney's Office to vacate the indictment and let Mr. Stavros go on with his life, which first and foremost will be to unseat the current district attorney of New York."

The judge looked at the prosecution team. "Good morning, Mr. Karp and Mr. Guma," he said. "Which of you will be speaking on behalf of the people?"

"Mr. Guma," Karp replied quickly. "He is lead counsel in this case. I'm here as Sancho to his Don Quixote."

The courtroom tittered and even the defense lawyers allowed themselves to smile. "I see you haven't managed to keep him from tilting at windmills," Anderson joked, half turning in his seat to see if the members of the media were taking notes that might state something about his commanding presence in the courtroom. He'd spent a lot of time at the gym to keep his body toned and more than a few bucks with a "cosmetic surgeon" to make sure the face remained taut and youthful, and he looked like he got dressed at the dry cleaner's. He checked the effect by winking at a pretty blond television reporter and was rewarded with a blush. Have to buy her a drink later, he thought absently. Wonder what she'd do for "an exclusive."

"Indeed," said the judge. "Very well, Mr. Quixote-slash-Guma, are you ready to proceed with your evidence?"

"I am, Your Honor," Guma replied as he rose from his seat. "But first I wanted to note something about Mr. Anderson's innuendo stated for the benefit of the press specifically that the District Attorney's Office chose to pursue this case prior to the election. Your Honor will recall that it was the defense that insisted on their client's right to a speedy trial, and in fact chose the date in September as 'most convenient' for their busy schedules. As Mr. Anderson, this court, and anyone somewhat cognizant of the judicial system is aware, he could have delayed this trial until after the election. Indeed, we were prepared for that likelihood. In that case, only Mr. Karp's political opponent would have benefited from the timing of this indictment as an opportunity to attack Mr. Karp through the only too willing members of the media—long before a jury renders a verdict that we believe will justify the timing as, in fact, long overdue."

"Thank you for that aside, Mr. Guma," the judge said sardonically. "But your boss is a big boy and plenty capable of taking care of himself. Please address the legal issues in front of this court today."

"I was just getting there, Your Honor," Guma replied. "My first response to counsel's diatribe is to note that this is a system based in part on the law of common sense. Every juror is told that when deliberating, they are free to use their experience, their common sense—that when trying to ascertain what is meant by reasonable doubt, they are to use the same standards as they would when making an important decision in their everyday lives . . . their common sense. Mrs. Teresa Aiello Stavros, a devoted, thirty-five-year-old mother, disappeared fourteen years ago, fifteen in August. Since that time, there has been no evidence—not a clear photograph, not a conversation with a credible witness, not a handwritten letter. And in fact, as the defendant well knows, based upon all the facts contained in the affidavit that supported the issuance of the search warrant, at trial the people plan to call a handwriting expert who will testify that the signatures, allegedly of the deceased Mrs. Stavros, that appear on the so-called credit card and bank withdrawal slips—evidence the defense maintains is proof that she was still alive as of nine or ten years ago—were in fact forged. Moreover, we have a witness who says he saw Emil Stavros strangle his wife. So if the body, discovered after having served a legally justified search warrant issued by this court, isn't that of Teresa Stavros, whose would it be?"

"Exactly," Anderson replied, not waiting his turn as he shot to his feet. "Who? But that isn't for my client to determine, or this court.

It's the state's burden to prove that the body 'found' in the back-yard is that of Teresa Stavros. And I've seen nothing that conclu-sively says it is. How does the state plan to prove beyond a reasonable doubt that my client killed his wife if they can't even prove that the remains they plan to parade in front of the jury be-longed to her? Or that she's even dead? From what I understand, essentially what they found was a skeleton—no fingerprints or flu-ids to test DNA."

"If I might continue, Your Honor," Guma said testily. "Even if this body turned out to belong to Amelia Earhart, we'd still go for-ward with our case. The evidence presented to the grand jury that handed down the indictment in this case was more than sufficient to permit a trial jury to convict the defendant as charged."

"Grand juries don't hear the other side of the story—"

Guma ignored Anderson's remark. "The means that led to the discovery of the remains at the Stavros residence, as well as the sci-entifically valid measures we've taken to positively identify the re-mains, will be presented at trial for the jury to weigh."

Anderson rapped his knuckles on the defense table. "The state is well aware of the emotional impact that presenting a body, any body, would have on jurors," he said. "By the time Your Honor grows tired of the testimony by their so-called experts, it will be too late. The jury will have heard that the bones belonged to Teresa Stavros, and no matter what I say, or what instructions you may give them regarding the burden being on the prosecution to prove it beyond a reasonable doubt, they will believe what Mr. Guma here has told them. It's just human nature to want to solve a mys-tery and bring some closure for Zachary Stavros. But my client has a right—"

"—and so did Teresa Stavros," Guma shot back.

"Your Honor, Mr. Guma is being disingenuous," Anderson said. "Without the body, they know and I know that what they have left is a foray into carnival sideshow hypnotism and a bunch of circum-stantial evidence that doesn't prove a damn thing. The truth of the matter, one that the NYPD reached years ago, is that this woman walked out on her family, drained her accounts to get even with a cheating hubby, and is probably dancing the salsa with some hot young Latin lover as we speak."

"Your Honor, what this hearing proves is that my counterpart is either an idiot or assumes that we're idiots to believe that these remains belonged to anyone other than Teresa Stavros," Guma said hotly, his face flushing. "However, we recognize that the burden of proof in this matter rests with the prosecution. But we contend that the weighing is rightfully something for the jury to undertake."

"The jury cannot be expected to weigh fairly," Anderson retorted just as angrily, "when faced with this quasi-scientific jargon and guesswork meant to confuse any layperson—at least that's my motion from the papers I've been given so far, which I might add are very limited. I can't even prepare my own expert witnesses because God only knows what the prosecution's witnesses will claim."

The judge held up his hand. "Okay, gentlemen, you've both had your say. I am going to wait to render my decision until after I've heard from two of the prosecution's experts today. In the meantime, I have a small matter to take up in my chambers, and we'll recess for thirty minutes."

Karp remained standing after the judge left, but Guma plopped down in his seat where he doodled manically on a yellow legal pad. "You okay?" Karp asked.

"Yeah, I just thought that the 'young lover' remark was below the belt," Guma said. "She should have left that bastard Emil; he was the one fucking around on her. But she couldn't because she would have lost custody of Zachary. It just pisses me off that some slime-ball attorney can disparage a victim's character without any proof whatsoever, but say one unkind remark about their client and they want a mistrial."

Karp patted his friend on the shoulder. "Hey, if I didn't know you better, I'd say you're getting personally involved with this case." He meant the remark in jest to lighten the mood, but immediately regretted it when he saw Guma's eyes smolder and jaw tighten.

"I know what it takes to do my job," Guma replied, balling up the sheet from his legal pad and tossing it toward the waste can near the witness stand and missing. "Damn. I'm just trying to see a little justice done here."

"I know you are," Karp apologized, walking over to pick up the paper and toss it in the can. "I was just trying to take the edge off before you cross the aisle and beat that smarmy bastard to a pulp. . . . How you feeling these days?"

"What is this?" Guma asked but only half as irritably. "I look like I'm going to keel over? Is the Grim Reaper standing behind me?" His eyes grew big with mock fear as he quickly looked over both of his shoulders.

Karp laughed, but they both knew that the only reason he was sitting next to Guma at the prosecution table was as an insurance policy. They hadn't announced that Karp would be second chair and let the media find out on their own at a run-of-the-mill motions hearing.

As expected, Rachman had blown a fuse. *What is this?* she'd demanded to the press. *A Joseph McCarthy witch hunt? Oppose me and we'll pull out all the stops to see that your name is besmirched, your reputation destroyed, and your freedom imperiled.*

Meanwhile, Stavros's lawyers went to court demanding that the judge impose a gag order to keep Karp and his team from *using this bit of grandstanding for political gain.* Of course, they'd immediately ignored the gag order themselves. In fact, Stavros soon had a dream team of celebrity lawyers, all of them well-known TV talking heads, each of whom held his own press conference where they announced, among other things, that they'd sliced their fees in order to work on a case that was so obviously a miscarriage of justice.

"I'm okay," Guma reassured Karp as Judge Lussman returned to the courtroom and asked him to call his witness in opposition to defense's motion.

Addressing the judge, Karp said, "Your Honor, for purposes of a complete record, the people suggest that the court consider the testimony of our experts as part of a Daubert hearing. As the court is well aware, a Daubert hearing tests the scientific reliability and acceptability of the evidence in question. Also, Your Honor, we will ask for a similar Daubert hearing with respect to the repressed memory testimony that we intend to present to the jury."

The way they'd laid out the workload of the trial, Guma was to give the opening statement, while Karp would sum up the people's case for the jury. The reason was that the rigors of the trial might be too draining on Guma, and he might not have the energy for a lengthy closing argument on the final day. As far as the rest of it, Guma was going to handle the testimony of Zachary Stavros, and they would both take turns with the expert witnesses.

Guma then called Swanburg to the stand. After establishing Swanburg's credentials qualifying him as an expert, Guma proceeded. "Dr. Swanburg, were you able to identify the remains through standard scientific means, such as those named by defense counsel?"

Swanburg shook his head. "No, the remains had skeletonized; there was no flesh on the hands for fingerprints. Nor was it possible to identify the deceased through dental records."

"And why is that?" Guma asked.

"Well, it seems that some ten years ago, the office of Teresa Stavros's dentist was burglarized and many files, including hers, disappeared," Swanburg replied.

"Objection," Anderson said. "*If* Your Honor allows any of this testimony about the remains, I insist that the witness be prohibited from testifying about why Mrs. Stavros's files are missing. They're obviously trying to imply that those records were removed as part of a coverup. There's no evidence that this burglary had anything to do with her files in particular, or anybody else for that matter."

"It's a simple fact, Your Honor," Guma said.

"Overruled," the judge said. "Mr. Anderson, you may make all the appropriate motions *in limine* prior to trial. As far as we are concerned at this hearing, the witness simply stated that a burglary occurred and files were missing, among which were Mrs. Stavros's.

For the record, Mr. Guma, you can satisfy this point concerning the burglary by producing a police report."

Guma nodded and scribbled a note on his yellow legal pad.

"Very well, please proceed," the judge directed.

"Yes, Your Honor," Guma replied and turned back to Swanburg. "What about DNA comparison?"

Swanburg shook his head. "We weren't able to come up with anything there either," he said. "Again we were hampered by the deterioration of the remains due to weather, insect activity, and the normal processes. We did attempt to compare hair found in the site with that of Mrs. Stavros's only known blood relative, her son, Zachary, but all we can state is that they are 'scientifically similar,' but the same can be said with too large a percentage of the population to say 'to a scientific certainty,' which is the forensic standard. We also tried to extract marrow left in the bones, which can be used for blood typing as well as DNA testing, but again we were stymied by decomposition. We even attempted to extract pulp from one of her molars for the same purpose, but with the same result."

Guma turned to his next question. "Dr. Swanburg, can you tell the court how long, within a time frame, the remains had been in the grave."

"Objection," Anderson called out. "Here is another point, Your Honor, at which the prosecution witness will be testifying about guesswork that has not been accepted as standard in the scientific community. In fact, any two scientists could debate these suppositions indefinitely without reaching an answer that satisfies the threshold of reasonable degree of scientific certainty."

"Well, that's what we're doing here, Mr. Anderson," the judge said. "I'm listening to this gentleman, and any other witnesses, to determine whether it will be allowed into evidence at trial. Now, I'd like to hear what Dr. Swanburg has to say. I'll rule on it then." He looked at Swanburg. "You may answer the question."

"I can't give you an exact day, but we have ways of getting pretty close," Swanburg said. "For instance, we know that the body was buried for a number of years before cement was poured over the gravesite. We know this because when we exhumed the remains, my colleague in the back of the courtroom, Dr. Charlotte Gates, noted plant roots that had grown through the rib area. As it turns out, the roots were from a rosebush; however, the rosebushes formerly above the site had been removed when the cement was poured, at which point the roots stopped growing and died."

Swanburg turned in the witness seat and looked over at the judge. "Are you with me still?"

Amused, the judge nodded. "So far, Dr. Swanburg, even if my wife accuses me of doddering senility."

"Know what you mean, Your Honor," Swanburg chuckled. "Anyway, we know from the growth rings of the rose roots—roots have rings just like a tree that indicate age—that they had pierced the wall of the grave and grew into the corpse for at least two years before the plant was removed. We also know that the cement for the patio was poured in 1994, according to records from Manhattan Concrete, Inc. So that would mean that the roots had been growing in the grave since at least 1992. And, of course, after the grave was dug, it would have taken one to three growing seasons—depending if the plant had been disturbed by the digging—to reach the wall of the grave. So that pushes our timetable back to the grave having been dug sometime between 1989 and 1992."

Guma didn't have much more for Swanburg and turned him over to Anderson. "Let's start with the last issue first," the attorney said. "Do you know within a scientific certainty that the roots in the grave are the roots of a plant removed when the cement was poured?"

"It's the scenario that makes the most sense."

"Is that a yes or no?"

"That would be a 'no,' not absolutely certain."

"Then the roots in that grave could actually be much older than a plant killed by the pouring of cement in 1994?"

"Yes, I suppose."

"In fact, the grave could have been dug, and the victim interred at some point in the distant past before Mr. Stavros even purchased the home. Those roots could have 'pierced the grave,' as you put it, years before Mrs. Stavros left her home."

"I suppose it is possible but we—"

"Is 'I suppose,' a 'yes,' Dr. Swanburg?"

"Yes, a qualified yes, but a yes."

"More like a qualified guess, Dr. Swanburg."

Swanburg looked somewhat bemused but let the aside go without comment.

"Let's move on, Dr. Swanburg," Anderson said. "Essentially, what you told Mr. Guma is that the standard accepted methods of human identification were not available to you."

"Well, no, that's not what I said at all," Swanburg replied. "I testified that two methods—granted, the most common known to laypersons such as you—were not available to us. And I'll concede that these other methods are less exact, but I believe that my colleague will be testifying that these other methods have been used in courts throughout the world for years now."

When Swanburg stepped down, Karp called Charlotte Gates to the stand. After the exchange of pleasantries and establishing her expertise, he began by asking her for a short version of the excavation process. When she finished, he noted Swanburg's testimony regarding the lack of fingerprint or DNA evidence. "Does that mean we have no other scientific means of identifying these remains?"

"Not at all," Gates replied. "Those are just two."

"Would you care to elaborate?"

"Sure. For one thing, even though we don't have dental records, the deceased's teeth can still give us clues to her identity."

"How so?"

"Well, through a subspecialty of dentistry called forensic odontology, something I've studied in my practice as a forensic anthropologist. There are several reasons why the dentition is valuable for human identification. Tooth enamel is the hardest substance in the human body, which makes teeth capable of surviving conditions under which other human tissues, including bone, deteriorate. Dental work such as fillings, crowns, bridges, and root canal therapy are individually customized for each patient; plus, individuals lose or damage teeth, as well as the bone that holds them. It is these unique qualities that enable forensic odontologists to compare dental restoration work, through X-rays or even anecdotal evidence, with the remains to identify, or exclude, a possible missing individual with a very high level of probability. However, as you've heard in this case, there are no dental records for comparison."

"And so?"

"And so we move on to a less exact but nevertheless valid means to 'narrow the field,' so to speak," Dr. Gates said. "We all know that we lose our so-called baby teeth at certain points in our life—give or take a year or two. But actually, we can make determinations as to age well into adulthood because dental development is tightly controlled and protected against disturbances through a process known as canalization. The disadvantage of age estimates, based on dental development, is that most adults have completed the process by age twenty-five."

"So from what you just said," Karp asked, breaking up the sequence to make it more understandable, "what can we say about the remains found in the defendant's backyard?"

"We can say the deceased was at least twenty-five years old," Gates replied.

"Can you be any more exact?" Karp said.

"To a lesser but still scientifically valid degree I can," Gates said. "As strong as they are, our teeth don't last forever. We wear them down by eating hard foods and grinding them against each other. We also tend to lose some of the bone around the roots as we grow older, and we experience more gum diseases, some of which can be seen in the bone of the jaw as well as the teeth themselves."

"Well, do all people wear out their teeth at the same rate?" Karp asked.

Gates shook her head. "No, and as a matter of fact that can vary greatly according to culture, socioeconomic status—i.e., such as the availability and frequency of dentist visits—and some physical cause, such as a tense person who grinds their teeth a lot. However, a fairly large body of evidence has been gathered comparing thousands of people—both living and deceased—in any one age, gender, social class, and area. The end result is the ability to say that the average person in a certain category can be expected to demonstrate particular aspects in regard to their dentition. For instance, the teeth of the average wealthy white male in the United States will look different at age fifty, than the teeth of the average impoverished Asian, fifty-year-old female in Cambodia."

"So using this comparison system, can you estimate the age of the remains in question?" Karp asked.

"Yes, these comparison studies have been fed into computers, which I've accessed," Gates replied. "The remains fall into the category of adult, Caucasian females of upper-middle to wealthy economic status with an age range of between thirty and forty-two years."

"And do you recall the age of Teresa Stavros when she disappeared?"

"I've been told that she was thirty-five years old."

"That's correct," Karp nodded. "Is there anything else that might indicate the age of the victim in this case?"

"Objection," Anderson said. "There's no foundation that the remains are those of a crime victim."

"I see," Karp said. "Then perhaps we should call the Smithsonian Institution to let them know that we may have discovered the ancient burial grounds of Pocahontas—she having died of natural causes."

Anderson chuckled and shook his head as if greatly amused while pouring himself a drink of water. The rest of the courtroom laughed as well.

"Let me rephrase that," Karp said, smiling. "Is there anything else you can tell us about the age of the person whose remains just happened to wind up in the backyard of Emil Stavros?"

"Yes," Gates nodded. "When we're young our bones are very flexible because they have not hardened. This process begins at the growth places on either end of the bone and works its way toward the center until they meet and we have the stronger but more brittle bones of an adult. Bones can tell a story if you know how to read them. For instance, in adulthood we can see where someone broke his leg as a child. But there are more subtle clues as well, such as the onset of age-related arthritis. Or, in the case of women especially, who have difficulty maintaining bone density as they age due to a lack of calcium, the onset of osteoporosis."

"And how does that help you determine age?" Karp asked.

"In a way that is similar to the comparison studies of teeth," Gates replied. "By comparing the bones of thousands of females whose age at death was known, we can say with a strong degree of scientific certainty that the remains we exhumed belonged to a woman in her midthirties to early forties."

Karp took a sip of water from a cup on the prosecution table and looked at Emil Stavros, who quickly let his attention be drawn to his notepad. "Now, Dr. Gates, a moment ago you said that the remains belonged to a woman. Was it possible to establish the gender by looking at the bones?"

"Yes, there are several means," Gates said. "The easiest was looking at the bones of the hips. I'm sure we're all fairly aware that a woman's hips are anatomically different from a man's, in large part so that a woman can give birth."

"Speaking of hips, Dr. Gates," Karp said, "is there something more you can tell from the hip bones found in the grave?"

"Yes, she'd given birth to one, perhaps, two children," Gates said. "Babies do not pass through the birth canal easily, and the pressures of childbirth cause the bones to move and scar."

"So in summation, what can you tell us to a reasonable degree of scientific certainty about the remains?"

"That they belonged to a woman who gave birth to at least one child and was between the ages of thirty and, let's say, forty-five tops when she died."

Karp studied his notes. He actually knew exactly where he was going next but wanted to let Gates's testimony sink in before adding more. "Let's move, on," he said at last turning on a slide projector as Guma stood to turn down the lights in the courtroom. The photograph of a skull appeared on the screen set up in front of the jury box.

"Your Honor, for the purposes of this hearing, may we have these slide photographs marked sequentially starting with people's exhibit one," Karp said.

Anderson glanced up at the slide and went back to scribbling notes on his legal pad. "No objection."

Karp pointed to the screen. "Dr. Gates, can you tell us what this is a photograph of?"

"It's a photograph of the skull we removed from the grave in this case."

"What can you tell us about it?"

"Well, firstly, all races have physical characteristics that differentiate them from another race," she said. "We can see this walking down the sidewalk outside of this building. People of one race may have differences in the shape of their skulls that determine their appearance. For instance, you have what I would call Slavic facial characteristics, Mr. Karp—"

"Very good," he said, surprised as this had not come up before, "my ancestors came from Poland. So can you make a similar statement regarding this skull?"

"Yes, well, in this particular case, the shape of the skull identifies its owner as a Caucasian woman."

Karp pressed a button and another slide appeared—this one showing the skull from the left side. Using a light pointer, he noted a small dark circle behind the ear hole. "Can you tell us what this is?"

Gates nodded. "It's an entry wound."

"Caused by?"

"A bullet."

"How do you know?"

"After we disinterred the remains, I carefully placed the skull in an evidence bag," she said. "I then took it to the Office of the New York Medical Examiner, who was gracious enough to allow me to work there, where I placed it in hot water to remove dirt as well as organic matter, such as any remaining skin or organs . . . not that there was much. After the clean skull was removed, the residue in the bottom of the pot was sifted through a fine mesh screen. There was no exit wound from the skull, and I was able to find bullet shards still inside; several pieces, as a matter of fact, that under the microscope turned out to be that of a .22-caliber bullet."

Karp turned to another slide. This one showed the skull from the front, next to a photograph of Teresa Stavros. "Is there any way to match this skull to this woman?" he asked.

"Yes, we call it superimposition," Gates said. She explained that more than one hundred physical points of the skull had been mapped out onto a graph.

"When we compare one person's face to another, we see things like high cheeks, or a long chin, or a wide forehead, or note that the distance between the eyes is greater or smaller than a person standing next to them. These characteristics are caused by the structure of the bones beneath the skin. So that when I lay the graph of the skull over a photograph . . ."

Karp switched to another slide that showed the graph from the skull on top of the photograph of Teresa Stavros.

". . . I compare the points from the graph to see if they match similar points on the photograph. And as you can see here, this is a very good match—ninety-two percent of the graph points match those of the photograph, plus or minus four percent."

"Is this method infallible?" Karp asked.

"Hey, that was my question," Anderson said and looked back to see if the blond reporter was laughing. But she, as well as the other courtroom observers, was too fascinated by the testimony to pay attention to him.

"You may ask it again in a minute," Karp said. "Doctor?"

"No," Gates conceded. "Photographs are not exact. A person may seem to have certain characteristics that may not be as pronounced in another photograph. Also, people gain or lose weight, which can disguise certain physical attributes. For that reason, superimposition is better at ruling someone out than saying with certainty that a skull matches exactly one person. We accept that super-imposition has a ten to fifteen percent margin of error."

"Which is like telling us that by using superimposition you are from eighty-five percent to ninety percent sure that this skull belonged to Teresa Stavros?"

"That's probably fair," Gates replied. "And when you add up the other things we know about the remains—age, gender, child-birth—I think I can state with a high degree of scientific certainty that the remains we exhumed in the defendant's yard belonged to Teresa Stavros."

Karp looked at the judge and back at the defense table. The celebrity attorneys were all making notes, then shaking their heads and whispering behind smirks, as if they'd seen through a parlor magician's trick. "No further questions," he said.

"Mr. Anderson?"

The defense attorney pursed his lips and looked up at the ceiling, turning his head so that the blond reporter could see his "good side." He stood up suddenly and walked partway across the courtroom toward the witness stand rubbing his chin. "Just one question, Your Honor," he said, looking up at the witness. "Dr. Gates, could these be the remains of someone other than Teresa Stavros?"

Gates shrugged. "Yes, I think it's highly unlikely, but—"

"Thank you," he said, cutting her off. "No further questions."

The courtroom was quiet as Anderson took his seat. Judge Lussman again bowed his head in thought. He looked up at Emil Stavros. "I think the people have established the foundation to allow the evidence to go to the jury, and I will allow it. We'll let the jury decide how much weight to give these expert witnesses, but Mr. Anderson, if I were you, I'd find some good ones of my own."

Court was adjourned. Emil Stavros was handcuffed and led away with a look of hatred back at Karp and Guma. "You'll pay for this, Karp," he shouted just before he disappeared through the security door that led him back down and through the tunnel to the Tombs.

"Whew!" Anderson said to the other defense attorneys. "I need a drink. How about we reconvene at Restaurant 222 on West Seventy-ninth?"

The celebrity attorneys left the courtroom laughing and arranging golf dates. "What do you think?" Detective Fairbrother asked as Karp and Guma gathered their papers at the prosecution table.

"I think Mr. Anderson mostly just wanted to see how our experts performed in a courtroom," Guma answered. "How about you, Butch? Butch?"

Karp heard his name being called but he was thinking about Kane's face turning blue with his hands around the man's neck. He tried to kill my kids!

20

THE THROBBING PULSE OF THE DRUMS ROLLING ACROSS THE high plains desert from the pueblo dictated the pace and nature of Marlene's sleep. Even the people in her dreams danced like Indians with stylized tribal masks of carved wood and feathers.

Despite the disguises, she knew who was behind the masks. Kane's demonic mask seemed to shift, his body a formless smoke, as he pursued Lucy, who wore a Corn Maiden mask and was dressed in a fringed white doeskin dress and knee-high white doeskin boots.

Butch danced after them in a Great Horned Owl mask that Jojola had once shown her, which was used by the tribe's warrior clan, while David Grale stamped along behind him wearing the gray-brown, mud-covered mask of a water spirit. Swirling around all of them was a woman, or the shadow of a woman in black whose raven mask covered only the top part of her face; Marlene assumed from the mole on her cheek that she was Samira Azzam.

Moving in and out of the assemblage, John Jojola soared and screeched like the golden eagle he represented. Eagles, Marlene thought in her dream, John believes that they carry prayers to the

Creator. The sight of the Indian police chief filled her with such an overwhelming sadness that she cried out in her sleep. Hearing her, he turned and winked before flapping his great wings and rising above the dancers, circling up and up until he was lost in the sun.

Then Vladimir Karchovski appeared in the middle of the dancers. He was not dressed differently than he would have been for any of his summertime walks along the Brighton Beach board-walk, just the usual linen suit and black beret. He gazed fondly at Marlene as he did whenever she came to visit, and held up a piece of paper.

Before she could reach out and take it, however, a shadow passed between them and stole the note. Marlene realized that the shadow was Azzam, who began trilling in the way of Arab women who have lost their men, circling the old man like a—

"—vulture, not a raven," Marlene said aloud as she sat up in the dark of the room of the mission house where she was staying on the Taos reservation.

She got out of bed and walked over to the door leading to the Spanish-style courtyard outside her room. The stars overhead shone brilliantly—not the weary specks of light she was used to in the East, but three-dimensional bodies of light that had substance and dimension. "Billions and billions of stars," she said as she entered the courtyard and sat down in a hanging chair next to a large clump of lilac bushes. The fragrance of the tiny lavender flowers permeated the predawn morning.

The drums from the pueblo were growing louder and seemed to be trying to match the syncopation of her heart . . . or maybe it's my heart trying to keep the beat. Holding her breath to listen, she heard the far-off high-pitched keening and chanted songs as the people of the Taos Pueblo mourned the death of their police chief and warrior John Jojola. A coyote's howl joined in the grieving from a bluff near the house.

She would have liked to have attended the funeral. But it was a private ceremony, part of the sacred rituals that the Taos Indians had kept secret from all outsiders ever since the Spanish conquistadores arrived in 1540.

The pueblo was thought to be the oldest continuously inhabited site in North America, and its people had been one of the only tribes that had not been forced from their lands by other Indians or whites. The seven pueblos in the Rio Grande Valley, of which Taos was the best known, even spoke a unique language, Tewa. They didn't teach the language to anyone else. However, Marlene's daughter, Lucy, a language savant, had a passing knowledge of it from listening to conversations as she helped out at the Catholic mission on the Taos reservation.

Even allowing Marlene to stay in a house on the reservation's Catholic mission grounds was a breach in tradition while the reservation's borders were closed to outsiders, as they were now. When she was dropped off at the house, she'd been told, politely, that she was to remain in the house until someone from the tribe arrived to escort her to the memorial service in the morning, now only a few hours away.

Closing the reservation to everyone except the Red Willow People, as the Taos people were known, wasn't unusual. It happened several times during the year for special ceremonies, as well as for most of the winter. About fifty families, including Jojola and his son, lived year-round in the actual pueblo—an apartment-like complex as high as five stories made of adobe, a mixture of mud and straw, that had been there for perhaps as long as a thousand years. Most of the rest of the tribe's population of nearly two thousand lived in houses and trailers scattered around the reservation. During the winter and on festival days, many of the families living outside moved into their ancestral homes in the pueblo to touch base as a people and pass on their extensive oral history to their children and grandchildren. The ceremonies and dances performed in those times were for themselves, not the tourists with their cameras.

The reservation was also closed sometimes during times of community trauma, or to discuss matters important to the future of the Taos people, or to mourn the passing of a leader like Jojola. At the word from the tribal council, police officers wearing the traditional black skirts over their pants maintained roadblocks at the reservation entrances and patrolled the roads to keep the curious and un-invited away.

Marlene knew that decision to let her stay she owed to the legacy of Jojola, and the thought of her friend's death brought tears to her eyes again. He'd once told her that he didn't fear death because it represented only the passing of his spirit from one world into the next. But it wasn't a world she could enter, not without leaving her family, and she missed her friend. The lethal rage she felt toward Kane, the old street justice anger at injustice and the evil of men who perpetrated it—an anger she'd tried to leave in the past with Jojola's help—threatened to blind her at a time she needed to stay levelheaded to protect her family.

The morning after Jojola's death, she'd flown to Albuquerque where she was met by a Taos County sheriff's deputy who drove her to the town of Taos. She'd insisted on going straight to the hospital where she found Lucy sitting in a chair asleep with her head on Ned's chest.

Ned had been wide awake but trying not to disturb her daughter. *Hello, Mrs. Ciampi,* he whispered when she walked in the room.

Hi, cowboy, heard you've been taking on the James Gang.

The young man blushed. *Tell the truth, I was scared, but it was either fight or die,* he said. *Lucy was the brave one. And John and Tran who got there just in time . . . for us.*

And that, of course, is pure hogwash, said Lucy, who'd awakened. *Ned was better than John Wayne ever dreamed of being.*

Ned was now turning a dangerous shade of bright red, which only got worse when Marlene kissed him on the cheek. *Thank you for saving my daughter's life . . . again.*

Lucy burst into tears. *But John died saving us.* They'd all cried then, even Ned.

What about Tran? Marlene asked, wiping her eyes.

He's okay, Lucy sniffed. *You know Tran. He didn't want to be there when John's men showed up. I think he's gone back to New York.*

She'd left Lucy with Ned, not that she would have been able to coax her away, and was driven to the house on the reservation, where she'd called her husband. She'd told him that Jojola would have understood, but in reality she was relieved that Butch had remained in New York. Her relationship with Jojola—call it teacher to student, brother to sister, one old soul to another—had been a private one, and she preferred to say good-bye to him in her own way. When the memorial service was over, she hoped to watch the sunset on a rock outcropping above the Rio Grande Gorge where they'd spent many hours talking.

A thin gray line was separating the sky from the black silhouette of the mountains to the east, and the coyote howled again, much closer. Getting up from her chair, she wondered if she might see the animal if she went over to the gate leading to the desert beyond the courtyard. In Indian folklore, the coyote was known as the trickster—always playing practical jokes, not all of which turned out well for himself or his subjects. Jojola had a special affinity for the animal.

A second coyote howled, only differently. She hesitated, the second coyote sounded to her like a person trying to imitate a coyote. Slipping into her room, she retrieved her gun from beneath the pillow on her bed and returned to the courtyard. Marlene aimed at the gate. Then a voice said, "Oh please don't shoot honorable Vietnamese man, Missy." The voice's owner laughed.

"Tran! Goddammit," Marlene whispered, trying not to wake the Franciscan monks who lived in the house. "I might have shot you!"

She ran up and threw her arms around the thin shoulders of the former schoolteacher turned Vietcong leader turned gangster. A sob escaped her. "I can't believe he's dead."

Tran shrugged. "What is death? You're talking to a Buddhist. This was preordained, his karma; he will return soon in another body to continue the journey. His own beliefs also had him on this path where death is only a doorway into the next room."

"Nice you can be so matter-of-fact about it," Marlene sniffed.

"I miss him, too," Tran said. "We still had many things to talk about . . . some issues still to resolve from our old enmity. But there is nothing I can do; it was his fate. I expect to meet him somewhere down the road so we can continue our discussion and friendship. I expect you will find him in the future as well."

Tran nodded toward her room. "John's men are spread out all around here and a snake couldn't get through without them knowing. But Kane has eyes and ears all over this town."

Once they were in the room, Tran described what happened after they discovered the dead agents. "They looked like they'd been dead for at least an hour, maybe more," he said, "and I was worried we might already be too late. But then I heard the shooting from the direction of the cabin, which meant someone was still fighting. As John thought when he talked to you, we couldn't get through to his office on his cell phone."

With the sun setting, they'd driven the remaining few miles to the cabin until reaching the last hill providing cover and hid Jojola's truck off the road. "I was surprised that they'd left no one to guard the rear, but I don't think that they expected Ned to put up such a fight. We were about a mile away, but the first thing we saw was a truck overturned off the road with several bodies lying around."

There seemed to be a lull in the fighting, which they thought meant that the terrorists were waiting for it to get completely dark. "Which gave us about a half hour to cover the mile between us and them without being spotted," Tran said.

By following ravines and moving from rock outcropping or patch of mesquite brush to the next, they'd made it to within fifty yards of the attackers without being noticed. But they still weren't close enough. The only weapons they had were Jojola's police department–issued 9 mm Glock in the glove box, which he gave to Tran, and his hunting bow and hunting knife. None of the weapons had the range to be of much use against automatic rifles, which meant they too were going to have to wait until dark to close with the enemy.

They split up; agreeing that their signal to attack would be when the assault on the cabin commenced. "It wasn't going to be easy," Tran continued. "We were moving in the dark, but we had seen that the attackers had night-vision goggles. I was lucky that their attention was focused on Ned and Lucy because there was a patch of open ground I had to cover and would have surely been seen if they were looking behind them."

However, the attackers were caught off guard when one of their number who'd crept up close to the cabin was shot and killed by Ned. "He barely made it back to the cabin."

The action had then moved quickly. Under covering fire, the main body of attackers began to rush forward. Then someone inside the cabin—"I learned later it was Lucy"—shot a flare into the bales of hay. "Two guys got caught in the open and Ned picked them off like shooting fish in a barrel.

"I saw the hay bales catch fire, and I took off running to reach my targets," Tran said. "The first guy heard me coming, but I think the fire had also ruined his night vision because he was looking right at me but his shots went wide. I shot him and didn't stop running until I got to the next guy, who never saw me coming."

Jojola had also sprung into action. His first target was a man kneeling next to a rock and firing at the house, trying to keep Ned pinned while the others rushed in. The former commando didn't bother to use an arrow but instead drove his knife into the base of the man's skull as he ran past.

Notching an arrow as he moved, Jojola shot another of the terrorists just as the man was throwing a grenade at the cabin. Instead of going through the window the device—"a flash-bang type"—bounced off the outer wall and exploded. "Lucy believes that the men had orders to try to take her alive.

"Another terrorist reached the door and appeared about to shoot when John put an arrow through his chest. Then it was over, or so we thought."

The man Jojola had shot was still alive, but he refused to answer questions Lucy put to him in Arabic, Chechen, and Russian. "We were stupid. We failed to check him for a secreted weapon," Tran said sadly, not quite as much the Buddhist as his initial comments to Marlene.

Suddenly, the terrorist had raised a small pistol he'd palmed and pointed it at Lucy. *Poshyelk chyerto,* he'd cursed her.

"John was closest and jumped in front of her," Tran said. "He took the bullet before I could knock the gun from his hand."

Marlene wiped at her eyes and nodded. That part she'd heard from Lucy.

Jojola had died instantly. With her dead friend in her arms, according to Tran, Lucy said something back to the man in Russian.

"I asked her what the man had said," Tran recalled. "He'd told her to go to hell. I asked what she'd said back. . . . She told him that a saint had just informed her that there was a special place already reserved there for him and other murderers. I've never seen a man's face so terrified, and that's how he looked when he died a minute later."

Jojola's men had arrived soon after. Together they'd searched the dead and found a packet of documents on a man they figured was the leader that included a photograph of Ned and one of Jojola.

"The two white knights," Marlene said. She told Tran about the latest chess pieces and her run-in with the terrorists in New York.

"Well, if someone's trying to warn you that an attack is imminent, they need to work a little faster," Tran said. "The three of us only survived because of the fight the kid put up. I have no doubt that the plan was to swoop in, kill Ned, and kill or abduct Lucy, after which they would have waited for John to arrive. I don't think they knew I was with him."

"So maybe Kane sent the knights, knowing he could count on me calling John to go check on her," Marlene said.

"Or, anybody watching John for the past few months would have known that he looked in on the kids every couple of days," Tran said.

Jojola's men had taken his body with them to the reservation to be buried by his people before federal agents arrived. "I'm told that the guy with Homeland Security was ticked off and gave John's guys a hard time for 'disturbing a crime scene.' They told him to go screw himself and that they were following their customs, which prohibit autopsies," Tran said. "This is all secondhand. I wasn't hanging around; as you know, I'm not fond of federal agents, especially right now."

"You suspect a traitor?"

"Well, something's fishy," Tran answered. "The federal agents who got shot were set up. How else would professionals allow two truckloads of armed men to drive up and shoot them without a fight?"

"Maybe someone else got there first and shot them before the trucks arrived," Marlene suggested.

"We thought of that, too," Tran said. "But Ned saw the trucks approaching and then heard the shooting. And don't forget the murder of Fey. Someone told the killer where to find him and that was something only the federal agencies had knowledge of. There's one more thing, John's guys swear that the photograph the terrorists had of him had been taken for his police identification card, which they said was only on file in their office and with the FBI. . . . I don't think they were likely to give it to anyone; they loved that man."

"I did, too," Marlene said. "And karma or not, Buddhist or Indian spirituality or not, I'm going to do my best to kill the bastard who did this. . . . Jaxon thinks there's a mole in either his agency or Homeland Security, too."

She recalled a conversation she'd had with the agent that afternoon. It was believed that the terrorists had entered New Mexico from Mexico near the town of Gallup.

About thirty thousand people are caught sneaking across the border there every year; many more aren't apprehended, Jaxon had said. *Most of them are just poor laborers trying to make a better life for themselves and their families. However, it's also popular with drug smugglers and apparently, as we just found out, terrorists. Two men with the Minuteman organization—a bunch of civilians down on the border trying to help the Border Patrol spot illegals— disappeared about five days ago, their bodies were found this morning; they'd been shot to death. Probably stumbled on the terrorists and paid the price.*

The deaths of the Homeland Security agents were being kept very hush-hush. Jon Ellis, who'd arrived in town with Jaxon, was positive that his men had been ambushed before the truckloads of terrorists arrived. He'd even questioned whether Jojola was playing "both sides of the field" until Marlene had angrily straightened him out.

Did they give you stupid pills? she'd said. *My friend died saving my daughter and her boyfriend after your guys were caught asleep at the wheel. I don't want to speak ill of the dead—those two men are gone and can't defend themselves—but you have to wonder why they're sitting there like clay pigeons when they're supposed to be keeping an eye on my daughter.*

Jaxon started to intervene, but Ellis apologized. *It's okay, she's right.* He added, *I'm asking myself those same questions.*

Tran nodded and thought for a moment. A coyote howled outside the gate. "I have to go," he said. "I'm leaving for New York; you know how to contact me there. But I wanted to warn you. The hospital is being watched. The reservation is being watched. You've been followed since you got to Albuquerque. So far these watchers haven't tried to infiltrate the reservation, and it wouldn't be healthy for them if they did. But take care, Marlene. Trust no one."

Marlene hugged her old friend again. "Thank you, Tran," she said. "In case I've never told you, I love you, too. So be careful; I couldn't stand to have you both on the road without me."

Tran nodded and smiled. She thought there was even a hint of a tear in his eye as he led the way out of her room. "Don't grieve too much," he said, turning to her. "We need to look ahead, not behind. I suspect there will be many surprises still in store for all of us before this is over."

With that, the former guerrilla slipped out of the gate and into the gray light just before the dawn. A coyote, the one who sounded like a man imitating a coyote, howled and was answered from farther away by, she thought, the real animal.

Out in the sagebrush, a shadow emerged and joined Tran. "You need to work on your coyote-speak, my friend," the shadow whispered, "she almost shot you."

21

July

DETECTIVE CLARKE FAIRBROTHER DROVE SLOWLY DOWN Eden Street in Bar Harbor, Maine, looking for the address he'd located by calling a pal with the NYPD union's pension fund and asking where they sent retirement checks for former Detective Brian John Bassaline.

He didn't remember Bassaline, even though they were about the same age and had come on the force about the same time. But that wasn't all that unusual, they'd worked out of different precincts and Bassaline had mostly stayed with homicide, while he'd spent the bulk of his detective years chasing after the mob—racketeering, vice, drugs, with of course a few murders thrown in.

At last he spotted the house number on a mailbox outside of a light blue cottage near the waterfront. He could see the gray-green waters of the harbor fifty feet beyond the house and a small quay with a sixteen-foot sailboat tied up next to it, but it was difficult to see much farther as the fog left over from the night before had not yet melted away in the morning sun. Getting out of the car, he inhaled deeply, catching the salt air mixed with a slight tinge of fuel oil. Somewhere in the fog a buoy bell tolled. It was peaceful, almost a throwback to a simpler time, and he understood why a former NYPD homicide detective might want to retire to such a spot.

Fairbrother had considered the retirement thing himself. He was eligible, but after his wife, Marge, took sick and passed away a few years back, there was nothing for him at home. They hadn't been able to have kids, so it was just a big empty house without even the sound of his wife puttering around in some corner. He and Marge had talked about selling their old place in Yonkers when he retired, buying a Winnebago and then traveling around the country, but it wasn't something he wanted to do by himself.

Trouble was, he didn't feel like he fit in down at the precinct either. In fact, he felt like a dinosaur with all the new hotshots coming in with their college degrees in "criminal justice" and the newfangled technology and ways of doing things. The officers humored him, but it was clear that they were all just waiting for him to toddle off to the old folks' home or maybe keel over at his desk.

So he'd jumped at the chance when V. T. Newbury called and asked if he wanted to work in the DAO's office for his anticorruption unit—with the option of staying on even after the department eventually kicked him out. He hooked up with Ray Guma, a tough, hard-nosed prosecutor he'd done a couple of mob prosecutions with back in the day, to work on cold cases—icing on the cake. Real detective work again.

Still, ol' Brian has got himself a nice place here, Fairbrother thought as he walked up the path toward the cottage. He was glad to see there were only a couple of stairs to the porch as the arthritis in his hips had been acting up. Reaching the steps, he looked up as a man appeared at the screen door accompanied by a large German shepherd.

A low-throated growl emanated from the dog as the man with him, a pug-ugly archetypical Irish cop with a face as gnarled as the piece of driftwood decorating the front lawn, said, "Whaddya want?" The dog growl even louder.

"If you're Detective Bassaline, and I'm guessing by the Bronx accent that you are, I'd like to ask you a few questions," Fair-brother answered, holding up his gold detective badge. "Clarke Fairbrother. I'm working with the DAO."

"I got nothin' to say," Bassaline replied and started to turn around. "Come on, Fred."

"It's about the Teresa Stavros case," Fairbrother continued.

Bassaline hesitated at the door. "I still ain't interested."

Fairbrother knew he was losing the battle and decided to take a chance. "I guess not," Fairbrother retorted, "since you dropped the ball the first time."

The detective thought perhaps he'd taken too great a chance when Bassaline whirled and snarled, "Who the fuck says that?" The dog picked up on his master's anger and lunged at the screen door in full-throated roar with his teeth bared.

"Fred, down!" Bassaline commanded. The dog immediately stopped and lay down.

"K-9 unit," Fairbrother said. "Didn't know you worked that division."

Bassaline looked down at his dog with undisguised affection. "I didn't," he said. "Fred here is a hero. He took a bullet for his handler, but it made him shy of loud noises . . . unfit for duty. They were going to put him down. But I heard about it, and there was no way I was going to let them kill one of our own after he'd given himself up for another cop . . . I didn't care if he was a dog. That was ten years ago, about when I retired, so we've been hanging out together ever since."

"A man with integrity," Fairbrother said. "A rare breed these days, which means you didn't drop the ball on the Stavros case, did you . . . at least not because you wanted to."

Bassaline looked at him hard for a moment, but then the look softened. "Nice technique, Detective," he said and chuckled. "Used it once or twice myself. Get them talking about their dog, or their kids, or their car, then toss 'em a compliment. Well, can't let that kind of effort go to waste. Come on in and let me buy you a drink."

Fairbrother looked at his watch. "At ten o'clock in the morning?" he asked.

Stavros in the late afternoon before she disappeared and she didn't act like she was planning on running away from home. He knew her marriage wasn't a happy one; he'd heard them arguing pretty energetically on a couple of occasions, usually about money—she had a lot of it and Emil always seemed broke. But she had her kid and couldn't have cared less if Emil had his little mistress; in fact, it was probably a relief. But she was also Catholic and wouldn't divorce the bastard. Anyway, as Kaplan was leaving that afternoon, she stopped him to talk about plans she had for changing the garden that she wanted to begin the next week. That's when I figured she didn't just take off."

"You heard we found her body?" Fairbrother pointed out.

"Yeah, Bar Harbor's a quaint little place, but I still pick up the *Times*—saw the story about the hearing," Bassaline said. "How they going to explain that?"

Fairbrother shrugged. "They haven't said. I expect we'll hear at trial."

"Yeah, well, I figured she was in the backyard," Bassaline said. "I called Kaplan a few months after she disappeared to see if he could remember anything else, and he was all upset. He'd gone back to work the next week and somebody had messed with some of the rosebushes. . . . Wasn't anything you or I would have noticed. In fact, I'd been in the backyard right after she disappeared and, heck, the whole place just looked like a jungle of flowers and bushes to me. But apparently they were some special sort of rose— a hybrid he and Teresa had developed and were going to name after her. He swore they'd been moved."

Bassaline swirled the ice around in his glass for a moment, then looked up. "You might be right about me dropping the ball on this one—"

"Hey, I was just yankin' your chain, I didn't mean nothin'—" Fairbrother started to say.

"Nah, it's okay, but you're right also that I didn't want to," Bassaline said. "It was enough for me. I wanted to get a search warrant and dig up the yard . . . even went to my division chief, but he wouldn't go for it. Gave me a line about how Stavros was a big muckety-muck and we were going to need a whole lot more than some, and I quote here, 'dim bulb ex-con killer's opinion about some rosebushes' before we went to a judge. I pointed out that I thought I had a pretty good circumstantial case. I mean: the woman's gone, leaves her kid and most of her stuff—except a suitcase and a few clothes, which probably ended up in the ocean, plus her husband's got a mistress and money problems. All I wanted was to dig up a few rosebushes. But my chief wasn't going for it, and I might have gotten a little out of hand, called him a fuckin' ass kisser because this guy Stavros was a big politico. He took me off the case and gave it to some nimrod detective who couldn't find his ass with both hands. Kaplan got canned, but a month or two later, he calls me and says that he heard from the gardener next door to the Stavros place that they'd ripped out the rose garden and cemented the place over."

"Why wasn't this stuff about the gardener in the file?" Fairbrother asked.

Bassaline's thick brows knitted. "Whaddya mean it's not in there? It's all there, including the affidavit I filled out for the search warrant."

Fairbrother shook his head. "Nothing about a gardener named Jeff Kaplan, no affidavit either."

Bassaline was quiet for a moment, then nodded. "Well, guess that makes sense considering who they turned the case over to—"

"Who was that?" Fairbrother asked.

"Guy's been in the news quite a bit lately," Bassaline answered. "First, last fall when he went down for whackin' that rap singer and them hookers, which is why I figured he got his comeuppance in prison. Still, got the story taped to my refrigerator."

"You telling me that the detective who took over this case was Michael—"

"Flanagan," Bassaline finished the sentence. "Yeah, little holier-than-thou prick, at least that's how he tried to come off—though there were a lot of rumors floating around the precinct that he was handing out his own brand of justice, him and some other little hyper, self-righteous, religious pricks. Didn't surprise me at all that he was workin' for that a-hole Andrew Kane."

Fairbrother's mind was racing and suddenly clear of the effects of the alcohol. "You know where I can find Kaplan?" he asked.

Bassaline laughed but it wasn't a pleasant sound. "Yeah, he's easy to find, but it won't do you any good. He's buried in Acacia Cemetery over in Queens."

"What happened to him?"

"You tell me," Bassaline said. "Guess Jeff liked to fish for stripers almost as much as he liked his roses. About nine years ago, they found his boat out in the Long Island Sound. His body washed up a few days later. He had a nasty knock on his head, but the ME said he drowned. They ruled it accidental."

"My ass," Fairbrother said.

"Got that straight," Bassaline replied and chugged the remainder of his drink.

Fairbrother stood up and shook Bassaline's hand. "We may want you to testify about the gardener."

"Figured as much," Bassaline said. "Tell you the truth, that one's weighed on me for a while. I should have gone over my chief's head, but I didn't know Flanagan was dumptrucking the case or even that he was dirty . . . not until that stuff with Kane went down."

22

KARP WAS POLISHING OFF A HOT DOG FROM THE STAND IN front of the Criminal Courts building when the newspaper vendor with the coke-bottle eyeglasses and a nose like Pinocchio began cussing at him from his stand next door.

"Okay, asswipe Jesus," the man with a sly smile said. "I got one for you."

Karp rolled his eyes. Ever since he'd known "Dirty Warren," they'd played a game of movie trivia with Warren asking the questions and Karp answering them. So far, the score was: Warren zero and Karp about four thousand and three . . . not that he was counting.

"Don't you get tired of losing?" Karp asked, which elicited a stream of profanity and epithet-laced challenges that had little to do with Warren's affliction with Tourette syndrome, a short circuit in his brain that was manifested by profanity-laced speech, and everything to do with his irascible and competitive nature. But Karp just laughed, which irritated Warren all the more.

There were precious few things that Karp felt he knew with any degree of certainty. More often than not, Karp felt that his expertise was limited to where to find the best pastrami sandwich and hot dog in New York—Second Avenue Deli and Nathan's at Coney Island. But to Warren, there were two things at which Karp had no equal: his knowledge of movie trivia and anything and everything to do with the Yankees.

Karp got the first trait from his mother, who had loved movies and theater and often took him to both. As a boy growing up in Brooklyn, he looked forward to each weekend to the Saturday matinees down at the Avalon and Kingsway theaters, where for twenty-five cents he could catch double features. He preferred Westerns, but he saw them all, and gleaned, filed, and stored anything he could get from magazines, newspapers, and word-of-mouth rumor about the stars and making of the movies, including the unusual and the little known. It was a hobby he'd carried over into his adult life—probably more as something he could, in a way, still share with his mother. With his mother, Saturdays also meant the Broadway theaters; it had long been their goal to see all of the best shows listed in the *New York Times* theater guide.

Karp's forte was older movies, and the unwritten rule was that Warren was supposed to draw his questions from at least a couple decades back. But Karp had kept up with the latest stuff, too, because every once in a while, Warren would cheat and try to rattle him with something newer.

Today, Warren was playing fair, and even gave him a true or false question, though he tacked on a second part.

"When they made *The Godfather,* shit, there were 'post notes' all over the sets, including in Robert Duval's mouth because Marlon Brando couldn't remember his lines, true or false, scumbag bitch," Warren said. "And why?"

"Why what?" Karp asked as he turned to look at a crowd of reporters gathering near the top of the stairs of the building.

"Damn penis, why is it true, or why is it false?" Warren replied, peering around Karp's shoulder to see what was going on.

Karp turned as the crowd of reporters shouted a question to someone coming out of the building who he couldn't see yet. As long as it wasn't somebody from his office, he didn't really care; he didn't like his ADAs to grandstand in front of the press or leak tidbits in dark, smoky bars. He believed in trying cases in courtrooms, not the court of public opinion. He left that to the defense lawyers.

"I stumped you, didn't, fuck me, I, turd?" Warren said with a smug look on his face. He gazed around hoping that there would be a crowd to witness his moment of glory and was disappointed to see that everyone's attention was turned to the gaggle of press.

Karp moved to the side and closer until he could see that the reason for the media frenzy was the sudden appearance of Bryce Anderson, Rachel Rachman, and a tall, middle-aged body-builder type he quickly recognized as Dante Coletta, the Stavros chauffeur. He noticed Murrow standing off to the side; his aide saw him and hurried down the steps.

"What's up, Gilbert?" Karp asked.

"It seems that the defense has produced a 'witness' who claims to have seen who killed Teresa Stavros," Murrow said. "They filed an amended motion to dismiss the indictment."

"And I suppose Rachman's presence is a coincidence," Karp said.

"As is the sudden appearance of the media, despite the gag order following the last blood frenzy," said a voice coming from behind.

Karp glanced over his shoulder. "Hello, Ray. Yeah, I need that like I need a new hole in the head."

Funny how the press worked. The terrorist attack on his daughter and the death of John Jojola had made the front page of the *Times* for a day and then subsequent stories faded toward the inside pages until they'd disappeared. After all, anything west of the Hudson grew less important the farther one got from Manhattan. But the discovery of Teresa Stavros's skeleton in the backyard of the family brownstone had been on the front page for a week following the court hearing.

The press had gone to town, digging up the old stories from when Teresa first disappeared and the subsequent story about well-known missing persons. They'd talked to the neighbors, past and present; attempted to talk to Dante Coletta, who'd said what appeared in the papers as *[expletive] off and die.* Enterprising reporters had even gone to Denver and Albuquerque to speak with members of 221B Baker Street only to be referred to the court hearing transcripts.

The defense, of course, had railed on and on about having questions about the *quackery* used to identify the remains found in the grave. *And even if they prove to be those of Teresa Stavros,* Anderson said, *it only goes to further our contention that someone has set Mr. Stavros up to take the fall for his wife's disappearance and now, her "presumed" death, which I might add is still in question. And if it proves that she's dead, I am one hundred percent, positively comfortable knowing that a jury will realize that my client, Mr. Emil Stavros, philanthropist, dedicated father and husband, community leader, is not a murderer. He is as dedicated to finding out what happened to his beloved first wife as anyone and that includes those bureaucrats at the DAO or NYPD.* Now it appeared as though Emil Stavros was so dedicated that, through his attorneys, he had announced a $100,000 reward for information regarding how the skeleton found in his backyard came to be there.

"Did you know about this?" Karp asked.

Guma shook his head. "Nah, I was just grabbing a bite to eat at a Chinese place across the park when Murrow called with the news. Apparently, Anderson wants to meet to give us this apparently earth-shattering information."

The three prosecutors sidled closer to the back of the press herd to listen to the "impromptu" press conference. Anderson was talking and they caught him in midsentence. "—produce a witness, Mr. Dante Coletta, who is standing here to my right." The lawyer nodded to Coletta, who glared at the crowd. "However, you have caught me between a rock and a hard place as I intend to honor the gag order imposed by Judge Lussman. That being said, if the district attorney insists on proceeding with this ludicrous case, suffice it to say that Mr. Coletta will set matters straight in court as to the real killer of Teresa Aiello Stavros nearly fifteen years ago."

Anderson turned to go but paused to allow the press to shout after him. "Mr. Anderson! Mr. Anderson!" the young blond reporter shouted. She had thus far resisted his attempts for "a quiet dinner someplace where I might be able to illuminate some of the more complex issues surrounding this case."

He sighed as if he were being dragged back against his will but pointed to the reporter. "Yes, Jeanne?" he said. "One last question."

"Mr. Anderson, does your witness have any evidence to prove that what he is saying is true?"

Anderson paused and gave her his best "I know what I'm doing here and aren't you impressed" smile. "Let's just say Mr. Coletta was present when Mrs. Stavros was cruelly murdered by someone other than my client," he answered, then turned forcefully on his Guccis and strode into the building.

The press was left with Rachel Rachman, who was dressed, as usual, in loud colors . . . today purple and a sort of Granny Smith apple green. "Ms. Rachman do you have any comment?" a decidedly less interested press asked.

Rachman glared over the reporters' heads at Karp, which had the effect of turning some cameras his way. "I hesitate to comment on an ongoing case—" she said.

"Then don't," Guma muttered.

"—but this sort of rush to judgment, coupled with political gamesmanship that should have no part in the actions taken by the New York DAO, is exactly why I decided to run for this office," Rachman says. "We have murders, rapes, and other violent crimes every day, but our current district attorney is more interested in making headlines with a fifteen-year-old case aimed at destroying a man who dared to speak out by supporting a candidate who wants to bring integrity back to the once-proud tradition of the DAO. I say shame on Mr. Karp for jumping into this tar baby with both feet before he had all the facts . . ."

"Let's go," Karp said, ignoring the cameras and shouted questions from the press as he walked through them up the stairs.

"Shit fuck your sister, what's your answer, Karp?" Dirty Warren yelled. "You got ten seconds or I win!"

Karp turned, his face stern. Even the press went quiet. Then he smiled.

"Ah, shit!" Warren howled, having seen the smile before.

"False," Karp shouted. "There were notes with Brando's lines all over the sets, but it wasn't because he forgot his lines. He didn't read scripts beforehand because he thought his first read was the best one. So notes with his lines were placed where he could see them during filming."

"Aaaaaahhhhhh, piss!" Warren said stamping his feet.

Karp saluted with his index finger to his brow and turned, walking into the building followed by Murrow and Guma, who were smiling like their boss had just won an argument before the U.S. Supreme Court. They all stopped smiling when they saw the reporter who stood blocking their way.

"Hi, honey!" Gilbert said. "I didn't think you were getting in until tonight."

"Hi, baby," Ariadne Stupenagel said. "I was jonesing for my Gilbert the Great, so I caught an earlier flight. Just in time to learn that you've been holding out on me with the latest Karp and company caper. I'm about to go home to your apartment where I intend to slowly undress this magnificent body in front of a mirror before I step into a blazingly hot shower where I intend to lather up every last curve and crevice—"

"I didn't need to hear that," Karp said.

"I did," Guma and Murrow replied in something of a lather themselves.

Ariadne Stupenagel was one of Marlene's former college roommates. Probably the best freelance newshound in New York City— and elsewhere as she traveled the globe, most recently London to chase a story about Islamic extremist imams in the wake of the bombings. She was six foot and a bit, which made her a head taller than her boyfriend, and built—as she herself described—for lust. She bedded the rich and powerful in her time, as well as ("regrettably") Guma, but for reasons beyond Karp's ken, she'd seemed to settle on Murrow.

"Well, Gilbert," she said, ignoring Guma, "if you hurry home, you might get to watch. But first, I need to put on my reporter hat . . . so a comment, please, on Ms. Rachman's speech out there."

She pulled a tape recorder microphone out of her purse and shoved it toward Karp, but Murrow stepped in between.

"Not withstanding Ms. Rachman's grandstanding in a court matter that is none of her business, it is the policy of the New York DAO to seek justice in front of a jury consisting of honest, hardworking citizens of Manhattan, not in front of the press. Ms. Rachman was released by this office for a reason . . . a reason, I meant to say, that I am not at liberty to discuss. But let's just say a leopardess does not change her spots or a skunk her stripes."

"Murrow," Karp growled though inwardly he was thinking, Nice zingers, Gilbert. "I think that's quite enough. Welcome back, Ariadne."

An hour later, they were sitting in the DAO meeting room with Bryce Anderson and Dante Coletta. "Just in case your mind was not closed, and you were willing to take the blinders off—"

"Save the speeches, Bryce, the press ain't here," Guma said.

Anderson looked at Guma like he was looking at a bum and returned his gaze to Karp. "As I was saying, we're here so that you can listen to Mr. Coletta's version of what happened and judge for yourself whether to accept his story or we can wait until he testifies for the defense."

Karp looked at Guma. "Well, Ray, you want to hear this guy out or should we savage him on the witness stand or both?"

Coletta, who'd been sprawled in his chair smiling, sat up with a scowl. "We'll see who savages who."

"Whom," Guma corrected him

"Huh?"

"Never mind, I take it they didn't require English grammar as part of the GED you received in prison, according to your records," Guma said, looking at the file he'd asked Murrow to pull while they stalled Anderson and Coletta.

"If this is going to turn into an insult contest, we're out of here," Anderson said, making a move as if to stand.

Karp put his hand up and motioned for him to remain seated. "I think Mr. Guma, who is lead counsel for the prosecution in this case, would love to hear Mr. Coletta's 'version of the events.' Mr. Guma?"

"Yeah, let's hear it," Guma confirmed.

"Yeah, well, if this is the way a citizen gets treated for trying to do the right thing, no wonder there's so much crime in Manhattan," Coletta said. "But anyway, yeah, I was there when he did it."

"When who did what?" Karp said.

"What?" asked Coletta with a smirk. "Am I being tag teamed here? . . . Look, I ain't comfortable talking to The Man, con's code of honor and all, but I don't want to see Mr. Stavros go down for something he didn't do. He's a legit guy, gave me a chance after I did my time, and I've worked for him ever since."

"So you're saying, you owe Mr. Stavros," Guma asked, looking at his fingernails as if they might need clipping.

"Nah, it ain't like that," Coletta countered. "I just wanted to explain why I would turn on a guy who I was pretty tight with at one time."

"So who are we talking about?" Guma asked. "Who are you saying you saw kill Mrs. Stavros?"

"His name is, or rather was, Jeff Kaplan," Coletta said. "He was Mrs. Stavros's gardener. But I understand he died in a boating accident or something."

"Start from the beginning. Where did you meet him?" Karp asked, recalling the report he'd read from Detective Fairbrother regarding his conversation with former detective Brian Bassaline.

"I met him at Auburn Prison. He was in for killing some guy—not that he meant to do it; it was a fight in a bar, Jeff one-punched him and turned out the guy's lights forever. Guess it was sort of a freak thing. Anyway, next thing Jeff knows, he's doing time for manslaughter."

"And Mr. Kaplan was a gardener?" Guma asked, although he had also talked to Fairbrother and read the report.

"Yeah, he got into it in prison, said it calmed him down," Coletta said. "Anyway, we were cellies for a half year or so before I got out. When he was released, I talked to Mrs. Stavros, who was struggling with her roses, and got him a job."

"You'll excuse me, but this is the first we've heard of the gardener," Karp said. "But there's nothing in the file about him."

Coletta shrugged. "That's not my problem. I know he was questioned. Guess it's just sloppy work on your part."

Guma asked if Coletta had much time to observe the relationship between Emil and Teresa Stavros.

"Yeah, whoo boy, she was an A number-one bitch," Coletta said, before crossing himself superstitiously. "Excuse me for speaking unkindly of the dead. But I watched Mr. Stavros take a lot of shit from her, and it wasn't right."

Karp noticed Guma stiffen at Coletta's description of Teresa and quickly interjected. "But Mr. Stavros was, by his own account, carrying on an affair with Amarie Bliss."

Coletta nodded. "Yeah, I knew all about that. Hell, I drove him to her apartment all the time—that's how I know he wasn't around when his bitch wife got what was coming to her."

"This is a bunch of crap—" Guma snarled.

"Ray!" Karp cautioned.

Coletta's brow was furrowed. "What? You callin' me a liar?"

"Yeah, a liar and a—" Guma started in.

"Ray . . . let's hear what the man has to say," Karp said.

Guma looked like he was going to say something else. But instead he leaned back in his chair and looked at the ceiling.

Karp looked at Coletta. "Go on, and please, forgive Mr. Guma . . . this is the first we've heard that sort of description of the victim. Anyway, you were commenting on Mr. Stavros's affair?"

"Yeah, well, I don't know how much I want to say if I'm just going to be called a liar," Coletta said, but went on anyway. "Yeah, Mr. Stavros was bangin' Amarie. Can't say I blame him considering his wife was one cold fish." He looked at Guma as if expecting to be challenged. "Although she was plenty warm around Jeff."

Guma sat up with his dark eyes burrowing into Coletta. "But you just told us that Mr. Kaplan was the killer."

"Yeah, that's what I said," Coletta replied. "Them two were going at it hot and heavy. He was boning her whenever Mr. Stavros went out, which was plenty. She was just using Jeff to get back at Stavros, but when Jeff wised up and decided to call it quits, she wasn't going for it. 'Nobody leaves me,' she told him that night—"

"Which night?" Guma asked.

"The night of the murder," Coletta answered. "Anyways, she told him that night that if he left her, she would go to the police and say he raped her when her husband was gone."

Coletta said he was in the garage, putting the limo away when he heard Kaplan and Teresa arguing. "She was screaming at him and then she pulled a gun . . . this little .22 jobbie . . . and pointed it at him. But he took it out of her hands, so she turned and said she was going to go call the cops. Jeff freaked and shot her. That's when I came out of the garage and saw him shoot and her fall."

Kaplan turned and saw Coletta and was going to shoot. "But I put my hands up and said, 'Hey, no worries, she was a bitch and deserved what she got.' Then I helped him bury her in the rose garden. We even put the rosebushes right back on top of her grave."

"Why didn't you go to the police?" Karp asked.

Coletta rolled his eyes as if some rube had asked him a stupid question. "Come on, I just told you, I didn't like the bitch, and Jeff was a friend. And besides, I got paid pretty good to keep my mouth shut."

"By who?" Karp asked, wondering if they were about to hear the name Andrew Kane. When Detective Fairbrother returned from Maine and wrote up the conversation he'd had with Bassaline, the name Michael Flanagan had jumped at him like a rattlesnake in one of the old Westerns he'd loved.

Guma's thinking had turned the same way. *Do you think this is another Kane thing?* he'd asked.

Hard to say, Karp replied. *Sort of fits the "No Prosecution" MO. Pulls a few strings for a wealthy and well-connected socialite, gets his people on the force to quash the investigation.* But Newbury had found nothing in the files.

Could be this was just Flanagan freelancing, too.

"Who paid me? Kaplan, of course," Coletta said. "He came up with this scheme to say she disappeared, ran away from home, and kept her credit cards and bank shit. She'd shown him how to get into her private safe, so he had her PIN numbers and passwords, the whole schmear, including her jewelry. No woman was going to leave her jewelry. He had a girlfriend, sort of looked like Teresa, and he had her travel around a bunch, buying shit and then selling it, plus cashing big checks. They were living pretty high off the hog and sending me checks nice and regular, until the money ran out."

"Mr. Coletta, did you remember seeing Zachary Stavros at the time of the shooting?" Guma asked.

Coletta shook his head. "Nah. That kid's a basket case; I think he's making it all up. Been on just about every kind of pill there is."

"Do you remember what Teresa Stavros was wearing that night?"

Coletta scrunched his eyebrows and put a hand to his chin as if trying hard to recall an old memory. "Yeah, I think it was some white sort of see-through thing," he said. "That was one thing she had going for her . . . she was quite a looker and didn't mind show- ing the goods, if you know what I mean."

After a few more questions, Anderson held up his hand. "I think that's plenty. I hope you'll give Mr. Coletta's statement care- ful thought. It's obvious this makes much more sense than Mr. Stavros somehow escaping his mistress's apartment to sneak home, kill his wife, bury her in the backyard, and then sneak back into the apartment so that he could be seen leaving by the doorman in the morning."

"We'll let you know." Karp smiled. "Until then, nothing has changed."

Anderson and Coletta stood to leave. "Uh, sorry, just one more question," Karp said. "I'm trying to picture how this happened. You say Kaplan grabbed the gun from Mrs. Stavros and she turned to go call the cops . . ."

"Yeah, that's right," Coletta said.

"Would you mind, using Mr. Anderson there as a stand-in for Mrs. Stavros, showing me about how far away, Kaplan was standing . . . how he pointed the gun . . . you know, sort of act it out—"

"I'm not sure I approve of this—" Anderson started to say, but Coletta turned him around.

"Come on, Bryce, this will be fun," Coletta said. "He was about this far away." Coletta raised his arm and pointed it at the back of Anderson's head from a distance of a couple of feet. "Then *boom!* And she went down like a sack of rice."

"Boom? One shot?" Karp said.

"Yeah, boom, just once was all it took," Coletta said. "Ain't that what the newspaper story said a little while back?"

Karp grimaced. Somebody in the ME's office had leaked some of Dr. Gates's findings to the press. "Yeah," he said. "That's what it said."

After the attorney and chauffeur left, Karp turned to Guma, who was leaning back in his chair again with his eyes closed. "Guess I don't need to ask what you think."

"He's totally full of it," Guma said. "I haven't met a single other person who says that Teresa Stavros was anything but a kind, loving woman and that her husband was a dirtbag with money problems. No mention of Kaplan and Teresa having an affair, which just doesn't fit anyway."

"There's also Detective Bassaline's comment that Kaplan told him that the rosebushes had been disturbed in the backyard. Why would Kaplan say something like that if he didn't want to get caught?"

"And let's not forget this whole thing with Teresa supposedly skipping the country and living the high life somewhere else was a pretty sophisticated operation. But Bassaline said Kaplan was no rocket scientist, took too many left hooks to the head."

Karp agreed with the assessment. "Yeah, I guess it's a good thing Fairbrother's report is still on my desk, waiting to be sent to the defense." But, he cautioned Guma, the defense had just drawn a pretty tough hand to beat. "Our star witness was five years old and says he remembers his mother and father fighting, a couple of pops that may or may not have been gunshots, and the sound of someone digging. They have an adult, granted one with a sheet, who says he saw the whole thing. Nice that the statute of limitations for conspiracy to obstruct and accessory after the fact is up. But he did get the caliber of the gun, which wasn't mentioned in the newspapers, right."

"Don't tell me you buy this crap?" Guma said. "Isn't it just a little too convenient that this guy is popping up now?"

Karp nodded. "Ray, I think this guy's totally full of it, too, but we're going to have to counter him. We can't just ask the jury to believe our version based on our mutual good looks."

Guma laughed. "Maybe you can't, but I've won plenty of cases on that very notion."

23

THE BURLY GUARD AT THE GATE LEADING UP TO VLADIMIR Karchovski's house gave Marlene a suspicious look but let her in. He was the same gorilla who'd been there when she and Butch visited and his disposition wasn't much better that afternoon. Then again, the Karchovskis don't pay him the big bucks to be nice, she thought. She glanced quickly over her shoulder and saw that he was still watching her.

"Don't let Boris put you off," a male voice said as the door to the house opened. "He's a dangerous man when necessary, but shy as a lamb around women. Not that he doesn't appreciate the sight of a beautiful woman such as yourself."

Marlene smiled as she looked up at Yvgeny Karchovski. Butch with an accent, she sighed inwardly, but not the integrity, nor could anyone ever understand me the way Butch does. Karp had been wonderful after she got back from Jojola's memorial service—strong and supportive when she wanted to cry on his chest, fun and engaging when she needed a night out to get her mind off of her friend's death and the threats against her family, as well as her vow to someday, somehow seek and exact her vengeance against Andrew Kane.

It had been some time since she'd seen the Karchovskis. Yvgeny, she understood, had been traveling—she figured in Russia, although his father, Vladimir, had waved his hand vaguely and said it was "to see old friends." So that remained a mystery as did how Yvgeny, who was in the United States illegally, traveled so freely.

The old man had also been quiet for several weeks, since before Jojola's death until that morning when he called on her cell phone. *If you have a few moments,* he'd said, *I have some information that, perhaps, you can make sure gets in the hands of the proper authorities.* The call had reminded her of the dream she'd had while at the pueblo in which Vladimir had tried to hand her a note, but the woman in black had snatched it.

Yvgeny asked her to come in. "Vladimir is out for his walk," he said. "But he should return in a half hour or so."

"Let's go catch up to him," Marlene suggested. "I could use the fresh air."

"As you wish," Yvgeny said, and they stepped back out of the house and walked down to the gate.

"You leaving?" the guard asked.

"*Da,* Boris," Yvgeny said. "Open the gate."

"You are not waiting for Mr. Karchovski to return?" Boris asked.

"No, we are going to meet him," Yvgeny said. "Now if you don't mind, we'd like to leave."

"Yeah, sure," Boris responded and opened the gate. "Um, Mr. Vladimir Karchovski has to me give orders, 'Watch out for Yvgeny.' So I must go with you."

Yvgeny shook his head. "That's all right, Boris, stay here," he said. "I'll be okay."

"But Mr. Vladimir Karchovski, he give me this order—" The man looked like he might weep.

"Okay, Boris, okay," Yvgeny said, rolling his eyes at Marlene to whom he muttered under his breath, "Doesn't say three words in a week, but now he's my shadow."

With Boris lumbering along twenty feet behind and talking on his cell phone, Yvgeny and Marlene headed for the Brighton Beach boardwalk where Vladimir took his walks. Along the way, Yvgeny told her he'd been "snooping around" in Moscow and Chechnya to see if any of his associates with the black market had heard anything about what Samira Azzam was doing in the United States linking up with Andrew Kane.

"There's nothing much more than rumor," Yvgeny said. "However, one of those rumors is that an agent with the FSB—which used to be KGB—a woman named Nadya Malovo, is also rumored to be in this country. I actually met her once, many years ago after Afghanistan; she was with senior agents questioning officers about defections and anti-Soviet sentiments in the army. I thought she was a—how do you say—a cold one then, but I hear she may be much worse than that. Some claim she was with Azzam at the Nord-Ost theater and later Beslan. That is not for sure and even if she was, there could be a legitimate reason if, say, for instance, she is trying to work her way close to the Islamic extremist hierarchy." Yvgeny hestitated a moment as if working things out in his head.

"But?" Marlene asked.

"Excuse me?" Yvgeny said.

"You didn't say it, but there was a 'but' on the end of your last sentence," she said. "You're not sure you buy that theory."

Yvgeny shook his head. "I am not sure. However, if the theory that I was talking to you and Butch about the night you were over for dinner—that the Russian government, or at least some rogue element in the government, and the Islamic hard-liners are working together for the moment to discredit the Chechen nationalists—"

"Then this Nadya Malovo might be working with Azzam and Kane," Marlene finished. She whistled. "Which means the Russian government, or some rogue element, as you say, within the government or its secret police, is working with an Islamic terrorist and an American megalomaniac killer on some terrorist act on U.S. soil? That's the stuff—"

"—wars are made of." Yvgeny was the one to finish the sentence this time.

"So you think they're still after Putin?" Marlene asked.

"It makes sense," Yvgeny said. "Or at least, a staged attack directed at Putin with plenty of deaths among the UN ambassadors and staff to blame on the Chechen nationalists. The FSB isn't the only spy agency in Russia. The army has its own network, some of whom are still my friends. Of interest while I was there was the apprehension of an Arab courier on the border between Kazakhstan and Chechnya. He killed himself before he could be questioned, but a CD data file was found sewn into his jacket. It was encoded, however, the army had recently broken that particular code. The only thing on the CD was a blueprint of a building."

"Don't tell me," Marlene said. "The building was the United Nations."

"*Da* . . . yes," Yvgeny said. "Of course, the army cannot come out and accuse anyone of plotting to kill the president, or against the Chechen nationalists, not without proof. After all, no one knows how high this conspiracy goes. But put it all together and the signs are pointing to something big happening in September."

"So is this the information that Vladimir wanted to pass on?" Marlene asked.

Yvgeny shook his head again. "No . . . well, not entirely," he said. "It is perhaps for you to judge who might make use of this information. Though you do not need me to tell you that not everyone involved in all of this can be trusted. But that I leave to you. Me and my people will continue our own 'investigation.' However, what my father wanted to pass on to you, while related, is of a more personal nature."

Yvgeny and Marlene arrived at the top of the stairs leading down to the boardwalk. Below them a woman in colorful Lycra jogged along the boardwalk pushing a baby stroller. Farther along toward Coney Island, a young couple was buying hot dogs from two Hispanic female pushcart vendors. Twenty-five yards beyond them, Vladimir Karchovski strolled, throwing bread crumbs up in the air for the hovering seagulls as his two bear-sized bodyguards walked a few yards behind. He spotted Marlene and Yvgeny and waved as he stopped feeding the birds and walked toward them.

Marlene smiled when she saw the old man, but it was with a small feeling of guilt. Vladimir was a little older than her own father, and she found herself looking forward to visiting him more than she did Mariano Ciampi these days. Where the old Russian was still sharp, engaged, and living in the real world, her father seemed to be slipping more and more into doddering senility.

The other day Mariano had given her quite the start when he "confessed" to killing his wife, Marlene's mother, Concetta. *I've lived with the woman most of my life,* he cried as she stood behind him, cutting his hair at the kitchen table. *I used to know if she got up in the night or was having a restless sleep. I knew the sound of her heart through the mattress. I should have known, even in my sleep, that she was in trouble. I failed to take care of her.*

Relieved that her own worst fears had not suddenly been realized, Marlene had rumpled his hair and kissed him on the top of his head. *Nonsense, Poppa,* she said. *Mom had a stroke, there was nothing you could do.*

It unnerved her to watch her father's decline. He was often weepy over the smallest things. A memory. Or losing something. Or something as silly as a television commercial for diapers. *I remember when I used to change your diapers,* he said. *Funny how cleaning up such a horrible mess was such an act of love.*

Occasionally, he called her by one of her sisters' names, which frightened her as that had been one of the effects of Alzheimer's on her mother. But it was more how he refused to take care of himself, or the house—content to watch television for hours at a time amid a heap of television dinners, potato chip bags, and empty beer bottles. She even had to clean him up and chase him out of the house to the VFW post four blocks away—something neither she nor her mother, who'd always known to look for him there, had ever had to do before.

Meanwhile, Vladimir was still the emperor of his empire even if the heir apparent, Yvgeny, ran much of the show. He was up on world events, played chess, could identify obscure operas, and loved to debate the meaning behind the meaning of Anton Chekov.

Marlene waved back and started down the steps, when Yvgeny suddenly grabbed her by the arm. "Wait," he said. "Those women—the vendors—what are they doing?"

Marlene looked where he was staring and saw that the two women were walking away from the stand, toward a park that ran parallel to the boardwalk. Then she noticed that one of the women was wearing a sling, as if she'd injured a shoulder or an elbow. The woman looked back at the hot dog cart and Marlene caught a brief glimpse of her face . . . most notably, the mole on her face.

"It's Azzam!" she shouted and began to run down the stairs, her eyes on the women and the cart where the young couple was still fixing their hot dogs, just as the woman with the stroller was passing. Vladimir was still twenty feet away but closing fast on the cart.

Above her, Yvgeny also saw the danger. He'd also recognized Azzam, as well as the woman with her, Nadya Malovo. "Stop!" he shouted at his father, pointing at the cart. "It's a bomb!" He started to shout again but was cut off by a loud bang and a blow to his back. He tumbled down the stairs.

Standing at the top with his gun drawn, Boris tried to draw a bead on the tumbling Yvgeny. This wasn't the way it was supposed to happen. He was only supposed to keep track of the Karchovskis and report back anything unusual. There had certainly been enough of that over the past few months, which had helped his bank account swell many times over. After all, young prostitutes were expensive.

The string of unusual events began when he recognized the district attorney of New York as the dinner guest of his employers, the Karchovskis. That alone had been worth more than Vladimir paid him in a year. There had been an additional bonus when he reported that, according to the butler, who'd been eavesdropping but innocently as he simply liked to gossip, the Karchovskis had given a photograph of a woman named Azzam to the woman, Marlene.

Today, he'd called the telephone number he'd been given for such things to report when the old man was going on his walk and who would be with him. The implication was that he shouldn't expect the old man to return . . . ever. The son would then die in an apparent "mob shooting" that the police would write off as a battle between rivals. But the arrival of the woman had caught him by surprise, as had their sudden decision to walk to the boardwalk to find Vladimir. He'd called on the way to the boardwalk to relay the news.

You'll have to kill him, the man on the other end of the line had said. *He can't be allowed to interfere.*

Nyet! Boris, frightened, had said. *I would be a dead man.*

You will be a dead man if you don't, the other man said. *Kill him and then go to the house in Brooklyn and await further instructions. We will take care of you then.*

What about the woman? Boris asked.

The other man was silent for a moment before sighing, *Well, she was supposed to live a bit longer . . . but this is as good a time as any. She is too great a threat. I don't know what she has been told by your target.*

Boris had weighed who frightened him the most—Yvgeny Karchovski or the man on the telephone—and decided that at least he could kill Yvgeny and maybe survive. Betray the other man and death would not only be assured, it would be drawn out and painful. So when Yvgeny yelled his warning, he'd pulled his gun and shot him in the back. He aimed again to finish the job when his attention flicked to the woman at the bottom of the stairs. Too late, he realized she was pointing a gun at him.

Marlene pulled the trigger, killing the big Russian at the same moment that the hot dog cart exploded. Surrounded by a case filled with thousands of ball bearings, the C4 plastic explosive tore the young couple and the mother with her infant apart.

Twenty feet away, Vladimir would have met the same fate, except that hearing Yvgeny's shout followed by the gunshot, the first of his burly bodyguards had grabbed the old man and thrown him to the sand off the boardwalk. The bodyguard had jumped on top of Vladimir, while the second bodyguard turned his back to the hot dog cart, both men using themselves to shield their boss.

Marlene wasn't knocked off her feet by the blast but had heard the deadly missiles as they'd whistled past her. She saw the two women running across the park and took off after them. However, they had too great a head start and reached a car that was waiting for them, jumped in, and with tires burning, took off down Atlantic Boulevard.

Everywhere was pandemonium, some cars had screeched to a halt on the street. People were running in various directions, most away from the explosion, but many toward it as well. Screams, shouts, sirens shattered the boardwalk's usual serenity.

Cursing, Marlene turned back for the boardwalk. She saw that Yvgeny had already reached the spot where she'd last seen Vladimir. He was kneeling in the sand as she ran toward him; he'd removed his coat to place it under his father's head and that's when she saw the body armor. She paused only long enough at what re-mained of the young woman, her infant, and the young couple to see that they were beyond help, and kept running to Yvgeny.

The first bodyguard was dead. His pants had been torn off by the blast and his legs looked like someone had put them into a meat grinder; however, the fatal wounds had been to his head. The second man was severely wounded and moaning on the sand as Yvgeny turned him gently over, speaking softly in Russian. Even their heroics might not have been enough, except that both men had been wearing Kevlar body armor, which had absorbed the worst of the ball bearings and blast.

Other than a hard fall for an old man and some scrapes, Vladimir had survived the blast. With his bodyguard no longer weighing him down, Vladimir was picking himself up off the sand.

"I am all right," the old man said. "You two must leave. Yvgeny cannot be here when the police arrive and neither can you, Mar-lene. It would be too hard to explain. But first here . . ." The old man reached into the inside pocket of his linen suit and handed her a note card on which was written an address. "If it's not too late, I believe that you may find Mr. Kane at this address in Aspen, Colorado. But hurry, Marlene, events are moving quickly and as you can see, these people will stop at nothing."

24

SPECIAL AGENT S. P. JAXON PEERED OVER THE ROCK WALL with his field binoculars. There was no movement in the mansion on Red Mountain, the aptly named rust-red ridge opposite the town of Aspen. But he knew there were anywhere from a few to a half dozen or more armed terrorists inside the house, as well as the owners—a Saudi prince and his family who were being held hostage. He also hoped that one person in particular had been trapped when agents of the FBI, the Department of Homeland Security, the Aspen Police, and a Pitkin County Sheriff's Office SWAT team surrounded the property.

The various federal law enforcement leaders had arrived at the Aspen Square Hotel in downtown Aspen singly or in pairs, ostensibly tourists in the Wild West town of movie stars and wealthy tycoons ready to party. With the help of the hotel manager, a former FBI agent who'd retired young to run a high-end ski lodge, they'd assembled in the hotel meeting room where a sign on the door proclaimed that the room was closed to all but The Greater Cleveland Rotary Club members and their spouses. They'd also been joined by Homeland Security agent Vic Hodges, who'd apparently worked his way into the terrorist cell and was reporting to them *at considerable risk to his life if one of the bad guys spots him with us,* assistant HS director Jon Ellis noted to the others.

"Think he's in there?" Marlene asked.

Jaxon lowered his binoculars and looked over at Marlene Ciampi, who'd walked up to kneel beside him at the wall. "That's the information you gave us and Agent Hodges confirmed. Kane's supposed to be in the main house with the hostages." He paused to glance back at the mansion. "You ever going to tell me where you got this address? I mean, Aspen was on the list because the Green Opal jewelry store is one of only a dozen in the country that sells Carlos Torres chess sets. But the owner didn't remember the pieces we showed him."

Marlene smiled grimly. "I could tell you but—"

"—you'd have to kill me, I know. Isn't everybody tired of that one yet?" Jaxon said. "Maybe someday when we're old and gray, you'll tell me."

"I'm already gray, but it's a deal," she replied and thought, If you only knew.

Immediately after the bombing, Vladimir had insisted that they leave before the police arrived. So Yvgeny and Marlene split up, agreeing to meet back at the Karchovski house as soon as they could work their way there without being noticed. There, they'd argued about the next step, including what to do with the address she'd been given by Vladimir.

The old man had been the one to track down Carlos Torres, who was on vacation aboard a yacht in the Mediterranean, and had his man hand deliver one of the knights sent to Dugan that Marlene had taken with her. She'd figured that the FBI had the others, so when Vladimir had asked to "borrow" one, she'd consented. Funny, she'd thought when she handed it over, I trust an ancient Russian gangster more than I do anybody in the FBI, except Jaxon.

Torres had identified the piece as belonging to set *Numero Dieciocho . . . I know each of these pieces as though they are mem-*

bers of mi familia. This exquisite creature is lost from his family, which I believe resides at the Green Opal jewelry store in Aspen, Colorado.

When Vladimir's men visited the Green Opal, the owner had again claimed amnesia—until he was taken for a midnight helicopter ride and held upside down out the door over a thousand-foot drop above the Roaring Fork Valley. Then he'd suddenly regained his memory and said that a certain Saudi prince had purchased not one, but two of the Torres sets. The prince had been accompanied by a beautiful young woman whose only imperfection was a large mole on her cheek. She'd warned the store owner to avoid discussing the purchase of the chess sets with anyone, and something about the way she looked at him said it was worth his life to cross her.

Further investigation by Vladimir's men had noted a great deal of unusual traffic at the prince's home by an unusually large number of serious, fit, Arabic-looking men, some of whom had been seen carelessly handling automatic rifles when they slipped out at night to smoke cigarettes.

After getting back to the house following the bombing, Yvgeny had led Marlene into the library where he poured them both a shot of chilled vodka. *I will take care of this now,* he said. He reached for the telephone and punched in a number, then spoke rapidly in Russian before hanging up and saying to Marlene, *Forget the note my father gave you.*

Sorry, I want this guy to pay as much as you do, but I think I better give this address to a friend with the FBI, she replied.

Yvgeny was visibly seething—not that she blamed him; she was angry, too. Angry about Jojola. Angry about Vladimir. Angry and sick to her stomach for the woman and her child and the young couple who'd been murdered.

Nyet! Nyet! NYET! Yvgeny had roared and threw his glass at the fireplace where it shattered. *Who do you trust there? A friend with the FBI? He is going to go after these vermin by himself? No, he will have to tell others, and there are spies in that agency. No, I have tried it my father's way and I have tried it your way, and it almost got my father and myself killed; a woman and a child . . . those young lovers . . . were butchered by animals. My father wanted to give you this address so that what needs to be done could be done the quote "right way." But I am through with this right way. I will take this son of a bitch down to hell my way! And then I will hunt those two whores down and gut them myself like that young mother was gutted by their bomb!*

Look, Yvgeny, Marlene said trying to keep the anger she felt out of her voice. *I can hardly believe this is me arguing against taking the law into your own hands. I mean, I'm already in deep shit for leaving the scene without telling the police what I saw, and I'm ashamed to say I did it because I was worried that being connected to the Karchovskis might hurt my husband's political chances. When Butch hears, he'll drag me down to the precinct by my ear. But think about this: say you go to Aspen and kill Kane and foil his plot, no one will know the depth of this conspiracy. It will just be a gangland killing where, as far as the public is concerned, you're all bad guys—somebody ends up dead, somebody else probably winds up in prison—and I'd be surprised if you do this without innocent people being put in harm's way, too. But also, if you're right about this conspiracy, won't the Russian government and the terrorists just come up with a new plan?*

And why wouldn't they even if your FBI catches Kane and kills Azzam?

Because maybe Jaxon can get to the bottom of this and expose it for what it is, Marlene said, scrambling to come up with reasons that she didn't necessarily believe. In fact, while her mind was debating him, her heart was telling her to go with Yvgeny and settle this score with Kane. *But it goes beyond that. There needs to be a message sent that civilized nations don't have to revert to lawlessness or to military rule to combat terror. The public needs the reassurance that the people with the duty to protect them are out there doing their jobs. Besides, if you kill Kane, the moles go deeper, the plans next time are better.*

Yvgeny paced to the window. He smashed a fist into his hand, his whole body trembling in anger.

It's what your father wants, Marlene had said not knowing what else to say.

She's right.

Marlene turned and saw the old man in the doorway of the library. He looked somewhat worse for wear in his torn and bloody linen suit, a bandage on his forehead and another on his hand, but otherwise appeared to be okay.

Vladimir! she said and rushed over to hug him. *Are you all right? What did you tell the police?*

He patted her on the back. *I am physically fine,* he said. *But my heart is broken for the innocent blood spilled because someone wanted to kill me. The police were hardly interested in what an old man who didn't see much except sand had to say. . . . Now, I just want to clean up a little, then go to the hospital to check on Petre; it was his brother, Sasha, who was killed, and Petre may never walk again, though I believe he is too strong to die.* He turned to address his son.

Marlene will carry the address to whomever she believes should take care of this problem, and you will do nothing in Aspen, he said. *These savages follow no rules, they have no honor—even criminals such as we do not behave like these animals. If we fight them, and men like Kane, on their level, then we must stoop and become like them.*

Then I will stoop, Yvgeny insisted as he walked over to plead his case. *What do I care what people think of me, even though this would be for their welfare as well as my revenge. I will risk that the entirety of civilization does not follow me down this road to savagery, but sometimes only violence is capable of stopping the violent.*

This is true, Vladimir had said. *But there are differences in how violence is administered. Was it in compliance with the rule of law? A policeman who shoots a man about to kill someone, for instance. Or an army fighting to end slavery, which reminds me of a quote attributed to the great American president Abraham Lincoln: "Let us have faith that right makes might, and in that faith, let us, to the end, dare to do our duty as we understand it."*

Might for right and my duty is to kill Kane, Yvgeny growled, but his anger had gone from a hard boil to simmering.

And you may still be required to do your duty, Vladimir said. *But first we will allow this system of justice to do its. However . . .* he said, turning back to Marlene, *. . . if your friend and his FBI are not up to the task, then I give my son permission to seek justice in his own manner with this* zasranec, *excuse my language, Marlene, but this* zasranec *Kane—an appropriate surname, as the mark of Cain, the killer of brothers, is upon him.*

As Marlene turned to leave, Yvgeny's scarred face had softened and, surprising her, he'd reached out and hugged her. *Forgive my outburst,* he'd said. *You saved my life, killing the traitor Boris, and I repay you with a tantrum.*

Marlene hugged him in return, then stood back and smiled. *It's okay. Kane has a way of putting everyone on edge and wondering who to trust. Maybe that's part of his plan. But it won't work with us, will it?*

Yvgeny shook his head. *No, not so long as cooler—and prettier— heads prevail.*

Marlene punched him on the arm. *Flattery will get you everywhere.*

Everywhere? Yvgeny said, theatrically raising an eyebrow.

Well, how about a kiss on the cheek . . . between cousins by marriage, Marlene laughed.

Yvgeny sighed dramatically. *I believe the saying is, "Beggars shouldn't be choosy," correct?*

Close enough, Marlene said and gave him the promised reward.

On the way home, she called Jaxon and gave him the Aspen address and its importance without telling him the circumstances of its discovery.

That evening when Butch got home from work, she told him about what had happened. He'd wondered when Murrow came rushing into his office with news of the bombing if she was somehow involved. But seeing her face when she described what happened, he'd forgone any lectures on leaving the scene but won a promise from her to give her statement to Fulton, who passed it on to the detectives investigating the bomb.

She'd left out how and why she happened to be at the boardwalk other than "to meet an old friend," and just happened to be "in the right place at the right time" to shoot one of the terrorists as he fired at members of the public. Her target had been identified as one Boris Nabakov, a Russian national in the country illegally. What his connection was to the terrorist bomb remained unclear, according to the press.

Citing safety issues for a witness to a capital crime, the police had refused to disclose the name or even gender of the armed civilian who'd shot and killed Nabakov. Witnesses had told members of the press about seeing an armed woman chasing two other women, possibly the terrorists responsible for the bomb. Meanwhile, the National Rifle Association had jumped at the chance to laud the mystery woman's actions as a victory for the Second Amendment and urged all citizens to be ready to join the War on Terrorism by being ever vigilant.

Four days after the bombing at Brighton Beach Jaxon turned his field glasses on the SWAT teams making their way toward the mansion, dashing from one place of cover to the next. One team had already reached the guesthouse but reported it empty. Agent Hodges had confirmed Marlene's information; he'd seen Kane in the house within the past week.

Speak of the devil, he thought as he looked behind him and saw Hodges trotting down the gravel road away from the house. Jon Ellis swore by the guy, but there was something about him that Jaxon didn't like. It went beyond the Southern accent that he obviously laid on a little thicker whenever he was around Marlene or her daughter, Lucy, who'd driven up from New Mexico with her boyfriend. The guy's just a little too slick, he thought. Maybe that came with the territory of being a deep plant; maybe you had to have a plastic, malleable personality to fit into whatever situation arose, but Hodges seemed to think this was all something of an amusing game.

The object of Jaxon's inner debate continued jogging down the road. Agent Vic Hodges, aka Andrew Kane, found that he enjoyed keeping in "fighting trim" and took daily runs, which seemed to help him think more clearly.

It also seemed to help with his migraines. The headaches were nothing new—he'd had them off and on since puberty—but they'd been increasing in number and severity since his arrest the previous fall.

Kane giggled as he thought about the headlines in the *Aspen Times* back in June when the body of noted Aspen plastic surgeon Andre Buchwald had been found in his Mercedes off a mountain road. The body, according to the newspaper, was badly decomposed, but the good doctor had apparently been stabbed to death. The town worthies speculated that Buchwald must have picked up a hitchhiker who wasn't quite "all there." A side story noted that serial killer Ted Bundy had once been a prisoner of the Pitkin County Sheriff's Office until he escaped by jumping out of a second-floor window of the local courthouse.

Wait a little longer and they're really going to have something to talk about, Kane thought and laughed out loud as he ran past the mailbox next to the long driveway leading up to Prince Bandar's house. He wondered how the prince was faring. Bet he never thought that he'd end up a hostage of al Qaeda . . . not a pleasant prospect for him or his pathetic little family.

The arrival of the federal agents had caught Kane by surprise and would have messed up his plans if he hadn't received a warning. Somehow that fucking bitch Marlene Ciampi had figured out where he was hiding. Probably those fucking Karchovskis, he thought. Should have killed them sooner . . . after that idiot Boris told me about the photograph of Azzam.

All such photographs were supposed to have been purged from federal files, yet one had suddenly appeared in the hands of some grubby Russian gangsters. It had become much more dangerous for Azzam to walk the streets, especially after Karp made copies and had them distributed to the police and federal agencies.

The Russians were proving to be a bigger thorn in his side than he'd anticipated. It had taken many years, but Kane had managed to find someone he could compromise close to the inner circles of most of the big gangs in the Greater New York area. Mostly, these people were kept on "retainers" to feed him information on their employers' business interests, weaknesses, and peccadilloes. Humorously, Boris Nabakov had a weakness for young girls, but it was an expensive habit, so he'd agreed to spy on the Karchovskis for him. He'd been pretty much worthless until the day he'd called to report that the Karchovskis had a photograph of Samira Azzam, and . . . oh it's almost too delicious to contemplate . . . had given them to their relative, Roger "Butch" Karp. The frickin' Boy Scout of the NYDAO was related to a member of the Russian mob! Kane had yet to decide how best to use that information. But he just knew he'd find a way to work it into his vengeance.

For the most part, the plan had been a thing of beauty. The death of the Indian cop was wonderful. He had been afraid of the man, who'd shown up out of nowhere . . . a fucking third world Indian reservation for God's sake . . . like some sort of avenging angel. His death had been almost too good to believe. But his spies had reported that the Indian had been given some elaborate funeral ceremony, full of wailing and superstitious nonsense; then he'd had the Ciampi woman followed, but again his spies told him that her grief was real—that she'd actually been seen on a park bench near her home and then again on the Coney Island boardwalk in tears. He didn't understand such emotional reactions to somebody else's death. He wasn't even a lover, he thought. Women are such idiots.

The cowboy, too, though perhaps due to his age and relative inexperience, was not quite as dangerous, and therefore, Kane had not been as disappointed that he lived.

Kane had hoped that the teams sent to Taos would also abduct Lucy Karp. They'd been under orders to spirit her out of the country through the Mexican border and take her to his future home. He'd spent many evenings fantasizing about raping and torturing her while it was all being filmed to send back to her parents—if they somehow survived the coming days. However, there would be other opportunities to capture Lucy Karp.

Some of the plan was purely revenge motivated. However, he wasn't so blinded by vengeance that it overrode his other motives. Fey died because he'd proven to be a traitor, but also there was a small possibility that under questioning he might unknowingly give the authorities a clue as to the major focus of the plan. The same with Flanagan. Of course, his intent had been to distract Karp and his wife, as well as the federal agencies, from the real purpose of his plan. It was the larger plan that interested Samira Azzam and al Qaeda.

Kane turned around and headed back up the road. The assault on the mansion was scheduled for dusk, and he wanted to catch it all as Agent Vic Hodges.

It had taken some balls to suddenly "come in from the cold," so to speak, and try out his disguise on the others. So far it had worked perfectly, even Marlene Ciampi, whom he'd met before, didn't show any sign that she recognized him.

The only one he worried about was Lucy, and they'd never even met face-to-face before this little soiree. But he'd caught her looking at him with a frown on her face several times in the past couple of days, as if she suspected something. He'd even wondered if he'd made a mistake not to have the assassination teams try to kill her along with the Indian and the cowboy.

Speak of the devil, he thought as he looked ahead and saw Lucy standing near the mailbox at the bottom of the mansion driveway. "Going to check the mail?" he smiled as he trotted up to her, laying the Southern accent on thick.

"What? No," Lucy answered as if he'd caught her daydreaming. "Mind if I ask you something?"

Kane gave her his best smile. "Not at all."

"What's with the phony Southern accent?" she asked.

Kane's heart froze. Kill her, a little voice in his head yelled. Quiet you, we'd be caught, he replied. "Phony?"

"Yes," she said. "It's sort of hodgepodge of Mississippi Delta,

Arkansas hillbilly, and Virginia plantation owner. Not bad. You have a gift for mimicry, and most people wouldn't notice. But I have an ear for these things."

Better kill her, the voice said.

"Caught me," he conceded. "I was actually raised on the East Coast, but my family was Army and we moved around the South a lot, too. Then I had to sort of become a 'redneck' to fit in with the Aryan Brotherhood, so to tell you the truth, I'm not surprised I'm a potpourri of dialects."

Time to get out of here, he thought. It's dangerous to talk to her.

She's a witch, the voice said.

"Don't be stupid," Kane said, realizing too late he'd spoken aloud.

"I beg your pardon?" Lucy asked.

"I'm sorry, I mean don't take a chance when the shooting starts," he said. "Just came out wrong."

"Freudian slip, eh?" Lucy said with a smile.

"Something like that, I guess," he said.

"Well, guess I better get back to the action," Kane said. He nodded at the mailbox. "Just remember, stealing mail is a federal offense, ha ha." A funny look passed over his face, but he turned and started trotting back up the road.

Lucy stood for a moment watching Agent Hodges. When she turned to look up the drive toward the mansion, her gaze was drawn to the mailbox.

I think you should look inside, Saint Teresa said.

"Why?" Lucy asked aloud, feeling a little foolish about talking to a voice inside of her head.

You never know, the saint answered, a bit flippantly for a holy person, Lucy thought. There's something not quite right here, and you know it.

"What do you mean?"

Agent Hodges gives me the willies.

"I didn't know saints got the willies. Which just goes to prove you're not real."

Well, he does. You don't buy that bit about the crappy accent, do you?

"As a matter of fact, I think it makes perfect sense. And it might also be why you and I find him a little creepy, like the guys in that racist organization he infiltrated. Sort of like the Stockholm syndrome where the hostages became empathetic with their captors."

I suppose it's possible. But you know and I know that he's been watching you when he thinks you don't notice.

"Can I help it if I'm an extremely attractive woman?"

Go ahead, laugh it off. Just keep an eye on him. In the meantime, why don't you see if there's anything interesting in the mailbox?

Lucy walked two steps closer to the mailbox and stood looking at it for a moment. Without realizing that she'd formed a conscious thought to do it, she reached for the mailbox door and opened it. There was a small box inside, wrapped in brown paper. She was about to close the mailbox door when she saw that the box inside was addressed to her mother. She grabbed the box and took off running to where her mother was kneeling next to Espey Jaxon.

Marlene took the wrapped box and shook it lightly. She started to open it, but Jaxon grabbed her hand.

"What if it's a bomb?"

Marlene got up and ran back to the command tent where a federal agent with a German shepherd stood. "Bomb dog?" she asked.

"Yes, ma'am."

"Mind if he gives this a sniff?" Marlene asked, holding up the package.

"Not at all. Put it on the ground and step back, please."

Marlene did as told. The dog and his handler approached the box. The dog sniffed it curiously but otherwise didn't react. "You're good to go," the man said.

Marlene ran back to the wall with the box and tore the end open. She tilted the box and poured out its contents. Eight white pawns. She looked at them for a moment, then her eyes grew wide. She turned to Jaxon. "Call it off!"

When the federal agents surrounded the mansion, they'd tried to approach the house to demand that those inside leave the house with their hands up. The federal negotiator had retreated from the resulting gunfire and the siege was on.

Soon after, the Saudi ambassador in Denver had arrived at the scene and placed a call to the home. He'd then demanded that the federal agencies pull back. *A prince of the royal family, as well as his wife and children are hostage. The captors are demanding safe passage to Iran.*

Assistant director Jon Ellis had nixed the request. *The terrorists have the option of laying down their arms. No one will be allowed to leave the mansion with hostages.*

Further attempts to negotiate the surrender of the terrorists had broken down. The federal agencies had been given until nine o'clock that night or Prince Bandar, his family, and their servants, some of whom were American citizens, would be executed, one every hour, until the demands were met or all the hostages were dead.

Ellis had decided then to rush the mansion at dusk. *We cannot allow Kane to escape,* he had said. *We need to try to capture him and find out how deep this plot goes. Or, failing that, kill him.*

"Call it off," Marlene insisted again. "I think this was a warning."

"It's Ellis's call," Jaxon said. "Let's go talk to him."

At that moment, a middle-aged man emerged from the mansion. He was wearing a long trench coat and shouting in English.

Jaxon fixed his binoculars on the man. "It's Prince Bandar," he said.

"Help me!" the man screamed, as he walked toward one of the SWAT officers, who had his rifle trained on him. Bandar opened his coat to reveal that he had a bomb strapped to his chest. "Help me!"

Two members of the FBI SWAT team edged forward, one of them spoke into his radio, which went to the rest of the team including Jaxon. "Looks like C4. Pretty crude. If I can get close enough, I bet I can disarm it."

"Allah be merciful," Prince Bandar cried. "They have my family inside—"

Whatever the man was going to say next was lost in the explosion. He simply disappeared in a flash. As the smoke cleared, Marlene could see the two FBI agents on the ground. One was motionless, the other was writhing in pain.

At that moment, Agent Vic Hodges ran up with his gun drawn. "Ellis wants to know what the delay is."

"I think we need to call it off," Marlene said. She pointed at the chess pieces. "I just got those, and I think someone's trying to tell us something."

Hodges looked at the white pawns lying on the ground. "What the hell?" he said. "Chess pawns?"

Before anyone could answer, there was the sound of shooting from the house and women and children screaming. A girl, perhaps twelve, darted from the front door screaming. A masked man appeared behind her and shot her before an FBI sniper killed him. Another child screamed inside the house. The federal SWAT team started to rush toward the house.

"Tell your men to wait, Jaxon!" Marlene yelled. "It's a trap!"

"This is Jaxon, stand down! Stand down!" the agent yelled into his radio.

But it was too late. Driven by the terrified screams of women and children, the SWAT teams were running for the house to try to save the hostages. One paused long enough to throw a flash-bang grenade through the front window, just as other officers were reaching doors and windows on all sides of the building.

Instead of the flash bang of the grenade, however, the entire house went up with a roar. Fifty yards away, Jaxon, Marlene, Lucy, and Hodges were flung to the ground.

Debris rained down on them for what seemed like minutes. When they looked back over the wall, it was at a scene of complete devastation. The house was gone, except for part of the stone fireplace and exposed foundation. A dozen fires burned among the debris of the house and scattered about the yard. There was no sign of the SWAT teams, the hostages, or the terrorists.

The whole world seemed stunned. No one spoke. There were no sounds . . . except those of Lucy crying.

✦   ✦   ✦

Three days later, after the SWAT teams and the agency leaders and the postmortem investigators and Marlene, her daughter, and Ned were gone, Agent Vic Hodges—aka Andrew Kane—sat in a dark corner of the bar at the Hotel Jerome off Main Street in Aspen. He was soon joined by Ajmaani, also known as Nadya Malovo.

"And how's the lovely Samira Azzam?" Kane asked.

Malovo shrugged. "She lives for the day she gets to die in a blaze of glory."

Kane shook his head. "Save me from true believers," he said.

"So she has no idea it was a near thing," Malovo said, "the attempt on the old man. His son recognized me, and that woman—"

"Marlene Ciampi," Kane filled in helpfully.

"Yes, Ciampi," Malovo said, ". . . a dangerous woman. She recognized Azzam. She chose first to kill your man, otherwise she might have shot one of us."

"Hazards of war, I guess." Kane smiled.

Malovo didn't return the smile. "Be careful, Mr. Kane," she said coldly. "I am not one of your toys. I represent very powerful people who can put a stop to this little plan and turn you over to your friend, Mr. Karp."

Kane blanched but then laughed as he regained his color. "Don't threaten me," he sneered. "Your people want my plan to succeed as much as I do. You need to blame this on the Chechen nationalists so that you can keep your little army in place, while your puppets supply you with oil and fat bank accounts. It is a good thing for both of us that others want us to succeed for their own reasons, isn't that right, Mr. Ellis?"

Malovo looked up to see the compact, dapper figure and face of Jon Ellis of Homeland Security. "Yes, Mr. . . . Hodges," Ellis said. "But enough of these little sideshows—we've gone along with your little personal vendetta, and now we want you to focus on the real task at hand."

Ellis sat down at the table and ordered a double-malt Scotch on ice. He hated drinking with the psychopath Kane and the Russian agent almost as much as he was revolted by the idea of helping

Islamic extremists accomplish another act of terror on U.S. soil. However, he and certain others—rich and powerful men and women from many walks of life and areas of the country—were dedicated to protecting the United States of America from enemies within and outside the borders. They were concerned that the American public was growing complacent about the dangers of international terrorism. Safe in their little homes with their big cars and big-screen televisions, they second-guessed actions that men such as Ellis needed to take if they were to win the War on Terror. Hell, they didn't really get that it was a war . . . they saw bombings and beheadings as unrelated criminal acts by some shadowy, deranged people, not a battle of Armageddon proportions of Western civilization against the mongrel hordes of the third world. Even September 11, 2001, had been reduced to a three-digit call for help, 9-11, and the subject of anniversary specials on television.

The citizens of the United States just weren't scared enough anymore. Which made them harder to control and manipulate.

So the rich and powerful people Ellis worked for had decided that the American public needed a new wake-up call. When the Russians had broached the idea that Kane had come up with, it seemed the perfect vehicle for the lesson plan. After this, Americans would realize just how dangerous these Islamic maniacs were and quit questioning the money spent on Homeland Security and the use of the American military to "stabilize" certain parts of the oil-producing world.

Of course, there was the side benefit of keeping the Russians involved in the War on Terror. Sooner or later, as soon as they quashed the pesky nationalists, they'd have to take on the Islamic extremists in Chechnya. And they could hardly complain about the use of the American military while occupying another country themselves.

"As you wish," Kane said. He raised his glass. "Here's to focusing on the 'real task at hand.'"

"Good, then it's settled," Ellis replied, raising his glass. "To the real task."

They all drank, then Ellis looked thoughtfully at Kane before asking, "I'm curious. What's with the expensive chess pieces? It almost got you nailed by Ciampi, who I bet got it from Karchovski. If Jaxon didn't have to run everything through me, your ass might be on its way back to New York attached to a U.S. Marshal."

Kane frowned. "What in the hell are you talking about?"

25

September

"The people call Zachary Stavros." Guma looked to the side door panel through which the young man entered. He smiled in encouragement as his witness passed looking pale and shaky.

Sitting to Guma's left, Karp watched his old friend, searching for signs of how he was holding up. The month preceding the trial had been particularly grueling as they prepared, searching for weaknesses, plugging gaps, working on witness prep and preparing their opening and closing statements.

After one particularly long weekend, Karp asked Guma how he was feeling. He said it lightly but was concerned as the circles under his friend's eyes seemed more pronounced every week, and at other times, he didn't seem to be quite in the same room, though he was well prepared for the trial, his opening remarks simple, to the point, and powerful.

Don't worry, I'm not going to kick off during my opening or fall asleep, unless it's during your closing, Guma had replied with a smile.

Hey, I didn't say anything about your obtuse opening, Karp laughed. *And to be honest, I'm probably more likely to keel over than you. It's been a long month.*

Master of the understatement, Karp thought. Hell, it's been a long year, although maybe the worst of it is finally over. Ever since the debacle at Aspen, in which eight law enforcement officers had been killed and a half dozen others seriously wounded, there'd been no sign of Kane. The official view, according to a briefing he got from Ellis, was that he'd died in the blast.

Crime scene technicians had found very little in the way of identifiable human remains, particularly from inside the house. *Bits and pieces, blood splatters, that's about it,* Ellis had said. However, a single Gucci loafer with enough blood inside to be tested had turned out to be a *positive match for a blood sample taken from Kane when he was incarcerated.*

It was better than nothing, but Karp would have preferred a body—something along the lines of the Old West days when the local sheriff would pose next to the coffins and corpses of deceased outlaws. Not usually the bloodthirsty type, in Kane's case, he'd been willing to make an exception.

The Saudi embassy had registered a complaint with the U.S. Department of State alleging that "law enforcement cowboys had, through their precipitate actions, negated the possibility of a peaceful resolution to the hostage situation, resulting in the tragic deaths of innocent members of the royal family." The State Department, according to Jaxon who had a friend at State, had essentialy told the Saudis to "stick their complaint where the sun don't shine" considering that the "innocent" royal family had been harboring armed terrorists and a fugitive on the FBI's "Ten Most Wanted" list.

Still, even the assumed death of Kane did not necessarily mean the long year was over. There was a chance that whatever plan he was working on was still in place. After all, Azzam had last been seen in New York, running away from a bombing at Brighton Beach, and there'd been no report of her having been in Aspen during the siege. Jaxon had told him that his agency, the FBI, and Homeland Security were going forward as if there were still a threat against the United Nations during Russian President Putin's visit toward the end of the week.

When Karp told Jaxon that his source, "the same one that gave me the photograph of Azzam," believed that the second woman accompanying Azzam was in fact a Russian agent named Nadya Malovo, the FBI agent grimaced. "Christ, that's all we need," he said, "Russians plotting with Islamic terrorists to commit crimes on U.S. soil. A little tough to believe considering the enormous ramifications, even for the former KGB, but not without merit either. Without going into areas that I'm not allowed to discuss, the concept that the Russians are looking for reasons to remain in Chechnya has been discussed in the highest circles."

He'd asked Karp to keep the information under his hat for the time being, which he was only too happy to do. As far as he was concerned, with the exception of his friend Jaxon, all the spies, and agents, and terrorists were welcome to take their games out of Manhattan permanently.

Especially as there were plenty of other distractions that week, both in Manhattan and at home. As previously announced, the Pope would be attending the installment and celebratory mass for Cardinal Nicolas King as the new Archbishop of New York on Saturday. Even though the Vatican's public relations office had gone to great lengths to note that the Pope's visit would be short and limited to the events at St. Patrick's, an estimated one hundred thousand more visitors than usual had deluged Manhattan hoping for a glimpse of the pontiff or to simply be in the same city.

Police Chief Denton and Jaxon had both assured Karp that security for the Pope's visit would be every bit as tight as it would be for Putin's speech the following Friday. "But the 'chatter,' at least according to Ellis, still focuses on the United Nations theory," Jaxon said. "And if the Chechen nationalists are trying to make a point about Russian intervention in their country, attacking the Pope would seem counterproductive. An attack on the United Nations wouldn't exactly be a public relations coup, especially if a lot of innocent people were killed. But at least the attack would be seen as political and might even garner some twisted understanding by people of the sort who sympathized with the Irish Republican Army's tactics as the only way for so-called freedom fighters to defeat a military power. Not to mention, there are a few people in this country who wouldn't be too terribly upset if the United Nations was bombed."

"Either way," Denton added. "We'll be ready."

Security measures were in place, or so it was believed, that assured Karp that everything that could be done had been done. Good thing, too, as he planned to attend the event at St. Patrick's with his family, including Marlene, the twins, and Lucy, who'd returned to New York with her mother after Aspen, and Ned, who'd flown in to JFK that morning.

With the election only two months away, Murrow was working himself into a tizzy trying to line up speaking engagements and, as Guma and Newbury liked to tease, "baby- and ass-kissing events." But Murrow was adamant that Karp needed to get "face time" on the television and in the newspapers.

The polls still showed Rachman running a distant second, though she continued to outspend Karp four to one in advertising and it was reflected in small gains she'd made, especially in neighborhoods where being seen on television was more important than what you said. However, the nearer the November election, the more desperate Rachman was becoming; her attacks were growing ever more virulent.

While touting her credentials from her time as head of the Sex Crimes Bureau, she did all she could to portray Karp as "soft on sexual predators." She'd even managed to dredge up old allegations that Karp was a closet racist. And perhaps, she hinted, even anti-Catholic, as evidenced by his "personal investment" in the case against Archbishop Fey and other local parish priests who were part of the "Kane conspiracies." She was smart enough not to come right out and say it was because he was a Jew—that wouldn't have played well in New York—but left the idea swinging in the wind for the anti-Semitic crowd to grasp onto.

As Zachary Stavros was sworn in, Karp looked over at Emil Stavros, who actually caught his eye and smiled. The banker was dressed in a gray conservative two-thousand-dollar suit, his wavy pewter hair combed back in perfect rows from his tanned face. He oozed confidence and looked immaculate, like he just walked out of the dry cleaner's.

I'm sure we look like chewed-up dog toys by comparison, Karp thought. Of course, Stavros was probably well rested and well fed, having been released to his home with a monitoring bracelet in early August.

The defense had made a motion to dismiss the indictment based on the proffered testimony of Dante Coletta. Skirting a fine line with Judge Lussman's admonition to watch the pandering to the press, as well as attempts to poison the jury pool, Anderson had worded his argument in such a way as to infer that the DAO was not acting on Coletta's story due to politics.

The judge dismissed the motion with a meaningful glare at Anderson. But the lawyer had not been cowed.

Barring the outright dismissal of the charges, Anderson argued, at the very least, his client should be allowed out on bail. "The unfortunate incident that led to his present state of incarceration was due to a momentary lapse in judgment," he said. "Imagine, if you will, the shock of a body being discovered in your backyard when you had no idea it was there. I would remind Your Honor of his own words that Mr. Stavros is still presumed to be innocent and viewed in that light, one can understand why he got in a car and told his driver—a man who did know the truth—to 'just drive.' "

Judge Lussman had agreed to let Stavros out on a substantial bail. However, he'd insisted that Stavros remain at his residence and that his movements be monitored with an electronic bracelet. If Stavros left his home, a signal would be sent via the telephone line to an officer with the probation department.

Hell, even Martha Stewart probably knows how to get around electronic monitoring devices, Guma groused. But there was nothing else he could do.

As Guma checked his notes one last time at the lectern, Karp looked down at the prosecution table. The calm before the storm, he thought. The witness the press has been falling all over themselves to interview with no success.

They'd made a decision to call Zachary to the stand immediately following Guma's opening, which had kept the jurors riveted with their eyes following his every movement, many of them taking notes. All good signs.

The thought was that instead of saving Zachary for the emotional impact wrapping up the state's case would have had, they would present his testimony as it fit into the chronology of events. After he testified about his childhood memory, he'd be followed by former detective Bassaline to describe the original efforts to investigate Teresa Stavros's disappearance, including his interview with the now-accused gardener, Jeff Kaplan. Detective Fairbrother would then be called to describe the subsequent cold case investigation, taking particular care to note that the false credit card statements and reported "sightings" had all been part of an elaborate scheme—with emphasis on the idea that it was unlikely that a punchy ex-fighter-turned-gardener was able to pull it off.

At that point, Drs. Swanburg and Gates would be called to the stand to describe their roles in the discovery and identification of Teresa Stavros's body. Then Fairbrother would be recalled to testify about the subsequent arrest of Emil Stavros in upstate New York. Unfortunately for the defense, Judge Lussman had ruled in the prosecution's favor to allow the defendant's flight north to be brought into evidence as something the jury could weigh regarding his consciousness of guilt.

If Zachary Stavros had wrapped up the case, Karp and Guma decided, it would put too much emphasis on the questionable science of recalling repressed memories, which the defense was sure to attack. Instead, his recollections told in the proper chronology would simply be a small piece of the overall puzzle that would be reinforced with the remaining testimony.

"Good morning, Mr. Stavros . . . Zachary," Guma said. "Would you please tell the jury how you are related to the defendant and the deceased in this case?"

Karp glanced at a photograph Guma had left on the prosecution table next to his yellow legal pad. In it, Teresa Stavros and her son were playing in the surf at Fire Island. Teresa looked beautiful in a loose sweater with her hair pulled back, but it was the adoring smile of the boy as he looked up at her that caught the eye. Now, that's love, Karp thought. He was suddenly reminded of Marlene and his own sons, and his heart went out to the young man on the stand.

At an earlier motions hearing, Guma had to fight for the right to show photographs of Teresa Stavros. The defense attorneys had, of course, wailed and gnashed their teeth that photographs were prejudicial and meant to sway jurors with emotion rather than evidence dealing with the actual crime their client was accused of committing. So Lussman had compromised; Guma was allowed to pick a single photograph, and he'd chosen the one on the beach, which he now showed the jurors as a slide on a projection screen.

Guma had prepared Zachary for the photo presentation. But it was immediately clear that Zachary had become overwhelmed while sitting in a courtroom full of people. Notwithstanding the witness preparation, when shown the photo in the antiseptic, staid courtroom setting, Zachary was emotionally impacted.

"Is this a photograph of you and your mother?" Guma asked.

Zachary nodded and reached for a glass of water.

"You'll have to answer into the microphone," Judge Lussman said, adding, not unkindly, "my court reporter doesn't know how to write a gesture."

Zachary tried to speak but couldn't clear his throat. He took a drink of water.

Come on, kid, Karp thought. You can do this.

"Yes, that's my mother and me," Zachary replied, staring at the photo.

Zachary then lifted his head, glanced over at the jury, and then directly at Guma. The witness prep, perhaps, was starting to kick in.

It was like the first warm breath of spring after a cold winter. Relieved, Karp imagined that he could hear a sigh from the other people in the courtroom, except the defense of course.

Zachary settled into the witness chair and let Guma take him through his testimony. "What's your earliest memory, Mr. Stavros?"

"The earliest I can remember is lying in my mom's arms, looking up at her face," he replied. "I can still see her eyes—green—and feel this silky blue dress or nightshirt she used to wear."

Karp looked over at Emil Stavros, who was doing a passable imitation of a man hurt to see his son on the witness stand. A man who'd lost the woman he loved, and now also his son.

Guma continued. "Do you remember a night when you saw and heard your mother and father arguing?"

Zachary nodded but quickly added, "Yes, I remember a night when I saw and heard my mother and father arguing."

"What do you remember about that night?"

"Objection. Your Honor knows what problems I have with this witness's so-called memories, and I want to make a record of it," Anderson said from his seat.

"So noted, Mr. Anderson, and overruled," Lussman replied automatically, then said to Zachary, "You may continue." The defense objections to the use of Zachary Stavros's repressed memories had already been taken up in the Daubert hearing with the testimony of forensic psychologists. At that time, Lussman ruled that evidence was sufficiently trustworthy to be weighed by the jury. It would, he said, be up to the defense to cross-examine and counter with their own expert witnesses regarding the reliability of repressed memories. Anderson was just making a record for future appeals and, in the process, casting aspersions on the witness's testimony, hoping a juror or two might see it his way.

Guma stood by the jury rail, which was an extension of the jury box area directly in front of the jurors. Generally, lawyers placed their notes on the rail during opening and closing arguments and while questioning a witness.

Guma gave Zachary a slight nod to let him know that it was all right to continue. Zachary looked back to the jurors. "I remember having gotten out of bed to get a drink of water when I heard them fighting. . . . I remember my father slapping my mother—"

"Objection," Anderson said, shaking his head indignantly.

"Mr. Anderson, the record will reflect your continued objection to this witness's testimony," Lussman said. "No need to further interrupt. Please continue."

"I remember him putting his hands around her throat and . . . " Zachary swallowed hard but couldn't quite get the next words out. He reached for the glass of water and knocked it over. "Oh damn," he said and started to cry. "I'm sorry . . . sorry."

"That's all right," Guma said. "Take a moment to compose yourself." When the young man had wiped his eyes and nose, Guma asked, "Ready?"

Zachary nodded his head. "Sorry, yes, I can go on." He straightened his shoulders, shot a look at his father, and then back to Guma. "My father grabbed my mother by her throat and started to shake her. I remember how angry and mad he was . . . his face was red and his eyes looked . . . crazy. He was very loud, and I was very frightened."

"What happened next?"

"He had her backed up against the wall that led to the patio. She was pulling at his hands." As he described the scene, Zachary's hands went up to his neck as if trying to pry invisible hands away. He said something so quietly that the court reporter had to ask him to repeat it. "It seemed like a long time, but she went limp, and he let her fall to the ground."

"What did he do next?"

"I don't know," Zachary replied.

"Just tell us what you recall, please," Guma asked, though they'd been over the testimony many times before.

"I didn't see . . . I don't remember seeing anything more. The next thing I remember is lying in my bed with my sheet pulled up over my head. I was afraid my father would come for me next."

Out of the corner of his eye, Karp saw Emil Stavros shake his head and then cover his face with his hand. A Tony Award–winning performance, he thought.

"Is there anything else you can recall from that night?"

Zachary shook his head and quickly added, "At some point I heard two 'pops' and later I heard the sound of digging."

"Digging?"

"Yes, digging . . . from the backyard. My room was above the yard."

"Did you get up and go to the window to see who might be digging?"

"No."

"Why not?"

"I thought my dad might get mad at me if I got out of bed."

Guma now waded carefully into the area the defense was sure to attack. "Now, are these memories you've had since you were a small child?"

"Well, in a way, but I had repressed them."

"Repressed? How do you mean?"

"Well, as I understand it, sometimes people repress memories of a traumatic event—things that are too scary or bad—especially if they were children when it happened. You lock them away in a safe place in your mind where they can't hurt you, at least that's what Dr. Craig says."

"Who is Dr. Craig?"

"Dr. Craig is my psychologist. I was diagnosed as bipolar—some people call it manic-depressive—to the point where I was cutting myself with razor blades. Some people call that 'self-mutilation,' but really it's more self-injury. It's almost like releasing the steam from a pressure cooker. I had pretty low self-esteem, hated myself actually . . . I'd been told most of my life that my mother left me—"

"Yes, we'll get to that in a moment," Guma said. "Did your father suggest that you go to Dr. Craig?"

"Well, he tried sending me to a lot of different people. He didn't want to deal with me. But I think a friend of his recommended that I go see Dr. Craig.

"Anyway, Dr. Craig suggested that he hypnotize me and see if there was anything in my past—repressed memories that might explain some of my psychological problems."

"And that's when you recalled this fight between your mother and father . . . him choking her?"

"Yes . . . and the pops and digging." Zachary nodded.

"Do you have a recollection of when this fight occurred?"

"Well, I know that it was right before my mom—" suddenly in tears again, Zachary blurted out the rest of the sentence, "disappeared. My father told me she'd left us because she didn't want to be a mother anymore."

"Is that another repressed memory . . . what your father told you?"

Zachary shook his head. "No. I heard that until I stopped asking what happened to my mother."

"After that night, did you ever hear from her again?"

Again, Zachary shook his head. "Not directly. I received some Christmas and birthday cards . . . but obviously, they weren't real."

"Objection. The witness is testifying in an area he has no expertise. It has not been established that the cards in question were falsified," Anderson said.

"Sustained," the judge said. "The jury will disregard the statement about whether the cards were real or not."

"Did you ever see your mother again?" Guma asked. "Or hear her voice?"

Zachary bowed his head and sat quietly. It was soon obvious that he was weeping. He shook his head.

Kindly, Judge Lussman said, "Let the record indicate that the witness replied in the negative to the questions asked by the people."

"Thank you, Your Honor," Guma said taking his seat. "The people have no further questions."

Bryce Anderson rose slowly from his chair as his finger traced across the notepad where he'd been writing during Zachary's testimony. With his tailored suit, handmade ties, and two-hundred-dollar haircuts and hundred-dollar manicures, he almost looked airbrushed. His manner was deliberate, thoughtful as he approached the lectern. He hoped the blonde in the back, who'd finally agreed to dinner at the Tribeca Grill on Friday, was taking note.

For all of his flourishes, however, Anderson was no slacker as an attorney. He knew that he was going to have to tread lightly around Zachary. He was obviously a sympathetic figure on the witness stand.

In his opening, he'd portrayed Teresa and Emil Stavros as having once been very much in love—a love that had produced a fine young boy. However, trying to provide for them, Emil Stavros had worked long hours, *and, perhaps, failed to provide the emotional support for his beautiful wife and much-adored son. . . . The marriage became strained . . . BOTH parties strayed from their vows of fidelity. Mr. Stavros met a young woman who replaced the love that Teresa was giving now to another man—a former convict who'd served time for manslaughter and been hired to attend the family rose garden but tended another man's wife instead. A man named Jeff Kaplan.*

Anderson had asked the jury to keep *an open mind* regarding the skeleton found in the Stavros backyard. *Remember there is no proof that Emil Stavros killed or buried anyone. In fact, we will present a witness who will tell you that he knows who killed and buried Teresa Stavros—her lover, Jeff Kaplan. However, the prosecution will attempt to sway you with a pseudoscience . . . a quackery . . . called "repressed memory recovery," using the Stavros's son, a troubled young man if there ever was one, to "prove" the unprovable. But we will present expert witnesses who will tell you that it is far more likely to actually "plant" false memories than it is to recover real ones. It is not the young man's fault; he lost his much-loved mother and, due to the cruel hoax perpetrated by Mr. Kaplan, who was anxious to loot Teresa's bank accounts, he was unfortunately led to believe that she had abandoned him and his father.*

Anderson smiled sympathetically at Zachary, allowing him time to pull himself together. When the young man looked up, the lawyer inquired, "Are you ready to continue, Zachary?"

"Yes," the young man answered.

"Fine. I know this is tough, and I'm not here to try to make you suffer more than you already have," Anderson said. "But a man's life, your father's life, is at stake here, so I must ask my questions."

"I understand."

"Good. Now, how do we know that what you've claimed is a 'repressed memory' fourteen years after the fact is the truth?" Anderson asked.

Zachary shrugged. "How do we know any memory is the truth? Two people remember the same thing two different ways even a day later."

"Thank you for that," Anderson said, "but that doesn't really answer my question."

Zachary sighed. "We don't. All I can tell you is what I believe to be true."

"Thank you," the lawyer continued. "Now, when you 'recalled' this memory, were you aware that your mother had been having an affair with a man named Jeff Kaplan?"

"I don't believe that is true," Zachary said.

"That wasn't my question," Anderson said. "Were you aware she was having an affair?"

"No."

"Do you remember Mr. Kaplan?"

"I was five years old when my mom disappeared."

"I take that to mean, 'no.' "

"Yes . . . no."

"Thank you," Anderson said. "Now, Mr. Stavros . . . Zachary . . . until you were 'hypnotized' by this Dr. Craig, had you ever told anyone about seeing your father choke your mother?"

"No."

"Or about hearing 'pops' or the sound of digging in the backyard?"

"No."

"Thank you." Anderson turned, glanced briefly at the blond reporter, and said, "No further questions."

On redirect, Guma asked Zachary if he'd ever been shown any reports regarding the remains found in the backyard of his father's house.

"No. I asked, but you said it would have to wait until after the trial."

"Yes, I did," Guma said. "Now, is there anything else you remember from that night? For instance, what your mother was wearing?"

It sounded like a simple question, but it was one they'd discussed several times, including the offhand way it was asked.

"I remember that she was wearing a blue dress . . . or because it was night, I think it might have been a nightshirt. She wore it a lot."

"Yes."

"Anything else?"

"No, not really."

"And you believe that the 'repressed memories' you've recalled are true?"

"Yes."

Asked if he wanted to ask any questions for recross, Anderson looked bored and hardly rose out of his seat. "Just a couple, Your Honor," he said. "Again, Zachary, there is no way of knowing if these 'repressed memories' really depict what happened on the night your mother disappeared?"

"I believe they're real."

"Or, even if they were real—that what you witnessed of your mother and father having a fight occurred on the night your mother disappeared?"

"I believe they're real."

"If these memories are real, it could well be a memory from a month before, or a year. Isn't that correct?"

"I can only tell you that after that night, I never saw my mother again."

Zachary stepped down without looking at his father. He wiped at the tears on his face and glanced at Guma, who winked and said quietly, "I'm proud of you."

26

"YOUR HONOR, THAT IS THE PEOPLE'S CASE."

As Guma announced the end of the prosecution case in chief and sat down, Karp glanced over at the defense table. It was now their turn to proceed. Karp wondered about the worried looks and the agitated confabbing between the lawyers and Stavros.

"I don't think they were prepared for us to be done quite so soon," Karp whispered. "It seems to have thrown them for a loop."

"Good," Guma whispered back. "Anything that's bad for them is good for us."

The night before they'd talked and decided to move as fast as possible to finish. *We might be able to finish this before the weekend,* Karp said. *Maybe even get a jury decision by Friday.*

What? And deprive Emil of one last weekend boinkin' the former Miss Bliss? Guma laughed.

Yeah, let's pick up the pace, and see if we can rattle them a little, Karp said. They had a plan for dealing with the defense's star witness, Dante Coletta, but it was going to take some finesse and a dash of distraction to spring the trap.

Beginning at 9:00 A.M. sharp, Guma summoned former detective Bassaline to the stand to testify about his investigation into the disappearance of Teresa Stravros.

When he began to testify about what the gardener, Jeff Kaplan, had said about the rose garden, Anderson had objected. *Mr. Kaplan is deceased, Your Honor,* he said. *We won't have the opportunity to cross-examine him. And who knows if this witness's recollections after fourteen years are accurate or something he may have . . . dredged up after talking to the prosecution.*

Guma had smiled at the remark and turned to Bassaline. *Detective, you wouldn't have happened to keep any notes of your discussion with Mr. Kaplan, would you?*

Bassaline smiled back and produced a detective's notepad. *As a matter of fact, I'm something of a packrat,* he answered. *Especially in regard to this kind of case . . . it sort of eats at me, and I can't bring myself to throw away my notes, just in case. So I spent a chunk of last week up in the attic until I found this.* He held up the notebook.

The defense objection is overruled, the judge had said. *You may continue, Mr. Guma.*

After Bassaline left the stand, Guma called Detective Fairbrother to the stand to testify about the subsequent investigation, including the credit card and bank statement hoax.

In his opening statement, Anderson had already alluded to the hoax having been perpetrated by Kaplan and his alleged girlfriend, a mystery woman no one seemed able to locate. So there was no need to bring up the handwriting analysis that showed the signatures did not match those of Teresa Stavros. However, Guma went into some detail to demonstrate how elaborate the plan had been while Detective Bassaline's description of Kaplan as a punch-drunk former fighter was fresh in the jurors' minds.

After the detectives, Karp had quickly moved through his witnesses, Swanburg and Gates. Then Fairbrother had been recalled to testify about Stavros's flight when the grave was discovered.

When he left the house, did he say anything? Guma had asked innocently.

He said he had errands to run, Fairbrother replied.

Did he say those errands were in Canada? Guma asked.

Objection, Anderson complained. *My client was not in Canada when he was arrested.*

Close enough, Guma retorted. *But I withdraw the question.* He'd then waited until Fairbrother left the courtroom and declared that he had concluded the people's case.

"Very well," Judge Lussman said. "Mr. Anderson, are you prepared to call your first witness?"

There was still quite a bit of head shaking going on as Anderson rose. "Uh, Your Honor, we'd like to make a motion outside the hearing of the jury."

Lussman sent the jury out of the courtroom. "All right, Mr. Anderson, make your motion."

"The defense moves for a directed verdict of not guilty," Anderson said. "The state has not proved its case beyond a reasonable doubt."

Guma stood and started to speak, but the judge waved him back to his seat. "No need, Mr. Guma," he said. "I find that the prosecution has provided enough evidence that a jury could, at this point, find the defendant guilty as charged. Are you ready to call your witness?"

"Well, Your Honor," Anderson said, "I'd like the morning to prepare a brief on why we believe that the prosecution has not met its burden . . ."

Karp scowled. It was normal for the defense at this point to make the motion to dismiss the case on the ground Anderson cited. However, the "time to prepare a brief" was just a silly attempt to stall.

"I've made my decision, Mr. Anderson," the judge said. "Now, do you have a witness to call?"

Anderson twisted his lips as if trying to weigh how far he could push the judge. "Well, we were expecting the prosecution to take up all of the morning, as well as most if not all of the afternoon. I'm not sure—"

"He's stalling," Karp said under his breath to Guma. "In fact, seems a little desperate."

"Yeah, wonder why," Guma agreed. "Maybe our theory about wanting one more weekend with Amarie was on the money."

"I believe, Mr. Anderson, that I requested that you have your witnesses ready to go this morning," Lussman said. "I believe you've tried cases before me in the past and should know that I don't like delays. We have asked the jurors to put aside their lives and should respect their time. Not to mention, but I will, we have an enormous backlog of cases before this court—you were the one who insisted that an expedited trial take place on this particular week because of your busy schedule—and there's no time to waste."

One of the other lawyers tugged at Anderson's sleeve and said something. "Yes, Your Honor," Anderson said. "I was just caught a little off guard is all."

"Good, then we'll proceed," Lussman said. "I'll ask the jury to return, and you may call your first witness."

A minute later, Dr. Peter Oatman, a psychologist who taught at the University of California–Santa Barbara, was on the stand to testify about the pitfalls of "repressed memory." With his bleach-blond—and probably dyed, Karp thought—hair, perfect tan, and heavy gold chain around his neck, the middle-aged psychologist was the stereotypical California beach boy, which gave Karp an idea as he listened to the man testify.

Having noted that he'd been an expert witness at more than three hundred trials, Oatman knew his role. He listened carefully to each question from the defense as if he were hearing them for the first time. Then looking thoughtfully first at the ceiling, he'd drop his gaze to the jurors and give his answer.

"Dr. Oatman, is there any such thing as repressed memory?" Anderson asked.

Oatman allowed himself a small chuckle and shook his head as if he'd been asked if he believed in Santa Claus. "If you're talking about the sort of small things we all 'forget' in the course of our daily lives, then something 'jogs' our memory, then yes," he said. "Our brains can be very selective about ordering up which memories are necessary to get us through the day, such as how to drive a car. We might head out one morning, not quite sure of where to turn, but we see something that reminds us—a street sign or a building—then 'poof,' we recall the memory of how to get where we're going."

"Do you recall reading about the supposed 'recovery' of repressed memory of the prosecution's witness, Zachary Stavros, such as it applies to my client Emil Stavros and the crime with which he's been charged?" Anderson asked.

"I have."

"Is that the sort of 'jogging' of the memory you were talking about?"

Oatman rolled his eyes and again shook his head. "No. This quasi science that some of my colleagues in the psychology business profess is very unreliable. It's more likely, in this case, that the 'memory' is a combination of the boy's imagination—a way for him to deal with the sad loss of his mother and the idea that she might have abandoned him—and, perhaps, something his therapist may have suggested accidentally . . . or not."

"Are you saying this 'memory' could have been planted, Dr. Oatman?" Anderson asked as if the idea had never occurred to him.

"Yes. When someone is under hypnosis, they are very suggestible. It's sort of like having a dream where you wake up and wonder if it really happened. Of course, with a dream, we quickly realize that it wasn't real. But it's not as easy with a memory we pick up while under hypnosis. It may continue to be viewed as 'real' unless we are disabused of the notion."

Anderson turned over his witness to Karp, who noted that while Oatman had the same superficial smile plastered on his face, he had difficulty looking him in the eyes. Nervous, he thought, with good cause.

"Good morning, Dr. Oatman," Karp said. "If I may say so, you look like you spend a lot of time in the sun."

"I'll take that as a compliment, Mr. Karp. But don't worry," Oatman replied, turning to the jury with a smile, "it hasn't addled my brains."

Karp laughed with the rest of the courtroom. Smarmy bastard, he thought, but that ought to help. "I suppose not. Are you a surfer?"

Oatman looked surprised and glanced at Anderson, who was smiling but looked as if his brain was grinding trying to decide if he ought to object.

"Why yes, I try to get out a few times a week, as a matter of fact," Oatman said. "I'm not as young as I used to be, so I have to work a lot harder to stay on board."

"I see," Karp said. "Then you'd be familiar with the term 'goofy-footed'?"

"Yes, I've heard of it," Oatman said, shrugging as he addressed the jury. "Most surfers, like most of the population, are right-footed so the most comfortable or standard stance is with the left foot forward. Standing the opposite way is therefore 'goofy-footed,' though most surfers will switch back and forth."

"So do you switch back and forth from standing left-footed and goofy-footed, too?"

Anderson saw the danger and jumped to his feet. "I object, Your Honor. He's trying to bait the witness into saying something that isn't relevant to this case."

Judge Lussman looked at Karp with a half smile. "Is there some sort of relevance to this line of questioning, Mr. Karp?"

Karp smiled. "As a matter of fact, there is, Your Honor, and I'll get to the point, if I may proceed."

"You may, Mr. Karp," the judge said. "But do so quickly."

"Yes, Your Honor. Dr. Oatman, you told the jury that you've testified in more than three hundred cases. Is that true?"

Oatman was on guard. "Yes, more than three hundred cases."

"Ever testified as a prosecution witness regarding repressed memory?"

"Yes, I have appeared for both the prosecution and the defense," Oatman said. "I consider myself a scientist . . . the facts are the facts. My clients, whether the prosecution or the defense, know going in that I will state my opinion without regard for how it impacts their case."

"I see. And have you ever testified to the effect that there *is* scientific validity to recovery of repressed memory?"

Oatman's eyes flashed with alarm. "I may have early in my career when I was still somewhat on the fence."

"How long did you say you've been a practicing psychologist?"

"Approximately twenty-five years."

"So if you said something that supported repressed memory as scientifically valid in, say, the last five years, would that have been early or late in your career?"

Oatman gave a weak smile. "Ah, you must be talking about the seminar in Canada . . . I can explain—"

Karp interrupted. "Please, first answer my question. Would that have been early in your career?"

"Well, uh, no, not really," Oatman said. "But—"

"Then why, Dr. Oatman, would you have told the audience at the University of Toronto in May 2000 that, and I quote, 'the science of recovering repressed memories can no longer be considered in the same vein as witchcraft or past-life regression . . . time and again, hypnotized patients in clinical studies have recovered memories that could be proven with empirical facts."

"Well, taken out of context—"

"Out of context, Dr. Oatman? Didn't this appear in a professional magazine that ran the report of your speech past you before publication?"

"Well, yes, I didn't mean 'out of context' like that . . . I meant that I was playing the devil's advocate," Oatman said, his smile beginning to resemble a grimace.

"This was a debate?" Karp asked, looking back at his notes. "I saw nothing to indicate that you were debating someone who was playing the other side of the devil's advocate."

"Well, perhaps I could have put that better—"

"Yes, perhaps," Karp said. "So do you recall telling your audience that, and again I quote, 'the science of repressed memory' could be an important tool for attorneys on both sides of the aisle?"

"Yes," Oatman said sullenly.

"Who paid for you to give that speech, Dr. Oatman?"

"Relevance!" Anderson shouted, jumping to his feet.

"Overruled."

Oatman glared at Karp. "The speech was given to the Toronto Bar Association."

"So you told a roomful of lawyers that repressed memory was scientifically valid and an important courtroom tool?"

"Yes, Mr. Karp," Oatman said. "That's what I said."

"So based on today's testimony that would make you goofy-footed when it comes to your views on repressed memory?" Karp asked, thinking that one never knew when perusing one of Zak's skateboard and surfboard magazines might come in handy.

"Objection!" Anderson shouted.

"Sustained," the judge said shaking his head at Karp before turning to the jury. "You will disregard the last question from Mr. Karp. . . . And Mr. Karp, please restrain yourself."

On redirect, Anderson made a feeble attempt at rehabilitating his witness, who claimed to have reached his current feelings about repressed memory recovery "in the past year or so." But the defense attorney was also aware that none of the jurors were taking notes, and in fact, some were watching Oatman with their arms crossed.

Not a good sign for Dr. Oatman, Karp thought. He didn't even bother to look up from his notes when Anderson turned the psychologist back over to him for recross. "I have nothing further for this witness, Your Honor," he said. He didn't bother to conceal the contempt in his voice, even though personally, until this case, he hadn't given repressed memory much credence either.

The defense called its expert witnesses to counter Drs. Swanburg and Gates, but their testimony was so weak that Karp didn't bother to cross-examine them. "I have no questions," he said with a little nudge. "The people will let the jury weigh who to believe."

He enjoyed watching the defense lawyers look up at the clock and then huddle. "They don't like the pace of the trial," Karp said to Guma when the court recessed for lunch.

"Then maybe we should pick it up," Guma replied with a wicked smile.

The spectator and press sections of the courtroom were buzzing when Karp and Guma returned from lunch. The defense's star witness, Dante Coletta, was going to be called to the stand where—just like in a Perry Mason movie—he would finger the man who "really" killed Teresa Stavros. The crowd expected fireworks, and Karp knew that Guma was ready to give it to them.

When the judge returned and the jury was seated, Bryce Anderson called Coletta to the stand. The man swaggered to the stand, looking back and forth from one row of spectators to the other, nodding and smiling like he'd just been named best actor at the Academy Awards.

The swagger remained as Anderson led him through the story he'd told Karp and Guma about the murder of Teresa Stavros. He shook his head at the conclusion of Anderson's questioning and said, "I feel terrible about this. I should of said something at the time, but I was trying to protect a friend and was worried about taking the rap, too. Still, it weighs on my conscience, you know."

When the other attorney took his seat, Guma remained still with his eyes closed. Karp wondered if he'd fallen asleep and was about to prod him when his friend opened his eyes, took a quick look at the photograph of Teresa and Zachary on his desk, and then stood abruptly to walk to the lectern.

Karp smiled. The bulldog is back, he thought. They'd gone over the strategy the night before and again at lunch, and it could best be summed up with giving Coletta "enough rope to hang himself."

"So, Mr. Coletta, is it fair to say that you owe Mr. Stavros a lot?" Guma began.

"Yeah," Coletta said, looking up at the ceiling as if he'd discovered something interesting there. "Mr. Stavros gave me a chance when I got out of prison."

"For what?" Guma asked.

"Objection!" Anderson said.

"Mr. Anderson, I will allow it on the issue of the witness's credibility," said the judge.

"Assault and robbery," Coletta replied.

Guma checked his notes and looked up. "Anything else?"

"There was a rape charge in there, too," Coletta muttered.

"Oh, was that a repressed memory?" Guma asked as the courtroom spectators laughed and whispered.

Lussman gave Guma a sharp look. "We get your point, Mr. Guma. Please continue to another area."

Then, after several questions regarding Coletta's version of events, Guma acted as though he was winding down but then remembered something else. "Refresh my memory, Mr. Coletta," he said. "Was Mrs. Stavros standing when Mr. Kaplan shot her?"

Coletta furrowed his brows. The defense attorneys had coached him to think before he answered the prosecution's questions and answer as generally as possible.

"I think that's right," he said.

"Think? Well, let's see—if you'd turn to page 153 in your Q&A given to Clarke Fairbrother on—"

"Yeah, yeah, that's right," Coletta said. "She was standing up."

"And how many times did you say Mr. Kaplan shot her?"

"Uh, once, like I said," Coletta said. "He grabbed the gun from her and she turned to go call the cops, and he shot her once. Bang. Just once."

Coletta's brain was working overtime. There was a lot at stake, including his own future, and he worried that he'd already messed up more than was good for him. But he did remember that the lawyers had told him that there was a single bullet hole in the bitch's head. Emil Stavros had scratched his head at that but shrugged. *I thought I pulled the trigger twice,* he had said. *But it was dark and my hand was shaking. I could have missed.*

"With the court's permission, Mr. Coletta, I wonder if you'd mind stepping down from the witness box to demonstrate how this shooting occurred," Guma said, doing his best "slightly addled older attorney" act.

"I object," Anderson said. "This isn't a theater."

"Mr. Guma?" the judge said with his eyebrows raised.

"Mr. Coletta did this once before for my partner, Mr. Karp, which I think helped us understand how this could have happened," Guma said. "So I'm just trying to paint a clear picture for the jurors. As you know, Mr. Coletta's, uh, version of these events came in rather . . . late . . . in the game. I'd like a refresher myself."

"I'll allow it. But keep it short and to the point, Mr. Guma."

"Of course, Your Honor." Guma waited for Coletta to climb down from the witness stand. "Now, pretend your fingers are a gun. I'll turn my back, like so . . . and if you would, show the jury about how far Mr. Kaplan held the gun from the back of Mrs. Stavros's head."

Coletta did as told and stepped back a pace as he pointed his fingers at the back of Guma's head. "He was about this far away."

"And then 'boom,' right?"

"Yeah, yeah . . . boom . . . he shot her, she went down . . . end of story."

"End of story," Guma repeated. "Yes, well, you can retake the stand, Mr. Coletta."

When Coletta was settled, Guma looked up and stated, "Your Honor, for the record, the witness indicated the shooter was about a foot away from the deceased at the time of the shooting and shot the deceased in the head one time."

"The record will so reflect," Judge Lussman said.

Then Guma asked, "Is there anything else you can recall from that night? Some detail?"

Coletta tried to look thoughtful, then shrugged. But before he could answer, Guma slipped in, "Such as . . . what was she wearing?"

Coletta paused to remember what he'd told the prosecutors back in July. Then his face brightened. "Yeah, I think it was one of those white filmy negligee things. She was a pretty hot looker, if you know what I mean."

Guma appeared to bite his lip. "Yes," he said dryly, "I know what you mean. So it was white, sort of see-through?"

"Yeah, that's what I remember."

"Not blue?"

"Oh no," Coletta said. "Definitely not blue."

"And after Kaplan shot her, you helped with the burial?"

Coletta glanced quickly over at the jury. Anderson had told him this would be the dicey part and that he needed to look like a man consumed by guilt when he answered. "Yeah, like I said, I feel real bad about that," he said. "But back then I was like, 'Well, it's done. Jeff's my buddy . . . it's done . . . ' and I thought the cops would try to pin the rap on me, too."

"And what we also have is that you felt like you owed Mr. Stavros because he gave you a job—part of which was to ferry him back and forth to his mistress—after you got out of prison?"

"I—"

"Yes, or no, Mr. Coletta. True or false . . . if you know the difference."

"Objection! Your Honor, that comment was entirely beyond the pale!" Anderson was red-faced with anger.

Karp looked at Guma, knowing his friend was walking a fine line and hoped that his personal investment in the case wasn't going to carry over into the courtroom and destroy their good work. But when their eyes locked, Guma winked.

"Mr. Guma," the judge lectured. "You know and I know that comment was beyond the scope of cross-examination. I will not tolerate another such breach of good conduct. Am I understood?"

Guma bowed his head and nodded. "Yes, Your Honor. Sorry, Your Honor." He stood so that only Karp could see that his fingers were crossed.

The judge turned to the jurors. "As you can see, at times even fine attorneys such as our Mr. Guma can get carried away in the emotion of the moment. I'll remind you that offhand remarks and comments by either side are not to be considered evidence. The evidence is what you see and hear from the witness on the stand and from whatever exhibits may be marked and received in evidence. Please disregard Mr. Guma's uncalled-for remark. Now, Mr. Guma, do you have any other questions?"

"None, Your Honor. However, we do have a matter to take up with Your Honor out of the presence of the jury."

"Very well, Mr. Guma," the judge said. "The witness may step down."

After Coletta left with considerably less swagger than when he entered, the judge sent the jury out of the room. "All right, now what is this matter you wanted to bring up?"

It was Karp who stood to respond. "My esteemed colleague was referring to our intention to call three witnesses to the stand for impeachment purposes regarding Mr. Coletta's testimony during the people's rebuttal case."

Anderson scowled. "I object strenuously. They don't get to retry their case just because they messed up and forgot to ask the right questions the first time."

"There was no 'mess-up,' Your Honor," Karp said. "Again, I'd remind the court that Mr. Coletta was something of a 'witness out of the blue.' We simply want to present witnesses who can give the jury something with which to weigh his truthfulness."

"I'll allow it," Lussman said. "But keep it very straight and narrow, Mr. Karp."

"I promise, Your Honor," Karp said. "Now, we'd like to recall the jury and continue. I believe we have an hour left in the day."

The defense attorneys and Stavros immediately put their heads together. Anderson turned back. "Your Honor, we were prepared to present our case as requested on a shorter notice than we'd anticipated. We simply are unprepared to consider what these 'impeachment' witnesses will bring to the table. We're requesting that the court recess until tomorrow morning."

The judge nodded. "Very well. We'll call the jury back in and adjourn for the day. Mr. Guma and Mr. Karp, have your first witness here and ready to go at nine sharp."

"With bells on our toes," Guma replied, "with bells on our toes."

Lussman smiled wryly. "I'm sure that won't be necessary, Mr. Guma. Shoes will be sufficient."

27

"RELAX, GOOM, YOU SET THEM UP PERFECTLY. NOW WE come in tomorrow like Mariano Rivera and mow 'em down one, two, three. Game over."

They'd just returned to the office after court was recessed to discuss the next day's plans when Guma wondered aloud if he'd handled the Coletta testimony effectively. Karp wasn't used to having to give Guma pep talks.

"You know and I know that you can present the best case in the world and all it takes is for one juror to not 'get it,' and the slimeball walks," Guma replied. His shoulders slumped as he sat in the leather chair near the bookshelf.

Karp pulled open one of the side drawers in his desk and reached inside. He removed a silver flask. He unscrewed the top and sniffed. Karp grimaced and took out two glasses and poured several ounces of brown liquid into each. "I believe you left this here some time ago, but I'm assuming that whatever you had in it wasn't damaged by age," he said. He walked over to hand his friend the drink.

"Probably improved with age, unlike me," Guma said, gulping

his down and holding out his glass for another. He thought for a moment, then said, "It is sort of funny how desperate they are to slow this down. What's up with that?"

Karp looked into his glass as if into a crystal ball but came up empty. "I don't know," he said. "But I don't trust 'em any farther than I can toss 'em. So if they want to slow things down, let's be quick tomorrow."

Whatever Guma was going to say was interrupted by a panicked squawk on the intercom as Mrs. Milquetost tried to warn him about the men coming through the door. But before the words were out of her mouth, in walked Jaxon and Fulton, who was still using the braces, though his legs appeared to be gaining strength.

"Well, it looks like the cavalry has arrived," Guma said.

"Yeah, but to save you or me?" Karp replied, though he already knew the answer from the look on Fulton's face. "Gentlemen, you have the floor, as they say."

"Just making sure your ass lives to fight another day," Fulton said to Karp.

"A few days ago, we suddenly picked up an increase in some of the email 'chatter' and telephone calls with certain al Qaeda sympathizers we keep track of in this country," Jaxon explained. "Not a lot of details, just something big and soon."

"I thought we assumed that would be Putin," Karp said.

"Yeah, and he's still high on the list," Jaxon said. "But then I got a call from your wife."

"Marlene?" Karp asked.

"Well, unless you've taken up polygamy, that would be the one. Anyway, yes, Marlene called and asked me to come over to your loft—"

"I knew I couldn't trust her," Karp joked, but he didn't like the way this was going.

"Boss," Fulton said and put a finger to his lips, "shhhhhh . . . this is important stuff."

Jaxon continued, "Yeah, well, if she'd have me, I might give into the temptations of the flesh . . . don't tell my wife I said that. But like Clay said, this is important. I buzzed on over to your loft and this is what she had waiting for me." He held up a plastic bag with two objects inside.

Karp felt the chill in his spine that he thought might have disappeared for good back in July. "The white king and white queen. Kane?"

Jaxon shrugged. "Yeah, might be," he said. "I've never been real happy with the 'evidence' that he was dead. However, it could also be someone still trying to warn you that even if Kane is dead, his plans are still in motion."

"So who are the white king and queen?" Guma asked. "Butch and Marlene?"

"Well, so far the chess pieces have been sent before an attempt on the life of someone involved in Kane's downfall," Jaxon said. "So that's probably our best bet. Maybe as a distraction from the big plan to hit Putin."

"Oh, so whacking me is the 'little' plan?" Karp said lighter than he felt.

"Don't be offended," Fulton said. "Whacked is whacked."

"So when do we anticipate the whacking?" Guma said.

Jaxon shrugged. "We're really not sure. These little warnings have always come without much time to react. So soon, I'd guess, maybe tomorrow, or maybe Saturday, when all the attention is focused on the Pope. Anyway, we'd like you, Marlene, and the kids to take a little trip to the countryside with us. We have a safe house until this is— what?"

Karp was shaking his head. "Sorry. Not going. I have a trial to finish tomorrow. And Marlene and I are supposed to sit in the VIP section at St. Patrick's on Saturday, and she's looking forward to it."

Fulton swore. "Dammit, Butch, the trial can be postponed a few days. And if you go to the cathedral, maybe that's where they're planning the hit, which means you could be endangering a lot of innocent people even if you're willing to chance getting your own ass shot off. Now, you put me in charge of your security detail, so I insist you listen to me."

Karp clapped his hand on the big man's shoulder. They'd been together a long time, and he knew that Fulton was doing his job.

But he still shook his head as he said, "Not going to do it, Clay. How would it look if halfway through a murder trial and during the Pope's visit, the chief law enforcement officer for the County of New York cut and ran because some wacko or terrorist or combination of the two threatened him. Everybody in this city has known since 9/11, if not before, that Manhattan is one big bull's-eye and that we're all at risk. I'm not going to hide."

They all argued for a half hour before reaching a compromise. Karp would finish the trial, but he wouldn't go to St. Patrick's because of the risk to others if he was targeted. But neither would he be leaving the city for a safe house; he'd remain in the loft or at his office until the threat passed.

Fulton wasn't happy, but he accepted the deal. "Except going to and from the courthouse—at which times I will have my men sitting in your hip pockets—you and the rest of the family are under house arrest, and I don't want to hear anything more about it."

28

I{N AN OLD BRICK APARTMENT BUILDING ON THE NORTH END} of Manhattan Island across the street from Columbia University's Baker Field, Andrew Kane paused for a moment to look at himself in a mirror hanging from the wall of a room converted into an office. He sometimes missed the more refined look he'd had, but he was generally pleased with his new more rugged appearance . . . especially as it seemed to have everybody fooled.

God, I love you, Andrew Kane, he thought as he contemplated the fact that his plan had almost reached fruition; there were only a couple of issues he'd had to resolve and come to grips with since Aspen.

The first was the traitor in his midst who had been sending pieces from an expensive chess set he'd purchased, apparently as some sort of fuzzy warning about his plans for revenge.

When Ellis told him about the traitor at the Hotel Jerome, he'd acted like it was no big deal. However, upon his arrival in Manhattan at the apartment building, he'd immediately located the Torres chess sets he'd shipped. The first had been intact, and for a moment, he wondered if Ellis had got it wrong. But then he'd opened the second set. Missing from the black side were the bishop and the knight; gone from the white side were the pawns, the two knights, a bishop, and the king and queen.

In a rage, he'd flung the set across the room, frightening his al Qaeda bodyguards, who, while more than willing to blow themselves up for Allah, were scared to death of Kane. He knew that they referred to him as Iblis—the chief of the *shayateen,* the evil *jinn,* aka Satan. Their superstitious fear had both amused and flattered him; the part of himself that at times seemed to have a mind and purpose of its own laughed with delight every time he heard the whisperings.

No part of him was laughing when he discovered the betrayal. But who? he wondered. There weren't many who had access to the chess sets, which he'd kept in the guesthouse until the warning from Ellis and the decision for "the new, improved Agent Hodges" to have his coming-out party. Even fewer of them knew about his plans for vengeance.

Samira? No, as much as she hated him, she was devoted to seeing that the plan—along with her glorious martyrdom—came off.

Ajmaani/Nadya? Unlikely. The Russians wanted this as much as he did. They also could not chance her role in the plan being exposed.

Ellis knew about the plan, including the revenge murders. In fact, he'd been the one to turn FBI agent Michael Grover into a traitor. But he hadn't been in the house.

Prince Bandar? The man had never been privy to the plan. However, if he'd found a way to listen in on some of Kane's conversations—despite efforts to sweep the premises for eavesdropping devices and cameras—he might have heard enough. But why the oblique warnings instead of just contacting law enforcement and spelling it out? Unless he, too, was playing a little game, Kane thought. Perhaps, the little toad had more of a mean streak in him than I thought. Maybe sending the chess pieces—which hadn't really arrived in time to do much good—wasn't to warn, but to tease and torment.

It was an act of maliciousness that Kane could identify with, and he'd decided that Bandar was the traitor. If so, there was certainly nothing more to worry about from the man whom he'd personally turned into a million bits and pieces with the remote control detonator button he'd carried in his pocket. However, he was also keeping an open mind that the traitor might still be alive.

Kane's thoughts were interrupted by the whining voice of Bryce Anderson. "I'm worried we might lose this case," Anderson said. "They've got something up their sleeve with these impeachment witnesses."

"Whatever are you talking about, Bryce?" Kane asked coldly. If there was one thing he hated more than all the many other things he hated, it was people who whined about or questioned his plans.

Anderson caught the edge in Kane's voice and stopped himself. "Uh, well, I was just cautioning you that we could very well lose this case."

"Bryce, are you an idiot?"

Anderson felt the knot in his stomach tightening into a solid mass. "No, I don't believe that I'm an idiot," he said meekly.

"Well, then stop acting like one," Kane snarled. "It doesn't matter if you win or lose this case. It's all just a distraction, remember? All you have to remember is that whatever it takes, this better not go to the jury tomorrow. None of us can afford to have the jury come back early with a guilty verdict. Emil Stavros cannot be in prison this weekend. If he is . . . unavailable because he is in prison, I would not be a very happy man. Do you understand what that would mean to you?"

Anderson glanced quickly at the young woman in the corner. She was very beautiful but looking at him in such a predatory way that he thought he might faint. He nodded quickly. "Yes, I understand completely."

Kane smiled, but his eyes were as cold as any serpent's. "Good, because I don't care if you have to shoot yourself to delay the trial. . . . Besides, come Monday, you won't have to worry about Butch Karp or Emil Stavros."

After the lawyer was gone, Samira nearly spit when she said,

"This game you play is stupid. You put our plan in danger of failing."

"And you forget your place, Samira, darling."

"My place is to see that this mission is completed. But this personal vendetta against Karp jeopardizes that."

"That's none of your concern. Without my help this 'mission' cannot succeed anyway."

Kane admired himself again in the mirror. Stupid bitch, he thought. On a mission to kill herself, as if it will matter one little bit in the grand scheme of things.

The whole reason that Emil Stavros was being tried for his wife's murder was part of his glorious plan. He'd come up with the idea while in the Tombs and knew then that he was going to need a banker with access to international financial transfer wires.

That's when he thought of Emil Stavros.

Kane had known Stavros for nearly twenty years, having met him at various high-society functions. Always on the alert for weaknesses in others that he could exploit, he'd learned that Stavros not only cheated on his wife, and cheated on his various mistresses, he also had a bad gambling habit and was heavily indebted to some very bad people.

Kane had purchased the bad debt and then told Stavros who his new master was going to be. Originally, it was so that he could use Stavros's bank to launder money from his criminal enterprises. But he didn't trust the man, so he'd insisted that Stavros hire *a good friend of mine, who is getting out of prison* as his chauffeur, Dante Coletta.

Then came the night when Coletta called Kane and said that Stavros had choked his wife into unconsciousness during a fit of rage when she announced that despite her Catholic faith, she was going to divorce him, taking their son and her bank accounts with her. Kane had thought about it for a moment, then instructed Coletta to give Stavros the .22 Teresa Stavros was known to carry.

Make him shoot her, and make sure his fingerprints are on the gun, Kane had said. *Then bury her in the backyard. Don't touch the gun yourself; just carefully put it in a plastic bag and bring it to me.*

Kane had taken the gun to a bank and placed it in a safe deposit box. It was insurance against the day he might want to blackmail Stavros into something a bit more dramatic than questionable banking transactions. He'd then come up with the elaborate plan of making it appear that Teresa Stavros was alive and running about the world, using up her credit and bank accounts.

It had been easy enough to hire a woman who resembled Mrs. Stavros. Then when that nosy detective Bassaline started getting too close and especially after he'd talked to the gardener, Kane had decided to put a stop to it. First, he'd gone to Bassaline's boss, a man who'd been on his payroll for years, and insisted that the case be turned over to Detective Michael Flanagan.

Flanagan, who at the time thought Kane was giving him orders on behalf of the archdiocese, was told that certain anti-Catholic interests in the city were trying to frame Stavros, a big supporter of the church. Those interests had corrupted Bassaline and paid off the gardener in an attempt to destroy "a good man's, a good Catholic's" reputation. It was Flanagan who'd shelved the case after removing anything that some later detective might "misconstrue," such as the gardener's story.

Meanwhile, Coletta made sure Kaplan's story went no further. He'd called the gardener on the pretext of wanting to talk to him about *some shit I've learned about what happened to Mrs. Stavros.* Feigning that he was afraid he was being followed and might be overheard, Coletta had insisted that they make it appear as if they were going fishing. Out on the boat, when no one was close enough to see, Coletta had hit Kaplan with a fire extinguisher, knocking him unconscious; then the fire extinguisher and the gardener were dumped overboard. Coletta then used the boat's radio to call his ride back to shore.

For fourteen years, Mrs. Stavros had remained buried in the backyard, and the gun used to kill her stashed in a bank deposit box. But at last the day that Kane had anticipated had come.

However, given the magnitude of what Kane wanted to do, and the chance that Stavros would panic and run to the authorities to spoil it all, he'd decided a more subtle route than just straight-up blackmail.

While still a politician running for mayor, Kane had often been in the company of Stavros, whose rise in the political machine he'd funded. Over drinks, Stavros, who thought he had a confidant of sorts in Kane, confided that his son was driving him crazy with all of his psychological problems. He wouldn't have minded if the kid disappeared, but barring that, did Kane know anyone who might *straighten the little shit out.*

Kane remembered the conversation while in the Tombs and called Stavros, pretending that as a friend, he'd been giving Zachary's situation some thought and that, as a matter of fact, he did have someone in mind. He'd suggested sending Zachary to Dr. Craig.

Of course, what Stavros didn't know was that Dr. Craig was another of his thralls. The good psychologist had been charged with sexually assaulting his patients. But due to Kane's magnificent defense, which included threatening the victims, he'd been acquitted.

Although reluctant, Dr. Craig had finally agreed to Kane's plan to "plant" a memory in Zachary Stavros while the young man was hypnotized. It was meant to be a simple memory—of his father choking his mother into unconsciousness and then hearing the sound of digging in the backyard.

When Kane asked Dr. Craig where the stuff about the blue dress and hearing gunshots came from, the doctor shrugged. *He has probably associated the blue dress with his mother since childhood,* the doctor said. *And who knows about the gunshots; maybe he really did hear them, or once the planted memory took hold, his imagination added to it. He is a pretty troubled young man.*

Kane had also made the anonymous call to Guma, who he'd learned was working cold cases, and suggested that he contact Zachary Stavros. And, as planned, the whole thing had snowballed from there.

In fact, it had worked better than he hoped. While the main purpose was to put Stavros over a barrel—a barrel his good friend

Kane had promised to help him get over as long as he cooperated with *a few small requests*—he'd also hoped the political implications would prove to be a big distraction for Karp. It was a dream come true when Karp actually joined the case.

When Stavros learned what the "small requests" entailed, he'd balked. *I'd have to leave the country. I'd be ruined.*

Nonsense, Kane had cajoled him when Stavros visited him in Aspen before the body was located in the backyard. *We make it appear that you were blackmailed and threatened into helping me. And, my dear Emil, you become a very wealthy man.* He explained how Coletta would "confess" that he'd witnessed the murder and pin it on Jeff Kaplan.

Still, Stavros had refused to cooperate. *It will never work,* he'd wept.

That's when Kane lost all patience and decided to play hardball. *Look, you little shit,* he snarled as Stavros blanched. *Who the fuck do you think you're talking to? Pause just a fucking second and ask yourself what would happen if I give the gun you used to kill your wife to the authorities?*

The remaining color had drained from Stavros's face. *You kept the gun?* he asked incredulously. *You've been planning to blackmail me all of these years?*

If necessary, Kane said. *So you don't really have a choice, you piece of shit. Do what I say and you stand a good chance of beating this charge and getting wealthier than you've ever dreamed with all your gambling debts forgiven. Refuse—or worse, go to the cops—and you'll spend the rest of your life in prison, wondering when one of my people is going to show up and gut you like a fucking trout.*

The rest is history, Kane thought. There had been some issues to take care of and some that had arisen in the course of events that followed his escape. Killing Flanagan had been part revenge, but also a necessity to prevent any chance that the former detective, if questioned, might link him to Stavros.

Kane had been surprised that Guma had been able to win an indictment based on the circumstantial evidence he had; in fact, he'd been prepared to have a "little bird" inform Guma of the grave's location, but it hadn't been necessary.

The bigger problem had been when Stavros took off for Canada. The plan—the one involving Samira, the Russians, and Jon Ellis—required that he not be incarcerated, but the idiot had panicked when the body was discovered and had his bail revoked.

Fortunately, you're a genius, Kane thought. He'd simply told Coletta to "confess" a bit earlier than planned, and then informed Bryce Anderson that his life depended on his ability to get Stavros out of jail on bond again. The motivated defense attorney had done just that; just as he'd followed the plan to have the trial set for this particular week so that Stavros would remain over the proverbial barrel until the plan was a done deal.

Kane had toyed with the idea of killing Stavros after he was no longer necessary. But there was no telling if the man would find a way to leave a trail to the financial windfall Kane expected to reap. So for the time being, the plan was to let him live; perhaps his banking services could be used again . . . if he beat the rap.

All was going according to plan. However, his nemesis Karp and Karp's sidekick Guma had breezed through their case. And Anderson wasn't prepared to delay! Well, he better get it done, or I will have him shot.

"Kane! Kane!"

Hearing his name called, Kane looked away from the mirror. "What, Samira?"

"I hope you're not going to do that when it matters," Azzam said furiously. "I've been talking to you for five minutes, and you haven't heard a word."

Kane felt his face flush from the criticism. He hated being criticized. He laughed to cover up his embarrassment. "I heard what I needed to hear. And by the way, your services will be required again tonight if you can tear yourself away from that other bitch."

"I'd rather not," Samira said. "I have a lot to do to be prepared and rested."

"Well, that's too bad," he replied. "I like having sex when I'm stressed. Or perhaps, you'd rather I not allow you to attend the 'festivities.' In fact, maybe I should call my friends with al Qaeda and tell them that I've decided to keep you around awhile longer. Then your precious martyrdom will be put on hold."

Samira knew she'd been put in checkmate again. "Fuck you, Kane."

He smiled. "Exactly what I had in mind."

29

"YOUR HONOR, THIS MORNING THE PEOPLE WILL BE CALLING three impeachment witnesses to the stand, or actually, recalling two of them—Dr. Charlotte Gates and Zachary Stavros—as well as Dr. Sally Thoms. With your permission, the people now call Dr. Thoms."

"Objection," Anderson said, his voice monotone compared to Guma's bright-eyed and bushy-tailed delivery. He was only making a record as they'd already haggled over the state's rebuttal witnesses earlier that morning in the judge's chambers.

Normally, he would not have risked the judge's ire as he had in chambers with the vehemence of his protests and silly arguments. He'd known within the first five minutes how the judge would rule; however, the important thing was that it had taken a good forty minutes off the clock, and it was now almost ten. He had no idea how long the prosecution would take with these witnesses, or the length of time to allow for closings, but whatever it took, he was desperate the case not go to the jury. Chances were, they'd need more than a day to deliberate. But he'd seen juries come back in an hour, and if Emil Stavros was sent to prison any time before Monday, Anderson knew he'd be a dead man.

He wondered what Kane meant by not having to worry about Butch Karp come Monday. No, I don't want to know, he told himself. I just want this trial to be over, but not just yet. At the same time, this was a high-profile case that he wanted to win; both to beat Karp and Guma, something rarely accomplished, and because Stavros, who didn't trust Kane's plan, had promised him a quarter-million-dollar bonus for an acquittal.

Anderson glanced at the back of the courtroom to check on the blond reporter. He tried to set up their date that night after court the day before, but she'd hemmed and hawed and said "something came up" and she might not make it. Bitch was saying you took a beating in court, lost your manhood, and is going to see how you do today, he thought. Fuck her. What I need to do today is survive, then I'll worry about the blonde.

As everyone else in the courtroom waited for Thoms to enter, Anderson looked over at where Karp sat reviewing notes on a legal pad. Mr. Clean, he thought, but not without a twinge of envy. He, too, had come out of law school with high ideals, driven by the sense of purpose that every accused person deserved a competent, vigorous defense. That it was solemn duty to make the state prove its case before it took that most precious commodity, a man's freedom. But he'd also been driven to do whatever it took to become a partner in a prestigious law firm so that he could afford a lifestyle that included cocaine and beautiful women. If that had meant conflict with his conscience, well, it had become easier over time. He'd even talked himself into considering it a sort of strength that he'd learned to accept that he was one of the bad guys; the idealistic young lawyer had been suffocated by poor choices and buried where no one would ever find him, not even the scientists with 221B Baker Street, Inc.

"I'd like to get this into the hands of the jury this afternoon," Judge Lussman said as they waited. "I have another homicide trial on the docket with jury selection scheduled for early next week."

Anderson felt his heart skip a beat. Not if I can help it, he thought. However, he said, "My client would like that as well, Your Honor. The election is a little more than a month away, and there's a lot of work to do."

"He'll be fine," Guma said. "There aren't many distractions in a prison cell, though he may be limited on his use of the telephone."

Lussman cleared his throat meaningfully. "Okay, now that we've drawn this morning's line in the sand, gentlemen, let's knock off the cat fighting. Ah, I believe Dr. Thoms has arrived."

A short, attractive woman with what appeared to be prematurely gray hair entered the courtroom nervously looking around until she saw Karp, whom she first met in person that morning, smiled, and walked forward. The judge indicated with his hand the witness stand and invited her to have a seat where she was sworn in.

"Good morning, Dr. Thoms," Karp began. "Would you tell the jury a little about yourself?"

"Yes," she replied. "My name is Sally Thoms, and I am a professor of fashion design at Colorado State University in Fort Collins, Colorado."

"Do you have any particular area of expertise?" Karp asked.

"Yes. My specialty is fashion history—trends, styles . . . sort of who wore what and when," Thoms said.

After several more questions to establish her area of knowledge, Karp asked that the court accept her as an expert in the area of fashion history. Normally, the request would have been ignored by the defense with little or no questioning. However, Anderson spent an inordinate amount of time questioning Thoms until the judge grew irritated, at which point the lawyer said, "No objection that I haven't registered before."

Karp frowned for a moment as he looked at Anderson. The tactics were an obvious part of the delay game. But why? He turned back to Thoms.

"Were you asked by the prosecution to review evidence in this case?" he asked.

"Well, Dr. Gates asked me to look at some items that I understand were located in a grave," Thoms said.

"And what were those items?"

"Buttons," Thoms said. "Snap-type buttons approximately a half inch in diameter."

"Were you asked to look at any other items of clothing?"

Thoms shook her head. "No, just the buttons."

"There was no cloth? Nothing to which the buttons were attached?"

"No, nothing else. It's my understanding the . . . remains . . . had been in the ground for approximately fourteen years which, depending on the type of material, it's very likely the material would have decomposed given New York's climate, as well as insect activity, chemical additions to the soil. . . . I understand the grave was dug in a garden."

"So there is no way of knowing what sort of material, or article of clothing, the buttons were attached, too?" Karp asked.

"Well, no, actually, I did have some luck in that area," Thoms said. "If you would show the first slide, please."

Karp did as told and a photograph of a half dozen buttons appeared on the screen. Several had what appeared to be mother-of-pearl faces, but the facing had fallen off the rest revealing rusted metal underneath.

"These are the buttons as they were discovered in the grave," Thoms said. "As you can see, there is no material around the edges, the material having disintegrated. Next slide, please."

The second slide showed the buttons as having been pried apart. "When these buttons are created, the tops—the part with the mother-of-pearl inlay—is snapped over the cloth onto the portion with the 'nub' that would be on the inside of the piece of clothing. The nub is the part that snaps into a hole in a third part of the button ensemble to hold the article of clothing, such as a shirt or dress, together."

"Why is this important?" Karp asked, as if he were hearing this for the first time and had not received the report from Thoms more than a month earlier and questioned her both on the telephone and, that morning, in person.

"Well, because the inlay and metal on the top part of the button, when snapped into the second part, actually protected the cloth between them," Thoms said. "Next slide, please. . . . Here you can see the small circular pieces of cloth I removed from the interior of two of the buttons. They are about a half inch in diameter and blue in color."

"So the piece of cloth the buttons were formerly attached to was blue?" Karp asked. He turned to catch the reaction at the defense table and was pleased with what he saw. Emil Stavros looked stunned, while Anderson's mouth hung open.

"Yes," Thoms agreed.

"Is there anything you can add to this?" Karp said.

Thoms pointed to a large object on a stand that was covered with a sheet. "Would you reveal—"

"Objection!" Anderson said, gathering himself. "Foundation? I have no idea what the prosecution is attempting to uncover here, and I'd prefer the jury didn't see it until we've established that it has anything to do with this case."

Judge Lussman looked at Karp. "Counselor?"

"Very well, Your Honor, let's lay a little foundation," Karp said. "Dr. Thoms, can you illuminate us on what you did after prying apart the buttons and finding the pieces of blue material."

"Yes," she said. "Actually, it was quite a fun detective story. First, I determined that the blue material was silk . . . a very expensive type of silk imported from China."

"You can tell that?" Karp asked as though surprised.

"Indeed," Thoms said, warming up to the subject. "Like many other things in our lives, there are different qualities of silk both at its inception—i.e., the silkworms that produce the raw material, the quality and density of the weave, those sorts of things."

"So did that lead you somewhere else?"

"As a matter of fact, it did," Thoms said, enjoying herself now. "The mother-of-pearl inlay was very nice, as was the quality of the silk. And, very helpfully . . . next slide please . . ."

Karp hit the projector button and a magnified back of one of the buttons appeared on which several numbers were identifiable.

"This is the back of one of the 'female,' if you will, parts of the button—the part the nub fits into, thus the gender identification," Thoms said, blushing slightly. "You can see a number; it's a lot number. Now, believe it or not, fifteen years ago, there were not all that many companies producing the metal parts for buttons like these, especially with that sort of expensive inlay. I was able to trace the lot number to a company in Ohio, which produced the buttons for a clothier in New York whose designs were sold in Manhattan at Macy's."

"Were you able to determine what sort of design these buttons had once been part of?" Karp asked.

Thoms nodded. "Yes. It's sort of a long, flowing shirt . . . not evening wear but comfortable, the sort of thing a woman with some means might wear to the park, or even around the house."

"As a nightshirt?" Karp said.

Thoms pursed her lips. "Well, you're talking to someone who likes flannel," she said. "But it would be very comfortable in the summer. Silk from China, you know, was considered a very precious commodity in feudal Japan because of its comfort in hot, humid conditions."

"Like summer in Manhattan," Karp said.

"Yes, like summer in Manhattan," Thoms agreed.

"So were you able to locate a similar shirt at Macy's or elsewhere?" Karp asked.

Thoms shook her head. "No. The line was discontinued. However, I was able to talk the clothier into giving me the pattern from which I sewed my own version using a silk of the exact same color and quality."

Karp turned to Lussman. "Your Honor, I believe we've established foundation for the evidence beneath the sheet, which is the replica shirt sewn by Ms. Thoms."

With that, Karp walked over to the object on the stand and removed the sheet. Beneath it was a dressmaker's dummy on which was draped a blousy blue silk shirt. He then offered the exhibit into evidence. He turned back to Thoms, smiled, and said, "Thank you, Professor. I have no further questions."

"I object," Anderson said. "How do we know that these buttons were only used on this one particular type of shirt?"

"Dr. Thoms, would you like to respond to that?" Lussman asked.

"Yes, I would," Thoms said. "Actually, the buttons with this lot number were used only on this design."

"Very well," Lussman said. "I'll admit the exhibit. You may show it to the jury."

The jurors then examined Dr. Thoms's artistry.

Anderson did little on cross-examination except go over the same points Karp had addressed. More stalling, Karp thought.

The next witness called was Charlotte Gates. When she was settled, Karp asked, "Dr. Gates, remind me, did you testify that there was a single bullet wound in the skull of Teresa Stavros?"

"No," Gates said. "That's not what I said."

Karp was pleased to see the jury, which had paid rapt attention to Thoms, sit forward again and start writing in their notebooks. "No?" he said, as if surprised. "Could you explain?"

"Yes," Gates said. "What I testified to was that there was a single entry wound. But I did not say it was caused by a single bullet."

"Do you have reason to believe otherwise?" Karp asked.

"Yes, I believe the entry wound was actually created by two bullets," Gates replied.

There was a murmur in the spectator gallery even as Anderson jumped to his feet and angrily objected. "What is this?" he demanded. "This isn't impeachment. He's trying to introduce new evidence, which I might add was exculpatory and yet this is the first I've heard of it."

Karp smiled. When he'd first been told about this turn of event by Gates, he'd been just as surprised as defense counsel. Back in July, the forensic anthropologist had asked him to send the remains and the ballistics evidence to her laboratory in Albuquerque in preparation for the trial. *Nothing against the New York ME's lab, but they're not as well equipped* she'd said by way of explanation.

About a week later, and just before the sudden introduction of Dante Coletta into the mix, she'd called with the news that Teresa

Stavros had been shot twice. When during the interview with Coletta, the chauffeur claimed that Kaplan had shot the woman once, he'd formed the idea of a trap . . . the rope for Coletta to hang himself with. However, it was evident that someone in the ME's office had leaked Gates's initial findings to the press and, he assumed, Anderson used it to tailor Coletta's story. So he had Gates submit her latest finding to him—delaying until a week before the trial—and then turned it over with a bunch of other paperwork, counting on Anderson to turn the material over to an inexperienced lawyer or even law student who wouldn't know what to make of it.

"If defense counsel will turn to people's exhibit page one thousand, four hundred and sixty-five, he will find Dr. Gates's addendum to her original report," Karp said. "Please note that someone in Mr. Anderson's office signed for it more than a week ago, but he apparently failed to read the material. And for impeachment, this evidence will unequivocally demonstrate that Mr. Coletta's testimony is a pathetic fabrication."

"Proceed, Mr. Karp," Lussman said.

Anderson sat down like he'd been slapped. Stavros leaned toward him and began whispering furiously.

Would love to know what that's about, Karp thought with a smile. He looked at Gates, who sat waiting expectantly. "Please explain to the jury how you reached your conclusion that the deceased was shot not once, but twice in the head."

"As I was saying, I originally believed that the wound was caused by a single bullet. When all of the physical evidence and ballistics evidence was delivered to my office, I took all the bullet fragments found in the skull and weighed them—which, to be honest, I should have done originally, but knew that I would be taking a deeper look later in the proceedings. Anyway, the weight of the fragments was slightly more than the total weight of a single .22-caliber bullet. So I decided to take a closer look at the entry wound—this time with a high-power electron microscope. Would you mind showing the slide, Mr. Karp?"

"Not at all," Karp replied.

A photograph of the entry wound that the jury had already seen appeared on the screen. "And now the second slide." Suddenly, the wound appeared the size of a basketball. "As you can see, there is a circular wound from a bullet here with the resulting 'chipping' around where bone shattered," Gates said, using a light pointer. "But look at what would be the northeast quadrant and you'll notice another semicircular indentation with its own 'chipping' pattern. This is the second entry wound—so close to the first as to be very difficult to see with the naked eye and even a decent magnifying glass. But there's no denying it's there and what it means."

Karp allowed the jury to digest what they'd just heard before asking his follow-up question. "So if Dante Coletta testified that he saw Jeff Kaplan shoot Teresa Stavros only once, it's fair to say he was mistaken?"

"Correct, Mr. Karp, then Mr. Coletta was mistaken. The deceased was shot twice in the head," Gates said.

"Is there anything else you can tell us in regard to there being two bullet wounds so close together as to be visible only with the aid of a microscope?"

"Yes. It indicates that the deceased was lying down. She wasn't moving and was probably unconscious or even already dead."

Karp looked at Anderson expecting an objection, but the defense counsel seemed to be doodling on his notepad. "How did you reach that conclusion?"

"If, for instance, the deceased was standing when she was shot, it would be very difficult to place the second bullet in almost the same spot."

Karp held his fingers out a few feet from the dressmaker's dummy. "Even from such a close distance?"

"I suppose anything's possible," Gates said. "But highly unlikely. There's a certain amount of recoil, even in a small gun fired in quick succession. The chances of hitting the same spot even on a nonmoving target would be astronomical. But the deceased would have been moving. According to Mr. Coletta's testimony, she had turned and was walking away from Mr. Kaplan. Also, the first bullet would have rocked her head forward and she would have probably started to fall as well."

"Would it be fair to say then that Mrs. Stavros, while unconscious or dead, was executed with two shots to the head?"

"Objection. Counsel knows it's speculative and he's using loaded words to sway the jury."

"Sustained. Mr. Karp, would you like to rephrase your question?"

Karp acted as if he were giving it some thought. "No thank you, Your Honor. I have no further questions for Dr. Gates."

Again, Anderson's questions seemed designed more to take up time than to win any points with the jury. In fact, from Karp's point of view, all he did was reinforce Gates's testimony.

After breaking for lunch, at which time Guma and Karp discussed trying to speed things up as it was so evident that Anderson wanted to slow them down, Guma recalled Zachary Stavros. But not before Karp replaced the sheet over the dressmaker's dummy.

"I believe you testified earlier in the trial that you have never read the reports regarding the exhumation of your mother's remains or subsequent reports by forensic investigators, is that true?" Guma asked.

"Yes," Zachary said, shaking his head. "Like I said, you asked me not to, and I don't have a way to get the reports."

"Has anybody ever told you what is in the reports?"

"No. You said I have to wait until the trial is over."

Guma approached Zachary and handed him several sheets of paper. "I am handing you letters, marked collectively People's Exhibit 17A to F, addressed to Dr. Donald Craig and dated February of this year. Did you write these letters?"

"Yes, they're letters I wrote to Dr. Craig. He asked me to write down any memories of my mother that came to me after the initial sessions when I was hypnotized."

"Zachary, you'll see on the first page I handed you some text that I've highlighted in yellow. Would you read that, please?"

"Yes," Zachary said, clearing his throat. "It says, 'I can even remember what my mother was wearing that night—it was a blue, silk or some other material like that, shirt or maybe a dress. Very loose. I liked how cool it felt on my cheek. And I liked the buttons, which were shiny.'"

Guma looked at Karp who stood and walked over to the dressmaker's dummy. Karp gently pulled the sheet off.

"Does this look familiar?" Guma asked.

Zachary sobbed and nodded.

Gently, Lussman began to remind him, "Sorry, but you'll need to—"

"Yes, it's my mother's shirt," he blurted out and began to cry.

"I'm sorry, Zachary, that was a tough thing to do to you," Guma said, his own voice husky. "This isn't your mother's shirt. It's a replica. Your mother was buried with her shirt."

Guma turned to the judge, fighting the tears in his own eyes. "I have no further questions."

Lussman nodded and looked at Anderson, who had his face in his hands. "Mr. Anderson, do you intend to question the witness?"

Anderson looked at his watch. One o'clock. Closings could take a couple hours, maybe less. The jury might get the case. Stavros is going down for this, he thought, and if he does before Monday, I might as well go jump in that grave in his backyard. I have to stall. "May I approach the bench?"

"By all means," Lussman said.

With Guma and Karp present, Anderson angrily hissed, "They've been sandbagging me with their 'late-arriving' evidence and witnesses. All of this could have been presented during their case in chief."

"Nonsense, this only became necessary when you put a witness on the stand who I think you knew was lying," Guma shot back.

"You're accusing me of a pretty serious offense, Mr. Guma!" Anderson snarled.

"Handsome is as handsome does, Anderson," Guma retorted. "Let's get to closing arguments and see who the jury believes. Then Mr. Stavros can spend the weekend behind bars where he belongs!"

"Mr. Guma, Mr. Anderson, let's keep this civil," Lussman said.

Anderson held whatever he was about to say to Guma and

turned to the judge. "I am obviously going to have to digest what we've all heard here today and perhaps make an application for surrebuttal to recall Mr. Coletta to explain the divergence in theories here."

"Explain why he perjured himself, you mean?" Guma said.

"Your Honor, at the very least, I need some reflective time to respond in my summation to this new turn of events. Please, in the interest of fairness to my client, I'm asking for a small delay until Monday morning," Anderson said. "We'll still have the case to the jury by noon, if not before."

Lussman looked at the lawyers in front of him. The prosecution had obviously torn the defense to pieces, but Stavros still deserved the benefit of the doubt. He was still innocent until proven guilty beyond a reasonable doubt. . . . For a few more hours anyway. "Okay, Mr. Anderson, you have the weekend. Gentlemen, return to your seats."

Fifteen minutes later, Karp and Guma were alone in the courtroom. "Something's going on with Anderson," Karp said. "It's almost like I can put a finger on it, but not quite."

"Yeah, know what you mean," Guma said. "This isn't about one more weekend of freedom. He was sweating bullets to get this trial delayed until Monday. I wish I knew what he was up to."

Karp looked at the dressmaker's dummy and suddenly the words of an old saw popped into his head. "Sometimes it is the blind who see what the sighted cannot though it is right in front of him." Yes, it's right in front of me, he thought, but I can't see it.

30

KARP LEANED AGAINST THE WINDOW OF HIS OFFICE, LOOK-
ing down on the sidewalk outside the Criminal Courts building.
His thoughts drifted to Zachary Stavros's comments months back
about wishing he could be any one of the people on the sidewalk
except himself.

Do you ever wish that, Karp? he asked himself. Do you ever
wish you could choose to be one of those other people on the sidewalk? A cowboy visiting from New Mexico? A professional basketball player with the Knicks? A Navy officer? At one time or another
in his life, he'd wanted to be one of those three. But that wasn't
what Zachary was saying, was it, Karp? He said he'd trade places
with anybody else down there. The bum. The messenger boy on
the bicycle. The madman. Or, God forbid, a defense lawyer!

Karp chuckled at his own joke and turned back toward his desk.
There weren't many people on the sidewalks in and around 100
Centre on a late Saturday afternoon anyway, and he was procrasti-
nating. He'd come to work on his summation for Monday in peace
and quiet until going back to the loft to get ready for the evening's
festivities at St. Patrick's. But he couldn't keep his mind on the

trial. Not with the white king and white queen from an expensive Carlos Torres chess set sitting in an evidence bag on his desk and so many unanswered questions as to what that meant.

However, it wasn't just the sudden possible resurrection of Kane, if indeed it was Kane who had been sending the pieces. Nor was it only the thought of a dangerous terrorist running around Manhattan with the president of Russia due to speak at the United Nations on Friday. It was more of a feeling of not being able to see the big picture of what all of it put together meant because he was standing too close to it. Or smack dab in the middle of it.

All night he'd tossed and turned with a voice in his head. *Sometimes it is the blind who see what the sighted cannot. . . .*

At one point in his fitful dreams, Marlene had wakened him and they'd made love more out of a need to touch base and take comfort in the familiar than any great passion. He'd never tired of her lithe body and had always been amazed how she could make each time different than the thousands of times before. When they at last fell asleep, she was lying on top of him, nestled in his arms. But when he woke in the morning it was with the voice echoing forward from his dreams.

So what are you not seeing, Karp? Come on, use that analytical mind that's seen through a zillion defense strategies and out of a gazillion tight corners. . . . Nothing . . . Some genius you are.

Karp reached down and absently traced his finger across some of his summation notes. He came to a crossed-out name. Detective Michael Flanagan. They'd never figured out a way—mostly because it wasn't necessary—to introduce him into the trial as the cop who shut down the initial investigation. So his name had been crossed out for the closing argument.

Karp tapped the notepad. Although open to the possibility, he hadn't put much stock in the theory that Kane was connected to Teresa's murder through Flanagan. It was just too big a coincidence that fourteen years ago, Stavros killed his wife and called upon Kane to help cover up the crime. If that's true why would the murder suddenly come to light at this particular moment in time with Kane and an international terrorist group threatening?

Karp furrowed his brow and wiped his hand across his face. Let it roll, Karp. What if the trial of Emil Stavros really was part of some larger plan festering in the mind of Andrew Kane?

A distraction?

Maybe, but for what purpose? I'm not all that involved with Putin's appearance. That's not it, and it's more than just a distraction aimed at me and the feds. . . . Emil Stavros has to know that it's Kane pulling the strings that has placed him in jeopardy. Why wouldn't he try to make a deal with us in exchange for helping us catch Kane?

Karp's conscious and subconscious minds jumped to the same conclusion. Kane is blackmailing Stavros to help him . . . something to do with the murder. Something that could put him away, if it fell into the "right" hands.

But Stavros is already dead meat.

That might be the literal truth. Would Kane leave him alive? But I think Guma and I surprised them. I think Stavros was told not to worry about it, as long as he cooperated, he would be acquitted . . . that's why the little smile at the beginning of the trial.

Why would Kane need Stavros?

Stavros is a banker. Criminal masterminds need bankers, secret accounts, wire transfers. Cash.

Okay. So Kane has blackmailed Stavros into helping him . . . something to do with banks . . . but what?

Revenge?

What's that got to do with banks?

Bank robbery?

Using terrorists?

Then money to pay for terrorists to help Kane do something else? Kill me and my family? I don't know.

Don't let your ego get in the way of your brain, Karp. So al Qaeda, which by the way is loaded with oil money, is so impoverished and eager to help kill you that first they murder a half dozen schoolchildren and another half dozen officers of the law, then a former Catholic archbishop, a former detective, a couple more New York cops, then two Homeland Security agents, and the police chief of the Taos Pueblo, then another . . . at last count . . . dozen feds . . . Oh, and let's not forget between ten and twenty—it was difficult to tell from the pieces—hostages and captors in Aspen.

Not to mention all the attempts on my family and friends. Okay. Okay. I get it. This is more than vengeance aimed at me.

Brilliant, my dear Holmes! But the questions remain. What? When?

Karp tapped his finger on the notepad again. It reminded him of watching Guma doodle on his own notepad in court after lunch the day before as they waited for the judge. He'd written the word *stalling* and surrounded it with a variety of squiggles and arrows.

Stalling. Anderson had been so desperate to stretch the trial to Monday, knowing there'd be no delays after that. So it was important to make sure there was no way Stavros would be in prison this weekend.

Which means it's not Putin the terrorists and Kane are after . . .

His eyes caught sight of the white king. Nope. We're not talking the terrorists being after the white king of the Jews here, Karp, my man . . .

Karp grabbed the telephone and punched in the cell phone number of Special-Agent-in-Charge S. P. Jaxon. "Espey, I know this is going to sound like it's coming out of the blue, but we've got it all wrong," he said. "I think it's the Pope they're after. And if I'm right, it's going to be inside St. Patrick's. We have a mole in security inside that church. It's the same problem we had starting with Michael Grover, the traitor bastard responsible for the slaughter of those children and cops and Fulton getting shot."

"Hold on a second," Jaxon said. "I'm outside the cathedral standing near one of the television trucks. There, that's better. What do you mean . . . did you get new information?"

"No, just looking at old information in a new way," Karp replied and explained how he'd come to his conclusions.

"I have to admit, it makes sense," Jaxon said. "I'll run it by Ellis."

"No."

"What?"

"It's your call, but I'd like to keep this to as few people as we can trust with our lives," Karp said. "I don't know how much I trust Ellis, but for sure I don't know him well enough that I'd put my life in his hands. Do you?"

There was silence and then, "No."

"It's just we all know there's a mole in his agency or yours, maybe both," Karp said. "So let's just keep this as quiet as possible . . . need-to-know basis only. . . . Hey, I've always wanted to say that. Who's in charge of the inside security?"

"Vic Hodges," Jaxon said. "Former ATF agent, works for Homeland Security now. He was in Aspen. He has an HS team working with him."

"Yeah, I think Lucy mentioned him," Karp said. "She doesn't like him much."

"He's a little strange," Jaxon agreed. "But I did a background on him after Aspen . . . don't tell Ellis. He seems straight up. Has a wife and kid in the Midwest. Decorated. Shot in the line of duty . . . twice. Was deep undercover in an Aryan gang. Bound to be a little weird."

"Why is he doing the security?"

"He can recognize Samira Azzam and some of her associates. If they somehow manage to get in as part of the spectators or the church types—there's a bunch of them—he's seen their faces. I also have a few of my guys inside. . . . Think we ought to tell the Pope's people to call this off?"

Karp thought about it. "Tough question. But what would we tell them? There might, or might not be, a plot against the Pope by a supposedly dead psychopath and his gang of cutthroat Islamic terrorists? We don't really know how they plan to get past security or how they plan to pull this off. If I'm even right about this."

"The Pope would be safe."

"And every time anybody wanted to throw a panic into the public and force us to live in holes, they make a threat . . . viable or not. And if Kane is alive, this might be our best chance to bring him out, as well as Azzam and any Russian involvement."

"Do we have a right to risk the life of the spiritual leader for a billion or so people? The consequences of something happening to the Pope are enormous."

"I realize that. Maybe we could quietly get word to his top security guy and just let him know that the threat has increased today more than it was yesterday."

"I might be able to do that. And to be honest, if the target is the Pope, it would be easier to try something outside the cathedral, maybe when his motorcade is on the way to the airport. Security around St. Patrick's is going to be tighter than a rusted nut for blocks around the cathedral. No one in without law enforcement or church credentials, or VIP passes is going to be allowed on the streets within three blocks of the cathedral. No pedestrians. No cars that aren't official. As far as the adoring masses, this is a media event. The mayor's office is installing giant-screen televisions on the streets for all the pre-, during, and post-ceremony action."

Karp picked up the evidence bag. "Yeah, you're probably right. But then what's Stavros's role?"

"He's home with an electronic bracelet, isn't he?" Jaxon asked.

"Yeah . . . so maybe this is something he can do on a computer from home," Karp said.

"What if there was a sudden brownout that affected his electricity only?" Jaxon said.

Karp laughed. "I thought you guys didn't do that sort of thing anymore."

"Vee half vays, my friend," Jaxon said. "What about you? Going to stay home now?"

"Nope," Karp said. "My kid . . . Lucy . . . is already at the cathedral with her boyfriend, and soon so will two thousand more people. Marlene's going. You couldn't stop her with a cathedral full of terrorists. This is her one and only chance to get that up close and personal with His Holiness. So I want to be there if anything happens. Besides, if I don't think the Pope should call it off, how could I stay home? I'm going."

"Figured as much," Jaxon said. "Well, I'm going to talk to a couple of my guys who, like you said, I'd trust with my life. And then go find the head of the pontiff's Swiss Guard security detail."

"Swiss Guard? I thought those guys were ceremonial? The metal helmets and pikes."

"Some of what they do is ceremonial and medieval," Jaxon said. "But they've changed with the times, too. They're all former elite Swiss military and well trained."

"Trust them?"

"Yeah. These guys are the Vatican's version of the Untouchables. All Catholic. Impeccable reputations. Five hundred years of dedication to the Pope. If we can't trust them, we might as well just give the world to Kane. Anyway, I want to find one of my best guys, K. C. Chalk, ex-Navy SEAL, and let him in on this. . . . What's next for you?"

"I'm going to make a couple of calls, one to Denton," Karp said. "He'll know what to do as far as security outside the cathedral and on the motor route without tipping anybody else off."

"Who else?"

"Detective Clarke Fairbrother. I think he was taking the day off, but maybe he'd like to keep an eye on his old friend Emil Stavros after the electricity goes out."

"See you in a bit, then. . . . Oh, if you're not the white king, then Marlene probably isn't the white queen. So who is?"

This was the conclusion that Karp hadn't wanted to reach. But his conversation with himself had served as a reminder that the terrorists in New Mexico weren't just trying to kill John Jojola and Ned Blanchet. "That's a big part of why I want to be down there. . . . I hate to say it, but I think the white queen is Lucy."

31

AFTER HER HUSBAND LEFT FOR THE OFFICE, MARLENE SPENT most of the rest of the afternoon pacing and occasionally scowling at the rooftop of the building across the street where she could from time to time see the guys from the Homeland Security sniper team. Two more feds from the agency were stationed on the street outside the loft and another on the landing outside her door.

Jon Ellis had stopped by personally to ask that she and the rest of the family remain inside until it was time for her to go to the cathedral. "My guys have a lot on their hands today and, well, I've heard you're more than capable of taking care of yourself," he said. "But having you on the streets with the kids will make it that much tougher."

Marlene had reluctantly agreed. The weather wasn't so nice anyway. Indian summer had for the day anyway turned overcast and drizzly with wet gusts of wind blowing north from the harbor. Still, she didn't like being kept like a tethered goat waiting for the tiger to show while the hunters sat in their blinds.

Whenever she got tired of pacing, she watched the pageantry leading up to the arrival of the Pope at St. Patrick's Cathedral at about noon on the television. The twins had watched with her for a bit but quickly had grown tired of it, whined about not getting to go out, and retreated to their bedroom when she snapped at them to "quit driving me nuts."

The ceremony wasn't scheduled to begin until seven o'clock that evening, and the Pope was said to be resting in the archbishop's residence attached to the rear of the cathedral. However, that didn't deter the networks from wall-to-wall coverage of "The Pope Visits America." They'd filmed every foot of his movements after he'd transferred into his bulletproof "Pope Mobile" following the initial drive in from LaGuardia so that he could wave to the faithful already lining the streets leading up to the police barricades several blocks from the cathedral. The white space between his arrival at St. Patrick's and the evening's event they were breathlessly filling with interviews with tourists and cuts to talking heads discussing various church issues, such as the impact the conservative Pope's visit would have on wayward American Catholics who supported abortion rights and the ordination of female priests.

Some dignitaries—ranging from politicians, to stars of stage and screen, to the fabulously wealthy—began arriving in midafternoon. Perhaps thinking they might get a private audience with His Holiness if they arrived a bit earlier than the others. Their arrival gave the bored television reporters, who treated each occasion of a recognizable celebrity pulling up like Oscar night, something to do.

Marlene wondered if Lucy and Ned got in okay, but she hadn't heard anything to the contrary. She was sure Father Dugan wouldn't have a problem; he was resourceful that way. And she wished again that her father had been willing to get dressed up and attend.

Father Mike could get you in with Lucy and Ned, she'd told him the day before. *Your one and only chance of a lifetime to get that close to the Pope.*

Mariano Ciampi had been a good Catholic his entire life, rarely missing a mass, going to confession at least once a week, and arguing with his youngest daughter, Marlene, about being *a pick-and-choose Catholic.*

We aren't Methodists . . . or New Agers. You don't get to dabble a toe here and a toe there to see how you like the water. Being Catholic is jumping in feet first, he'd lectured her once during her college days. *You don't get to say, "I like the pretty music, so I'll go to church, but I don't like what the Pope says about premarital sex, so I'll sleep around."*

Marlene had known better than to argue with him—though in her younger, self-righteous years she'd done plenty of that, as her mother, Concetta, clucked around, asking her to *not rile your father.* Later, she'd discovered the benefit of keeping her mouth shut on matters of religion, especially as it intersected secular issues like abortion rights. But as she'd grown older, she'd also found comfort in the steadfast, unbending, principles of her church.

In things secular, Mariano was a patriot. Even if he didn't vote for him, the president of the United States was to be respected—at least the office, if not the man. But in things spiritual, the Pope was infallible. So she was surprised when he turned down the offer to see the pontiff in person.

Nah, it's too much trouble, he said. *I'm going to stay here with your mother.*

Mom's gone, Pops, Marlene said gently.

I know that, the old man scowled. *I meant with her . . . memory. I think maybe she'd be jealous if I got to go see the Pope without her.*

I'm sure she wouldn't mind, Marlene said. *Come on, I'll stop by and help you get ready and you can sit with Lucy and—*

No! I don't want to go, Mariano said, standing up out of his easy chair, suddenly angry, or panicked, she couldn't tell. *I don't deserve to go without your mother.*

Okay. Okay, calm down, Marlene said, taking him by his shaking shoulders and easing him back into the chair. *It's going to be on television anyway. You'll probably see more.*

Yeah, yeah, we'll be more comfortable here, Mariano said. He'd settled down then, but as she turned to leave, he'd grabbed her by the hand, which he kissed and held next to his cheek. *Please, if you get the chance to speak to him privately, would you ask him to say a prayer for your mother . . . and for me.*

She leaned over and kissed him on top of his head. *Yeah, sure, Pops. A special prayer for Mariano and Concetta Ciampi . . . a special place for them to be together in heaven.*

Mariano had laughed at the image. *A small home in Queens with your mother when she and I were young, and all of you were babies . . . that's what I'd call heaven.*

Marlene managed to get to her car before she broke down and started crying. Recalling the discussion the next afternoon, she had to catch herself to prevent the tears from falling again. She turned back to the television where a reporter was describing all the extraordinary security precautions—helicopters overhead, police officers on horseback, plainclothes police officers working the crowds around the barricades, metal detectors for anyone going into the cathedral. "Even Russian president Vladimir Putin's appearance at the United Nations later next week won't be seeing this kind of attention," the reporter gushed as he turned to a tall priest with a pitted, scarred face while the camera followed.

"I'm speaking with Father Aidan Clary, who is normally responsible for securing St. Patrick's," the reporter said. "A little different scenario today, eh, Father?"

The priest looked uncomfortable, like he didn't want to look in the camera. "I'm really not supposed to talk about it, but yes, it's different. Today will be different."

Today will be different. Something about the way the man said it made Marlene take notice. The scarred face. Tall. Wasn't that the description of the killer priest who'd murdered Fey and Flanagan?

Her mind raced ahead. *So the plan is to kill Butch and me at the cathedral? The white king and white queen.* She thought about calling her husband or Jaxon. But what? Tell them a priest who'd once had bad acne as a teenager and now spent his life as the custodian of a cathedral might be an assassin? Even if he was—and maybe whatever Kane or Azzam had planned was already in place—her daughter was in St. Patrick's, and if something went down, Marlene was going to be there.

She picked up the telephone and dialed a number. "I need to talk to him," was all she said to the man who answered.

A half hour later, the Homeland Security agent on the landing stood up as Marlene appeared at the door with her dog. "I know I'm not supposed to go outside until my husband arrives to take me to the cathedral, so would you mind giving Gilgamesh a quick walk before his bladder bursts?"

The agent looked at the dog like he'd just been asked to handle a rattlesnake. He was a big man, and well armed, but it was the biggest canine he'd ever seen in his life. Damn thing could take my arm off with one chomp, he thought.

Marlene noticed the hesitation and smiled. "Don't worry, he's well trained and really just a big baby. Come on, give him a pet."

Nervously, the agent put out his hand and gave the dog a scratch behind the ears. Gilgamesh responded by leaning against the agent and moaning with pleasure.

Marlene smiled sweetly. "Please."

"Sure, why not," the agent said taking the leash. "Come on, boy, let's go for a walk."

As soon as the agent got on the elevator and it started down, Marlene rapped lightly on the door with a spoon. A moment later the door sprang open, a hanging ladder appeared, and then Tran pulled himself up onto the landing, followed by Yvgeny. Someone on the floor below removed the ladder as the three quickly slipped into the loft and shut the door.

Tran had formerly owned the Chinese restaurant food and equipment store on the first floor of the loft building, as well as the space on the second, third, and fourth floors. He'd used it as both a front for some of his nefarious activities, but more as a way of keeping an eye on his friends in the loft. He still owned the building but had moved in a new tenant on the bottom floor, an import company that did very little importing—at least nothing much that was reported to U.S. Customs. It came in handy when he wanted to use a secret way into the building from the basement and then up to the fourth floor below the loft.

After the twins had greeted the "guests," Marlene had sent them grumbling back to their room. Then she explained to Tran and Yvgeny why she'd suddenly focused on the ceremony at the cathedral as the most likely time for an assassin to try to kill Butch and herself. "It might not be more than a woman's intuition, but I want to get inside but stay in the background until I can figure out what's going on. . . . I know it's asking a lot, but I'd like some company if I can arrange this."

Tran smiled. "I didn't have anything better to do today." He shrugged. It was the unspoken truth that he had a crush on Marlene and would have walked into the fires of hell if she was going.

Yvgeny nodded, too. "I have—how do you put it—a dog in this fight, too," he said. "However, I have been troubled by how Kane was playing his game, and you might not be correct on who they plan to target."

"What do you mean?" Marlene asked.

"Andrew Kane is supposed to be something of a chess master, no?" he began. "He buys elaborate chess sets and prides himself on his game."

"Yeah, so?" Marlene said.

"Well, I was asking myself recently, Why is he playing like such a rank amateur game?"

"You're losing me," Tran said.

"Let me explain. Chess is not about how many of your opponent's pieces you can take," Yvgeny said. "The object is to place the other's king in checkmate in as few moves as possible. Great players take pride in piercing to the heart of the enemy's defenses without making it a war of attrition. And for the truly great players, taking your opponent's king when the other side did not see you coming is an even more satisfying achievement."

"I know you just said something important," Marlene said. "But I still don't get it."

Ivgeney laughed. "Kane, who may or may not still be running the show, has played like a beginner. He kills the black bishop. He kills the black knight. He tries to kill the white bishop, kills a white knight, and tries to kill another. Then all those pawns, black and white. It's sort of a 'last man standing' strategy that no chess master would pride himself on, unless—"

"Unless what?" Marlene and Tran said together.

"Unless he is using the Naranja gambit . . . once used by the Spanish chess master, Orlando Naranja, in a world championship match," Yvgeny said. "Essentially, it entails sort of an all-out attack, a war of attrition in which he even sacrificed his queen. But it was meant to distract the opponent and force him to defend against, while Naranja's real purpose was a simple three-move strike from another direction."

"So what we think Kane or someone is trying to accomplish— the assassination of the district attorney of New York and his pesky wife," Marlene said, "is really a distraction for the true purpose, which is to—"

"—place in checkmate the real white king, the Pope," Tran finished. "And the white queen?"

Marlene looked at the television set. "Lucy," she said.

Ten minutes later, the Homeland Security agent knocked on the door of the loft. "Sit, boy," he said, pleased that the dog had followed his every command.

The door opened and Zak poked his head out. "Yes?"

"Oh, hi, where's your mother?" the agent asked. "I brought her dog back."

"She's napping," Zak replied, "and doesn't want to be disturbed." He took the leash from the agent and pulled the dog inside. "Thank you," he said and shut the door on the bemused agent.

32

ANDREW KANE APPROACHED THE SHORT, COMPACT MAN WITH the tidy black mustache and held out his hand. "Colonel Grolsch," he said to the head of the Swiss Guard security team. "Good to see you again."

"Ah, Senore Hodges," the man replied, shaking his hand. "Your people are in place, I assume?"

"Yes, indeed," Kane said with a smile. "My people are in place. And yours?"

"*Si* . . . yes, two here in the back," Grolsch said, pointing to each of two men at the back of the cathedral near the main doors where guests were passing through metal detectors and having their bags searched. "Plus two along the sides. And there will be two more up beyond the altar, along with myself, out of sight, but ready. Oh, and, of course, the two you can see standing behind where the pontiff will be seated, dressed in our traditional uniforms."

Kane looked to where Grolsch indicated the two men clad in Renaissance helmets and blue, red, and yellow tunics. He knew from the Catholic history books he'd been forced to read as a child that the colors were those of the Medici family and the uniforms supposedly designed by Michelangelo. The men were armed with swords and halberds—a combination spear and battle-ax. Not much of a threat, he thought.

"It is a small group"—Grolsch shrugged—"but with all the other security efforts outside and inside, I am comfortable. And your people?"

"Similar placement," Kane said. "But also two—females—among the nuns in the choir."

"But can they sing?" Grolsch asked.

It took Kane a moment to realize the man had made a joke. "You know, I've never asked," he said and did his best to chuckle.

"And where will you be, Senore Hodges?"

Kane smiled. "Why, right next to you. Just in case the unthinkable happens, we will be able to coordinate our response."

"Buono," Grolsch replied. "His Holiness would prefer no guards at all. Alas, we live in a world in which the man who represents peace and God's love to so many must be defended from men of violence. . . . Now, if you will excuse me, I must speak with my people before I take my place."

Kane returned the man's small bow and watched him walk off. Thanks to Grolsch's candidness, he was aware that the four men in the cathedral proper carried SIG P-210 pistols beneath their suit coats, and the two men out of sight behind the altar were also armed with Heckler & Koch submachine guns.

Not that it will matter, Kane thought, suppressing a giggle behind his hand. His plan was marching forward swimmingly with its twin purposes coming together at the appointed hour—soon the Pope, as well as Karp, his bitch wife, Marlene . . . and dear Lucy . . . would be in his grasp. He'd been told the twin boys wouldn't be attending, which was a small disappointment—he'd hoped to kill them in front of their parents. But no matter. He'd make sure the parents understood that they were dead before the evening's festivities were over.

He was so happy, in fact, with the way his plan had worked, he wished he could give himself a hug. The plan had been a masterful work of art, and he'd tinkered with it throughout. Even the death of the terrorist Akhmed Kadyrov during his escape had worked to his advantage when he had the number to the Iranian ambassador—who everyone knew was a tool of the Russians—placed in his pocket. Even the attempt on the old Russian gangster and his son, both known to be sympathetic to the Chechen nationalists, was meant as much for distraction as retribution.

Fey died for his treason, but also because it had been the former archbishop who'd told him the secret last fall that the Pope intended to visit New York to counter the bad publicity of the sexual offenses by priests. If Fey had been questioned about what Kane was up to, he might have given it away. And Flanagan could have recalled hearing the news from him as well.

There'd been a moment of rage and fear when Ellis told him about the king and queen chess pieces arriving at the Karp residence. Who was the traitor? Who was trying to warn Karp? Could Bandar have staggered the arrival of the pieces before his death? Was it the Russian, Malovo? He didn't trust her—the Russians were always full of intrigue and playing one party against another for their own ends. How about Ellis? Was the cooperation of the two just a lie to get what they wanted while preparing to sacrifice him? But no, he'd made sure that they understood that if something went wrong due to betrayal, he'd salted away plenty of evidence to take them down with him.

Who then? he wondered as he watched the guests enter and take their seats. Behind his smile, he was sneering at their excited faces and small talk as they soaked up being among the chosen. Once they'd shown him those same smiles, talked the small talk, when they arrived at his dinner parties, flattering him with their empty compliments and contributions to his campaign when they thought that he was going to be the next mayor of their precious city. They'd disappeared after his arrest, quickly distancing themselves before he'd even been tried and convicted. Now, he could hardly wait to see their faces when he revealed himself and they realized that their lives were in his hands.

Samira was the most logical choice for the traitor. But that didn't make sense either. When he last saw her with Malovo—both of

them dressed as nuns and mixing in with the choir, who'd been told they were there for the Pope's protection—her eyes glittered like black diamonds with the knowledge that at last she would become a martyr, striking a blow for Islam that would never be forgotten. He couldn't imagine her risking the operation . . . unless her purpose was to ruin the personal aspects of his plan.

But then, Kane thought, what if it really is Samira playing a little game as a way of getting back at him? His fear, after Ellis informed him of the king and queen, was that Karp and Ciampi, along with Lucy, would remain home or locked away in some safe house. It wouldn't have ruined the larger focus of the plan, but it would have taken a good chunk of the fun out of it. Just what Samira might enjoy.

Wouldn't have mattered in the long run, Kane thought as he took out his cell phone. I would have killed them someday in some other manner. And as it turned out, they were going to attend despite the threat, or warning, or whatever it was.

Kane was honest enough with himself to recognize that he feared Karp and Ciampi, as well as their odd assortment of friends. It was like some book from his childhood where a group of unlikely heroes comes together to battle the forces of darkness.

From the first moment he'd seen Karp, he'd recognized the man as the proverbial nemesis. He was the leader, the moral center around which the others gathered and found strength.

Marlene Ciampi was dangerous because she was so unpredictable, and as fully capable of using violence as he was without worrying about the niceties when doing what needed to be done. She was like the repentent gunslinger in Western movies who had given up the life until forced into one last showdown to save the townspeople from the bad men.

Superstitious and aware that there were forces at play he didn't understand, Kane wondered how such a fellowship of Goody Two-shoeses had ever come together. Take the Indian. He'd never met the man but recognized that he drew strength through his spirituality and was as fully cognizant of the play between light and dark as he was. The Indian's death had been a great relief.

And what about the cowboy? A seemingly insignificant hick from the sticks, and yet weren't cowboys the American equivalent of the knights-errant? It troubled him that the boy had survived the attack and saved Lucy from falling into his clutches sooner, causing him to slightly revamp his plan for the evening. Doesn't matter, the cowboy's ride is over tonight as well, he thought.

After this, though, I want to get the hell out of Dodge. Some unknown presence stalked him in Manhattan. His spies quavered when they talked about a shadow, or shadows, that watched and sometimes did more than watch, slitting throats and carting bodies off into the dark places. The two men assigned to follow the Karp brats had disappeared. Others left the apartment complex across from Baker Field to purchase a pack of cigarettes or scout the neighborhood to watch for the presence of federal agents or the NYPD and never returned. Even Samira, who didn't seem to fear anyone, was uneasy. But the scouts who did return had shrugged and said they'd seen nothing on the streets and in the park near the apartment except university students, harmless residents, and the usual assortment of homeless bums, including an obnoxious drunk Indian who had been hanging around, rummaging in the building's Dumpster, and begging for handouts.

There was one person who frightened him more than Karp, or Ciampi, their friends, or even nameless shadows. The most unlikely source of fear: Lucy Karp. He was both fascinated by her and afraid of her because she seemed to sense that he was something other than what he portrayed. He imagined that she could see beneath his skin and knew what squirmed there in the dark recesses of his mind. He was sure she'd seen through him in Aspen and almost waited for the feds to pull their guns and arrest him, laughing at how he'd been done in by a twenty-one-year-old girl. That was why she now figured so prominently in his plans.

He'd seen her when she and her cowboy entered the cathedral. In fact, he'd turned around and found her looking directly at him from thirty feet away. His first inclination had been to turn and run. But he'd managed to smile and nod. Instead of returning the greeting, she'd leaned toward her boyfriend and

whispered something, then they'd headed for their seats in the sixth row of pews.

The sooner this is over and I'm back to living the life to which I am accustomed, the better, Kane thought as he punched in the number for another cell phone and stepped into a corner of the cathedral where he could talk privately.

"Emil," he said when it was answered. "Is everything ready?"

Five blocks away at his bank on Fifth Avenue, Emil Stavros sat in the international wire room on the twenty-fifth floor with Dante Coletta. The bank was, of course, closed on Saturday, but the guard at the desk downstairs had hardly bothered to make Stavros and his chauffeur sign in.

Stavros was sweating bullets. The monitoring device set up in his home would have already sent a signal to the cops when the electronic bracelet he wore moved out of the prescribed range. However, that wasn't what had his stomach all tied up in knots.

After all, there was a plan in place to clear him. After he'd done what he was supposed to do, Coletta would tie him up with phone cords and duct tape his mouth shut before going back to the lobby, shooting the guard, and leaving.

Stavros's story would be that he'd been forced to cooperate with Kane or face death for himself and Amarie, who was already home and tied up on the bed. The whole murder case would be portrayed as a setup to blackmail him with a taped confession of Dante Coletta admitting to the murder. Poor Coletta, who thought he would be escaping the country with Kane, didn't know that the plan was for Kane's terrorist friends to shoot him and make it look like a suicide with the tape on the bed next to him.

Better him than me, Stavros thought as he'd waited for Kane's call.

He hadn't meant to kill Teresa that night. But when she refused to help him with his gambing debts, something clicked and the next thing he knew, his hands were around her throat and he'd choked her into unconsciousness. His first thought had been to call an ambulance. But then Coletta had appeared out of nowhere.

If you call an ambulance, the chauffeur said, *they'll call the cops. It will at least be attempted murder, and if she dies, you'll go away for life . . . if they don't give you the death penalty.*

What do I do? he'd pleaded.

Let me make a call, Coletta said. Then when he returned he said, *You're going to have to finish this. Shoot her and then we'll bury her and make it look like she got tired of you fucking around on her and left.*

I couldn't, he'd stammered.

It's that or the electric chair. The chauffeur had shrugged.

Then the gun was in his hand, and he was leaning over with the muzzle a foot from his wife's head. *Closer, Emil,* the chauffeur had whispered. *Put it right on her fucking skull and pull the trigger. You don't want to miss.*

Stavros had looked at his wife and was struck by how beautiful she was; there was a moment's regret, a thought of returning to the first option of calling for an ambulance. But then there was Coletta whispering again, *Shoot her, Emil. Or your life is over.*

He didn't remember pulling the trigger, or whether he shot once or a dozen times. The next thing he knew, he was on his knees throwing up with Coletta patting him sympathetically on the back. "You did what you had to do, Emil," he said.

They'd pulled up the rosebushes and buried her. After replacing the plants, Coletta had told him to sit tight for a couple of days and then report his wife as missing. *Everything will be taken care of,* the chauffeur said. *Just remember, you are indebted to Mr. Andrew Kane from this day on.*

Fourteen years later, Stavros had been angry when he learned that Kane had set him up in order to force him to cooperate with his plan. But there was nothing he could do—Kane had the gun with his fingerprints locked away in a safe deposit box.

The plan to absolve him of the murder should work, Stavros thought. Plus, Karp will be dead, and there will be a mistrial. If I'm worried about it, I'll leave the country. I'll have plenty of money from my share of this.

No, what really frightened him—as a Catholic who on occasion gave some thought to the hereafter—was Kane's plans for the Pope. The first time he heard about the plan, he'd been staggered by its audacity. *You're insane,* he'd said.

The blow from Kane, who'd been standing in front of him, had knocked him from the chair on which he'd sat. *You ever call me insane again, and I'll really show you what happens when I'm feeling a little crazy, you little motherfucker,* Kane snarled.

Stavros had never questioned him again. Nor did he now when Kane asked if he was ready. "Yes, Andy."

There was a moment when Stavros wondered if he'd lost the connection. Then Kane said quietly, coldly, "Emil, if you don't want me to rip your tongue out and feed it to a dog the next time I see you, don't ever call me Andy, again."

"Yes, sir, Mr. Kane. Sorry. Yes, everything is ready."

"Good. Now just sit tight and wait for the transfer. You know what to do after that."

Kane laughed as he closed the cell phone. What an idiot, he thought. He thinks he's going to live? But he did love hearing fear in men's voices when he spoke to them. It made him feel all warm and fuzzy inside.

A voice suddenly spoke in the radio receiver in his ear. "Yes," he said.

"This is Gregor at the back of the cathedral. We have three priests and a nun who say they are with the Pope's medical team."

"You check them over with a wand?"

"*Da,* they're clean. No guns."

"Then let them in. We don't want to do anything that might cause a fuss."

At the back of the cathedral where it joined with the building that held the archbishop's living quarters, as well as some of the archdiocese's offices, the Chechen terrorist posing as a Homeland Security agent allowed the four late arrivals to pass.

He hardly glanced at the men: an older priest he'd seen in the cathedral directing other priests and nuns to their places for the ceremony; and two men he'd not seen before. One of them was a short, middle-aged Asian, the other a tall, rugged priest with a patch over one eye and a scarred face. However, as the nun went past, he got a good look at her face and thought, What a waste of a fine woman to make her a nun. Too bad there is no time for rape, or I would choose this one. But who cares? After tonight, I will be in paradise with my every need fulfilled by virgins.

33

As Marlene surveyed the cathedral from her place among a crowd of nuns who'd assembled behind the altar near the Stations of the Cross sculptures, she wondered if she'd been mistaken. Nothing seemed out of the ordinary. She'd spotted the security detail—four back near her and others scattered throughout the cathedral—who she assumed to be a mix of the pontiff's private force and federal agents. But they seemed to be relaxed, calmly chatting as they watched the last of the spectators hurrying in to take their seats.

While still in the loft, she'd called Dugan. *I need you to help me and two friends get into the cathedral without anybody knowing I'm there,* she told him, explaining her reasons.

Dugan was alarmed. *If you think there's a danger to the Pope, I should tell the authorities.*

Well, I don't know if there is a danger to the Pope, she'd replied. *This is all guesswork. And to be honest, I'm not sure which authorities you can trust. Definitely not the feds, unless you see Espey Jaxon. I just want to be able to watch for any dan-*

ger to my daughter, and I might be able to spot trouble and give a warning to the security teams without alarming anyone.

Although still not happy with the plan, Dugan agreed to meet the threesome at St. Malachy's; he knew Marlene well enough to trust her instincts. Before leaving the cathedral *to pick up the Pope's medical team,* as he told the police captain at the security checkpoint, he'd asked two trusted priests and a nun to borrow their security clearance cards, which they'd given with arched eyebrows but no questions.

At St. Malachy's he'd found enough extra clothing for Marlene, Tran, and Yvgeny to pass as a nun and two priests, though the Russian's pants rode up three inches above his ankles. *I don't think you're going to get past the metal detectors with any weapons,* he'd said.

Thanks, Father Mike, Marlene said. *We'll have to deal with that if and when the time comes.*

Back at the police checkpoint, the three had presented their passes while Dugan explained. *Father Karchovski,* he said, nodding to Yvgeny, *is a Jesuit and a physician. The smaller priest, Father Tran, a visitor from Vietnam, treats the Pope with acupuncture for his arthritis. The sister is a registered nurse who will be assisting Father Karchovski.*

Then at the rear of the cathedral, they'd been stopped by the federal agent, who'd at first refused to let them in. *No one told me of these people,* the man said in accented English.

That's all very well and good, young man, Dugan said. *But I am responsible for the Holy Father's comfort and safety. Do you want to risk him having a health problem . . . causing an international incident?*

The man decided to call in on his radio. Apparently, whomever he reported to told him to let them pass.

After that, Dugan left them to attend to his tasks. Which left Marlene and her comrades faced with a problem of what to do next. The cathedral would hold more than two thousand visitors and there were a couple hundred more priests, nuns, and other church dignitaries wandering about or receiving last-minute instructions on their roles in the ceremony.

Marlene could no longer see Tran, who'd moved off to stand near the main entrance to the cathedral, or Yvgeny, who'd gone back toward the rear to see if he could spot anything out of the ordinary. However, she could see her husband, Butch, who'd entered the cathedral with the mayor, looked around—obviously trying to find his wife—then sat next to his daughter and her boyfriend. They had not spotted her yet.

She also saw Agent Vic Hodges, standing in a small alcove off to the side of the altar with a dark-haired, dark-mustachioed man where they were out of sight of most spectators but close to where the pontiff would be sitting. Hodges had turned toward her once before she could duck, but he hadn't seemed to recognize her in the habit of a Carmelite nun.

Marlene glanced at the acolytes who were standing behind the Swiss Guards positioned at the sides of the pontiff's seats. Then she did a double take as she locked eyes with one, who seemed a bit older than the others. Alejandro Garcia gave her a quick smile, then went back to imitating the actions of his fellow altar boys.

Marlene was thinking about finding a room and changing back into the civilian clothes she was wearing beneath the habit and then taking her seat with her family, when suddenly the nun's choir began to sing. They were facing away from her, otherwise she might have noticed that two were not singing and that one of the two had a recognizable mole on her cheek.

Too late, she thought, then got caught up in the murmur of excitement among her fellow "sisters" as the pontiff and the soon-to-be new Archbishop of New York passed by. The Pope raised his hand and blessed them, his merry blue eyes for a moment resting on Marlene's face so that she momentarily forgot why she was there and joined the others, as well as the spectators in the cathedral, in applauding the Holy Father.

The Pope stood before the crowd for a minute, making the sign of the cross and blessing those assembled. He then took his seat and the crowd grew quiet as a priest began the mass in Latin. However, he was almost immediately interrupted when two nuns stepped from the choir, brandishing handguns with silencers attached from beneath the sleeves of their robes.

The first walked up to the Pope with the gun pointing at his head, while with the other hand she pulled off the headdress of her habit. With shock, Marlene recognized Samira Azzam, who shouted at the Pope, "You are my prisoner in the name of the Islamic Jihad and al Qaeda in Chechnya!"

Several things then happened at once. Marlene saw the man with Hodges rush forward pulling his gun. But the second false nun had anticipated this and calmly shot the man in the forehead. She then held her gun on Hodges, who made no attempt to draw his own gun but raised his hands instead.

The two traditionally dressed Swiss Guards next to the Pope attempted to place themselves between Azzam and the pontiff. But she shot them dead, their halberds clattering to the floor in front of the stunned altar boys.

Marlene turned at the sound of two more pops behind her and saw that two of the four security detail members, who'd been waiting in the background, were on the ground with the other two standing above them with their guns drawn. The killers then walked forward, training their guns on the priests and nuns.

We knew it, and we still got caught, Marlene thought ruefully. But this was too easy. Who was the traitor? Her first inclination was to go to the Pope's aid as well, but she knew that to do so would be to die and that would be of no use to anyone. Wait, she told herself, at the moment, they want him as a hostage.

Elsewhere in the cathedral, the remaining four members of the Swiss Guard had been shot by the "federal agents" standing near them. The television crew swung their camera to the terrorist with the gun on the pontiff but was ordered to shut it off by another terrorist who came toward them with his gun pointed. When the reporter, a well-known broadcaster who'd pulled rank to do the live shots from inside the cathedral, complained, the gunman shot him through the eye. He was dead before his body crumpled to the floor.

Meanwhile, two more faux agents had swung the doors of the cathedral shut and locked them. Then they picked up the automatic rifles with the folding stocks they'd secreted behind curtains early that morning when the traitor priest—the one with the scarred face—let them in.

As the stunned spectators reacted with screams and cries, and by standing as if to flee, Azzam removed the silencer from her gun and shot a man who'd stepped into the aisle. "Sit down and listen," she shouted, pointing her gun back at the Pope's head, "or the leader of the Crusaders will die first, and then the rest of you. . . . Listen to my instructions if you wish to live. They are: you will not attempt to use cell phones, or you will die. You will remain seated and quiet, or you will die."

As if waiting for this cue, a middle-aged woman got up from her seat stating, "I'm not going to stay for this," and began to leave with her nose in the air as though she'd been insulted by the hostess at a bridge party. One of the terrorists near the entrance stepped into the aisle and fired a quick burst that caught the woman and laid her out on the carpet where she lay twitching.

"This," Azzam shouted, "is the penalty for ignoring my instructions."

The Pope, who'd remained seated as if he was trying to understand what sort of theatrical production was being staged, tried to stand. "Please, what is the meaning of this? Do with me what you will, but in the name of God, do not harm innocent—"

Azzam shoved the Holy Father back down in his seat. "Shut up, old man. You are nothing to me but a symbol of my people's oppressor." She turned to the television camera crew, who had remained motionless in slack-jawed terror staring at the body of the former anchorman. Neither of them had liked the man, a pompous ass who liked to treat fellow employees like his personal slaves, but they weren't prepared to see him staring sightlessly at the ceiling with blood trickling out of his ruined eye socket.

"You," Azzam said, commanding their attention, "you will now turn your camera back on and train it on me. No one else . . . or you will die."

The cameraman and the soundman nodded and picked up their equipment. From the folds of her robes Azzam pulled a written statement that she began to read into the camera. "On behalf of the struggle of Muslim peoples in Chechnya, as well as throughout the world, your Pope, a criminal and Crusader representing the centuries of oppression against Muslim people, is the prisoner of al Qaeda in Chechnya, as are all other people in this building. Any attempts at rescue, and this man will be the first, but not the last, to die. My people have already taken control of the security cameras monitoring the outside of this building; we will know of any attempts to use force against us. There have already been numerous deaths; your security people are dead. If you wish to prevent any other unnecessary deaths, you will wait until further contact. That is it for now."

Azzam signaled for the camera crew to cut, which they did, dutifully placing their equipment back on the ground. Then the terrorist turned back to where Agent Hodges, aka Andrew Kane, still had his hands up. "It is done," she said.

The other woman with the gun lowered it as Kane strode forward wearing a big smile as if he'd been named Homecoming King. He'd almost laughed looking at the astonished faces of the crowd when Azzam first announced that the Pope was her prisoner. "Let's get started then," he said clapping with glee.

Half the terrorists put their guns down and picked up bags they'd stored at various spots around the cathedral and began removing the contents. A frightened murmur ran through the spectators when some recognized the materials for making bombs.

"Ladies and gentlemen, please," Kane announced. "My people are just taking out an insurance policy. If all goes well, and everyone cooperates, you'll all go home and sleep in your own beds tonight."

Kane leaped down the stairs and approached the camera crew. "See my face?" he asked the cameraman. The man nodded. "Good.

If you ever photograph my face, you will die. Is that clear?" The man nodded again and mumbled, "Yes, sir."

Kane smiled and patted him on the shoulder. "Good. Good. Then we'll have no problems. Now, think of me sort of as your director-slash-off-screen-commentator. You'll carry my voice, but no face. Now, we're about to go live again. I want you to open with a nice shot of my friend Samira Azzam with her gun pointed at that ridiculous little old man in that silly costume."

"The Pope?" the cameraman asked.

Kane rolled his eyes. "Yes, of course, you idiot. The Pope. . . . Then we'll switch to a shot of those fine young men rigging the explosives. Got that? Good, good . . . hey you might even win an Emmy out of this! All right, hand me that microphone . . . oh good God, wipe the blood off of it first . . . that's better. You ready? Okay, lights, camera, action."

Kane cleared his throat. He couldn't remember the last time he'd had this much fun. "Good afternoon," he said. "We're sorry for any inconvenience, but we've interrupted your regularly scheduled program to bring you a special report. He turned to face Karp, Lucy, and the cowboy, all of whom had remained calm, and said, dropping the Southern accent and assuming his normal voice, "My name is . . . drumroll please . . . Andrew Kane."

Kane paused to let it sink in. He was pleased by the gasps of the spectators in the cathedral and absolutely overjoyed to watch Karp realize the implications. He was less enthused by the reaction of Lucy. He'd expected some mix of shock and horror, but instead she just looked at him steadily, as if she'd known all along and was prepared. It sent a shiver up his spine that he had not anticipated. Well, I will see fear in her eyes before this is over, he swore to himself and tore his gaze away from hers.

"As you've been informed, His Pope-ness and all these fine people are prisoners of al Qaeda," he said and motioned to the cameraman to switch from the Pope to the bombers, who were attaching their devices to the columns of the cathedral and running wires down the aisles toward a panel near the Pope's chair. "Failure to comply with our few rules and our small requests . . . and we'll blow this place to, pardon the pun, Kingdom Come. Oh, and by the way, that goes for any attempt to interrupt this broadcast now or at any time in the future. We are in contact with friends on the outside who will let us know, at which point I will have no choice but to kill someone for every minute we are off the air."

Kane laughed. "Our demands are pretty simple. First, the Vatican will direct its bank to transfer by wire the sum of five hundred million dollars into an account the numbers of which will be given when the Vatican is ready and it had best be within the hour or else"— Kane did his best James Cagney gangster voice—"the Pope gets it, you dirty rats. . . . Next, when our demands have been met, we'll be leaving this fine establishment and traveling to LaGuardia with His Eminence—just to make sure there's no trickery—at which point we'll board a 747 and fly to a country of my choosing. At that point, the Popester will be released to that government, which I'm sure can be negotiated with to allow his return to the Vatican."

Kane pointed to the dead woman lying in the aisle and signaled for the cameraman to focus on her. "This bitch wouldn't follow directions," he quipped. "Now, she's dead. So you can see that I am absolutely serious. Stay tuned for further updates in the near future. Oh, the clock starts ticking as . . . of . . . now."

When the camera was turned off, Kane walked over to where Karp was sitting with his arm around Lucy. "Ah, my good friend Butch Karp," he said, then sniffed the air. "Is that Karp, or carp? Something smells like dead fish."

Karp said nothing so Kane pulled out his gun and waved it in his face. "What's the matter, Karp, cat got your tongue?" He put the gun closer to Karp's face. "So whatever shall I do?" he said. "Shoot you now or shoot you later." He began to dance a little jig. "Shoot Karp now, or shoot him later. Shoot Karp now, or shoot him later." He stopped dancing. "Shoot you now and splatter your fucking ugly head all over your little bitch daughter, or let you think about it?" He leaned toward Karp. "What shall it be?"

Karp continued to say nothing. He just looked in Kane's eyes until the psychopath quailed, but then snarled. "I think we'll wait. In the meantime, I have an hour to spare, maybe it's time Miss

Lucy and I became better acquainted. I've decided to make her my concubine, you know . . . mother of my children. Hey, how about that? We'll be related. Mind if I call you Dad?"

Karp moved his hand so that it gripped Ned's shoulder. Kane saw the move and said, "That's right. Sit still, cowboy, while I go rape the shit out of your girlfriend. Come on, Lucy, let's go."

Any thoughts Karp had entertained about staying calm and finding a reasoned way out of the difficulty were lost to the duty of fatherhood. With a snarl he shot up from his seat, and with one hand grabbed Kane's wrist so that he couldn't use the gun and with the other took Kane by the throat and tried to crush his larynx. He had the momentary satisfaction of seeing terror in the eyes of Kane before the blow from the butt of the gun of a terrorist who'd come up to support Kane, stunned him. The second blow knocked him out.

The terrorist pointed the gun at Karp's head to finish the job, but Kane stopped him. Still, clutching his injured throat and pointing his gun at Ned, who'd started to rise from his seat, Kane croaked, "No. I don't want him dead yet. Bring the girl."

Ned would have leaped and died anyway, but Lucy turned to him quickly. "If you love me, you'll sit back down," she said. "This isn't over." The cowboy remained poised for a moment, then collapsed into his seat.

"That's right, cowboy," Kane taunted. "No John Waynes in here, please. Any heroics would just get a lot of nice people killed. So Lucy and I are just going to go have a little fun, then we'll be right back."

"I'm going to kill you, Kane," Ned said.

"Oh, get in line, cowboy," Kane replied. "Of course you will. Isn't that what happens in the movies? Oh, but wait. This isn't a movie. This is real life and sometimes the bad guy wins!"

"And when I put a bullet in you," Ned whispered, "that will be real, too."

Kane looked at the cowboy for a moment as if weighing whether to end the threat. Then he laughed. "Yeah, but first I'm going to get the girl."

34

As Kane and his bodyguard ascended the stairs to the altar and prepared to pass, the Pope spoke up. "Please, leave the child alone," he said.

Kane shook his head. "Now, you just sit there like a good little Pope and wait for your friends to send me lots of money."

But the Pope continued, "Don't compound your sins by harming another innocent life. No man is so evil that he cannot find salvation through Jesus Christ."

"Oh pul-eeze," Kane said, rolling his eyes. "Take a look at the world, you clown, and tell me again that two thousand years of Christianity has improved things. And let's take the Catholic Church. You've been ignoring the rapacious nature of your priests for how long? Do you think raping little boys is something new? The Catholic Church is just another greedy, money-sucking leech, willing to do whatever it takes to keep the coffers full and the faithful in fear of hell if they don't do as you say. Did you know my father was also my grandfather . . . yes, that's right, he fucked his own daughter, and then your precious church hid the dirty little secret. I don't want your salvation or God's forgiveness. If anything, you should be asking for mine and every other child out there harmed by your crap."

"I am God's representative on earth," the Pope said. "If I beg for your forgiveness, will you give up this mad plan and let the child go?"

Kane looked up at the ceiling as if considering the offer. But then looked back at the Pope and said, "Hell, no. What do I look like, an idiot?"

As he began to pass from the cathedral, Father Aidan Clary stepped forward and clutched Kane by the arm. "I've done what you asked," he said. "I've killed, and now I'm about to become a mass murderer. Where are the woman and my child?"

Kane pulled his arm away from the scar-faced priest. "Oh, I expect you'll be seeing them soon enough," he said, then looked as if something else had occurred to him. "Of course, if there really is a heaven and a hell . . . maybe not."

Clary's face became such a mask of anger and grief that one of the terrorists pointed a gun and motioned him back. "You promised," the priest sobbed.

Kane looked amused. "Yes, so I did. But guess what? I lied. So long, Father . . . and thanks."

As Kane pulled Lucy into the rectory, he stopped at a room where one of his men was monitoring a bank of monitors showing the outside of the building.

"Damn," he said, looking back to smile at Lucy. "Looks like they got us surrounded. Whatever will we do?" He patted the terrorist on the back. "Anything to worry about?"

"Not yet," the man said. "They have called in their SWAT teams, but they seem confused as to what to do next. The infidels are never prepared to accept losses. But soon they will see how real men die, *Allah akbar.*"

"Yes, yes, Allah be praised and all that," Kane said. "Let me know if anything changes."

They continued until reaching the archbishop's apartment where Kane led the way to the sleeping quarters where he shoved Lucy down on the bed. "Leave us," he ordered the bodyguard, then turned to Lucy. "Sheesh, I am so tired of true believers. Don't you find them taxing, Lucy?"

"At least they believe in something worth dying for," Lucy replied calmly.

"At least they believe in something worth dying for," Kane mimicked. "How droll. I hope you're a better fuck than you are a philosopher. We have a lot of years ahead of us."

Lucy furrowed her brow. "What do you mean?"

"Just what I told your daddy," Kane said. "I'm taking you with me when I leave here, and you're going to spend whatever years I decide you have left bearing my children and servicing me whenever I feel like it."

"I'd rather stay here," Lucy said.

"What? And die when I blow this place into so much rubble?"

"If that's the choice, then yes, I'd rather stay."

Kane shook his head. "Sorry, not part of the plan. It is too bad that your dad is going to die here, and your mom and your brothers won't be around much longer, either. I'd give almost anything to see their faces when we send them baby photos. But like I said, almost anything. Fact is, I really can't be bothered with them anymore, I have a world out there that's just waiting for me to take over. I'll just have to get my kicks tormenting you for as long as it amuses me."

"You're insane," Lucy said.

"Well, duh," Kane responded. "But I really hate it when someone says that to me. So I guess we better get started. Take off your clothes, bitch."

Lucy launched herself at Kane, surprising him with the suddenness and ferocity of her attack. A year earlier, and she might have taken his gun. But his training in *Kali* paid off as he sidestepped and struck her in the solar plexus with the extended fingers of his right hand. She collapsed gasping for air on the floor.

Kane took his gun out of its shoulder holster and pointed it at her as he unzipped his pants. "Take your clothes off," he demanded.

"Fuck you," she replied.

"Exactly, but if you don't make this easier, I'm going to send for your boyfriend and blow his brains out all over the archbishop's nice quilt and then fuck you in the gore," Kane snarled.

Lucy got to her knees and nodded. "Okay, you win," she said.

"Good, now—" Kane stopped talking and grabbed his head with his free hand. "Ow, that hurts!"

"Good, maybe it's a stroke," Lucy said.

"Oh, oh," Kane cried out in pain, then he looked up as if frightened and held the gun out to Lucy. "Here, quick, shoot him."

"What?" Lucy looked around wondering who "him" was.

"Take the gun and shoot Kane," he said, shoving the gun toward her as she backed away.

"What's with the sick joke, Kane? And what's with talking like a little boy?"

"I'm not Kane," he replied. "I'm Andy, and I'm twelve years old. Now, take the gun and shoot before he comes back."

"You are one sick puppy, Kane."

Kane stopped offering the gun for a moment, his face a mask of sadness as tears welled in his eyes. "Yes, he is . . . we are." He tried to offer the gun again. "Please, Lucy, I'm a good boy, but I can't do it myself. Shoot us. I want to die."

Lucy stood up slowly and approached. The way Kane was holding the gun, she could have easily taken it out of his hand. "Wow, a complete schizophrenic break," Lucy said in awe and in spite of herself.

"A what?" Andy asked.

"Most so-called split personalities aren't really complete personalities within one body," Lucy replied. "Just variations or idiosyncracies that surface in one main personality. But sometimes the personalities are complete and distinct. Andrew Kane, the psychopath. Andy, the twelve-year-old boy. Of course, I happen to believe that it has something to do with the existence of good and evil in every person. My dad and I could debate this forever."

"There are others in here, too," Andy offered. "Some worse than Kane. They are getting stronger and someday will take over even from him if you don't shoot me. Then the world will be in real trouble."

Lucy looked at the gun. "I . . . I don't think I can, Andy, not while it's a twelve-year-old boy I'd be shooting, not Andrew Kane," she said.

"Please, Lucy, I'm scared," Andy cried. "I don't want to live with the others. They are mean to me and hate me. You have to do it. You're the white queen!"

Lucy's mouth fell open. "You sent the chess pieces," she said.

"Yes, yes, I was trying to warn you," Andy said. "Whenever I could get away from the mean people, like that Samira. I sent them to a friend. He's a bicycle messenger. He gave two to a janitor who works where your daddy does. He also brought them himself. He's my friend."

"What about Aspen . . . the pawns?"

Andy smiled. "That was me when he ran by the mailbox. He didn't see you coming down the driveway, but I did. I thought I could get you to look inside."

"Why not write a note?" Lucy asked.

"They wouldn't let me," Andy pouted. "I tried. But the inside Kane thought it was a fun game to send the pieces."

"He did know, then?"

"Not when he's the one in control," Andy said. "I can't explain . . . but sometimes we're all in here together, and it's all stirred up. He knows about the chess pieces only when he's back inside with the rest of us. So he let me send them when I was out, but nothing else."

"But why am I the white queen? Why not my mother?" Lucy asked.

Andy looked at her like she was kidding him. "You're mom's too old. Geez, I'm just a kid."

"Are you saying you have a crush on me, Andy?" Lucy asked.

Andy blushed. "I don't like girls. But you are good and nice. Once I tried to get out when your daddy and Kane were at a party, and Kane got a bad headache trying to keep me in, you asked if I was okay . . . or really, if Kane was okay. You felt my forehead to see if he, I, had a temperature . . . like a mom is supposed to." Andy shook his head sadly from side to side. "Like my mom never did."

"And that's why I'm the white queen?" Lucy said. "Because I'm nice?"

"Sort of . . . but mostly because the white queen is the most dangerous piece on the chessboard."

"Me? Dangerous," Lucy said. "Now, I do think you have me mixed up with my mom."

"No, I don't," Andy said. "Why do you think Kane brought you back here and wants to do bad things to you? He's afraid of you, and it's because he knows, deep down, that I would want to help you stop him. Now, will you please shoot me?"

Lucy shook her head. "I probably should, but I can't murder an innocent boy."

Andy stomped his feet. "Girls are so dumb."

Lucy smiled. "Sugar and spice . . . now what is he planning to do?"

Andy looked sad again. "He's going to leave here with you. He has a boat waiting for him at the Columbia University boathouse. Then he's going to take you to some place called Spite and Divel and meet a bigger boat to take you and him up the Hudson River to a safe place. But the others are going to stay and kill everyone."

"Spuyten Duyvil," Lucy said.

"What?"

"Spuyten Duyvil is the name of the place you just mentioned," Lucy said. "My dad once told me a story about it."

"I like stories," Andy said. "I wish my mother had read me stories. I . . . uh oh, he's coming back. Good-bye, Lucy, find a way to make him stop."

"Good-bye, Andy," Lucy replied.

Kane scowled. "I hate being called Andy. And I thought I told you to take your fucking clothes off."

Kane was interrupted by a knock on the door. "What is it!" he shouted.

The terrorist who'd escorted them back poked his head in. "The

Vatican has the money ready to transfer, but they are demanding that we release the Pope first," he said.

Kane glared at Lucy, then reached out and grabbed her by her hair. "Oh are they," he yelled as he pulled her out of the room and began walking back to the cathedral. "We'll see about that."

When they reached the altar area, Kane shoved Lucy over next to the Pope, who grabbed her hand. "Are you all right, my child?" he asked.

Lucy smiled. "Yes. I'm not afraid," she said.

"Good," the Pope said with a smile. "Because I am."

Kane said something to Azzam, who said something to the largest of the terrorists standing near the Pope. The man immediately pulled a large knife from a sheath behind his back. With one hand, he cupped the Pope's chin and pulled his head back, with the other he placed the knife at the pontiff's throat.

Kane jumped down the stairs and ran over to the camera crew. "Roll 'em," he screamed as he grabbed the microphone.

"Okay, assholes," he said. "I told you no breaking the rules. Send the money NOW! Or I'll fucking roll the bastard's head down the steps of St. Pat's."

The cell phone of the terrorist who had brought him the news rang. The man listened and then nodded to Kane. "It's done," he said.

"I'll be the judge of that," Kane shouted. He took out his own cell phone and called Emil Stavros. "Is it there? Give it a second . . . okay, good." Speaking back into the microphone, Kane was calmer. "Okay, just a little misunderstanding. But let's not have any more of those. In the meantime, get the plane ready, and we'll all get through this just fine. And as a gesture of goodwill for you coming to your senses, I'm going to send out your Agent Hodges and Lucy Karp. She will be unconscious but unharmed. When she wakes in a couple of hours—after my colleagues and I are long gone with His Pontificy—she will have the information on how to defuse the bombs we have set in the cathedral, and then everyone can go home. See, I'm not such a bad man."

Kane indicated to the camera crew to cut. He then walked up to where Lucy had been fidgeting beside the Pope. "Well, my love," he said to Samira. "It's time we parted ways."

"I am heartbroken," Azzam said. "Are you sure you don't want to remain with me to share the glorious end to this adventure?"

Kane smiled. "No. You see I have a new love . . . Miss Lucy here," he said. "And we're about to embark on our honeymoon with several hundreds of millions of dollars in the bank. Now, if you'd perform the honors."

Azzam produced a hypodermic needle and started to walk to Lucy, who turned to Kane. "Please, I won't give you any trouble if you let me say good-bye to my dad," she pleaded.

Kane looked ready to deny her request but got an odd look on his face and nodded. "Sure, one last good-bye between father and daughter. But mind you, no kissing the cowboy. I'm the jealous sort."

Lucy walked down the stairs to the aisle where her father sat propped up against one of the pews, holding a makeshift bandage made from Ned's shirt on his head. "Do whatever it takes to stay alive, I will get you," he said as she knelt to kiss him on the cheek.

"I know you will," she said, then bent as if to kiss him again. "Kane's taking me to the Hudson by way of Spuyten Duyvil from Columbia's boathouse. The plan is to blow this place up when he's gone."

Lucy stood and leaned over to kiss Ned. "You are not going to do anything to stop him from leaving with me," she said. "After that, it's all fair game, cowboy. I love you."

"I love you, too, Lucy," Ned said. "I'm going to marry you when this is over."

"Ned, you are definitely going to have to choose a more appropriate time to propose," she said and wiped at the tear that trickled down her cheek.

"Okay, okay, break it up," Kane said. "I told you, no mushy stuff with the cowboy. He's yesterday's news."

Azzam walked up to Lucy and deftly stuck the needle in her arm. Kane caught her and laid her on the floor. "All righty, then," he said. "Now you better work me over a little. After all, Agent Hodges wouldn't have let himself get captured without a fight."

Azzam smiled. "With pleasure." She struck him in the mouth with a fist that nearly knocked him over.

"Ouch, good one," he said, spitting out a tooth. "Now, a couple more, and we'll call it a day."

Five minutes later, the doors of the cathedral opened and Agent Vic Hodges staggered out—bloody, one eye swollen closed, his clothes torn—with the unconscious Lucy Karp in his arms. He made it halfway down the steps before sinking to his knees. Two members of the NYPD SWAT team scurried from the police barricade; one of them took Lucy from him and the other helped him to his feet and to a waiting ambulance where Police Chief Bill Denton, Special-Agent-in-Charge Jaxon, Clay Fulton, and assistant director of Homeland Security Jon Ellis waited.

"I think she's okay," Hodges said. "Kane said she'd wake in a couple of hours."

"What can you tell us about the situation inside?" Denton asked.

Hodges shook his head. He started to choke up. "It was a setup," he said. "Someone on the inside stashed guns. Most of my team and the Swiss Guard never knew what hit them." Tears sprang to his eyes. "I'm sorry. I fucked up. Azzam was with the nuns' choir. I never saw her until it was too late. A lot of people, including some civilians, are dead because I messed up."

Ellis stepped forward and patted him on the shoulder. "That's all right, kid," he said.

"No it's not," Hodges said. "I tried to get to my gun, but next thing I knew it was lights out. I'm still feeling a little woozy." As if to prove his point, his knees buckled again.

Ellis looked at the paramedic standing by the back of the ambulance. "Got room in there to get my boy checked out?"

The paramedic nodded. "Sure. The girl's out of it, but she doesn't seem to be in any distress," he said. "Still, I'd like to get going."

Ellis helped Hodges to the back of the ambulance. "Go get that head checked out. We can debrief you later. I'll send one of the boys by to keep you company."

"I'd rather stay, sir," Hodges replied.

"That's an order," Ellis said. "Whatever happened in there wasn't your fault. Now get out of here."

With that, Hodges climbed in the back of the ambulance. The paramedic was about to close the doors when Fulton stopped them. "I think I'll ride along," he said. "I'm not much use here, and I'd like to be there for Lucy when she wakes up . . . especially if things go bad inside." He looked at Hodges. "You don't mind, do you?"

Hodges looked at Ellis and then back to the big detective. "Not at all," he said. "I'm sure Lucy will want you there."

35

"WATCH HER HANDS," GIANCARLO SAID.

"What?" his brother, Zak, replied. "Watch whose hands?"

Giancarlo said, "Watch Lucy's hands."

Like a good part of the rest of the world, the twins were camped out in front of their television watching the events as they unfolded at St. Patrick's Cathedral. At the moment, a large man was holding a knife to the throat of the Pope while their sister stood somewhat to the rear but still in view.

If the twins had more at stake than some in what occurred, they were also somewhat used to their family going from the frying pan and into the fire on a regular basis. If it gave them a rather unusual childhood, they also developed a strong belief that things would turn out all right; after all, their mother and father were in the fray.

"So what?" Zak said.

"I'm watching Lucy's hands," Giancarlo said. "She's signing."

"Signing what?"

"Would you quit being dense? She's saying something in sign language."

"Cool! What's she saying?"

After he was blinded by an assassin's shotgun pellet, Giancarlo had taken up reading in Braille. Then when he regained his sight, he'd remained fascinated by how the blind, and then the deaf, communicated and started to learn sign language, which was one of the sixty-some-odd languages Lucy knew.

"Um, let me see," Giancarlo said. "I'm still pretty shaky at this, She's keeps signing the same thing over and over. 'Lucy hostage. Annoy Satan. Baker. Field. . . . Lucy hostage. Annoy Satan. Baker. Field.'"

"I don't get it," Zak said.

"Neither do I," Giancarlo replied. "But she wouldn't be doing it if it wasn't important."

"So who do we tell?" Zak said. "We can't get anybody on their cell phones."

"The guy outside the door," Giancarlo said and walked over to the front door. He opened it and invited the agent inside. "Um, we think our sister is trying to tell us something about what's going on at the cathedral?"

The agent glanced at the television just as Kane stopped the broadcast. "Like what?" he said.

"We don't know," Giancarlo replied. "That's why we want to go down there and tell somebody like Espey."

"Espey?" the agent replied.

"Yeah, Espey Jaxon, he's a G-man," Zak said. "He'll know what to do with the information."

The agent smiled. "Why don't you just tell me, and I'll relay the information," he said.

Giancarlo frowned. "No. I think we'll go to the cathedral. Our folks are in there." He started to walk to the front door, but the agent pulled him back and shut the door.

"Keep your mouths shut," he said, opening his coat enough to show them his gun. "Where's your mother?"

"Gone," Zak said. "What's it to you?"

"Shut up, kid, and have a seat."

"Shut up yourself. We're leaving, and if you try to stop us, our dog is going to eat you."

The agent looked over at Gilgamesh who was standing watching the conversation but wagging his tail. The agent's orders were to kill the kids and the mother, who had now mysteriously disappeared. He wasn't looking forward to it; then again, national security sometimes required small sacrifices. He laughed and put his hand on his gun, ready to pull it and shoot the dog. "Yeah, right. Gilgamesh, attack!" The dog just stood there wagging his tail. The agent laughed again, "Gilgamesh, sit!" The dog obeyed.

The agent looked back at the boys and pulled his gun. "Some guard dog. You little fuckers aren't going anywhere. Now, sit on the couch while I go check on your mom. If you try to get out of here, the agent at the front door will make things very unpleasant for you."

"You said it wrong," Giancarlo pointed out.

"Said what wrong?" the agent replied, walking over to scratch the dog's neck.

"His word for 'attack' isn't English," Zak said.

"No? He speaks other languages?" the agent smirked.

"Yeah, Italian," Giancarlo said. "The word is *assalire*."

Too late the agent heard the rumble start within the big dog's chest. He tried to reach for his gun, but the big dog already had his forearm in his mouth. The agent screamed as the dog bit down and screamed again at the sound of the bones in his arm being pulverized. He fumbled for the gun with his other hand and almost reached it when he noticed the dog had let go of him. There was a moment when he looked into the dog's brown-yellow eyes, just before the animal tore his throat out.

"Mom's going to be pissed about all the blood," Zak said as they walked out the front door.

"I think she'll understand," Giancarlo said. He rapped the code on the elevator door. A moment later, the door opened and the hanging ladder appeared.

A few minutes later, the agent on the bottom floor heard the elevator coming down. Job's finished, he thought. Figured that was what the scream was about. He waited for his partner to emerge after which they'd disappear—maybe take a month or two down in

Costa Rica until the dust settled. However, when the door opened, the agent took a look at the slaughtered body of his partner and threw up.

Ten minutes later, the twins showed up at the police barricade at Forty-seventh and Fifth Avenue and squirmed their way to the front of the anxious crowd. "We're District Attorney Butch Karp's kids," they told the officer at the checkpoint. "And we need to talk to the FBI guys at the cathedral."

"Yeah, right, kids, just like everybody else here," the officer said. "But sorry, no one gets through."

Zak and Giancarlo backed off for a moment. "You got to get through," Zak said.

Giancarlo agreed. "But how?"

"What we need here," Zak replied, "is a diversion. You ready?"

"What? Wait! No!" Giancarlo shouted, but Zak had already dashed through the checkpoint, followed by the officer and several others. The officers who closed ranks to prevent other dashes watched the mad chase as Zak darted this way and that, so they weren't ready when Giancarlo slipped between two of them and took off up Fifth Avenue.

Three blocks later, winded and barely ahead of the pursuing police officers, Giancarlo ran up to where he saw Jaxon and some other men who were watching a television screen. A pretty woman with dark hair and a mole on her cheek was speaking at the camera.

"We have increased our demands," she shouted. "We insist that all prisoners held by the criminal United States and its puppet allies captured in its illegal wars on Muslim lands be freed immediately. We also demand that all Muslims captured in the Russian war of aggression against Chechnya be released immediately and that all Russian troops leave Chechnya."

"She's building up to something," Jaxon said to Denton. "I think you better get your guys ready to go in. She knows nobody is going to go for these demands. And where's Kane in all this? He's not the sort to blow himself up for Allah or anybody else."

"Jaxon, Jaxon!" Giancarlo shouted. "I have to tell you something."

A police officer grabbed the boy and started to pull him away, kicking and screaming. The agent looked over and saw who was shouting at him and called out to the officer. "That's okay. Let him go."

When Giancarlo ran up, Jaxon leaned over. "Hey, it's okay. We're going to try to get your dad out of there."

"Mom, too," Giancarlo said.

"Your mom's inside?" Jaxon said. "I didn't see her go in."

"She snuck in with a couple of guys after she figured out something was wrong."

Jaxon smiled. "Smart lady, your mom."

"Yeah, but that's not why I came," he said. "Lucy was using sign language on the television to tell us something."

"What she say?" Jaxon asked.

"She said she's a hostage," Giancarlo replied.

Jaxon straightened up. "Not anymore," he said. "She's out and on her way to a hospital. She's going to be okay. Now, I need to get back to—"

"No," Giancarlo said tugging at his arm. "She said this when they were threatening to kill the Pope. So we already knew she was a hostage. She was trying to say she was still going to be a hostage. Sign language isn't that exact, especially when Lucy had to be careful no one would notice."

Jaxon furrowed his brow. Where is Kane? he wondered. Dead? Killed by the terrorists? Or gone? "What else did she say?"

"It didn't make a lot of sense," Giancarlo explained. "She just kept signing the same thing. 'Lucy hostage. Annoy Satan. Baker. Field.' That's it, but I bet it's a clue on where she was being taken."

Jon Ellis walked up. "We got a crisis going on over here, Jaxon," he said.

Jaxon gave Ellis a funny look. "This is Butch Karp's son, Giancarlo. He says Lucy was using sign language before she came out of the cathedral. He thinks she's still a hostage and was trying to give us an indication of how to find her."

Ellis scoffed. "Come on, that's crazy."

"Is it?" Jaxon asked. He strode over to Denton. "Hey, Bill, would you get your guys to check on that ambulance that was taking Hodges and Lucy to the hospital."

Denton got on the radio, then turned around and shrugged. "The ambulance isn't responding," he said. "It never arrived."

Jaxon whirled expecting to see Ellis. But the man had disappeared. He turned back to Denton. "We need to find that ambulance," he said. "I think Hodges is wrong."

"Wrong? As in a bad guy?" Denton asked.

"Yeah, I don't know how he pulled it off," Jaxon said. "But I think if we find Hodges, we'll find Kane, and he's got Lucy and Clay Fulton with him."

Jaxon ran the clues through his head again. Annoy Satan? Baker? Field? But just then the sound of gunfire erupted in the cathedral.

"Go, go, go!" Denton shouted into his microphone and immediately the NYPD and FBI SWAT teams surrounding the cathedral rushed for the entrances.

Inside the cathedral, two different women fought to keep their emotions in check. As she made her demands for the television audience, Samira Azzam had battled back tears. This was to be the best day of her life when she and the woman she loved would sacrifice themselves for the ultimate triumph of Islam.

When Kane left the building, she'd felt an enormous burden lifted from her shoulders. Never again would any man touch her. She turned to Ajmaani and smiled. "It is time, my darling," she said. But Ajmaani had walked up to her shaking her head.

"Perhaps for you, my little warrior," she said, kissing her on the cheeks. "But I have other duties. I will be leaving now for a part of the building that has not been booby-trapped."

Azzam had looked at her for a moment before comprehending what her lover was saying. "You intend to let them capture you?" she asked, aghast.

"Only for the moment," Ajmaani née Nadya Malovo replied. "I will be 'exchanged' later. Perhaps, if you wish, you could also survive this day with me."

Hot, angry tears flooded Azzam's eyes. Once again, she'd been betrayed. She considered killing Ajmaani, who turned and walked toward the back of the cathedral. But even as she pointed her gun, she could not pull the trigger. Instead, she'd allowed the hatred to boil up in her as she began to make her demands.

Across the dais from Azzam, Marlene had taken as much inaction as she could stand. It had taken every bit of willpower not to do something when the initial attack took place, and even more when her daughter and husband were assaulted. But she'd known that if she moved, she would have died without accomplishing anything. Her heart told her to defend her family. But her mind knew that if there was any way to save the Pope and the two thousand others in the cathedral, it had to take precedence.

Still, she also knew that Azzam was building toward the big moment. Soon she would have to take action and most likely die in vain. Jojola had once told her that a warrior wasn't someone who weighed whether he would survive the battle or not. "A warrior takes the necessary action on behalf of others, regardless of the consequences to himself," he'd said. "This sets him free to be a perfect weapon."

Marlene felt a hot tear spring to her eye. Several times over the past weeks, her mind had played tricks on her. She'd see a face in a crowd and start to cry out, "John Jojola!" But the face wouldn't be there when she looked again. Or from a distance . . . or when the lighting was unsure . . . she'd see some old bum walking away with that curious, bowlegged gait that her friend had. But she could never quite catch up and had finally quit trying, realizing that her mind was seeing what she wanted to see.

I wish I could see you here, now, John, she thought. You were the perfect warrior, and we need you. But I guess we'll have to settle for me.

The moment arrived when Azzam motioned for the big male terrorist to again take his place behind the Pope with his knife. Azzam was almost shrieking now as she began to read off a list of "crimes" committed by Christians against Muslims. Marlene had no idea where Yvgeny and Tran were, but she locked eyes with Alejandro and nodded. It was now or never.

Just then, a large priest with a scarred face—the one she'd seen have words with Kane as he was leaving—stepped forward and grabbed the terrorist behind the Pope in a bear hug, pulling him back and away from the pontiff.

Distracted, Azzam pointed her gun and shot the big priest whose treachery had brought her so close to the glorious martyrdom she sought. At the same time, Marlene pushed through the crowd of nuns and began to sprint for the terrorist leader.

One of Azzam's men shouted a warning and pointed behind her. Azzam whirled to confront the danger and was surprised to see that a nun had been moved to action. She was used to hostages going to the slaughter like sheep. She shouted at the assassin who was disengaging himself from the mortally wounded priest. "Kill the Pope!"

The man moved to carry out the command, but suddenly the top half of his head disappeared in a spray of blood, gray matter, and shattered bone. The sound of the .50-caliber sniper's rifle stunned hostages and hostage takers long enough for FBI sniper K. C. Chalk to slam another bullet home and shoot a terrorist who was drawing a bead on the nun charging the female leader of the group.

Like Marlene, Chalk had sat quietly in the back of the cathedral biding his time. Earlier, Jaxon had asked him to quietly find a spot in the cathedral with his rifle "just in case." The odd part of the request was to do it without letting the other security detail know he was doing it. So he'd disassembled the rifle and stashed it in a briefcase, which he'd hidden beneath the pew in front of him. With the help of hostages on either side of him who kept watch, he'd slowly reassembled the rifle, then kept it on the floor until the moment presented itself.

Chalk had almost gone for it the first time the terrorist put his knife to the Pope's throat, but held off. This time, he had been sure that it was now or never, so in one well-rehearsed move, he'd stood and blown the head off the Pope's assailant. He would have liked to kill the woman leader—chop off the head and the serpent dies—but other hostages had jumped to their feet and he couldn't get a clear shot so he'd taken the second man.

Any moment he expected to feel a bullet from the two terrorists behind him. He heard one shot and then another, but neither was directed at him. Instead, the second shot took out the terrorist over to his side who'd turned to find him in the panicking crowd. Chalk glanced behind and saw a small Asian priest with one of the terrorist's rifles taking aim at another. Sometimes one finds friends in the oddest places, Chalk thought as he turned and sought another target himself.

Tran, too, had waited, pretending to be a somewhat crippled, older priest as he worked his way toward the terrorist nearest to him. When the sniper stood and Marlene began her sprint, his target raised his rifle to shoot and so never saw him coming. Tran knocked the rifle up so that the bullet went harmlessly into the ceiling. He ripped the gun away with one hand and with the other delivered a killing *atemi* blow to the man's throat, crushing his windpipe. Without pausing, Tran raised the rifle and shot his target's partner, who seemed confused by the sudden turn of events.

One of the terrorists, who'd moved up the aisle to shoot Marlene, suddenly found himself on the receiving end of a left hook thrown by Karp, who'd appeared to be groggily out of action and leaning against the pew when the shooting started. The gunman went down hard, his head striking the floor with a sickening thud, like a watermelon dropped on a sidewalk. Karp jumped on the man and hammered him in the face with two more punches.

"Mr. Karp, watch out!" Ned yelled behind him.

Karp looked up and saw another terrorist on the other end of the pew aiming for him. He rolled off to the side just as the gun cracked, the bullet finding its mark in the man he'd been punching. He landed next to the handgun that had flown out of the hand of the gunman he'd knocked out. He tossed it to Ned, who put two bullets in the terrorist at the end of the pew, then turned and killed a man who was charging from the back of the cathedral.

Meanwhile, up on the dais, Marlene closed the distance to Azzam, who fumbled for her pistol only to have it kicked out of her hand by the crazy nun. "Blow them up," Azzam screamed to her man at the electronic panel that was wired to the bombs. He did as ordered but nothing happened. A moment later, he was dead with a hole the size of an orange through his chest from Chalk's .50 caliber.

"I know you," Azzam said to Marlene as she pulled her knife. "You were at the beach."

"Damn straight, sister," Marlene said. "And we have a little unfinished business."

Azzam feinted with her knife and kicked for Marlene's leg. But her target had moved and instead landed a kick of her own to the terrorist's jaw, spinning her around.

Marlene moved in with another kick, but had taken her opponent too lightly and felt the burning as Azzam's knife cut a small gash in her thigh.

Seeing her opportunity, Azzam leaped for Marlene. But again Marlene was fast and ducked beneath the flashing blade and delivered an upper cut that staggered her back toward the Pope. At the same time, a large-caliber bullet whizzed by her head and slammed into the pipe organ.

Azzam realized that her moment of ultimate glory had passed. The bombs had not gone off, the cathedral was still standing, and she was a moment away from her own death without having accomplished anything that would be remembered. I can still kill the Pope, she thought and whirled to cross the few steps to the pontiff and sink her blade into his heart.

Instead, in the last moment of her life, Azzam was surprised to see an ancient weapon, half-battle ax, half spear whizzing toward her. She didn't feel the halberd blade pass through her neck, there was no time for pain as her head fell from her shoulders and rolled down the stairs.

Marlene looked up in surprise at Alejandro, who stood looking at the headless body of Samira Azzam with the bloody halberd still in his hands. "Take that, you fucking bitch," he said. "You fucked around in the wrong city this time."

Suddenly realizing who was sitting in the chair behind him, Alejandro grimaced at Marlene and turned. "Sorry, Holy Father," he said. "I got a little carried away."

The Pope, looking a little pale, waved off the apology. "All things considered," he said, "I think you deserve a little grace. One Hail Mary, and all's forgiven."

36

TWO SETS OF EARS HAD BEEN LISTENING FROM THE STORM sewer beneath the street at Fiftieth and Fifth when Giancarlo explained to the FBI agent the message his sister had sent from inside the cathedral.

What else did she say?

It didn't make a lot of sense. She just kept signing the same thing. "Lucy hostage. Annoy Satan. Baker. Field." That's it, but I bet it's a clue on where she was being taken.

From his vantage point on the ladder, David Grale could see the feet of those speaking but not much else. But he could hear fine. He motioned with his hand to his accomplice below him on the ladder and they both climbed down.

Grale was troubled, indecisive. An hour earlier, he and the man with him had been preparing to check out a rumor of unusual activity by foreign strangers on the north end of the island near Columbia University's Baker Field when the news arrived that terrorists were holding the Pope and two thousand others hostage in St. Patrick's.

It was Dirty Warren who'd brought the tidings. *Kane . . .*

fucker . . . is leading them with that woman . . . shit, bitch, he'd stuttered after making his way to Grale's lair among the Mole People beneath Grand Central Station. *Karp and Lucy . . . aaahhh piss . . . are in there. . . . Marlene, Tran, and someone else—tall, patch over his eye—is too, son of a whore. But they're in disguise so they must have known . . . holy crap, holy crap . . . something was up.*

Grale and his partner had immediately grabbed their weapons and the long, loose cloaks they favored to keep out the moisture of life underground and departed for the cathedral. Grale cursed himself as they moved through the labyrinth of sewer tunnels for allowing himself to be lulled to sleep by the news that Kane had died in Aspen. He'd never really believed it . . . or, more accurately, he'd never felt that Kane was gone. Not in his soul, which told him that the man's evil presence was still alive and well . . . and had returned to New York City.

Grale arrived at the cathedral—actually almost directly below where law enforcement officials had established their headquarters—as twilight fell over the city. He chafed at the idea, but he was going to have to wait until dark to try to slip with the other man past the police and enter the cathedral through a secret door and passage that he'd used a year before to surprise the child killer priest Hans Lichner.

He'd felt some relief when Lucy Karp was brought out of the cathedral and apparently unharmed though unconscious. But his instincts told him something was wrong. Something about what the agent who brought her out said, or maybe it was just a gut feeling again. But his concerns about Lucy and her rescuer he put aside when Giancarlo raced up with his information.

"I think Giancarlo's right," Grale said. "I think Lucy's still a hostage . . . and now maybe Clay Fulton, too, if he's not dead."

"Which means there's something wrong with that guy who brought her out . . . and he's a federal agent," said his partner. "But the rest is still a riddle to me. Annoy Satan? Baker? Field? . . . And do we try to find Lucy and Fulton before something bad happens to them, or do we stick with the plan?"

John Jojola was suddenly filled with regret. His sister—not in blood, but in soul—Marlene Ciampi was in the cathedral, which was rigged to blow up and in the control of al Qaeda. If it blew up, he would have missed his chance to explain to her the subterfuge he'd planned after the terrorist attack in Taos.

He thought back to the night when he'd been listening on the other side of the courtyard wall to Tran and Marlene talking. His had been the first coyote howl to join the sounds of the ceremony his people were performing—not for his sham funeral, but to cleanse the land of evil spirits.

When Marlene expressed her grief for him, he'd almost had a change of heart and let her in on the plan. But like Tran had told her, Kane had eyes and ears all over Taos County, as well as spies in the various police agencies. It wasn't that he didn't trust her, but he needed her grief and reactions to his "death" to be real, so that anyone watching would "know" that he was indeed dead.

He'd come up with the plan after the last of the would-be assassins had died with the fear on his face still from Lucy's curse. Even then, it wasn't so much to fool Marlene so she could fool Kane, but so that Jojola could fly beneath Kane's radar. The psychopath wanted him dead, so he'd be dead and thus no longer a threat. They'd considered having Ned "die" too, but somebody had to have killed the last of the terrorists, and he was the likely choice. Besides, Ned had been reluctant to abandon his post as Lucy's bodyguard.

So Jojola had been spirited out of Taos in the luxury of Tran's private jet, after which the two friends had gone to the gangster's home on Long Island. However, he'd remained there only as long as it took to contact David Grale, who was the man who would have the best intelligence on the whereabouts and plans of Andrew Kane and his al Qaeda assassins.

The liaison with Grale had been Dirty Warren who, cursing and asking him if he knew any movie trivia, met him in Central Park one night and then led him underground through to Grale's hideout, where he had once been a captive. For more than a month, Jojola had mostly lived underground with his host, a roller-coaster affair at times due to Grale's wild mood swings. The former social worker at times brooded in darkness, unwilling to move.

In the worst moments, he pronounced that the "end of times" was near and that he welcomed the "coming of evil men" to the city so that the final battle could begin. Other times, he was a shadowy whirlwind of action, hunting "the Others," a different breed of Under-Worlders, as the Mole People referred to their home—evil men and women, devoid of humanity—as he gathered information about Kane.

Grale and Jojola both were committed to watching over the Karp-Ciampi clan—partly because of a mutual affection for the family, but also the knowledge that Kane would be drawn to them. Several times, Jojola had nearly been caught by Marlene, who seemed to have an uncanny sense for when he was near.

Now, with the possibility that she wouldn't survive the night, Jojola wished that he'd let Marlene know that he was alive. Suddenly, there was the sound of distant gunfire echoing down through the sewers from the cathedral above. Jojola started to climb the ladder back to the manhole cover to see if he could help, but Grale grabbed his arm.

In the dim light from above and the flashlights they carried, Jojola could just make out the other man's gaunt face and the small spot of dried blood at the corner of his mouth. Grale had been coughing a lot of late, and Jojola suspected tuberculosis. But at the moment, his eyes were bright with some inner fire as he tugged and said, "Come on, John. Whatever is happening up there, we're not going to be of much use now. Their fates are in the hands of God. But Lucy needs our help, and I think that if we find her, we'll find Kane."

Jojola looked down for a moment, then nodded. "Where do we go?"

"North, John," Grale said turning to run. "We catch a ride north."

As they moved swiftly, splashing through foul water of the sewers with only their flashlights for illumination, Grale explained that he thought he knew what Lucy was trying to say with her sign language. "It's as we suspected," he said.

His spies had reported an unusually large number of rough-looking men passing in and out of an old apartment building on the north end of the island near Baker Field. The strangers weren't the usual age for students; plus they all seemed unusually fit and didn't interact with anyone else in the multicultural neighborhood.

Grale had sent more of his people to hang out in the park—digging in Dumpsters, begging on street corners, and sleeping in stairwells—to keep their eyes and ears open. Even Jojola had visited the neighborhood, acting the part of a drunk derelict, but there'd been no sign of Kane. However, a Caucasian male, with chestnut hair, a scar beneath his right eye and a crooked nose was occasionally seen entering and leaving the apartment building where the others congregated.

"The building is across the street from Columbia University's track and football stadium," Grale explained as they emerged from a sewer into a construction zone that brought them to the tunnel between the Times Square station and the blue line subway station, the rail that ran north to the very end of Manhattan. "The stadium is called Baker Field."

"I get it," Jojola said. "But what about 'annoy Satan.' Was Lucy trying to say that Kane is Satan?"

Grale barked out a laugh. "Not a bad guess, but Lucy knows that Kane is just one of the minions," he said. "I don't think that's what she's saying. It took me a minute—and I had to think about the area around Baker Field—and that's when it hit me. As you already know, there's a big park on the far end of the island close to the stadium, as well as the Columbia University boathouse, where they store their crewing boats. The park has a lot of trails and softball diamonds, as well as a large, tree-covered hill that sort of juts out into the water—the northernmost point of Manhattan from which the Henry Hudson Bridge crosses the Harlem River to the Riverdale section of the Bronx. That's where the Harlem River meets the Hudson River—a turbulent stretch of water called Spuyten Duyvil."

As the two moved quickly through the tunnel toward the subway station, other pedestrians gave them a wide berth. Unshaven, lank haired, and pale from a lack of sunlight, with their long, dark cloaks billowing, they looked pretty rough. Probably smell bad, too, Jojola thought.

Just before reaching the station, Grale stopped for a moment to say something to an old black man playing the saxophone behind a beat-up hat in which a few dollars had been tossed. Jojola looked behind as they took off running again and saw that the old man was talking into a cell phone.

"Spuyten Duyvil? I still don't get it," Jojola said as they reached the stairs leading down to the subway platform.

"Wouldn't expect you to," Grale said. "It's tied to an early piece of New York folklore, but I think it's what Lucy meant by 'annoy Satan.' Another word for 'annoy' could be 'spite,' and, of course, Satan is the devil."

"And?"

"Spuyten Duyvil is sort of a bastardized Dutch from the original European colonizers on that part of the river," Grale said. "Some people think it translates to 'Devil's Whirlpool,' which is certainly apt for the water conditions. But the more accepted definition is 'in spite of the devil'—it comes from a story I'll tell you about some-time. I think Lucy was trying to sign 'spite the devil,' and I think she was trying to say she's going to be taken someplace near Baker Field and Spuyten Duyvil."

Jojola heard the rumble of an approaching subway. At the sound, Grale began taking the stairs three at a time, urging Jojola to keep up. "Come on," he shouted, "or we'll miss our rendezvous with the devil's pal, Kane."

Many blocks away, the people in St. Patrick's Cathedral jumped when there was a small explosion at the main door, followed by an invasion of rifle-bearing SWAT team officers. The new arrivals very nearly shot Tran, who quickly dropped his rifle and raised his hands, but K. C. Chalk had identified him as one of the good guys just in the nick of time.

The SWAT teams were surprised to discover that "the situation" was well in hand. The FBI's Chalk, as well as civilians, apparently including a small Asian priest, the district attorney of New York, a thin young man who spoke with a Western drawl, a nun, and an altar boy with an ax had taken on a well-armed team of terrorists and won the day. One of the terrorists had even been jumped and beaten senseless by spectators as he tried to draw a bead on the avenging nun.

Everywhere they looked, the officers were confronted by a grisly scene. Along with people killed by bullets, a woman's head lay at the bottom of the steps leading up to the altar.

One team quickly made their way to the Pope, who was kneeling on the floor, holding the head of a wounded priest with a badly scarred face.

"Leave me, Father," the dying priest begged. "I'm not worth your trouble. I have sinned against you and God for the sake of my love for a woman and a child. God turned His face from me for my sins."

"For the sake of love, I forgive you," the Pope said smiling and stroking a loose lock of hair from the man's face. "Now, for the sake of your soul, confess your sins and ask for God's forgiveness. But I want you to know that He has not turned his face from you. Indeed, He has a place for you and the woman and child."

Those watching turned away as the man confessed to the Pope. They knew it was over when they heard the pontiff call for holy water to perform last rites for the man.

They were all distracted by the appearance of a SWAT team that had entered from the rear of the cathedral leading a bloody-faced female prisoner and followed by two priests. Marlene recognized the woman as Nadya Malovo and that bringing up the rear were Father Mike Dugan and "Father" Yvgeny Karchovski.

"You wouldn't have had anything to do with the reason St. Patrick's is still standing," Marlene asked Yvgeny as she was joined by her husband and Ned.

The tall Russian held out his hand, which contained a key. "Let's say it was a close call," he replied.

Yvgeny had been with Dugan, who he'd discovered in a broom

closet into which both had ducked when the hostage crisis began. Leaving the older priest behind, Yvgeny had discovered the room where three terrorists were monitoring the bank of security cameras and hovering over an electronic panel he recognized was the computerized detonator. On the desk next to the panel was a small box with a key, which he believed would be turned to arm the bombs set in the cathedral.

Yvgeny had returned to Dugan, and they'd been trying to formulate a way to take out the team when they heard Nadya Malovo shouting at the men. It was apparently a pep talk.

Are you prepared to strike a blow for Islam? the Russian double agent had asked.

Allah akbar, the men yelled in reply. *We will die for Allah!*

As Malovo left the room, she'd rolled her eyes. But then caught sight of a priest at the end of the hall. He ducked to the left as she pulled her gun; she couldn't chance that someone would survive who might endanger her own escape plans.

Malovo raced to the end of the hall and was about to turn left when she heard a voice behind her. *Good evening, Major Malovo, or is it Colonel now?* She whirled, ready to shoot, but the man intercepted her gun hand with a grip like iron, then with a simple backward twist, broke her wrist, which sent the gun clattering to the floor.

Malovo looked up into the face of Yvgeny Karchovski. She recognized him just as a fist the size of a small ham struck her in the face, knocking her back and to the floor.

Yvgeny began to follow but was driven back by a shot from one of the men who'd emerged from the room down the hall. It gave Malovo a chance to scramble for her gun. She grabbed it with one hand and began to stand up, intending to finish off the man who could identify her to the authorities for who she really was, but found herself looking into the face of the first priest and, for the second time in a matter of seconds, at a fist on its way to her face. This time, she was knocked unconscious.

Dugan kicked the terrorist's gun across the hall to Yvgeny who picked it up just in time to shoot the man advancing down the hallway. Leaving Dugan to watch over Malovo, Yvgeny had raced back down the hall to the room just in time to hear a woman's voice on the radio shouting to detonate the bombs. His first bullet went through the temple of a man reaching for the key to arm the bombs; the remaining bullets stopped the second man from reaching it as well. He retrieved the key to keep it safe, just as the SWAT team came in through the back.

"I think it's time for this 'priest' to fade into the woodwork," Yvgeny said to Marlene. He winked at Butch and said, "Good luck, cousin," and left just as Jaxon arrived.

"Are you all right?" Karp asked his wife.

"No," she said. "My daughter's with Andrew Kane."

Karp turned to Jaxon. "Do you have a helicopter outside?"

"Yes. What's up?"

"Is there room for the three of us and you?"

"I think so. Want to tell me what you have in mind?"

Karp started running down the aisle, ignoring the pain in his arthritic knee. "I'll explain on the way," he said. "But I've got a bridge to cross."

37

KANE STOOD WITH LUCY JUST INSIDE THE ENTRANCE TO THE Columbia University boathouse just to the north of Baker Field to get out of the rain that had begun to fall with an accompanying rise in the wind. Lying just outside the door like a useless sack of potatoes was Clay Fulton, his wrists bound behind his back.

They were awaiting the arrival of two speedboats that would carry them up the Harlem River, beneath the Henry Hudson Bridge, through Spuyten Duyvil and past the Amtrak bridge to the Hudson. There they would be met by a larger boat that would take them up the Hudson—the least likely place for cops to be watching.

When he'd formulated the plan, Kane had expected that everyone's attention would be focused on the devastation of St. Patrick's Cathedral and the death of the Pope, as well as a couple thousand others, including Butch Karp. And the plan had continued to go smoothly from the moment the doors on the ambulance had closed and they were beyond the police barricade.

Then Fulton had sensed something when the ambulance pulled

over to the curb, but when he went for his gun, he found himself staring down the barrel of "Agent Hodges's" 9 mm Beretta. *I'm afraid you have the misfortune of finding yourself at my mercy again, Detective.*

Kane! Fulton exclaimed.

Yes, indeed, Kane replied. *And these gentlemen with the rifles pointed at you—and I might add just in case you're feeling heroic, at Lucy—would like you to disembark now. We need to get ready for a little boat ride.*

They'd all loaded into a couple of vans, which had driven to the apartment building across from Baker Field. There Lucy had been given another shot to wake her up while they waited for a call that the speedboats were at the boathouse dock.

When Kane got back to the apartment building, he'd been in a great mood. He was free, immensely wealthy again, and had brought ruin and despair to his enemies.

However, his mood had blackened when the dirty, bald man with the bulging eyes stepped out of the shadows of the stairwell outside the building. *Master,* he said, weeping and reaching out for Kane. *I've come to warn you.*

Warn me about what, you filthy pig? Kane said, backing away from the man's hand. Two of his al Qaeda bodyguards moved between them.

They know Dickens! the man cried.

What?

Dickens! They know Dickens! "Thus, cases of injustice, and oppression, and tyranny, and the most extravagant bigotry, are in constant occurrence among us every day." They know these things about you and are coming! the man cried, the smell of his rotting teeth wafting over Kane.

Who's coming? Kane had asked in spite of himself, wondering at the same time, Do I really want to know this?

Who? the man asked as if he'd thought the answer was obvious. *Who? Why, Karp, of course.* He fell to his knees, groveling as he wept.

Karp, of course. The three words sent a shiver up Kane's spine and formed a cold, tight fist in his stomach. "Shoot him," he directed the bodyguard closest to the man.

He'd hoped the quick, terrified scream followed by two silenced shots would make him feel better. But the knot was still in his gut when he entered his apartment and turned on the television, expecting to see St. Patrick's Cathedral in ruins and his nemesis Karp dead. Only to his incredulous eyes, the church was still standing and, as the broadcaster cheerfully reported, *The Pope is safe! . . . Two terrorists have been captured, but most are dead, as are an undisclosed number of civilians.* Another newscast indicated that *New York District Attorney Butch Karp, as well as his wife, Marlene, plus several unknown civilians, are credited with stopping the terrorists and rescuing the Holy Father . . .*

Nearly purple with rage, Kane kicked the television off the stand. *Goddamn, I hate that fucker Karp!* he shouted. *Every time I turn around, that son of a bitch and his frickin' wife are messing up my life.*

I'd suggest you surrender now, Lucy said with a smile on her face. *You know he's coming for me . . . and for you.*

Kane turned to her with his eyes looking like they might bug out of this head. He aimed his gun at her head and kept it there shaking in his hand for a full minute before he lowered it and laughed. *You know,* he said calmly. *This is even better. He gets to go home and find his precious little boys have been turned into worm food. And I still have his daughter . . . so I guess he will be thrilled to receive the baby pictures after all.*

I'll kill myself before I have your baby, Kane, Lucy said.

Kane tsked. *What—a good Catholic like you committing a mortal sin that would send you straight to hell?*

It would be worth it, she replied.

We'll see, he said just as the call came in that the boats were on their way.

The group had left the building and crossed the street where the fence into the boatyard was open. "My dad once told me a story about Spuyten Duyvil," Lucy said as she peered out into the dark night.

"Oh, really? I like stories. Why don't you tell me while we wait for our cruise ship," Kane said.

Lucy paused. She thought she'd heard Andy's childlike voice when Kane replied about liking stories.

"Well, the story goes that long before the Revolutionary War, a brave trumpeter—his name was Anthony Van Corlaer—used to blow his trumpet when the leader of the colony of New Amsterdam, Peter Stuyvesant, wanted to warn the people or call them together.

"One night, Stuyvesant heard that the English were going to attack New Amsterdam so he sent Anthony to warn the Dutch settlers along the Hudson. But a storm was brewing, sort of like tonight, so that when Anthony reached the tip of Manhattan, the ferry that should have been there to take him across was nowhere to be found. But he'd been given a mission, so he decided he would swim across at the spot where the Harlem River and the Hudson met. Even without the storm, the waters in that area were known to be especially turbulent with bad currents. But he vowed to swim across *'en spijt den duyvil.'* In spite of the devil."

Kane frowned. He did not particularly like the way this story was going. "Are you going to get to the point or bore me to death?"

Lucy smiled. "If it would bore you to death, I'd talk all night. . . . Anyway, Anthony dove into the water and began to swim across. However, the devil had heard his boast and reached up and grabbed Anthony's leg. The brave lad pulled out his trumpet and blew such a blast that it drowned out the storm and startled the devil so much that he let go of Anthony. The sound of his trumpet warned the settlers far up the Hudson that danger was approaching, so they were prepared when the English arrived. But poor Anthony was so exhausted by his efforts that he drowned."

"So the moral of the story," Kane said, "is: don't fuck with the devil."

"Or use his name lightly, Mr. Kane." Lucy smiled back. "You

never know when he might reach up and grab you by the leg and pull you back to hell."

Kane scowled but any comeback was interrupted by the sound of gunfire from across the road where he'd left a rear guard to watch for any cops. He could see flashes from the area of the park and more popping noises.

An Arab man came running up, obviously frightened. "We are being pursued by *jinn*," he said. "We must leave."

"*Jinn* with guns?" Kane asked. "Why am I surrounded by such fools?"

"They move like shadows, and when you shoot at them, they aren't there anymore. They are *jinn*," the man repeated confidently, which started several of the other men murmuring.

Kane raised his gun and shot the man in the stomach. "Now," he told the others as they watched their comrade suffering on the ground. "Let's have no more talk about *jinn* and get to the boats."

There was more gunfire. Closer. Kane looked down toward where the street rounded the corner into the park. It was hard to see in darkness through the rain, but he thought he spotted several shadowy figures run across the street.

"Move!" he shouted, suddenly afraid himself. "Get to the boats!"

"What about him?" one of the men said pointing at Fulton.

Kane considered shooting the detective. "Two hostages are better than one," he said. "Bring him. Two of you stay here and hold them off, then join us in the second boat."

With that they ran down the boat ramp for the floating dock. At Kane's direction, Lucy climbed in the front boat, followed by Kane. Two terrorists brought Fulton, who they dumped on the floor; then one moved quickly to the helm while the other untied the boat. The second man was about to get in when a bullet caught him in the back and he fell into the water.

"Go! Go!" Kane shouted.

"What about the others?" the man at the wheel shouted.

"Leave them," Kane said. "Just go."

The speedboat pulled away from the dock with a roar. Lucy

looked back and saw several men running for the second boat, firing over their shoulders at the shadow people who chased them.

One of the terrorists fell and lay still. Another was struck in the leg. He went down but got back up and was trying to hobble to the boat. But a tall shadow figure caught him. There was a piercing scream loud enough to be heard over the roar of the boat engine.

Grale, Lucy thought. And John is with him! Come on, guys. Here I am!

The last of the terrorists got to the floating dock and, throwing off the line, jumped in the boat. It looked like he was going to get away, but then another pursuer ran down the dock and leaped just as the boat was starting to pull away.

Jojola landed hard and rolled across the deck. The man at the wheel saw him land and left his post to meet him. Pulling a long, curved knife, he slashed at Jojola, who threw himself backward to avoid the blow. The man leaped for Jojola, intending to finish him, but instead impaled himself on the Indian's upraised hunting knife.

Jojola pushed the body off and stood, just as the wet figure of David Grale, who'd dived in after the boat, pulled himself over the side. Grale rushed forward and took the wheel and gunned the engine so suddenly that Jojola was thrown back and nearly overboard.

It was difficult to see with the rain pelting their faces, and the water was getting increasingly choppy as they sped into the Spuyten Duyvil area. On the subway, Grale had told him that although the waters could look calm, they were deceptive. *The Harlem River is affected by the ocean tide,* he'd said. *Especially at high tide, which it will be at tonight, the waters in the river actually push up against the waters from the Hudson that flow down from the north. Strong swimmers have been sucked beneath the surface and never seen again.*

Now, over the roar of the boat engine, Grale pointed ahead at a dark object in the middle of the river. "That's the Amtrak rail bridge," he said. "It's only about eight feet above the water at high tide. You can't go under it, but it swivels in the middle to let boats pass and then back again for the train to pass over. I'm not sure, but it looks like it's open for boats now. If they get through it and Kane's men close it before we can get there, we'll lose them."

Up ahead, Kane saw that the Amtrak bridge was open and smiled. His men had obviously reached the control office and forced the operator, who was undoubtedly now dead, to swing it open.

Some nemesis you turned out to be, Mr. Karp, he thought, happily. Yes, you managed to save your stupid cathedral and precious Pope, but your life will be one of never-ending tears when you find your sons butchered and have to live with the idea that your daughter is my whore. I'll ruin you politically as well when my friends in the media hear how you're related to Russian gangsters. My new good friend Rachel Rachman will be the district attorney, and I'll be able to return to the city . . . perhaps with a new face and identity.

Kane looked behind. The second boat with the shadowy pursuers would never catch him in time. We'll scoot through and then shut the door, he thought happily. But the smirk left his face when his driver sounded the boat's horn, which for the moment drowned out the sound of the storm, reminding him of Lucy's story.

"What in the hell!" Kane shouted.

His man pointed ahead. The bridge was swiveling to a close, and it was going to be a race to see if they could reach the opening in time.

"Faster!" Kane shouted.

"There is no more speed," the man shouted back.

They almost made it, but at the last minute, the driver had to cut the engine and turn the boat sharply to avoid crashing into the end of the bridge section. The drastic move caused the engine to stall and despite repeated efforts it wouldn't start up again.

"No!" Kane howled. "How did this happen?"

As an answer a spotlight suddenly stabbed down from a helicopter overhead. "This is the New York City Police Department.

Put down your weapons and remain where you are with your hands up."

Suddenly, the lights on the bridge were turned on. Kane shaded his eyes and tried to see who was on the bridge. He could just make out three figures standing on the edge of the bridge looking down at him. It took a moment for his eyes to adjust, and when they did, making out the features of the tall one in the middle, he screamed in rage. "Karp! I don't believe this!" He aimed his gun and fired until he was out of bullets, but his aim on the pitching boat was worthless and all his shots went wide.

"Shoot them, dammit," he yelled at his driver. The man obediently grabbed his AK-47 and jumped up on the bow of the boat. He aimed the rifle but never got a shot off before there were two flashes from one of the figures on the bridge and the terrorist fell back and into the water.

Up on the bridge, standing between his wife and Ned, Butch Karp picked up a bullhorn. "It's over, Kane," he said. "There's nowhere to go. The river's sealed off in both directions. The Pope is safe. So is the cathedral. And by the way, you don't have any money."

"You're lying, Karp," Kane said, suddenly turning to point his gun at Lucy. "Open the bridge or I swear I'll kill her."

Kane glanced over as the second boat pulled up twenty feet away. A tall, pale man stepped to the edge of the boat. He looked almost like a skeleton. Or the pale rider, a voice said in Kane's head sending a spasm of fear through his body.

"Nope, telling you the truth, Kane," Karp said. "Emil never got the chance to reroute the money into your foreign accounts. You got nothing, nada, zippo."

Kane's call to confirm the transfer of the money from the Vatican's bank had arrived with Emil Stavros already in handcuffs and Ray Guma holding the phone so he could speak. Dante Coletta was also handcuffed and sitting on the floor, somewhat worse the wear for having tried to duke it out with Clarke Fairbrother first.

Kane stood for a moment as if contemplating his surrender. But fast as a snake, he reached out and yanked Lucy to her feet and then held his knife at her throat.

"So this is how it ends, Karp," he said. "But first you're going to have to watch me cut this bitch's head off."

Karp spoke quietly. "Can you get him, Ned?"

Ned shook his head. He still had the terrorist's handgun from the cathedral, but it was an automatic, not what he was used to, and the boat was pitching. "I'm as likely to hit her as him."

"Open the bridge, Karp," Kane said. "Is it worth watching your daughter die?"

Down in the boat, Lucy was finishing her conversation with St. Teresa when Kane pulled her to her feet. For the first time in a long time, Teresa had appeared as a visual manifestation sitting on the seat at the back of the boat. But she looked different than she had in the past. Before, she'd appeared as a young, not particularly pretty woman in fifteenth-century robes; for unknown reasons, this time she was wearing a blue silk shirt over white cutoffs. She also looked to be in her midthirties and was very beautiful.

"I swam this once," Teresa said. "But I wouldn't try it at high tide."

"Why are you telling me this?" Lucy replied, though she realized she'd said nothing aloud.

"No reason," the woman said. "Just a memory of who I used to be. Andy's got memories, too, of your kindness once before. I suggest that the white queen make her move. Oh, and Lucy, when you see Ray Guma, tell him hi for me."

I'll do that, Lucy thought, then said aloud, "Andy, you need to stop him."

Kane tightened his grip and pressed the knife harder against her throat. "What the fuck are you talking about, you little whore."

"Andy. You have to be strong."

"Quit calling me 'Andy,' I hate that name, and you're giving me a headache," Kane snarled. "As soon as we get your daddy, I mean Karp, to open the bridge, I'm going to cut your fuckin'—"

"You shouldn't use bad words," a boy's voice scolded.

Lucy felt the grip on her loosen for a moment, then it tightened again.

"Shut the fuck up, you little wimp," Kane yelled.

"Let her go," Andy replied. "You're a bad man."

"Get out of my head!" Kane shouted again. "You're not real. You died a long time ago . . . worthless . . . stupid."

"Sticks and stones may break my bones," Andy rhymed, "but words will never hurt me."

"I'll hurt you, you son of a bitch," Kane said, letting go of Lucy who crawled over next to Fulton.

Kane slashed at the air with his knife. "Die, you little faggot," he screamed, slashing again. "You're weak. You're stupid. You're a whore's son."

"I'm just a little boy," Andy cried. "I want to be loved."

Kane slammed his left hand down on the gunwale of the boat. He raised the knife and chopped down, cutting off three fingers. "There, you weakling," he screamed. "Now, run and hide. You never could handle pain."

Blood pouring from his wounded hand, Kane turned to Lucy. "Nice try, bitch. But your little friend is gone. And now I'm going to finish you, too."

Kane took two steps toward Lucy with his knife in the air. A shot rang out from the bridge above, but the bullet whizzed past. He leaped for the girl, but even as he prepared to drive the knife into her chest, Fulton's foot lashed out and caught him in the stomach.

The blow knocked Kane to the deck. When he rose, the big detective was between him and the girl.

"Well, Detective." Kane smirked as he dropped into the *Kali* on-guard pose. "Guess it's like I said . . . I should have killed you back in February." He feinted with the knife for Fulton's eyes, then stabbed at his chest. But instead of his blade sinking into flesh, he was surprised when his hand was deflected outward; then the wind was driven out of him when the detective's other hand shot in and caught him in the solar plexus.

"This ain't my first knife fight, sucker," Fulton snarled. "And you . . ." the next blow caught Kane under the chin ". . . ain't that good." The right cross sent Kane spinning against the rail of the boat where he tottered for a moment and then fell over the side.

Fulton limped over to the side of the boat and looked down at the water. "You're right," he said to the bubbles rising to the surface. "The bad guy should always kill the good guy when he has the chance."

Over in the other boat, Grale also looked at the water. The police helicopter hovering overhead played its spotlight on the area around the boats. But there was no sign of Kane.

Grale dove over the side and down into the dark waters where Kane had disappeared. It was a fool's chance, the likelihood of finding the other man in the roiling, tumbling currents below was almost nothing. And yet, call it fate, call it faith, call it what you will, the two men found each other beneath the surface. They grappled and held on—one man with only a thumb and finger on one hand but strong in his insanity—each trying to locate the other's body with his knife.

Over and over they tumbled like socks in a dryer. Down they sank like rocks. Beneath and past the bridge. Their lungs screamed for air, but their brains focused on the death of the other.

Until at last, one knife finally found a home and sank deep into the ribs of the other, who stiffened for a moment, then sagged. The victor pushed the wounded man away and struggled to reach the surface, though in truth he had no idea which direction it was. So it was almost with surprise that he felt his hand break the surface and in the next moment sucked cool fresh air into his aching lungs.

Exhausted and too weak to do anything except float on his back with the current, he looked up to where the clouds were abandoning the sky and saw the stars. A hundred yards away, a police helicopter's search beam drifted over the waters near the bridge. He began to kick toward the shore . . . and smiled.

Epilogue

October

KARP GLANCED AT HIS WATCH. FOUR O'CLOCK. STILL, PLENTY of time to hear the verdict, congratulate Guma, then meet up with Marlene, swing by the loft to grab the kids, and make it to the synagogue in time for the twins' bar mitzvah class.

Word that the jury in the Emil Stavros murder trial had reached their verdict had come an hour ago . . . more than two weeks after summations and deliberations had been delayed due to the events at St. Patrick's.

Jon Ellis had wanted to make a deal with Stavros, who, according to his lawyer, had quite a bit of information on al Qaeda banking practices and the accounts he was supposed to send the ransom money to after the transfer from the Vatican bank. He'd be placed in a Witness Protection Program and given immunity from further prosecution for his role in the weekend's events, as well as the murder trial.

In a meeting with Karp, Guma, Murrow, and Jaxon, Ellis hinted that he didn't need "the locals' " permission "seeing as how this is a national security matter" but was asking as a "matter of courtesy." Karp told him where he could stick his courtesy and that Stavros was still a prisoner under the lock and key of the New York City criminal justice system and under the jurisdiction of the Honorable Paul Lussman of the New York County Supreme Court, Trial Part 34.

I'm sure the media will be interested in a story about how you vouched for "Agent Hodges," also known as Andrew Kane, and almost got the Pope and two thousand other people killed, Karp said looking the assistant director in the eyes until the man stood as if to leave.

This isn't the end of this, Karp, Ellis said.

Damn straight it isn't, Karp said. *So don't be surprised if you receive a subpoena to testify before a New York County grand jury.*

Ellis glared for a moment longer at Karp, then laughed and shook his head as he turned to Jaxon. *You coming?* he asked.

Jaxon kicked back in his chair. *No,* he said. *I have other matters to discuss with Mr. Karp.*

Ellis stormed from the room as Guma quipped, *See you in court.*

When he was gone, Jaxon gave the others the "official" explanation being handed down by Homeland Security's public relations office. *Agent Hodges came from another agency, and therefore wasn't personally known to Ellis, except by reputation,* Jaxon said. *Heads will roll . . . supposedly . . . but not Ellis's. Obviously, Kane went to great lengths to alter his appearance and was able to force the real Hodges to reveal information, including passwords and such, that only an agent would have. Ellis was as stunned as anyone . . . at least that's his story, and he's sticking to it.*

In other words, Ellis has "plausible deniability" going for him? Murrow asked. *But what about the Russian agent? Nadya Malovo.*

Jaxon shook his head. *She wouldn't say anything to us,* he replied. *The Russian government is, of course, denying any knowledge of her involvement in a conspiracy to blow up St. Patrick's and blame it on Chechen nationalists. They're labeling her "a rogue element" and making noises that they want her returned so that she can be prosecuted in Moscow.*

You guys going to go along with that? Karp scowled.

Jaxon shrugged. *I hope not, but it may not be up to the Justice Department,* he said. *Homeland Security and the administration are desperate to keep the Russians involved in the "War on Terror;" so saving the Russians embarrassment might trump federal charges of murder, attempted murder, conspiracy to commit murder, kidnapping, and various other crimes that fit under the terrorism label.*

And, of course, Putin canceled his appearance at the United Nations to explain the need for continued Russian occupation of Chechnya, Karp noted.

Yeah . . . and the rumors are that the administration is going to trade Malovo and keeping a lid on Russian involvement at St. Patrick's in exchange for the Russians sitting down for "meaningful dialogue" with the nationalists, Jaxon said, *which, if something came of it, would be a blow to the Russians and al Qaeda, but I'm not holding my breath.*

On a sad note, the bodies of the Homeland Security agents who had been assigned to work with the fake Agent Hodges on security inside the cathedral had been discovered in a parking garage near Columbia University. But on the brighter side, the real Agent Hodges had been found in the cabin of Kane's speedboat—bound and gagged, but alive. Apparently, Kane had planned to dump him in the Hudson as if he'd been abducted from the ambulance with Lucy and then killed. *He's been reunited with his family,* Jaxon said, *and a former priest who had an outstanding warrant out for sexually molesting children and was tailing the family for Kane, was arrested with Hodges's help.*

Karp looked around the courtroom. Guma was chatting amiably with detectives Fairbrother and Bassaline. With surprise he noted that Amarie Bliss Stavros was sitting on the prosecution side of the aisle with her arm around Zachary. Meanwhile, those sitting at the defense table appeared as if they were on their way to a good friend's funeral.

Anderson looked like the bully on the playground who'd just had the shit kicked out of him by the new kid he'd tried to pick on. He hazarded a quick glance back at the blond reporter and, Karp thought, probably wished he hadn't; she was staring at him with open contempt. Karp half expected her to mouth the word *loser.*

Unshaved and crumpled-looking in his jail jumpsuit, Stavros just sat morosely looking at the table. He'd tried claiming that he'd been blackmailed into cooperating with Kane and pointed to Dante Coletta as his wife's killer. But Coletta started squealing as soon as Fairbrother got him to the Tombs—admitting to his part in the murder and burial in exchange for eight to twelve years at Attica for conspiracy. Given the circumstances, Judge Lussman had allowed Guma to put Coletta back on the stand to recant his original testimony.

Hear that banging? Guma had asked Karp after Coletta's testimony.

What banging? Karp asked, puzzled.

The last nail going into Stavros's coffin.

There were still many unresolved questions from what Ariadne Stupenagel in a "special report" for the *Times* had called "The Siege at St. Patrick's." The biggest blank was whatever happened to Kane and Grale. The official view of the NYPD was that the two were "missing, presumed dead," but no bodies had been found after extensive searches of the banks of the Harlem and Hudson rivers. But Karp wasn't going to believe that either man was gone, not until he'd seen the bodies himself.

Now, Karp and everyone else in the courtroom jumped to their feet when Judge Lussman entered the courtroom and remained standing while the judge brought in the jury. "Ladies and gentlemen of the jury, have you reached a verdict?"

"We have, Your Honor," the foreman said. He handed the paperwork to the court clerk who took it to the judge for his perusal.

Lussman glanced quickly at the verdict sheet and handed it back to the clerk who walked it over to the foreman. "Would you read your verdict, please," the judge said.

"We find the defendant guilty . . ."

They all knew what was coming but spectators, lawyers, defendants, and witnesses held their breath.

". . . of murder . . ."

As the foreman read off the guilty verdicts for the remaining counts and reporters ran from the courtroom to file their stories, Karp turned to Guma and shook his hand as he pretended not to see the tears that had welled up in his friend's eyes. "Congratulations, pal, you did it again."

Guma nodded, too choked up to speak. He picked up the photograph of Teresa and Zachary, looked at it one last time, and then placed it in the file that would be stored in a vault. Karp recognized the act as a way of saying good-bye.

Ten minutes later, Karp found Guma again in the hallway speaking to a gaggle of reporters. "Hey, got to go," he said. "Marlene's meeting me outside. We'll catch up and have a drink over this later."

Guma nodded. "No problem," he said. "Actually, I have plans tonight as well." He made eye contact with the little blond television reporter standing with the rest of the pack listening to Murrow, who was happy as a pig in slop. Karp's lead over Rachman had skyrocketed in the wake of the attack, especially after Stupenagel's article which, he thought, overly dramatized his own small role in the cathedral and then on the bridge. The reporter smiled at Guma and blushed.

Karp raised his eyebrows. "I see that the Italian Stallion is back in the saddle, or will be. But I thought Teresa was 'the one.'"

Guma smiled and nodded to the reporter. "Maybe, she was," he said with a shrug. "And maybe I'll see her on the flip-flop, and we'll find out. But until then, a man's got to live, doesn't he?" With that, Guma walked over and separated the blonde from the others and was soon making her laugh with something he said.

"Yeah, Goom," Karp said quietly. "A man's got to live."

With that, Karp walked down the hall to the elevator and got on for the trip to the lobby. He was thinking about Marlene as he got off. When the dust settled, she and the others involved in the Pope's rescue had been granted a special audience with His Holiness.

Lucy emerged looking like she'd been told that her beatification was imminent. And Marlene also had been beaming, but she wouldn't talk about what had been said, except that *I got a chance to ask him for a favor for my dad.*

Karp sighed as he left the Criminal Courts building. All's well that end's well, he thought. Once again, his family had survived another brush with death, and now he was going to meet his beautiful wife, whom he saw waving on the other side of Centre Street.

God, she's as beautiful now as the day I first met her, he thought and walked toward the curb.

On the other side of the street, Marlene waved again and began to walk toward him. The days following the events at St. Patrick's had been surreal. First, she'd had to get used to the fact that John Jojola was alive and then forgive him for keeping her in the dark. She listened to his reasoning, accepted it, and then slapped him hard.

Don't ever do that again, she'd said. *I can keep a secret, and I'm a great actress . . . just ask Butch.*

Hey, hey, what do you mean by that, her husband scowled. Then they'd all shared a good laugh.

Jojola, Lucy, and Ned had all spent most of a week relaxing and seeing the sights. At Tran's insistence, they'd all then boarded his private jet for the flight back to Taos County Airport and were, as the saying went, now happily back home on the range.

Kane was probably dead—and she wasn't going to lose any more sleep over him. The Pope was safe and so was her family. Life just doesn't get any better, she thought as she approached the curb.

Karp was so fixated on his bride that he didn't see the sedan with the dark-tinted windows pull away from the curb and start to roll slowly toward him. But Marlene did and something about how it didn't pick up speed to join the rest of traffic warned her that something wasn't right. "Butch, watch out!" she shouted, pointing to the sedan and then reaching into her purse to pull her gun.

Karp saw her point but couldn't hear her over the honking of taxis and general sound of traffic. He looked and saw a sedan approaching and noticed the window on the passenger side come down. He glanced back at Marlene and saw her darting into traffic with her gun, and only then realized that he was a target.

Karp never saw the person who shot him, just flashes from the gun. The force of the bullets hitting him in the chest, the shoulder, the neck, and leg drove him back, landing on the sidewalk as pedestrians screamed and moved to get out of the way. He looked up at the sky, noticed how white the clouds looked against the blue background . . . heard more shots, more screams.

Then Marlene's face appeared above him. She was yelling something and crying. He wanted to tell her it was all right. Don't cry. I love you. But something was pulling at him, lifting him from the sidewalk and into the air where he could look down, surprised to see his body lying in a spreading pool of blood as his wife and a man he didn't recognize pressed at his wounds. He noticed the sedan was partly up on the curb, stopped where it had run into Dirty Warren's newsstand.

Marlene kept pressure on the wounds, but there were too many. She'd been too late, getting through the traffic and emptying her gun into the dark window on the driver's side. The first bullet had shattered the window, and she'd seen Rachel Rachman turn toward her, her former protégée's face a mask of hatred and rage. Marlene's second bullet had obliterated that face, the third turned it into a bloody mass, and the fourth and fifth pulverizing it until there was nothing much left.

The car had drifted past as Marlene ran to her husband and dropped to her knees and began applying pressure to his wounds. But there were too many. "Butch! Butch! Listen to me," she screamed. "You're not leaving me, Karp! Don't leave me, please, baby."

Lying on the sidewalk, Karp's eyelids fluttered then closed. His mind was filled with a white light. So that part's true, he thought. I wonder what's next. He was ready to go then, almost irritated by Marlene's screaming. His eyelids opened again. "What?" he said weakly. "Can't you see I'm sleeping?"